CHANGING TIMES AT HARPERS

ROSIE CLARKE

Boldwood

First published in Great Britain in 2023 by Boldwood Books Ltd.

Copyright © Rosie Clarke, 2023

Cover Design by Colin Thomas

Cover Photography: Colin Thomas and Alamy

Every effort has been made to obtain the necessary permissions with reference to copyright material, both illustrative and quoted. We apologise for any omissions in this respect and will be pleased to make the appropriate acknowledgements in any future edition.

A CIP catalogue record for this book is available from the British Library.

Paperback ISBN 978-1-80415-742-8

Large Print ISBN 978-1-80415-743-5

Hardback ISBN 978-1-80415-741-1

Ebook ISBN 978-1-80415-745-9

Kindle ISBN 978-1-80415-744-2

Audio CD ISBN 978-1-80415-736-7

MP3 CD ISBN 978-1-80415-737-4

Digital audio download ISBN 978-1-80415-738-1

Boldwood Books Ltd
23 Bowerdean Street
London SW6 3TN
www.boldwoodbooks.com

1

What a joy it was to see Harpers' shelves fully stocked again! More than two years had passed since the Armistice and it was now late spring 1920; gradually, the right kind of stock had started to appear once more. Instead of Sally Harper having to search for firms that were able to sell her small quantities, they were queuing up to offer her merchandise and she had a pile of catalogues and samples waiting on her desk in the office. At the beginning of the war, with her husband, Ben's absence and a shortage of male staff, she'd been obliged to take on more and more of the buying responsibility, but she was now able to concentrate on the departments she enjoyed most.

'I will be around a lot more now,' Ben had told her when he'd finally been able to walk away from the duties he'd taken on for the War Office during the long conflict. 'I shall oversee the men's department, though Mr Brown will continue to run it and we'll discuss the merchandise together. You've done too much these past years, Sally. I know you don't want to give it up, so go back to the departments you love and leave the rest to me – and the buyers I'll appoint for the other departments.'

Sally hadn't argued. They had discussed it at length and it seemed right that Ben, who was after all the owner of the business, should take on much of the work that had fallen to her. Harpers was a large store and if Ben had his way it would continue to grow, with more and more departments. He'd talked of increasing their floor space as soon as an adjacent building to the restaurant became free. No one person could be responsible for all that indefinitely. Besides, she had two lively children to care for, her daughter Jenny, six and a half years old now, and her son Peter, not yet two, and she was looking forward to spending time with them, as well as the other charitable work she did with Maggie Morgan and Beth Burrows, two of her closest friends. All three of them had started work at Harpers when it had first opened. Beth and Maggie were happily married, and no longer worked there, but the three had remained firm friends.

When the Armistice was signed, amidst all the joy and celebrations for the Allied victory, Maggie had made Sally aware of a serious problem for the men returning from several years at war. They were suffering from mental wounds as well as physical ones and a member of their own staff, Marion Jackson, had been affected. Her husband Reggie had been wounded more than once and recovered physically, but his mental state was fragile and he'd attacked her. If a man who loved his wife, as Reggie clearly did, had been so severely affected that he would hit her, then how many men were suffering untold horrors they'd seen during the war, and how many other wives were being subjected to the same distress? Reggie had shown his remorse and asked for help, which had led Marion to approach her friend Maggie.

Maggie had come up with the idea of campaigning for proper homes for soldiers suffering from war stress caused by the terrible death and destruction they had witnessed and endured for the sake of king and country. So Maggie and Sally had raised funds and gathered support, actually setting up as many homes as they could themselves. So far, they had three up and running, all with trained staff who understood that these men had been pushed beyond endurance. They were not cowards because they got the shakes if they heard a loud bang, nor were they bullies and wife-beaters by nature. Instead, they were ill with worry and fear to the extent that they might never be the same, often hiding their shame and pain behind closed doors. Now that people were becoming more aware of the problem, they were calling it shell shock, but many still thought it shameful.

* * *

'Mrs Harper – may I have a word please?'

Sally's thoughts returned to the present as she looked at the young woman who had spoken. Now in charge of the hat and bag department, to which Sally's meandering steps had brought her, Andrea Martin was in her thirties, attractive, intelligent and a war widow. Her only son was at boarding school, having won a scholar-ship that meant there were no fees, but she worked to keep her home going and to pay for his uniform and the other things he needed.

'Paul is as bright as his father was,' she'd told Sally when applying for the position of supervisor in the bag, hat and jewellery department. 'I want him to have a good education – the education he would have had if the war hadn't happened.'

'Your husband was a fighter pilot,' Sally had noted, reading her application letter. 'Yes, I see you say he was killed... his plane went down over the sea... I am so sorry.' She'd felt immediate sympathy with the young woman, who had some of the resilience of Rachel Bailey, the woman who had been in charge of the department until she'd retired to the country with her husband. 'You say you had experience at Selfridges before you married – why did you not return there?'

'Because I'd heard about Harpers and the opportunity for women here. Many of the other shops are only taking on men for senior positions these days.' She'd looked so earnest and anxious that Sally had felt her need. 'I am a good careful person, Mrs Harper. I can add up and I'm honest – but I've never done office work, nor do I have the skills to be a secretary. A shop girl's wage would not be sufficient for my needs. I could have gone on the counters at Selfridges, but I wanted a supervisor's position.'

Considering her to be the best applicant, Sally had taken her on. She looked at her now. Andrea was dressed in a smart black dress with a white collar and sensible court shoes, her dark hair cut short into the neck and styled in waves each side of her attractive face.

'Yes, Mrs Martin, how can I help you?'

'A man came to the department asking to see you earlier this morning. He said he was an old friend but... I wasn't sure...' She took a deep breath. 'I thought he might be... might not be what he claimed, so I didn't tell him you were coming in later today.'

'A man?' Sally asked, mildly intrigued. 'Was he disreputable or threatening?'

'It was just his accent.' Andrea frowned. 'I think he was Irish – and he spoke about you in such a familiar way—'

'Irish?' Sally stared at her. 'It might be Mick O'Sullivan; he is a good friend, but I thought he'd decided to settle in America. Oh, well, if it was Mick, he knows where I live. He will get in touch, but I'm surprised he didn't write to let us know he was coming back...' Mick had invested in Harpers at the end of the war, but it wasn't generally known and Sally had no intention of telling her new supervisor.

An embarrassed look flushed Andrea's face. 'I may have made a mistake, Mrs Harper. I was a little short with him – and if he is a friend—'

'Oh, don't worry,' Sally told her. 'Mick will be highly amused if it is him. He'd go away chuckling to himself – but next time, ask for the name please.'

'I think he did say it was Mick, but that is often used for Irishmen... I am so sorry.'

'No, you did the right thing,' Sally told her. 'Now, let's talk of business. You've been here a week – how are you getting on?'

'I like it very much,' Andrea told her, still a little embarrassed. 'Everyone is friendly and the girls you employ in this department seem polite and good at their jobs.'

'Most of you are new to the department,' Sally informed her. 'The girls I knew best have left for various reasons. Mrs Bailey left some time ago – she had your job and I've had two ladies in the position since, neither of whom were really up to it and both left to marry when their sweethearts returned from the war. I hope you won't leave me in the lurch, Mrs Martin?'

'Oh no, I am far too grateful to have the position,' she said. 'Well, Miss Brown is doing well on hats. She is the men's department head, Mr Brown's daughter, of course, and her father told her what was expected. He calls in for her in the evening and they go home together. Miss Fairley is suitable for the scarves and gloves. She has good hands and keeps them soft so doesn't snag the silk.'

'And Lilly Ross?' Sally asked, glancing at the young girl who had come as the junior to assist Andrea Martin. 'How is she getting on?'

'Lilly...' Andrea frowned. 'She is trying her best. I believe her to be honest, which is very necessary in this department, but she hasn't been trained for this kind of position. You did know she worked in a munitions factory during the war?'

'Yes, she told me,' Sally said and smiled at the girl who was helping Janet Fairley on the scarf and glove counter. Three customers were asking about merchandise, which was too much for any one assistant. 'She has an invalid mother and two younger siblings at home and needed a better job with a hope of promotion in the future. Her father is dead and two of her elder brothers were killed on active service...'

'Yes, I know. It was devastating for the family,' Andrea agreed. 'That's why I've given her the benefit of the doubt when she has been late for work a few times.'

'If it continues, send her to me and I'll get to the bottom of it,' Sally instructed. 'I know there is a lot of hardship, Mrs Martin, and I want to give all my staff a fair chance.'

'Yes, I understand that. All the girls think it a privilege to work here.'

'That is as I hoped,' Sally said. 'I will leave you to it, then. I am making my tour of the store. I like to visit every department once a week, just to be sure that everything is as it should be.'

Sally walked away smiling to herself. She sometimes regretted that Beth, Maggie and Rachel no longer worked at Harpers, but life moved on and her friends had other lives now. Beth had two little boys of her own – Jackie and Timmy – to look after, though the eldest was now at a preparatory school and she'd spoken of perhaps being able to pop into Harpers more.

'I'm not sure what I could do,' she'd told Sally when she'd asked her if she wanted her old job back. 'I couldn't come in often enough to be a supervisor and I don't have Mr Marco's flair for window dressing. I know Marion Jackson helps with that...' Sally had heard the wistful note in her voice and knew Beth missed her job sometimes.

'I can't go in every day myself, because of the children. Their nanny left me to marry and Mrs Hills has quite enough to do without my pair driving her mad. Jenny is at infants school for a few hours most days, but Peter is running around now and takes quite a bit of looking after.' Sally had reflected for a moment, then, 'I am looking for a nanny to take care of him while I am busy, but I still don't think I need to go in every day. What I have been thinking... well, some of the departments aren't looking their best. Would you like to do the job of a floor walker once or twice a week? Tell me what you think is letting a department down so that we can discuss how to make it look better?'

'You've just invented that job for me,' Beth had accused her with a laugh. 'It appeals, Sally, but are you sure you need me to help you?'

'It is just another pair of eyes,' Sally had replied, smiling. 'Perhaps it isn't enough for you but it would help me...'

'I'd like to help you, be your assistant,' Beth had told her. 'We could discuss anything that was bothering you and, if you don't wish to see a certain representative, I could do it for you – tell them to leave their brochures with me and look at the quality of their samples. I do know what you like, Sally.'

'You should do, you're my closest friend,' Sally had said and hugged her impulsively. 'I love Maggie, too, but I don't see her enough, and Rachel hardly ever. Maggie and Colin are in London as much as possible, because he likes to paint in his studio and she visits me and the soldiers' home we set up, but they take the children down to his father's estate in Devon for long holidays. Colin's father isn't always well, but Maggie says they are all getting on together much better now and she is quite fond of him.'

'She supervises the convalescent home down there, too,' Beth had agreed. 'It was good of her father-in-law to provide a house for those poor men. Maggie says he loves the children they adopted, though at the start he was against them doing it. Now, apparently, he dotes on them and has given them all the toys from Colin's nursery.'

'They are dear little things, so it is no wonder.' She paused, then, 'I suppose you know that the restaurant Jack and Ben are opening together is almost ready?' They had managed to buy a property close to Harpers store and were opening an exclusive restaurant very soon.

'Jack talks of nothing else. He is really looking forward to managing it.' Beth had laughed then. 'I'd begun to think it would never happen. It took ages to find the right premises and the alterations just seemed to go on and on – the builders were so busy...'

'There has been a lot of slum clearance going on,' Sally had pointed out. 'I suppose it is the right thing to do – but it must be hard being forced to leave your home.'

'Not if there are cockroaches coming out of the walls,' Beth had countered with a shiver. 'Those new terraced houses they are building to rehouse the displaced have bathrooms with inside toilets. Most of the houses that are coming down only have an outside toilet – and that is awful when you want to go in the middle of the night. There is still far too much poverty and bad housing in London.'

'Yes, I know you are right. My mother lived in some horrid houses before she married again. She told me about them when she came up to stay. Some of them actually had rats under the floorboards.'

'Ugh! No wonder she loves your house. You are lucky to have bought it when you did. We've found something we like at last, not too far from you in Hampstead, and it will be a relief when we move – for Fred and Vera as much as ourselves. Vera loves the children, but they must want a little peace sometimes.' Jack's father had at last married the lady he'd known for some years and they'd settled down happily together.

'Yes.' Sally had looked at her pensively. 'I was really sorry when Fred retired. We have a new man in the stores and he is very good at his job, but he isn't the same. He does his work but...' She'd shrugged. 'I always thought of your father-in-law as a friend.'

'Yes, and he still thinks a lot of you, but it was right for him and Vera to have some time together – to go out and enjoy themselves while they still can...'

'Yes, of course, it is and I don't begrudge him that time, I just feel something is missing when I go down to the basement,' Sally had reflected.

'I'll tell him he's missed, that will please him,' Beth had said, then, bringing her back to the subject of Harpers. 'So when would you like me to start my job?'

'I usually go in on a Monday and sometimes Thursday.' Sally had nodded. 'So Tuesday and Fridays for a start, but when the children are all in school, we shall probably pop in most days.'

'I'll start this week then,' Beth had looked pleased. 'I was beginning to wonder what I'd do with myself all day when Jack is at the restaurant and the children are in school.'

Beth would start the next morning. Sally was pleased because she was still not happy with several of the departments. They had plenty of stock now but were not always displaying it to the best advantage. Sally had spoken to her husband about it, but Ben looked at the bigger picture, not the small details. He hadn't seen what she'd seen. Sally would talk to Beth and see what she thought. They could have lunch together and look at some of the new-season catalogues too.

Yes, that would be a start. Sally knew she wanted some changes but wasn't yet sure what was needed. Jenni Harper, Ben's half-sister, had a good eye for stock, but she was busy with her own large fashion store in the north of England. When Sally had paid a flying visit earlier that year, she'd thought it very stylish and modern – and perhaps that was what was lacking a little in Harpers. You had to keep up to date with methods of display or the customers soon thought you were dowdy and old-fashioned and went elsewhere.

Ben wanted Harpers to be the biggest and best. Sally wasn't sure that they would ever be bigger than some of the large department stores in London, but they could certainly try to be the best...

2

'Have you got enough money for everything you need?' Marion Jackson's sister-in-law, Sarah, asked her as Marion was packing her basket with things she'd purchased for her husband, Reggie. 'Dan gave me extra this week so I can let you have some if you need it.'

'Sarah, you're a sweetheart and I love you,' Marion replied and gave her a quick hug. 'I'm not sure how I would have managed with Reggie in that hospital these past years without you and my brothers. You already do more than enough for us and I don't need anything else, thank you.'

Marion's wage was now almost double what she'd received on the counters at Harpers, because as an assistant window dresser, she was considered skilled staff, and she only went in three days a week. It was an ideal arrangement for her and she enjoyed working with Mr Marco. He had a lovely sense of humour and was a war hero. Marion admired him and they often talked about his son, Pierre. His wife had died during the Spanish Flu epidemic just before the war ended and he'd had to employ a nurse to care for his son at times, although most days he brought the boy into the store to be looked after in the nursery department, which Sally Harper had set up for her staff. Because she employed quite a few women, she'd made it possible for them to go on working even if they had a child – and with so many war widows, that was of huge benefit to Marion and to others.

It was because of Sally Harper and Maggie Morgan that Reggie had been given the help he needed to recover from the mental trauma he'd suffered in the war.

'It wasn't the actual wounds I got that made me break,' Reggie had told her when she'd visited the convalescent home the previous week. 'It was the lying in the trenches at night, wondering when the order to go forward would come and the relentless bombardment. It was seeing your friends and officers die right there beside you and knowing you might be next – and the fear of being a coward.'

'You were never a coward,' Marion had exclaimed. 'You did what you had to and you were one of the first to volunteer. No one could have known what it would do to you.'

Reggie had been such a bright, eager and upright young man when she'd first met him. She'd been reluctant to court him at first because of all her commitments at home, but he'd persisted and she'd fallen in love with him. They had married after her mother had died, though most of the time they'd been parted by the war – and then, when she'd looked forward to having him home, he'd had a nervous breakdown and hit her in sudden anger. Afterwards, he'd wept and begged her to forgive him. She'd told her friend Maggie and she and Sally Harper had come up with the idea of the rest homes.

Marion believed that her husband was making progress. The rest home near Epping Forrest was in a peaceful setting and the men were allowed to recover at their own pace. Not much treatment could be given, because so little was understood of the illness that many survivors were suffering, some in private at home. The lucky ones got a chance to talk their fears through with understanding nurses and doctors and, as some gradually felt able to go home to wives and families, perhaps rest, peace and quiet was all they needed.

'These men have been asked to bear more than any human can,' one doctor had told Marion. 'The mind is a strange thing, Mrs Jackson. A man's body is often strong and will endure terrible hardship, but the mind stores up trouble and then it comes out and he cannot control it.'

'Reggie was a gentle man before the war.' Marion had been fighting her tears. 'He hated himself for the way he was with me. Will he ever get better, sir?'

'I can't guarantee that,' the doctor had told her. 'But I believe he will – if you have the patience to wait for him and let him come back in his own time.'

'I will,' she'd promised. That had been at the start of Reggie's hospital stay and the many months and years between had been hard for Marion to bear. She'd had to be the main breadwinner in her family long before the war, caring for a sick mother and her siblings. One of her brothers had died in the war. Robbie, for whom her son was named, would never return, but Dan had come home to Sarah, and Dickon had done his duty to the family and her by working in the docks for long hours when he'd wanted to join up. He'd resented that and of late he'd started staying out with his friends at night, drinking or playing darts at the local pub. Her sister, Kathy, worked at the canteen at Harpers and was excited at the prospect of being promoted to the new restaurant as a junior chef.

'I've liked being at the canteen,' she'd told Marion when she'd heard she was being moved. 'But I'll get to do so much more at the restaurant.'

Yes, Kathy was happy and so was Dan. Married to Sarah and with a son of his own, he'd taken a steady job as a foreman in a biscuit factory, giving up his life at sea for his family.

As she caught her bus out to the rest home, Marion wished she could be as happy and settled as her sister-in-law. Dan and Sarah now had their own house. It was a few streets away from Marion's home and so they saw each other regularly. If Marion was visiting Reggie or working late at Harpers to get a window finished, her youngest sister, Milly, could go to Sarah for her tea. She could also go next door to Mrs Jackson, Reggie's mother, so Marion didn't have to worry that she was alone until she got home. Sarah would have willingly minded Marion's son, but Marion liked taking him with her to work. He was well looked after and she could pop in and see him, feed him during her own lunch break, and that was thanks to Sally Harper.

Marion never forgot Sally Harper in her nightly prayers. Had she not been fortunate enough to work at Harpers, she could well have been on the factory floor now, doing hard dirty work for much less than she earned in a job she loved. Not many would have given her so many opportunities. Marion knew she was lucky, despite her worries over Reggie. It wasn't easy to make ends meet with only one wage coming in, but it could have been so much worse.

* * *

Reggie was sitting by the window looking out at the pleasant gardens, waiting for her when she arrived. He waved and smiled and Marion's heart lifted. His face wasn't as thin as it had been and he was beginning to look more like his old self. Perhaps he would be well enough to come home soon.

He got up and walked to greet her as she entered the small

sitting room. The convalescent home was a real home, set in a nice but formal garden, not a cold hospital with the smell of starch and disinfectant. It was a large house that had been donated to the charity that ran it and the rooms were furnished with old, comfortable chairs and well-worn pieces that made you feel peaceful.

'Did you see the Queen has unveiled the statue to the memory of Edith Cavell?' he asked, indicating the newspaper beside him. 'About time if you ask me. She and others like her were marvellous out there.'

'I think all those nurses were brave to go out to the front line,' Marion said. 'Maggie Gibbs, as she was then, was one of them. It was Maggie that got you this place here, Reggie.'

He nodded but made no comment, seeming to drift off in a daydream for a moment before focusing on her again.

'How are you, love?' he asked as she put the basket down on the oak gate-legged table beside him. 'You shouldn't have brought all that – it looks heavy.'

'It wasn't too bad,' Marion replied and leaned forward to kiss him. He put his arm behind her head and pulled her in for a long kiss and she laughed when he released her. 'You're feeling better?'

'Yes, I am,' he agreed, his eyes lighting up in a way that reminded her of their courting days. 'The doctor says he thinks I'll soon be ready for a home visit – just a few days for a start to see how I manage... If you will have me?'

'Of course I will,' Marion said and touched his hand. 'You know I love you – and Robbie is growing up so quickly...'

'I hoped you might bring him today?'

'It isn't easy on the bus. If Sarah comes too, I can manage, but she was busy. She has an order for her sewing that has to go out in the morning.'

'You should've brought him and not the basket...' Reggie said, frowning.

'Your mum cooked some of your favourites – treacle tart and apple pies. I brought you some shaving soap and socks. You said you needed them?'

'Yes, I do,' he agreed, a shadow passed across his face. 'Sorry. I just want to see my son. It is a long time between visits, Marion. Time hangs in here. They give us things to do. I'm making a sewing basket for you... but it gets tedious. I had such plans for after the war. My father and brother... we were going to go into building...'

'It is happening, Reggie. Your brother sent you a letter. They are starting the business and you will be a part of it when you're well enough.'

Reggie shook his head. 'You don't understand. It is driving me mad just sitting around...' His voice rose a little and a nurse looked across at him. 'I'm not angry, Marion love, not with you – just myself for being such a fool.'

'It isn't your fault,' Marion assured him. 'I know how hard it must be for you, Reggie, just sitting here – as if the world is passing you by.'

Reggie's tension eased and he sat back in his chair. 'I was supposed to look after you, love. I don't even get a bloody war pension, because I am physically able to work. If I'd been killed, you would have got one.' He looked angry. 'You work and keep a home and visit me and all I do is complain. I want to take care of you. It's time someone did...'

'I'm all right. I can manage,' Marion said, her eyes meeting his. 'I just want you to be well and come home so we can be happy again.'

'Bloody war,' Reggie said and then laughed bitterly. 'I couldn't wait to get out there. I thought it was all going to be so simple. I'm a good shot and I thought I'd kill lots of the enemy and then come home. It's not like that...' He'd been sent home to recuperate and then back to the front twice; then given guard duty at the docks, where he'd been injured again.

'I know,' Marion replied. 'At least, I know that it has harmed you and lots of others. I can't know how awful it was, because I wasn't there. I didn't have to put up with things the way you did.'

'I'm lucky to have made it back.' Reggie swore softly. 'Why can't I just be normal again?'

'You will be,' Marion said. 'I know you will, Reggie – you have to because we need you, Robbie and I...'

Reggie sighed. 'I just want to be with him and you, to be a normal happy family.'

'You will soon,' Marion said and reached for his hand. 'Just try to relax and do whatever the doctors tell you – and then perhaps they will let you come home.'

'Sometimes, when one of us gets hysterical, they use chloroform to calm us down,' Reggie told her. 'It knocks you out and you feel a bit groggy when you come round – but it stops you being violent.'

'That doesn't sound very pleasant,' Marion said and frowned. 'What else do they do?'

'Nothing much, except encourage us to talk about what happened – and gardening. I like that, Marion...' An odd faraway look came to his eyes. 'I've never lived in the country. I think I might like it...'

Marion stared at him. 'What would you do there?'

'I'd work on a farm. I'd find a little cottage and I'd work on the land... When you do hard physical work, you can't think so much...'

'What about the building business? You were looking forward to that, Reggie.'

'They don't need me – besides, London is so noisy. I don't like the traffic. I don't like loud noises...' A shudder went through him.

'Is that what you want to do when you leave here?' Marion asked.

He nodded, still seeming distant, lost in thought.

'What about me – and Robbie, your mum and the others?'

'You and Robbie could come with me,' Reggie said. 'I'd like it if you did – but I think I shall go anyway...' As he talked, he seemed to have forgotten her, as if his mind had shut her out.

Marion was silent. How could he expect her to just leave everything – her whole life – and go somewhere she would know no one? She would have to leave behind her brothers, sisters and his large family too. She didn't feel she wanted to do that, but nor did she want to argue about it now.

'If it is what you want...' she said after a long pause.

'You wouldn't come though,' he said and turned his head to look out at the garden. 'I knew you wouldn't...'

'I haven't said no. It is a big decision for me. What about Kathy and Dickon and Milly?'

Reggie turned his gaze on her and the pain in his eyes made her gasp. 'What about me, Marion? Don't I count? You've looked after your family all these years – can't someone else take over? Don't you want us to be together?'

'Yes, of course I do...' Marion's throat closed with emotion. Reggie was her husband. She loved him and wanted him home and now she felt like crying. 'What about me, Reggie? Where does what I want come in?'

'I don't know,' he said and flopped further back in his chair. 'I can't think about all that... you'd better go. I feel tired and I might misbehave if you stay...'

'Reggie...' she began, but his eyes flashed at her. It was always the same. When she arrived, he was pleased to see her and talked of coming home and then he suddenly changed, turning sullen, as if she'd done something wrong. She got to her feet. 'I'm sorry if I've upset you. Shall I come next week?'

'Please yourself...' Reggie closed his eyes. She saw his right leg begin to shake. He clasped a hand over it and the nurse hurried towards him, kneeling down by his side.

'Reggie hasn't been too well for a couple of days,' she told Marion. 'Please leave now. Come next week. He will probably be better again then...'

Marion glanced at her husband, but his body was rigid as he tried to control his shaking. She walked away, her head down, tears springing to her eyes. Reggie had seemed so much better when she'd arrived, but he'd changed as they talked – perhaps because of her reluctance to give up her life and follow him to the country.

Would the peace of the countryside really be so much better for him than living in town? She knew that sudden loud noises could start him shaking, but she'd hoped the peaceful atmosphere of the convalescent home was making him better, but now...

Tears trickled down her cheeks. It was all so difficult and so sad. Other men had come home and been able to settle down in a short time, but many – and it ran into hundreds of thousands – were suffering like Reggie. As yet, there didn't seem to be a cure, nor was it universally accepted. Only a few doctors were trying to treat it. Marion thought it strange how some managed to fight their way back to normality and others didn't... was Reggie one of those? Would he always be this way?

Marion didn't know what she ought to do. Her duty as a wife was to go with Reggie wherever he went, of course – and perhaps it was time that she put her husband first. Milly was old enough to understand now. She could probably live with Sarah or Mrs Jackson...

Reggie's mother would be upset if he went away. She visited him once a week regularly. Perhaps it would be best to talk to her.

She was caring for Robbie while Marion visited the rest home. She
would talk to her when she got home.

'Go off to the country and work on a farm?' Mrs Jackson stared at
her in astonishment. 'I hope you told him not to be so daft, lass.
How could he expect it of you? Your family is here – and so is his.
His father and brothers are waiting for him to join the firm they
started.'

'I know and I told him so – but he is still unwell,' Marion said
falteringly. 'I thought he was getting better... he said he might
come home on a visit soon and then... he just said he wants to live
in the country and work on a farm. I ought to go if it is better for
him...'

'And what about your sisters and Dickon? Kathy will never do
what you've done, Marion. She has a good heart, but it takes more
than that – it takes guts to work the way you have and to put up
with all you've endured.'

'But I do love Reggie so much.'

'I love him too,' his mother said, 'but I won't stand for this
nonsense and so I'll tell him when I visit. I'd never see him or you
or my grandson...' Normally an easy-going woman she sounded
cross but Marion knew that when it came to it she wouldn't have
the heart to say much to her son.

'I like my job. It's good pay for three days a week,' Marion told
her. 'I've been lucky to manage all this time, but it's heartbreaking
to see the pain in his eyes. I'm not sure he can live in the town and
that means—'

'You'll not go?' Mrs Jackson cried. 'It's not right, love.'

'I may have to,' Marion replied. 'It means giving up a lot for me
– but I can't see what else I can do...'

'It's not a decision you can make now. He can't have one of his turns if you and Robbie are alone with him in the country – whatever would you do?'

'I don't know,' Marion admitted. She sighed. 'Perhaps he'll change his mind...'

3

'You look very smart,' Jack Burrows said as he looked at Beth. 'Is that a new dress?'

'Yes, I bought it for my job,' Beth replied, glancing down at the straight skirt of her dress that finished just below her knees. It was dark grey, had a squared neckline and a dropped waist with a little band of black satin that nestled on her hips and tied in a sash at the side. 'I wanted to look smart but formal – do you approve?'

'Of the style, yes,' Jack said, his gaze moving over her. 'You have good legs, Beth. You can wear the shorter length. I wasn't sure I liked it when I saw Vera wearing a dress halfway up her calves – but it looks good on you.'

'I hope you didn't say anything to Vera.' Beth glanced at her husband. He wasn't as tolerant of his father's new wife as she was, though he would never actually be rude or harsh to her. 'She was reluctant to buy that dress, but the salesgirl told her they were the fashion now and I thought it suited her.'

'I still think an ankle-length dress suits the older ladies better,' Jack said and laughed as he saw the sparkle in Beth's eyes. 'I know I am old-fashioned and so are a lot of men – but you look beautiful. You always do.'

Beth laughed. 'Charmer! I wonder why I married you...'

'Because I am handsome, delightful company and I'm going to be rich one day,' Jack teased. 'You're looking forward to this job, aren't you?'

'Yes. It will be fun,' Beth said. 'I loved working on the counters at Harpers, but I couldn't do that now. This is just a little job that I'll enjoy – and it means I'll spend more time with Sally discussing how we can improve Harpers...'

'I think the store looks good,' Jack said and saw a flash in her eyes. 'I'm not trying to put you off, Beth. I just think that Harpers was lucky to come through the war as well as it did – some businesses may never recover.'

'That wasn't luck, but hard work and determination on Sally's part,' Beth retorted. 'She held it together with pins sometimes, but she held on somehow. Imagine how many people would have lost their jobs if she hadn't. Ben was lucky. Without her, I doubt he'd have a store to come back to.'

'Yes, perhaps you are right,' Jack said. 'He has a lot of ideas for the future though. He isn't going to stop at one restaurant. We'll build a chain of them between us.'

'I'm glad you're happy, Jack.' Beth went to him and he put his arms around her, embracing her. 'I was afraid for a while that you never would be after—'

'After my brother's death?' Jack nodded. 'That was hard to take, Beth. Tim was too young to die that way – but I'm lucky. I survived and I have my beautiful wife and two wonderful sons. With the opening of the restaurant, I have all I could want.'

'Dad and Vera too,' Beth reminded him. 'We're lucky to have Fred. Vera is good for him. He is enjoying his retirement and we could never have left him alone, Jack. We wouldn't have our lovely new home...'

'I know you are fond of him.' Jack nodded. 'Dad thinks the world of you and the boys.' He glanced up at the clock on the mantel. 'We'd better get going or we shall both be late for work...'

* * *

'Good morning, Mrs Burrows,' Mr Marco smiled at Beth as she paused to watch him at work on a new window for the store; the theme seemed to be a fairground from what she could see. Mr Marco was always full of clever ideas. Sally didn't need to worry about the windows. 'If you will allow me to say so, that dress is very becoming.'

'Thank you, Mr Marco.' Beth raised her head a little higher. 'I bought it in the store and Minnie Stockbridge altered it to fit me... she made it slightly shorter.' Beth gave a little giggle. 'We have to keep up with the times.'

'Indeed, we do,' he replied. 'I think all the young ladies who work here should be wearing the shorter length – to show that we are a modern establishment.'

'Yes, that is an excellent suggestion. I shall make a note of it...'

Nodding to him, Beth continued to write on the notepad she had brought with her. The girls still wearing ankle-length dresses were a part of the problem; Harpers needed to move with the times. It would be much better if they all lifted their hems a little.

The lighting was a bit dull, too. Some brighter lights over the glass counters would make them sparkle, Beth thought and made a note of that, also. She looked around at the ground floor and frowned. Sally was right. There was something not quite pleasing in the way the counters were placed, but for a moment or so she couldn't quite see what was wrong – and then she realised that the counters were all spaced around the shop facing inwards, leaving a big hollow in the middle. It would look better if they were set at an angle so that customers moved between them.

Beth made some more notes on her pad and walked towards the lift, nodding to the friendly young man in charge. He smiled at her and asked politely which floor she wanted and she told him. As he turned away, she saw the scarring on one side of his face. Clearly, he had been wounded during the war.

She made a point of thanking him as she prepared to leave on the second floor. 'You're welcome, Mrs Burrows,' he said and she looked at him again.

'You know me?'

'I worked here in the basement with Fred Burrows before the war,' he told her. 'I remember you very well, Mrs Burrows. I'm Ernie...'

'Oh, you have grown up,' she cried. 'I'm sorry I didn't remember. Fred said you were the best helper he ever had.' She'd thought he'd been killed, but clearly, he'd survived his wounds.

'I wouldn't be any good these days – my leg won't let me lift a lot, but they thought I was a goner, so I'm lucky to be alive,' he said and grinned. 'So Mr Harper gave me this job...' He nodded his satisfaction. 'How is Fred then?'

'Enjoying his retirement. I'll tell him you asked after him. I know he'll say the same as me – well done for your service and for coming back to Harpers,' Beth said and saw him smile. 'I'll be going to the first floor next time.'

'Saved the best 'till last then...' He gave her another cheery grin and the lift went down in answer to a summons from the ground floor. Beth made another note on her pad and continued to the men's department.

She had no fault to find with it, because the rails were immaculate and the counters were neat. There were mannequins that normally went in the windows posed here and there and she noticed a beautiful evening suit that she thought would look wonderful on Jack. She didn't think much could be done to improve this department, so she spoke to Mr Brown, telling him how nice it all looked and then moved on.

The shoe department was next on Beth's tour and that made her frown. Apart from one small display of merchandise, it was just chairs and the stools the assistants used to sit on and fit the customers' shoes. It looked dull and Beth felt that something needed to be done. She knew there were many more designs of shoes than were on show and it meant the salesgirls would be backwards and forwards bringing out models to try to tempt the customers. How much better it could be if there were displays throughout. Glass cabinets all around the walls – or just shelves?

Perhaps that was a step too far, but if just one of a pair was put out, customers could look at styles they liked and ask to try on their size. Beth smiled at the idea and made a note on her pad.

From there, she went up a few stairs to the canteen, which all looked spick and span, and then summoned the lift to take her down to the first floor.

The bag, hat, scarf and jewellery department looked beautiful. Someone had arranged the hats in a lovely display. A stand displaying gloves and another with a scarf draped over it was eye-catching and the bags were displayed to advantage, as was the jewellery. Beth saw the new supervisor was just rearranging one of her counters and went up to her.

'Mrs Martin, isn't it?' she asked. 'I'm Beth Burrows. I'm helping Mrs Harper with ideas for the store. I must say your department looks beautiful.'

'Thank you,' Mrs Martin gave a smile of pleasure. 'I did have some experience of display, so I asked Mrs Harper if I could have the special stands and she got them for us.'

Beth nodded and looked about her. 'This department gets very busy at times. Do you have enough assistants?'

'Not really.' The reply didn't surprise Beth. 'We could do with another girl, especially when its break time. Either that or close for an hour – that might be easier.'

'That has never been Harpers' policy. We've always kept open. It isn't always as busy during the lunch hour.'

'It may not have been once,' Mrs Martin commented. 'However, of late, I have found it has been much busier than, say, two o'clock to three in the afternoon, and I've staggered the breaks more, though that isn't always popular.'

'I see...' Beth nodded. 'I know it can be very difficult. Sometimes I didn't take a lunch break at all.'

'But that isn't right, is it?' Mrs Martin lifted her head slightly.

'No, probably not,' Beth agreed. 'I didn't mind, but the girls must have their breaks, of course.' She hesitated, then, 'Would you like me to speak to Mrs Harper about it?'

'I was wondering... but, no, perhaps I shouldn't say...'

'Please do say what is on your mind,' Beth told her. 'It is what Mrs Harpers wants to hear – ideas that may improve the way Harpers is run. It is up to her and Mr Harper if they change anything, but I am sure they are open to suggestions.'

'I think it would be better to have another section for the jewellery,' Mrs Martin said. 'We need to keep the bags and jewellery separate and we need another display cabinet or even two. I have beautiful bags in the stockroom I have no space to display and it takes me away from the counters if I need to fetch them.'

'Yes, I do see that...' Beth looked around her. Most of the wall space was already in use. 'Perhaps the glass counters could be set differently and we could put another one or two in if they were slanted across like that...' She turned her body to show what she meant.

Mrs Martin looked puzzled. 'Would that not mean people could walk round them?' she asked. 'These things are expensive. It might mean some went missing...'

'Yes, we had a problem with stock being taken once before,' Beth agreed. 'I can't think how else it could be done – unless the bag cabinet was replaced by a taller one?'

'That might help but... would it not be possible to have a jewellery department elsewhere?'

'It has always been here,' Beth replied, a little shocked. 'It has worked well with the other things ladies like to buy.'

'They do have more room in the women's clothing department,' Mrs Martin persisted. 'Either they could have the jewellery or the bags or we could swop departments?'

'That is a rather radical change,' Beth said. 'I will speak to Mrs Harper after I've been to the women's clothing department, but I don't think it likely she would agree. The dressing rooms and the sewing room are all adjacent.'

'Yes, I suppose so,' Mrs Martin agreed. 'It just seems a waste of space...'

Beth nodded and left, feeling thoughtful. It was true that there was a lot of space in the women's dress department, but she knew that women liked to wander about looking at the clothes on rails and the seats set here and there were comfortable, making it a pleasant experience when shopping with friends and watching them try on different clothes. Somehow, she didn't think Sally Harper would want to change things that much, though the idea had its merits.

* * *

Sally listened to what Beth had to say when she visited her at home. She looked pleased when Beth made her suggestions about the shoe department and the ground floor.

'I had been thinking something similar, Beth,' she said, 'but I needed another opinion. Yes, I think we should have displays of shoes all around the department – and I was wondering if we should move the bags there?'

'Now that is a brilliant idea and it would kill two birds with one stone.' Beth explained what Mrs Martin had told her. 'She thought you had too much empty space in the clothing department and wanted to swap them over, but I thought that would be just too much upheaval.'

'If we ever get more floor space that might be a part of the refurbishment then,' Sally agreed. 'However, bags and shoes should match, so I think we might transfer them to that department. It will make the hat, scarf, glove and jewellery department easier to manage, too. I would like to expand the jewellery department. I think it could be completely independent and we should stock far more than we do, but we can increase the stock displayed once the bags are moved. I wonder...' She looked thoughtful. 'If all the stock was on display, apart from new stuff in the basement – would we need the stockroom?'

'You mean open that up and have it just for jewellery?' Beth nodded, catching Sally's excitement. 'I think the partition is just wood, so it could be done quite easily without too much mess.'

'I could have more hats where the bag counter stands now,' Sally went on and Beth laughed.

'You already had lots of ideas. Why did you need me?'

'Because I like to discuss things,' Sally replied with a smile. 'You are my closest friend, Beth, and it is easy to talk to you. Ben is so tied up with the restaurant at the moment and he is overseeing the men's department personally.'

'Is that why it was looking so good?' Beth laughed. 'It is very smart, Sally. There are several mannequins there now displaying suits and shirts – I noticed a smart evening suit that would look good on Jack.'

'You could order one for him if you have his measurements. It is Ben's new made-to-measure department. He thought the clothes were a bit dowdy so he has found some new tailors who came up with the idea. We take the waist and leg size, neck, shoulder and all the rest and then they make an appointment to come in and fit it before finishing. Ben had a new suit made for himself and it is so smart and elegant.'

'Then I'll order one for Jack,' Beth said enthusiastically. 'He was talking of taking me to the theatre for my birthday so it would be just what he needs. I don't think he has had a new suit since our wedding – except the one he had for work at the restaurant, but that is different.'

'Do order one,' Sally encouraged. 'It would please Ben. I think the orders have been a little slow, but I am certain it will catch on in time.'

'Men are often so careless about their clothes; they just buy whatever is available, unless they are used to having them fitted and then they have their own tailors. It is a new thing to come to a department store for a fitting.'

'I agree, but Ben liked the idea, so he'll see how it goes. After all, Minnie Stockbridge does the same thing for our ladies...'

'She does such beautiful embroidery,' Beth said and sighed. 'Unfortunately, it has rather gone out of fashion since the war. The new designs are much plainer in a way...'

'Plain but smart,' Beth agreed. 'I wasn't sure Jack would like the dress I chose for work, but he does.'

'I think it looks wonderful,' Sally told her. 'I've bought something similar – though mine is an evening dress, but it has the dropped waist and the shorter skirt. I haven't shown it to Ben yet.'

'He will love it,' Beth assured her. 'Long dresses are just so out of style now. I think all the salesgirls at Harpers should be told to take up their hems. Mr Marco thinks so too.'

A little laugh broke from Sally. 'He would say that because he is so stylish himself. Did you notice the little moustache he has grown? I swear it is because he saw Ronald Coleman as a sheik in that play *The Maharani* of something or other at the theatre...'

'Oh, Fred took me to see that during the war,' Beth cried. 'It was wonderful. I do love the theatre, Sally. We don't go often enough.'

'We must arrange something for your birthday,' Sally said affectionately. 'I know Jack is busy most evenings with the restaurant, but surely they can manage without him for once?'

'Oh, I think if it was on a Monday... the restaurant doesn't open on Mondays...' Beth laughed. 'I don't mind that he is busy, Sally. At least he is home and I don't have to worry that he is being shot at or that his ship will sink.'

'Thank God it is over,' Sally agreed. 'Ben wasn't often in danger, but he was always away for one reason or the other. It is so good to have him home.' The doorbell pealed and Sally looked at her. 'Maybe he has forgotten his key again...'

Mrs Hills came to the doorway. 'Mr O' Sullivan is here to see you, Mrs Harper.'

Sally was on her feet immediately as he followed her in. 'Mick – how wonderful to see you! When did you get back?'

'A few days ago,' he told her and moved forward to take her hands. 'It is so good to see you, Sally Harper. I went to the store, but I was told you were not available... to the likes of me... sure 'tis a hard thing when your friends won't see you...'

'Mick! You know that isn't true,' Sally cried. 'She was out of order speaking to you as she did – had I known, I would have asked you to visit before.'

'Sure, and don't I know that, my darlin',' Mick said and smiled. 'I've spoken to the lucky man who stole you from me – and he invited me to dinner this evening. I thought I would come to see you and make sure it's not putting you out?'

'How could it?' Sally told him. 'Come and say hello to Beth – you do remember her?'

'Of course I do. How are you, Mrs Burrows? Yes, I remember all your friends, Sally Harper,' Mick said and then, as he saw her look, 'My broken heart is mended. When I went to visit my folks in America, I wasn't sure I would come back, but I decided I missed you all and here I am...' They had been close friends a long time and for Mick it had perhaps been more once, but then he'd fallen in love with Maggie and when she'd rejected him to marry Colin it had broken his heart. Sally had been really worried about him then.

'I saw some of the merchandise you sourced for Harpers, Mr O'Sullivan,' Beth said. 'I like the silver jewellery.' He'd agreed to help source American goods for Harpers when he'd bought Jenni Harper's shares before leaving England.

'It is Aztec,' Mick replied. 'At least, it is based on the jewellery the Aztec tribes wore in their ceremonies and quite beautiful, I think.'

'Jenni Harper sourced some similar for us once and it sold out so quickly,' Sally said. 'We are going to expand our jewellery department, Mick. I shall be wanting a lot of different stock soon.'

'I've seen some stylish Art Decco designs right here in London,' he told her. 'I'm thinking of buying a workshop and starting up in the business.'

'That is a new idea for you,' Sally remarked. 'I thought restaurants were more in your line?'

'They were, but I met this young craftsman who designs in gold and silver and he needs a place to work,' Mick explained. 'His jewellery is so fine and delicate. Once you see it, you'll be wanting it for your department. It's just a part of what I'll be doing...'

'What else do you have in mind?' Sally was interested and Beth looked on curiously.

'Motorcars,' he said and grinned. 'I came into a little money while I was over there and I invested it in motorcars in America – and I'll be bringing them over here. They will be special cars, not the nice little black boxes on wheels that Mr Ford is making so popular, but individual, built to the specification of the owner. Mind you, if the government brings in the new tax of one pound per horsepower, they will be more expensive to run.'

'Oh, I doubt that will stop you.' Sally laughed. 'Mr Ford's cars are reliable, that is why they are popular with those who can afford them – but could you build a car to suit me?'

'What about a white one?' Mick asked. 'A nice little roadster you could drive to go shopping in?'

'Oh yes!' Sally's eyes sparkled. 'That sounds like fun. Are you going to race them? I've heard people are racing cars somewhere now...'

'Some of my customers will,' Mick told her. 'But I just want to build them and don't you go thinking about racing yours or I won't build it for you.'

Sally pealed with laughter. 'I have two children and a business to run, Mick O'Sullivan – don't you go putting ideas into my head.'

'She is only teasing you,' Beth said and looked at Sally. 'You wouldn't think of it, Sally. You mustn't – it is too dangerous.'

'It can be,' Mick agreed. 'Leave it to the men, Sally Harper.'

'Oh, you're a spoilsport,' Sally said and then a cry from the doorway made them all look as Mrs Hills brought in her son, Peter.

'I am sorry, Mrs Harper, but he woke up and heard your

voice...'

'Come to Mummy, darling,' Sally said and opened her arms as he darted towards her and then went plop down on his bottom just in front of her. She scooped him up and took him on her lap, kissing the top of his head, which was covered in soft curling locks. He smelled of baby powder and soap and his little face shone as he looked up at her.

'And this is for you...' Mick produced a parcel wrapped in brown paper and gave it to the little boy.

Sally helped him unwrap it and revealed a shining dark green model roadster car with an open-top and red seats. The child put it in his mouth straight away and she removed it.

'It is for looking at, not playing with,' Sally reproved. 'He's a little too young yet.'

'There is a doll with a porcelain head and some pretty clothes for Jenny in the hall,' Mick told her with a shrug. 'I brought you this...'

He opened his hand and she saw the delicate pendant lying there. It was a gold square with a small pearl at the centre and a z-like engraving round the mount. The chain also had geometrical shapes and was so unusual that she was intrigued.

'It is beautiful, thank you,' Sally exclaimed, examining the exquisite workmanship. 'Did your craftsman make this?'

'He did, especially for you,' Mick said. 'I thought you would like it – it is modern and new.'

'I haven't seen anything as pretty in ages,' Sally remarked and showed it to Beth.

'That is gorgeous,' she said. 'Imagine a counter in your new department filled with jewellery like that, Sally...'

'I am,' Sally replied, eyes lighting up. 'How soon can you show me more, Mick – and will you make some lines exclusive to Harpers?'

'You will have the sole rights to his work for a year,' Mick told her. 'Kavi is just getting started and he can only produce so much, but he has several pieces ready to show you. I'll bring him to your office at the store and you can see for yourself.'

'That is an unusual name,' Sally was intrigued again.

'He is Russian,' Mick said. 'Russian Jew to be exact and he escaped from a purge when many of his people were being killed in the upheaval after the war. He went to America but was unable to set up his own workshop there and could only find manual labour.'

'So, you persuaded him to come here?'

'He'd wanted to come to England for a while, because he has some family here.' Mick shrugged. 'I made it possible. He is a nice person but... you'll see for yourself when you meet him.'

'I shall look forward to it,' Sally said. 'Would you like some tea or coffee now – we were about to have some...'

'I'll be on my way,' Mick replied with his easy smile. 'We'll talk some more this evening.'

'I'll see you to the door...' Sally went with him and gave him a little kiss on the cheek. 'I am glad you are back, Mick. I wasn't sure you would ever return to us.'

'I wasn't sure either,' he told her and grinned. 'I'm like the bad penny, Sally Harper. I always turn up.'

She laughed as he went out into the hall and then returned to Beth. 'He seems better now. I think his time in America did him good.'

'In more ways than one,' Beth agreed. 'That necklace is very elegant, Sally. Isn't it strange how we were talking about making it a department on its own – and then this comes your way?'

'I find things happen like that,' Sally replied. 'Perhaps it was meant to be. I am very curious to see what this Mr Kavi is like...'

4

Kathy Jackson looked at the girl who had just sat down by the window in the Harpers' canteen with a cup of tea and a Chelsea bun. She was a little thing – attractive but sad-looking. Kathy believed her to be on the counters in the department that Marion had once worked in. Why wasn't she eating a proper lunch? Perhaps she couldn't afford it?

As she walked into the kitchens, Mrs Higgs, the cook, gave an audible sniff. 'Did you forget something?' she asked. 'I thought you was off to that fancy new restaurant?'

'I just went for a look today; I actually start tomorrow,' Kathy told her as she put on her long white apron. 'I met the chef – he is French and has a funny little moustache...' Mrs Higgs gave a snort of derision. 'I am only going to assist, but I wouldn't have been promoted if you hadn't helped me so much. I'll always be grateful...'

Mrs Higgs nodded but still looked grumpy. 'He won't treat you as well as I do,' she stated. 'I know them sort. He'll shout at you and have you doing all the worst jobs and you will wish you were back here.'

'I've loved being here, but I need to...' Kathy had been going to say that she needed to learn more, but that would upset her friend. 'I need to see how the other half live...' she finished lamely.

'Well, good luck to you, but don't go getting ideas above your station,' Mrs Higgs warned with another sniff. 'If you're here to work, get on with them bread-and-butter puddings. Once the lunch hour gets going, we'll have a rush on them, you'll see.'

Kathy nodded and did as she was asked, buttering the bread and lining the dish before adding dried fruit and then beaten egg. Her thoughts were still with the young woman she'd seen sitting in the canteen. The look in her eyes had reminded Kathy of a look she'd seen in her mother's eyes so many times – part distress, part hopelessness. Why was she so unhappy? Had her supervisor been on to her over some foolish mistake – or was it something in her home life that had given her that air of sadness?

'Well,' Mrs Higgs was at her side. 'Did you like the look of the kitchens at the posh restaurant then?'

'Yes, very smart and lots of working space,' Kathy told her. 'Why didn't you apply for a job there, Mrs Higgs?'

'Because I know my limits...' She sighed. 'If I'd had the chance when I was young and free like you, well, I might have gone further. I'm a good cook, but I haven't had the time or the opportunity to do all that fancy stuff...'

'I saw the menus,' Kathy told her. 'They do have some fancy appetisers and, of course, there is good meat – like steak and pheasant and all that sort of thing – but I bet they won't taste any better than your cottage pie and your bread-and-butter pudding.'

'Mebbe they won't at that,' Mrs Higgs said and gave a cackle of laughter, her good humour restored. 'It isn't that I grudge your good fortune, Kathy. I'm going to miss you, that's all. I know I've got another young girl coming to take your place, but it won't be the same. I'll have to teach her everything.'

'Thank you. I shall miss you, too,' Kathy said, but Mrs Higgs only sniffed. 'Maybe the new girl will be better than you think.'

Mrs Higgs sniffed again. 'You were a decent little cook before you came and I think you have a good chance of getting somewhere if you stick to your guns and don't go and fall in love and get married.'

'I'm never doing that,' Kathy said. 'I've seen the way men treat their wives. My father was a drunken old so-and-so – and Marion's husband...' She shook her head. 'I mustn't say it. He was all right before the war, but even then, he was on about her giving up the life she loves to do what he wants – stay home, mind the house and look after him.' Kathy's head went up. 'Why shouldn't a woman be independent and have a good life without being wed?'

'No reason at all if it's what she wants,' Mrs Higgs said. 'I was as happy as Larry with my Jeb, but he caught a chill and died when he was thirty. I had a young lad to bring up and a living to make, so I did the only thing I knew how – I cooked for a lady. It was long hours and my lad spent a lot of time round my sister's house, but I managed to give him a good education...' Mrs Higgs shook her head. 'He went off to join the navy before the war.'

'Where is he now?' Kathy was intrigued. She'd never spoken of her son before.

'Somewhere in the Mediterranean,' Mrs Higgs said with a deep sigh. 'His ship went down and...' She shook her head. 'No use in crying over spilt milk. I've still got me job and my sister, so I'm better off than a good many.'

'I'm sorry,' Kathy said. 'You've never said anything.'

'Well, I wouldn't, would I?' Mrs Higgs replied sharply. 'Get on with them veg now, Kathy. The orders have started to come in.'

* * *

Kathy forgot about the girl with the sad eyes until she got home that evening. Marion hadn't been to work that day and she'd cooked a big stew with carrots, onions, potatoes and cabbage. She'd also made rock buns and an apple crumble.

'How did you get on, it being your last day at the canteen?' Marion asked her.

'It was good,' Kathy said and smiled. 'How is little Robbie?'

'He's finally sleeping,' Marion replied. 'I think he plays me up – when Sarah has him, he is as good as gold.'

'Perhaps it is to pay you back for leaving him,' Kathy said as she washed her hands at the sink and was then sorry that she'd said it, as she saw Marion's stricken look. 'I didn't mean that you shouldn't...'

'Reggie did, though,' Marion said and sighed. 'He wrote me a horrid letter and said as much when I saw him last, accusing me of preferring my job to my family.'

'He didn't mean it, love,' Kathy said. 'You know what that doctor told you – Reggie does and says things he doesn't mean, because his mind is all jumbled up. He is desperately unhappy and so he takes it out on you.'

Marion nodded. 'I know, but it doesn't make it easier to bear, Kathy.' Her shoulders went back as she made an effort to change the subject. 'What did Mrs Higgs have to say about your new job?'

'She was a bit miffed – but only because she will miss me,' Kathy told her. 'I've said I'll visit her now and then. I think she is lonely. Her husband died when she was young and her son was killed in the war.'

'That bloomin' war!' Marion muttered. 'Yes, you visit when you can, Kathy. She has helped you with your cooking a lot.'

'I told her so...' Kathy paused then, 'Do you ever visit your old department, Marion?'

'Sometimes. I go in to have a look and also to borrow stock if we need more than we have for the windows.' She looked at Kathy. 'Why do you ask?'

'There is a young woman – well, about my age. I think she works there?'

'You mean Miss Lilly Ross?' Marion asked. 'She's a bit older than you but works as a junior helping on whatever counter needs her. Why do you mention her?'

'She looks so sad. I saw her in the canteen this morning. She had a cup of tea and a Chelsea bun, but she was just sitting staring out of the window.'

'I believe she may have some problems at home,' Marion said. 'I don't know much, but someone said her mother is an invalid and Lilly has younger siblings, so I expect she has a lot to do when she gets home.'

'The way you did when Ma was ill and...' Kathy shook her head. 'I thought things would get better for you when you married Reggie. They haven't, have they?'

'In some ways,' Marion said. 'I do love him, Kathy, despite the things he says – and what happened that day.'

'He hit you,' Kathy retorted. 'I know he isn't like Dad. It was his illness – but why take it out on you?'

'You know what they say, you always hurt the one you love,' Marion replied sadly. 'He is still my husband and I love him. I'm not sure he still loves me. He wants to go right away to settle in the countryside... that is what the letter is all about. He knows I don't want to go and he's striking out at me.' She pushed back a lock of dark hair from her eyes.

'You won't go?' Kathy burst out just as Milly came into the kitchen. She was twelve now and a leggy little girl, but bright and energetic.

'Is dinner ready?' she asked. 'I'm hungry.'

'Almost,' Marion told her. 'Just pop upstairs, love, and see if Robbie is awake. Don't wake him if he is asleep.'

Milly made a face but went off obediently.

Marion turned to Kathy. 'You'd manage here if I went, wouldn't you? I would take Robbie, of course – I'm not sure if Reggie would tolerate Milly, but if not, Sarah would look out for her while you're at work.'

'But... you'd have to give up your job,' Kathy said and grunted with disgust. 'You love that job – and you don't even know how Reggie would be with you if you went.'

'It's a chance I have to take,' Marion replied softly. 'I don't like leaving you in the lurch, but Reggie's mother finally agrees, after visiting him and seeing how much he wants it. She has offered to help you and Dickon all she can. Milly could live with her if she chose.'

'But...' Kathy shook her head. The thought of coming home to an empty house, to cooking for her brother and sister after a long day at work and having to find the money for rent and everything appalled her. 'I don't think I could manage here, Marion. My hours are longer than yours ever were and I couldn't look after the house alone. I might have to go into lodgings. Milly could go to Sarah or your mother-in-law and Dickon... he'll have to find lodgings too.'

'You would give up the house?' Marion looked thunderstruck. 'Oh, Kathy, no. You can't do that, after all...' She shook her head. 'It isn't fair, love. I've looked after you all for years...'

'I know and perhaps I'm selfish, but I can't do it. I won't,' Kathy said but felt awful as she saw her sister's face. 'Why should I? I have to work hard in my new job or I'll lose it. I haven't got the time or the energy to look after a home as well. Not all of it. I give you a hand now and then. Why do you want to leave us?'

'I don't – but if I say no, I'll lose Reggie. It will be the end for us. He needs this, Kathy. I don't have a choice...'

Kathy shook her head. 'I'm going upstairs. I don't want any stew.'

She rushed from the room, tears starting to her eyes. How could Marion be so selfish as to walk out on them – just when Kathy had the job she'd wanted for so long? She would need all her energy for the work ahead and just didn't have the time to look after her brother or her younger sister.

5

Lilly sighed as she saw the state of the kitchen. Her brothers had been at it again, throwing their work boots in the corner, dropping their filthy jackets on the tiled floor she'd scrubbed the night before. Why couldn't they take them off outside and save the coal dust getting everywhere? It was a decent job, delivering the coal and coke folk needed, but dirty work. Lilly's eldest brother, Ted, was forbidden to take his work boots and coat home – his wife refused to have them in her house.

'Lilly, is that you?' Her mother's voice sounded weary but urgent as she called from the other room.

'Yes, Ma, coming.' Lilly smothered a sigh and went through into what had once been a spick-and-span parlour hardly used but was now her mother's bedroom. The smell of urine and vomit met her instantly and she understood the urgency. 'Don't worry. I'll soon clear it up—'

'I'm such a trouble to you.' There were tears in her voice, but Lilly shook her head and smiled.

'You know I don't care, Ma. I want to look after you. I love you.'

'I know, but it isn't fair,' her mother said faintly, smothering a moan as Lilly rolled her to one side to remove the folded sheet beneath her. Under that was a rubber sheet to save the mattress, so it was a simple thing to slip another folded sheet under her. The vomit was in a bucket beside the bed, but some had gone on the cover. Lilly whisked that away, carrying the soiled items and the bucket through to the scullery. She dumped the sheets and cotton candlewick cover into a tub of cold water and left them to soak. Later she would wash them and, because it was a warm spring night, leave them out on the line to dry. She rinsed her hands, filled a basin with warm water and returned to the bedroom to bathe her mother's face, hands and her thighs.

'There, that feels better, doesn't it?' she said cheerfully after she'd gently patted her dry and helped her into clean nightclothes. 'I'll get supper on for the boys and then I'll bring you something. What could you eat? A nice soft-boiled egg or a bit of ham?'

'I only want a cup of tea,' her mother began, but the look Lilly gave her stopped her. 'All right then – I'll have an egg sandwich, please.'

'Good.' Lilly bent to kiss her cheek. Her skin was so papery thin and beneath the smell of soap, the odour of ill-health lingered. 'I'll get their supper cooking. Where are the young ones?'

'I heard them playing in the street earlier,' her mother told her with a faint smile. 'They will come charging in when they know tea is ready.'

Lilly nodded and went back to the kitchen. It was a long, wide room with a dark slate-tiled floor and two big pine dressers, one at either end. In the middle was a long pine table that her mother had used to scrub at least twice a day, and a hotch-potch of chairs were grouped around it. Under the window was the deep stone sink with a wooden drainer either side. Faded floral curtains covered the space beneath and it was there Lilly stored her vegetables.

She took out six large potatoes, a big cabbage, four large carrots with the dirt still on them; it was the best way to store them and out in the garden shed there was an almost empty sack of carrots that had been bought from the wholesale market by Ted and brought home on the back of his lorry.

Ted was the eldest and ran the family coal business. He had an ancient lorry that was a survivor from long before the war and had belonged to their father. The thought of her late father brought tears to Lilly's eyes. She'd loved him so much, because he was the kindest, best father a girl could want. His death from a sudden and fatal heart attack had hit Lilly hard and had almost killed her mother.

Annie Ross had been an invalid since the birth of her seventh child, all of whom had lived until the war, when Sam and Will had been killed. Young Stevie had been a large baby and she'd been too many hours in childbirth. Oh, she'd struggled on for a few years, doing her duty by her family, but, after the loss of Archie Ross, her much-loved husband, she had collapsed and been left paralysed down one side. Her illness had never been properly diagnosed and the doctor had told Lilly that her mother had gone into a decline because of a broken heart. Lilly wasn't sure she believed that, but she had no money to take her mother to the hospital to see a specialist and so all she could do was care for her.

'I'll look after you both,' Ted had told Lilly when he got back from the war. Unlike Sam and Will, he'd gone right through it without a scratch. 'You stay home now and look after Mum.'

Unfortunately, Ted had found it difficult to manage two homes on just his small profits. He had a wife and two children himself. Lilly had discussed it with her mother and a neighbour, who offered to pop in now and then to see she was all right.

'She can bang on the wall if she is desperate,' Effie Bates said. 'These walls are paper-thin, so I'll hear her.'

It wasn't ideal, but Lilly had seen the relief in Ted's eyes when she'd told him she had another job after she'd been let go from the munitions factory.

'It isn't much money at first,' she'd told him, 'but there is a chance of promotion at Harpers if I work hard.'

'You'll have to work 'ard an' all; it ain't right, but I can't give you enough,' Ted had said gruffly and looked slightly ashamed. 'I'll look in on Ma, too, when I'm this way and so will Joe. We'll help all we can, Lilly. I ain't abandoning you. I'll still give you the ten shillings a week.'

Ted was a good brother and Lilly was grateful for his help.

She heard a clatter of feet behind her and smelled the soap as her second-eldest brother, Joe, entered the kitchen. The first thing he did when he got home from working on the coal round was to strip off and head for the bathroom, which was behind the scullery. It was a grand name for the tin bath in an adjacent lean-to that they all used, but at least they had a private space instead of having to bathe in the kitchen like many folks.

'Hello, our Lilly,' Joe said and put his arm around her waist. 'What are we having for supper tonight?'

'Mash, cabbage, carrots and lamb chops,' Lilly said. 'I got a half-crown extra this week as a bonus, so I thought I'd treat us all. There's an egg for Ma and a little bit of ham, too.'

'The chops are a real treat.' Joe grinned at her. He flicked at her hair, which she'd had cut short so that it curled in her neck. 'Fancy our little Lilly being a Harpers' girl now... posh shop...'

'Give over,' Lilly said. 'I've got the veg on, so I'm going to make a pot of tea and take Ma a cup. If you want to be useful, give Stevie and Carol a shout.'

'They went next door to Effie's house,' Joe told her. 'She made treacle tart and you know what they're like for a treat.'

'I hope they haven't gorged themselves,' Lilly grumbled. 'I don't want these chops wasted.'

'They won't be,' Joe promised. 'Any chops left over will do for me tomorrow. I'll have 'em instead of sandwiches.'

Even as he spoke, the door opened and Lilly's youngest brother and her sister rushed in. Carol was nine, her fair hair in plaits that had started to unravel and Stevie was seven, his dark hair standing up like a brush on top where Joe had chopped it off too short. He had been the cause of his mother's decline in health, but no one had ever spoken of it in his hearing and never would. He was a lovely lad, always bright and cheerful, and the image of his father, with his dark hair and eyes. Lilly loved him the best, though she tried not to let the others see it.

'Is supper ready?' Stevie said. 'I'm hungry, our Lilly.' He came towards her and looked at the meat on a plate on the table. 'Are we having chops? Cor! I love lamb chops.'

Lilly ruffled his hair. 'Yes, I know you do, Stevie. It is a treat because I got extra in my pay this week.' She smiled at him. 'Can you take this cup of tea through to Ma for me, please?'

'I'll take it,' Carol said. 'He will only spill half of it.'

'Then you can carry Ma's sandwich, Stevie.'

Lilly sent them off and turned back to the range. Sometimes she wished they had a nice smart gas cooker like Effie's son had just had installed for her, but the range was useful, because it heated their water. She couldn't afford to buy a gas cooker anyway, so perhaps it was just as well as she'd still have needed the range.

She started to cook the chops and the smell was tantalising. Their supper was just about ready when both Stevie and Carol returned from their mother's room.

'I'm starving,' Stevie declared and rushed for his place at the table. Joe joined him and the two of them indulged in some play fighting as they waited for Lilly to serve them.

'Can I do anything?' Carol asked. She'd undone her plaits and her hair fell in little twists to her shoulders.

'You can carry Joe's plate,' Lilly offered, noting the subdued look in her sister's eyes. 'What's wrong, love?'

'Nothing...' Carol shook her head, but a hint of tears was in her eyes. She sniffed them back. 'I'll tell you later...'

'Right, I'll hold you to that,' Lilly said. She served up the food and silence fell as they all enjoyed their special treat.

* * *

Joe had gone off to meet some friends. Lilly suspected he was going to the pub, but as he normally made a half-pint last all evening, she never minded. He was a good brother and gave her a third of his wages every week.

Carol helped Lilly clear the plates into the sink and watched as she poured hot water over them.

'Now then,' Lilly said. 'What's upsetting you, love?'

'It's Ma—' Carol gulped back her tears. 'She won't ever get better, will she?'

'I don't know. What made you think it?'

'I heard Effie telling her married daughter that Annie Ross was in a bad way and likely to pass on sooner rather than later.'

'She shouldn't have said that.' Lilly frowned. 'You know Ma is paralysed down one side, that's why she can't get to the toilet or help herself when she feels sick.'

'I know – but I didn't think she was going to die soon.'

'I don't think she is,' Lilly said. 'Yes, she is an invalid, but that doesn't mean she will die. What else did Effie say about Ma?'

'Oh, nothing bad. She said she was the sweetest person alive and she liked looking after her. I think her daughter didn't like her coming in to look after Ma. She said she needed help with the kids if her mother had time to spare...'

'I see...' Lilly was thoughtful. She would have to pop round to see Effie, because if she regretted saying she would help, Lilly would need to find someone else.

She washed the last dish and decided to go round now. The dirty linen would have to wait for a bit...

* * *

'Lord bless you, love,' Effie said when she asked her if it was too much to pop in three times a day. 'Wherever did you get that idea? Annie is my friend and she would do the same for me if she could.'

'Carol heard something you said to your daughter—'

'Lor! I'm sorry, love. I never meant her to hear. I was just trying to get Marge off my back. I didn't think the kids could hear – they were playing games in the garden.'

'You don't think Ma is going to die, do you?' Lilly looked at her. 'Have you seen something I haven't?'

'No. I promise I'd tell you, Lilly. It's me and my wicked tongue. I just said that to make Marge think it wouldn't be for long. She will go on and on about me mindin' her kids and I'd far rather look after your ma. Marge's kids are proper hooligans.'

'That's a relief,' Lilly confessed. 'I'm not sure what I'd do if you didn't pop round, Effie. Ma can't manage for herself and I do need to work.'

'It's a cryin' shame what 'appened to yer dad,' Effie said. 'Archie Ross was a good man. He delivered the coal all round and there was never a bag short. If he *said* two bags, it was two bags.'

Lilly heard something in her voice. 'Ted is honest too, Effie – what makes you think different?'

Effie's neck went a bit red. 'It ain't me, love – but I've heard a couple of customers say he's short-changed 'em. Either the bags ain't full or he only delivered one and charged for two...' She shrugged. 'I know things are hard, but folk will go elsewhere if they think he's cheating them.'

'He wouldn't...' Lilly's neck prickled. Surely her brother wouldn't be such a fool? 'I know he's finding it hard to get enough business... someone must be spreading lies to harm him.'

'Mebbe that's it,' Effie agreed, but Lilly saw the doubt in her eyes.

'I'm glad you told me,' Lilly said. 'Dad would turn in his grave if he heard such tales.'

'Aye, he would. Archie Ross would have given you tuppence rather than steal a ha'penny.'

Lilly laughed. 'He so would! I'll speak to Ted – see if he can solve the mystery.'

She was deep in thought as she left Effie's house and went through the narrow passage that divided the two lots of terraced houses. Surely Ted wouldn't do anything dishonest? She couldn't believe it, but she would have to tell him when he came in the morning to see Ma.

* * *

'What?' Ted exploded with indignation when Lilly explained what was being said about his deliveries. 'It's lies, our Lilly. I've never cheated anyone in my life and I'll kill the bugger what said it!'

'You can't kill Effie and she only repeated what others had told her,' Lilly said. 'I told her it was lies, Ted. I knew you wouldn't do that – but someone is saying it, so be careful. Someone wants to ruin your business, though I don't know why.'

'I think I might,' Ted said, an angry expression in his eyes. 'There's someone else started delivering on the same streets. Young upstart, only got a handcart, but as cheeky as they come.'

'You'd best have a word with him,' Lilly said. 'Make him under-

6

'Have you seen Mrs Harper this morning?'

Andrea drew in her breath as the handsome man spoke to her. She'd watched him approach, wondering if he was Mr Harper, but she wasn't sure, because although she'd been working here some weeks now, she hadn't actually seen him before – except once at a distance.

'I arranged to meet her for lunch, but she didn't arrive and she isn't in the office. I wondered if she'd been into this department?'

'No, sir. I don't believe she has. I'd have seen her. I haven't left the floor this morning.'

'Ah,' He glanced at his watch. 'Aren't you due for a lunch break soon?' His words confirmed her assumption that he was her boss

'Yes, Mr Harper, when Lilly gets back... she is coming now, but if I can be of any help?'

'Well, yes, you might be able to – but don't let me interfere with your lunch break...'

'What might I do?' Andrea asked, feeling a tingle of excitement.

'I have a salesman waiting in my office. He is selling something I don't feel qualified to give an opinion on...' Mr Harper's eyebrows stand that two can play at the same game. You hear he's been calling you a cheat; you tell everyone his stuff is nutty slack.'

'Yeah, that would do it,' Ted replied with a grin. 'My coal is all good stuff and the coke lasts for ages. I'll make certain folk see what I deliver in future. You don't know who was saying they'd been given short?'

'Effie didn't tell me that,' Lilly said. 'You could go round and ask. If you tell her face to face it is a lie, she might remember the names.'

'You're a clever girl, our Lilly,' Ted said. 'Joe says you bought chops with your bonus last night. You should have kept a bit back for yourself.'

'I will one day. I need some shoes,' Lilly admitted. 'I get a discount at Harpers, but they are still too expensive for me. I'll buy a pair from the nearly new stall on the market when I've saved a few shillings.'

'Mebbe I'll get you a pair for your birthday,' her brother said and smiled. 'You're a good girl, Lilly, and I'm glad you didn't believe bad of me.'

'I never would,' she told him. 'You'd best get off, Ted. You've got work to do.'

'So have you, I dare say.' He nodded. 'It never stops for us, does it, Lilly? Perhaps the crooks have it best—'

'You wash your mouth with salt,' Lilly retorted. 'If Dad heard you say that, he would take his belt to you.'

'No, he wouldn't. He'd just look at me reproachful and that hurt more than the strap they gave us at school.'

Lilly nodded her agreement. Her father would never have lifted a finger to any of them; he hadn't needed to, when just a look said more than a thrashing ever could.

lifted in a way Andrea found totally fascinating. 'Ladies undergarments. I asked if he could come back tomorrow when my wife is in, but, apparently, he has a big round and will be on his way to the Midlands in the morning.'

'Then I shall come. I was only going to the canteen for a coffee and a bun.'

'Oh, that isn't very tempting,' Mr Harper replied. 'Order a lunch and tell them I said it was free.'

'I couldn't possibly...' Andrea protested.

He didn't answer, instead leading the way to the elevator and asking the operator to take them up to the top floor. Andrea felt a little nervous as she entered the office. A very young man was standing there with two large leather suitcases. He'd been looking at his silver pocket watch but seemed to breathe a sigh of relief, coming forward to offer his hand.

'Mrs Harper?'

'No. I am Mrs Martin. Mr Harper asked me to take a look at your samples. What are you selling?'

'We do some beautiful fully-fashioned silk stockings,' he said. 'Also, some wonderful silk underwear. Ladies cannot wear their old corsets with the latest fashions. They need these instead.' He produced a flimsy garment from his case with a flourish. 'A brassiere and matching silk French knickers.'

Andrea drew a deep breath, the colour rushing into her cheeks. She'd expected brochures of staid corsets, not these exotic pieces of clothing that were hardly there – hardly decent.

'Oh, I don't know...' she said, shocked that he had produced them so boldly. Surely, he could have been more discreet?

'Are they wearing them in Paris and London?' Mr Harper asked. 'They look a bit thin to me...'

'Oh yes, all the fashionable women will be wearing them and abandoning their corsets soon,' the young salesman said confidently. 'It's the new softer look for the twenties and we've got in on it early. These are going to sell like hot cakes.'

'I'm not sure our customers will approve—' Andrea began, only to have her words cut across by another voice from the doorway.

'I am. They are fabulous, Mr Thompson. I am sorry I'm late – and that I didn't keep our lunch date, Ben. I've been at the hospital for three hours. Jenny was hurt in the park. She climbed on a wall before I could stop her and fell off. She cut her forehead and it bled a great deal, so I took her to the hospital and she had three stitches.'

'Oh my God!' Andrea saw that Mr Harper looked horrified. 'Is she all right? Where is she now?'

'At home in bed. Mrs Hills is fussing over her,' Mrs Harper sighed. 'I went to meet you, but you'd left so came on here.' She turned to the salesman. 'May I see some more of that delicious lingerie please?'

'I'll take my break if it is all right?' Andrea looked at Mr Harper. He nodded but seemed to have forgotten her. She had the feeling that he was angry with his wife but trying not to show it in public.

She went straight to the canteen and was about to order her coffee and bun when she saw there was a nice pie on the menu. With a sudden change of heart, she ordered that instead and told them to put it on Mr Harper's account. The waitress behind the counter gave her an odd look but did as she was told; it wasn't unheard of for Mr Harper to do something like that, but the expression in the girl's eyes made Andrea wish she'd stuck to her usual.

The pie was good. She enjoyed it and then went back to her department. She saw the salesman on his way down from the office. He was looking pleased with himself, so presumably he'd been given a substantial order. Andrea would have sent him away without one. She still wore her corset and stuck to the longer-length skirt, even though the girls had all been told they could raise their hems to mid-calf if they wished. Her figure was fuller than these young girls. Andrea wouldn't be buying one of those flimsy things he'd called a brassiere or those shocking French knickers!

Andrea reflected that Ben Harper hadn't looked at all pleased with his wife after she'd announced where she had been. She wondered if he had a temper and what he was saying to his wife now the salesman had gone.

7

'What the hell did you think you were doing, letting Jenny walk on a wall?' Ben demanded the moment they were alone. 'She could have been seriously injured – she might even have died!'

'Do you think I don't realise that?' Sally said, distressed. 'I only took my eyes off her for a moment. If she had died, it would be my fault...' Tears trickled down her cheek. 'I don't know where she got the idea from. I've never allowed her to do it or put her up on any wall. I wouldn't—'

'Why would she suddenly get it into her head unless she'd been allowed to climb a wall before?' Ben looked at her, his anger simmering. 'I know you enjoy your work, but how could you leave our darling daughter to Mrs Hills when she has been injured, just because you had to meet a salesman?'

'Ben!' Sally gave him a hurt look. 'She is fine now, really. The doctor told me there was no problem, just a cut that will heal. She is quite safe with Mrs Hills.'

'Oh yes, anything is fine as long as you do as you please.'

The totally unprovoked attack made Sally gasp.

'That isn't fair, Ben,' she said, her voice scarcely above a whisper. 'I wouldn't have come to the office if I'd believed her to be in any danger. Surely you know that?'

'Do I, Sally? Most mothers couldn't bear to be parted from their children when they need them.'

'Are you accusing me of neglecting my daughter?' Sally's eyes flashed suddenly, angry that he had attacked her motives. 'If you are, that is damned unfair, Ben. I love her – both of them – and I spend a lot of time playing with them and reading stories to them. Yes, I like my job, and it's just as well I did or things might not be the way they are now. Don't forget that during the war I had to oversee the store *and* care for our children.'

For a moment longer, he glared at her and then he nodded. 'Yes, that was mean of me. I know you had to do too much during the war, Sally. I do appreciate it, of course I do, but I think you should cut back now. You have no need to work so hard, because I'm back at the store. A lot of women who went to work during the war are content to be at home again.'

Sally fixed him with a straight look. 'You married a working girl, Ben. I told you I wanted to continue working even if we had a family and you agreed. If you'd wanted a languid lady who was content to sit at home and embroider all day, you made a bad choice. Please do not go back on your word or blame me for wanting to do a job I love.'

He met her stare with one of his own and then inclined his head. 'Have it your own way, but employ a nanny to make certain my daughter is safe playing in the park or indeed her own garden.'

'Very well,' Sally replied. 'I'll see if a nanny can be found – one that you will approve of. Perhaps you would like to interview her yourself, to make sure she fits your exacting standards.' She turned and left the office without another word.

Ben realised that he'd hurt her and wished he could take back the angry words.

* * *

Sally could hardly keep from crying in frustration. Ben belittled her work by saying she could leave it to him or another buyer. She felt a surge of indignation that banished her desire to cry. Clearly, he'd asked Mrs Martin for her advice with the new underwear and, just as clearly, she would have refused the offer Sally had pulled strings to get. Sally had been told on the phone that Selfridges had wanted the exclusive rights to the line in London and had used all her powers of persuasion to be allowed the chance to stock underwear she just knew all the women under forty would be dying to own. A lot of ladies over that age would probably love it, too, if they thought their husbands would approve.

Recently, Ben seemed as if he was trying to shut her out – to push her into being just a dutiful wife and mother. It wasn't like the man she'd married; he'd always encouraged her to be independent. She loved him as much as she always had and she adored both her children, but she needed more. If she was selfish for wanting to keep the job that she loved, well, so be it. Yet his attitude irked her and she was still smarting from the way he'd spoken to her – as if it was entirely her fault that Jenny had fallen from that wall.

If anything, Ben was as much to blame, because he spoiled Jenny too much. She knew her daddy would give her almost anything and had a habit of defying Sally and running to him if she didn't immediately get her own way. However, Sally did blame herself for the accident. She'd turned away from her daughter for a few seconds to admire a dress a young woman was wearing. The soft lines and dropped waist had looked so elegant, even though the skirt had been barely below her knees. So daring! A lot of women and some men would think it shameless, no doubt. Sally had thought the young woman able to get away with it because she had lovely legs.

In that moment, Jenny had seized her opportunity to climb the wall and in the next she had lost her balance and fallen, her scream of fear making Sally lurch at her to break her fall. She'd hit the side of her head on the uneven coping stones as she fell, making a nasty gash along the flesh, which had bled profusely. Sally had staunched it as best she could but taken her little girl straight to hospital, her lunch with Ben forgotten in a rush of fear and anxiety.

Once Jenny was patched up and Sally reassured that nothing terrible would result from the accident, she'd taken her home and Mrs Hills had put her to bed.

'You get off, Mrs Harper,' she'd said with a nod and a smile. 'Jenny will be fine now,' and by the time she'd been settled into her familiar bed, she'd fallen asleep.

'I've missed lunch with Ben,' Sally had told her, 'but there is an appointment at the office.'

'If you're needed, I'll ring you, but Peter is still sleeping after I put him down for a nap,' Mrs Hills had assured her. 'Don't look so stricken. These things happen and likely it will slow her down a bit, make her think of the consequences of her actions.'

Sally had nodded, agreed and left. She'd wanted to see the salesman and it had been well worth her while – but the quarrel with Ben had spoiled things. Sally remembered once before when they'd had a small quarrel over Jenny but... She shook her head. Ben hadn't just been angry over Jenny's accident. That had been the touchpoint, but he'd been annoyed over a few small things lately. Was something wrong that he wasn't telling her?

Stopping to buy a newspaper, Sally saw that the star of the silent screen, Mary Pickford, had been seen out with Douglas Fairbanks, another famous actor, and a romance was rumoured. She smiled over it for a moment; it was nice to see something pleasant in the papers after all the misery of recent years.

Shaking her head, she decided to put the little scene with Ben out of her mind. He had been upset and that was understandable, but it still hurt that he'd turned on her that way.

8

Ben stood staring out of the office window at the busy street below. Oxford Street was thronging with folk, shopping or merely going about their business on this warm spring afternoon. Cursing softly, Ben blamed himself for the quarrel. He was a damned fool and he knew it. Sally had been right to remind him that she and her shop girls had carried the burden of his store during the war, when he'd given his time to the British Government. She hadn't complained and he'd come home to a business in better shape than he'd had any right to expect. So why did it irritate him that everyone still looked to her now that he was back?

Even Marco had insisted they needed Sally's input when they discussed the new windows. Marco, his long-standing friend, who he'd trust with any decisions, had put his foot down over it when Ben said it wasn't necessary.

'Forgive me for contradicting you, Ben,' he'd said with a smile to soften the statement. 'But Sally's input has proved invaluable. Besides, I don't want to hurt her feelings.'

'Well, if *you* need her ideas...' It was a low blow and Ben knew it.

He'd been feeling out of sorts for the past month or two. Didn't know what was wrong, just a queasy feeling and chest pain sometimes. Ben didn't like the idea that he might be sickening for something. Sally could take over again if she had to; he knew that, but it needled at him. He was her husband. It should be his place to take the heavy load of running a big store like Harpers – and it would grow if he had his way. Harpers of London was nowhere near as big a store as his uncle's family owned in America.

Jenni – his half-sister – would understand. Ben had never expected to be handed the store so soon. He'd expected his uncle to live a lot longer. It had been a fight to stabilise the situation after his uncle's sudden death, gain control of important shares. Then, just as Ben had thought he was making some headway, the war had started and he'd got involved – more deeply than he'd expected. No one, not even Sally, knew the real reason why he hadn't been able to enlist. He had tried after those women handed him white feathers, but he'd been told he had an inherited weakness in his chest. He could have been a liability to fighting men if his problem had flared up. It was something that ran in his family. His uncle and father had both had it, but his uncle had lived into his sixties. Ben had been told that he would probably do the same, but that didn't stop him feeling unwell at times.

He shouldn't take his frustrations out on Sally! Ben knew he loved her – loved her and envied her. She'd nearly died during the pregnancy that had given him his precious son, but she'd fought back and showed no signs of weakness, either physically or mentally.

He would send her some flowers to say sorry – and perhaps he would visit his doctor again, though the last time, it had been a waste of time. It was always the same story; he had a weakness in his heart muscle that might, if he was unlucky, cause sudden death, but at the moment there was no reason to suppose he would not live for many years to come. It was just that he felt so tired at times...

His thoughts came to a halt as his secretary knocked at the door. She entered as he invited her in and he raised his brows.

'Yes, Miss Hastings? What can I do for you?'

'Constable Winston is here, sir. He asked for Mrs Harper and then you...'

'Send him in,' Ben said with a nod. What did the police want with Sally?

'Sorry to trouble you, Mr Harper,' a cheerful-looking man dressed in formal uniform entered. 'Mrs Harper is always so generous to us – she usually buys some tickets to our ball; we hold it in the summer – it is for sick or retired police officers, injured in the line of duty or simply ill...'

'Ah, I see,' Ben said relieved. 'What does my wife normally give you?'

'Two guineas – for two tickets. She came with another lady once, just to say hello, but mostly she just supports us.'

Ben reached into his wallet and took out a crisp five-pound note. 'I will take four tickets, Winston. No, I don't need any change.'

'That is very generous of you, sir,' the police officer said and smiled. 'We in the force like to support decent business folk like yourselves. Give my regards to Mrs Harper and we'll hope to see you at the event.'

'Thank you,' Ben said and nodded to himself as the police officer left. He recalled Sally telling him about the police ball now. She'd taken Beth with her once, just to make an appearance; it was a good charity and Constable Winston's wife, Mary, knew Sally from her early association with the Women's Movement.

Feeling more in charity with himself, Ben thought again about buying his wife some flowers by way of apology. He would give her the tickets to the ball too and let her decide who she wanted to share them with.

* * *

Ben bought three dozen red roses at the florist's department and had them presented in a big basket, which would be delivered to Sally. Perhaps it was going over the top a bit, but he had to apologise. He didn't want to be on bad terms with the woman he loved.

As he left, he collided with a young girl. Lost in thought and wondering how his own little girl was, he hadn't looked where he was going and put his arms out to save her from falling. She was a slight, thin girl and, as she looked up, Ben found himself looking into the saddest eyes.

'I am so sorry. Forgive me,' he apologised. 'Did I hurt you, miss?'

'Lilly Ross...' she breathed. 'It's all right, Mr Harper. You just knocked me a bit, but I'm not hurt.'

'You know me?' He stared at her, feeling puzzled. 'I think I may have seen you – do you work at the store?'

'Yes, sir. In the department that sells bags and jewellery. I am the new junior.'

Ben nodded and saw that she was bending to pick up some parcels she must have dropped. Hearing her exclamation of distress, he realised that she'd been carrying eggs, which had broken.

'I've broken your eggs. I'm sorry – is there any more damage?'

'No, just the eggs, sir. I might save some of them...'

Ben felt in his pocket and took out his wallet, extracting a ten-shilling note. He thrust it into her hand. 'Will this buy you some more?'

'It's far too much, sir...' she protested and shook her head. 'I can't take that – it's nearly two weeks wages.'

'Good grief, is it?' Ben thrust it into her hand. 'You must accept it and I'll see about having you promoted to counter assistant, Lilly. You'll earn more then.'

'Thank you, sir...'

She was smiling in relief and Ben saw how pretty she was – or would be dressed in nice clothes with her hair done. 'It's the least I can do. I was thinking about my daughter Jenny. She climbed a wall and fell and hit her head...'

'Poor little love,' Lilly said. 'Our Carol was forever doing that when she was little. She broke her arm one time and Ma was fair out of her mind with worry – but it mended and you'd never know she hurt it. You can't teach them; they have to learn.'

Ben stared at her. 'Do you have several siblings at home, Lilly?'

'Yes, sir. My two older brothers were killed in the war. I'm the oldest all but one and he's married now. Joe is a year younger than me and Carol is nine. Steve is the littlest one, but he is a sturdy lad and not much trouble mostly.'

'Do you look after them all?' Ben's attention was caught.

Lilly inclined her head. 'Ma is an invalid – paralysed on one side. My neighbour looks in on her, but I do all the rest when I get home.'

'In that case, I mustn't keep you.' Ben tipped his hat to her and walked on, but he kept thinking about how sad Lilly's eyes were. She must find it hard to manage. Perhaps if she had more money, she would be able to get a little help. He nodded to himself. At least he could do that for her.

* * *

Ten whole shillings! Lilly could hardly believe her luck as she walked home. Mr Harper had broken eggs worth a shilling and he'd given her ten to make up for it. To Lilly that was a fortune and she was planning what she would do with her gift as she walked home. She would buy more eggs, but she could put the rest by for emergencies or buy a little something for Ma.

On the corner of her road, she saw a barrow boy packing up for the night. She knew he'd been selling flowers, because he always did, and at a far cheaper price than that florist she'd been looking at when Mr Harper knocked into her.

It was Lilly's dream to have a florist shop, but she knew she never would. Her hopes of becoming a counter assistant were as far as she would ever go. Running the last few steps, she called out, 'Have you any violets left, Jeb?'

'Lilly?' The young man turned to look at her with a smile that lit up his face and made him look almost handsome, though he had freckles, a slightly crooked nose and a shock of ginger hair. 'Yes, I've got a couple of bunches here...' He hesitated and then offered them. 'You can have them for tuppence. It is the end of the day and they won't be as fresh tomorrow.'

'Really?' Lilly beamed at him. Jeb had always been kind to her. At school, he'd stopped older children bullying her and he'd become her friend when they were growing up. She didn't see much of him now because he worked hard, but when they met, they always lingered to talk. Lilly knew that she'd carried a torch for him ever since she was a child, but she'd never given him a sign. If he felt the same, he would speak when he was ready. 'This is my lucky day. I know they were sixpence each this morning.'

She handed him the two pennies and received the violets, which smelled gorgeous. Before she could realise what he was about, Jeb darted a kiss at her cheek.

'What do you think you're doin'?' Lilly demanded, pretending to be outraged. 'I can't be bought for two bunches of violets.'

'Wouldn't want you if you could,' Jeb retorted. 'You're a lovely girl, Lilly. One day I'm going to own a florist shop and then you'll marry me!'

'And what makes you think that?' she asked, but her heart raced. It was the first time he'd tried to kiss her or said anything of the sort.

''Cos it is what you want and you like me just a bit...' he grinned at her cheekily. 'I'll make you love me, our Lilly. You see if I don't—'

'Go on with you! I wouldn't marry you if you was the King,' Lilly teased and ran away laughing. She liked Jeb a lot and she would marry him if he was serious, but he was just joshing her. She felt wistful. If only he meant it, but why would anyone want to marry Lilly? She had too much to do looking after her family to even think of it...

Arriving home, she sighed as she put the violets in a little glass jar and then carried them carefully into the parlour that was now her mother's bedroom. It had been a good day, even if Mrs Martin had been in a funny mood all the afternoon.

9

When the flowers arrived from Ben, Sally was sitting on her daughter's bed reading her a story. Mrs Hills brought them in and handed her the card. Sally took the card, opened it and smiled. She'd guessed it was Ben apologising for his uncalled-for remarks earlier.

'Yes, they are beautiful flowers. Daddy sent them,' she said as Jenny, now up and about and full of it once more, reached to touch the huge basket of fragrant blooms. 'Can you put them in the living room, Mrs Hills? Thank you.'

'Yes, Mrs Harper.' Her housekeeper hesitated. 'Is there anything more – I was meeting a friend and we're off to the picture house this evening to see Lillian Gish in her new film, but if you need me...?'

'No, I can manage now, and thank you for looking after Jenny earlier.'

'She was asleep most of the time. She's more awake now you're home.'

'Yes. Jenny likes to hear stories,' Sally agreed. 'Have a good evening.'

'I will – I've been looking forward to. It was Winnie's idea; she's my niece and a lovely girl. She's bored at home, though...'

'How old is Winnie?' Sally asked.

'Nineteen. She'd like to be at work, but her mother doesn't approve of girls working in factories or shops, and she has no skills, like typing, to help her find work, but she's a good girl and helps her mother at home.'

Sally nodded. 'That's lovely. You will enjoy a night at the cinema so much.'

'I like the old-fashioned musical hall the best,' Mrs Hills said with a smile. 'Most of them are either closing down or changing to become picture houses these days. People like new ideas, but I cling to the old ways and Miriam wanted to see the picture, so I said I'd go.'

'I like the motion pictures,' Sally agreed, 'but the musical hall is always such fun; joining in the old songs and calling out to the master of ceremonies is part of the entertainment.'

'You haven't been to the theatre for a while,' Mrs Hills remarked. 'You know I never mind looking out for the young ones if you want to go.'

'Thank you,' Sally replied. 'Ben is going to buy some tickets for the opera. I am looking forward to that.'

Mrs Hills nodded and left.

Sally continued reading to Jenny until the little girl fell asleep. She was just preparing to get up and creep from the room when Ben entered, carrying a beautiful doll. It was even more splendid than the one Mick had given Jenny recently. She smiled at him but put a finger to her lips, indicating that he should take the doll with him.

When they were downstairs, she poured a glass of wine for them both. 'You can give it to her in the morning, Ben. She will love that – where did you get it?'

'I had an appointment with a toy manufacturer and he gave me the doll for Jenny. I wanted to buy it, but he said it was a gesture of goodwill – apparently, you helped him get started early in the war and now he has a good business. He says thanks to you... a chap in a wheelchair?'

'Yes, I remember. He was making wooden toys by hand then,' Sally agreed. 'That was nice of him. And thank you for the beautiful flowers, Ben.'

'I shouldn't have blamed you for Jenny's fall,' he said. 'I know you are never careless with her.'

'She is so full of life and so reckless,' Sally told him. 'It was my fault though. One minute she was playing happily with Lulu and the next she was on the wall, showing her dog how clever she was. I did let my attention wander for a few seconds and if she'd been seriously hurt, I would have blamed myself.'

'No one can watch her every second,' he admitted. 'I know that – but we do need another nanny to look after her when you're busy. Can't you find anyone suitable?'

'I interviewed two a while ago and they were awful. Old-fashioned nannies who looked at me as if I were dirt. I suppose I still have my working-girl accent and they are used to working for the best families, as they both informed me.'

'I'm sure they didn't look down on you.' Ben frowned. 'Perhaps we do need someone stricter?'

'Jenny would be miserable if she was kept out of the way and brought down for ten minutes before dinner and then taken back to the nursery. Pearl was her nurse, not an old-fashioned nanny, and had such a lovely way with her, not too strict but not indulgent. I miss her.'

'Yes, I agree...' Ben hesitated, then, 'How much do you pay a nurse for looking after Jenny?'

'I paid Pearl three pounds a week. A nanny might be more.'

'And what does a junior get on the counters at Harpers?'

'Seven shillings and sixpence now. It was five shillings before the war, but I put it up. I doubt it is enough. I think we might pay ten shillings a week soon. Harpers can afford it. The girls on the counters get thirty-five shillings, but I am hoping we can increase that to two pounds soon.'

'But a nurse for Jenny would still be more. I wonder...' He frowned and then nodded. 'Do you know a junior called Lilly?'

'Yes, of course I do. I know all our staff by name – but Lilly works in my department. Why?'

'I nearly knocked her over when I left the florist earlier this evening. I was thinking about something... I broke her eggs so I paid for them and told her I'd have her promoted to the counters... if you agree?' Sally nodded. 'But – she has helped to look after young children at home and I wonder if that would suit her better...'

'You mean have her here to help with Jenny?'

'Lilly could look after Jenny and Peter sometimes – if that would make it easier for you.'

'Jenny goes to her little school three mornings a week,' Sally reminded him. 'I don't think Lilly could move in here as a children's nurse, Ben. She has too many commitments at home. Two of her siblings are still at school, but her mother is an invalid and she has to look after her.'

'Oh, I hadn't thought of that,' Ben said. He shook his head. 'It was just an idea.'

'Lilly wants to be a florist one day,' Sally said, making him look at her in surprise. 'If you want to help her, give her a job in your florist department.'

'How did you know she has that ambition?'

'I found her in there one day, asking if we had any violets. Her mother loves violets. I talked to her for a few minutes, asked her if she was happy at Harpers. She said yes, she loved working for us, but wanted to own a flower shop one day.'

'You really do know your staff,' Ben said and there was a strange expression in his eyes. 'I had no idea that she wanted to work with flowers.'

'Well, now you do,' Sally teased. 'So what will you do about it?'

'I could ask the supervisor in the florist department to take her on, train her. It would be a start for her...'

'But would she earn enough to help her family?' Sally asked practically. 'You were putting her wage up to thirty-five shillings on the counters, but you could hardly justify that as a trainee florist?'

'No, that would be a stretch too far,' Ben agreed and gave her a wry smile. 'It isn't that easy sorting out staff, is it? Yet you do it so easily...'

'I like Lilly too and I feel for her,' Sally said. 'Let me think about it and see what I come up with.'

'I'm supposed to take some of the burden from your shoulders.' Ben looked at her wryly. 'Yet here I am giving you more problems.'

'I don't consider Lilly a problem,' Sally said and smiled as it came to her. 'I think there might be a way... if she really wants to learn.'

'And that is?' Ben raised his eyebrows.

'She could take her lunch break and her tea break together and spend that time with the florist. If she ate her sandwiches watching at first and then she might try her hand at arrangements. I've noticed the hat display has been better again recently and I saw Lilly adjusting some hats when I paid a visit to the department. She isn't given any credit for it, but I was about to give her a raise in wages because of it, so we'll do as you suggested and promote her to salesgirl.'

'Do you think she would be interested in learning the florist's trade?'

'I imagine she would love it,' Sally replied and smiled. 'This is how it should be, Ben – us discussing things, sorting out little problems. We haven't done much of that this past year. I've felt as if... as if, you would rather I stopped working and became just your wife and mother to our children?'

'Good grief, no,' Ben said, running his fingers through his hair. 'I felt guilty because I left you to get on with it during the war and it must have been hard at times.'

'It was sometimes, but I love working at Harpers,' Sally said. 'I love you and the children, too, Ben. You do know that?'

'Of course I do,' he replied. 'Sorry, if I've been a pain in the rear lately, Sally. I've had a few things on my mind...'

She looked at him enquiringly. 'Are there problems with Harpers that I don't know about?'

'Not that I know of...' Ben sighed. 'I didn't want to tell you, Sally, because I know you'll worry – but I had some pains in my chest. At first, I thought it might be indigestion, but it kept on, so I went to the doctor...'

'And? Don't keep me in suspense, Ben.'

'There is a weakness in my heart muscle – much the same as both my father and my uncle had...' He hesitated, then, 'My father died too soon, early forties, but that wasn't due to his heart muscle, it was an accident. My uncle was in his sixties... so I should have quite a few years left to me if I'm lucky, but it does cause me quite a bit of discomfort.'

'Ben!' Sally stared at him with stricken eyes. 'I had no idea, my darling. You should have told me you were feeling ill!'

'I'm not, not really,' Ben said. 'It is just the odd bit of pain now and then, tiredness too – nothing terrible, but I've been worrying about you and the children... if anything should happen unexpectedly.'

'It won't,' Sally said quickly. 'It can't. I won't let it.' She got up

from her chair and went to put her arms around him. 'Stop worrying, Ben. If I lost you, I would be devastated. There would never be
anyone else for me – but I would take care of your children and
their inheritance. I would make sure they were happy and safe.'

'I know,' he said and sighed. He bent his head and kissed her
softly. 'It was stupid of me to hold it inside – but I thought it had
passed me by, that I'd got away with it...'

'You should see a specialist,' Sally told him. 'I don't know
anything about what is wrong with you, Ben, but I can find a good
doctor who will—'

'I've already seen a top consultant,' Ben replied. 'I suspected
what it might be of course, but thought it best to be sure.'

'What about a second opinion?'

'Mr Samuels is supposed to be the best in London at the
moment.'

'Why don't you ask Jenni's husband if he knows someone?'
Sally persisted. 'I wouldn't just take the word of one man, Ben.'

'My uncle went to the best doctors, in America, London and
Switzerland. They all said the same. It's just a weak heart muscle.
Although it may cause me some difficulty at times, I should be fine
for several years. Now, can we leave it – or I'll wish I hadn't told
you.'

Sally nodded. She wouldn't say anything more now, but she
would speak to Jenni's husband on the telephone and ask his
advice. Andrew Alexander was a brilliant surgeon and had helped
soldiers who had been badly burned during the war. He would say
the heart wasn't his field of expertise, but he might know someone
who could help. She wouldn't say anything to Ben until she had a
name and she would ask Andrew not to tell his wife, because if he
did, Jenni would come rushing down to London and Ben would be
annoyed with her all over again.

10

Andrea looked at herself in the mirror with dissatisfaction. She felt out of sorts and wasn't sure why – unless she was just a little bit jealous of Sally Harper? No, surely not! She chastised herself immediately. Mrs Harper, as she ought to think of her, had given her the job she needed; she'd been kind and generous and it was mean of Andrea to envy her. She seemed to have the world at her fingertips, so intelligent, poised and beautiful; she had everything any woman could want – including a handsome husband.

'Don't be foolish!' Andrea told herself severely. She would be stupid to let herself be influenced by a man's charming smile. Ben Harper had smiled at her when he'd come to the department, but then, when his wife had arrived, he'd forgotten her. Whether in annoyance or relief, she wasn't sure. 'He wouldn't look twice at you...' Surely she didn't want him to? She'd been strictly brought up and had high moral standards

It was just that her life was so empty these days. Now that her husband was gone, and Paul at boarding school, there was nothing left to fill her time, other than her job at Harpers. She was very grateful for the opportunity she'd been given and felt annoyed with herself for admitting to a slight yearning to see Ben Harper smile just for her.

Now she was being ridiculous! Making an effort to put such foolish thoughts from her mind, Andrea got out the unfinished dress she'd been making for herself. It was a dark blue, the material heavily embossed silk that would hang beautifully. The pattern was her usual style, shaped to the waist and gently flowing over her hips to ankle length. She had it all tacked together and held it up against herself in the mirror. A sigh broke from her. It looked staid and old-fashioned compared with the new look that was slowly coming in.

Andrea couldn't wear that low-waisted look. She would appear as mutton dressed as lamb. No, she would stick to the same style... but perhaps the skirt might be shortened a little. Andrea lifted her dress to admire her slender feet and ankles. Her husband had always said she had good legs – but he'd been the only one to see them.

Deciding that she would be daring, Andrea shortened the hem on her new Sunday dress. She would see what reaction that drew when she went to church and if it was favourable, she might take up the hem of her working dresses a little.

* * *

Andrea stopped to look at the headlines on the newspaper boy's board the next morning. A large black headline said that Troytown had won the Grand National and she nodded with satisfaction. Her husband Philip had liked horse racing and they'd always had a little flutter on the big races. Andrea had picked Troytown to win, but of course she hadn't placed a bet. She couldn't afford to do it these days...

The thought brought a frown to her brow. Life without her Philip was so much harder than she'd ever imagined it could be. Born into a decent working family where money had been tight but adequate, Andrea had married up and believed she would have a comfortable life, so much better than her parents or her brothers. Both her brothers had been killed in the war. Her eyes stung with tears. Her father had died of a broken heart, but her mother carried on living – bitter and angry at the world for robbing her of her family.

Andrea visited her every Sunday and took her a few groceries to help her. It was all she could afford. She had to keep Paul in his boarding school, because that was what his father had wanted. The uniform was so expensive and all the other things he needed, like rugby boots and a cricket bat. Andrea hadn't bought that yet, but he'd told her he wanted one, as he was the only boy who hadn't got his own, so she would have to find the money somehow.

Sighing, Andrea prepared to cross the road to Harpers. She liked to get in nice and early... Stopping in her tracks as she saw two people talking on the pavement outside the store, she stared in dismay. Lilly Ross was laughing and talking in an animated way to – Mr Harper! How dare she look at him like that? It just wasn't right. Just wait until she got her in the department! She would put her straight. Flirting with her employer that way!

'Good morning, Mrs Martin,' a voice said beside her.

Andrea turned and saw Mrs Burrows standing there. 'Oh, good morning,' she said. 'I was just admiring the window. Mr Marco is so clever, isn't he?' Now why had she lied?

Lilly had gone inside the store now and Mr Harper was looking at the windows.

'Good morning, ladies,' he said as they approached. 'I was just admiring Mr Marco's latest efforts. Really stylish, don't you think?'

'The windows are always interesting,' Andrea said.

'I love the background of the moon and stars for the evening wear,' Mrs Burrows said and Mr Harper nodded enthusiastically.

'Yes, exactly. He has caught the mood. Those dresses and the gentleman's evening suit are very elegant – softer and less formal than before the war.'

'Well, ladies couldn't cart heavy weights wearing corsets...' Mr Marco had come up to them unnoticed. 'There had to be a change – and this shows the way things are going. We all want to let go a bit, to have some fun – and the background gives us that hint of excitement and perhaps a bit of naughtiness we've all been missing.' His eyes twinkled with mischief. 'What do you ladies think?'

'I think it is wonderful,' Mrs Burrows exclaimed. 'Jack is taking me dancing at the weekend. He says we have to make up for lost time... it is a tea dance, because he is busy Saturday night, but that is fine with me. We went last week and it was fun.'

'And you, Mrs Martin?' Mr Marco asked.

Andrea couldn't think of anything to say. 'I'm sure you are right,' she managed at last and then hurried on inside.

She felt hot and a bit miserable. No wonder Mrs Burrows always looked so pleased with life. If her husband was taking her to tea dances. Well, she was lucky!

Lilly Ross was rearranging a few hats when Andrea reached the department. A sharp reprimand was on Andrea's lips, but then she thought better of it. It wasn't her business if Lilly chose to flirt with her employer.

'Why do you do that?' she asked. 'It isn't your job, Miss Ross.'

'I just thought they looked better.' Lilly gave her a guilty look. 'Should I put them back as they were?'

'No, I just wondered why you bothered. As a junior, you just have to assist where necessary.'

Lilly's smile lit her face. 'Mr Harper says I'm being promoted to counter assistant,' she confided. 'I start from tomorrow – that's when the new jewellery department will be ready. I am to be promoted and they will employ a new junior assistant – but I reckon with four of us on the counters we should manage...' Her face fell as Andrea stared at her. 'Don't you think so?'

'Possibly...' Andrea felt irritated. How dare they just promote Lilly without telling her first? It was wrong and it made her feel slighted. 'For the moment, you are still my assistant – until I am informed of the change...'

Her back stiff with annoyance, she stalked off to the small cubbyhole that was all they had to hang their coats now that their stock area was being prepared for the larger jewellery department. It was rude of Ben Harper to tell the girl of her change of position without first informing her supervisor.

She had been charmed by Ben Harper's smile – now she disliked him. Chasing after a young girl like Lilly... it was disgraceful!

Lilly must be warned somehow. Men like Ben Harper did not do nice things for girls of her class without an ulterior motive.

Andrea bit her lip. She had to be careful, because she didn't want to lose her job. Perhaps she wouldn't say anything just yet. She would just wait and watch...

Returning to the counters, she saw that a man had entered in her absence. Lilly was the only other member of staff there, because it wasn't yet opening time. As he turned her way, a smile on his face, Andrea saw it was the Irishman that Mrs Harper had claimed was her friend.

'Ah, the lady herself,' he said and the soft charm of his voice made Andrea relax despite her reservations regarding him. He was, after all, a good friend of Mrs Harper, as she'd been told after reporting his first foray into the department.

'Mr O'Sullivan,' Andrea said. 'What may I do for you, sir?'

'I've come to look at the new jewellery counters,' he said. 'I recommended them to Mrs Harper and I want to make sure they are all they should be. The jewellery you will be stocking is more expensive than in the past so they need to be lockable.'

'Very well, please follow me, sir.'

Andrea walked ahead of him. She was still a little wary of Mr O'Sullivan but now knew that he was someone both Mr and Mrs Harper trusted. Feeling a prickling sensation at the back of her neck, she glanced over her shoulder and saw an expression on his face that made her frown. He was enjoying watching her walk and she suspected him of eying her posterior.

'There you are,' she said in a cold voice – the kind of voice she might use to the coalman she suspected of short-changing her when he delivered.

'Thank you, my lovely,' Mr O' Sullivan said and that annoying twinkle was back in his eyes. 'Ah yes, these look fine. You can open them with the key, but a thieving customer can't—'

'Our customers aren't thieves,' she said indignantly. 'Well, of course one has to be careful – but in general the ladies I serve wouldn't dream of stealing.'

'I knew a young woman who stole once,' he said. 'To look at her, you'd think her an angel, so you would – but turn your back and she'd have your watch and your wallet.'

'Well…' Andrea sniffed. 'Of course that kind…'

'Oh no, she wasn't on the streets,' he contradicted. 'She worked in my restaurant, but I had to let her go when she stole the customers' change.'

Andrea stared. She hadn't seen him as a man of property, but you never could tell.

'You'll be all right then,' he said and nodded. 'Mrs Harper was telling me you are a widow. I am sorry for your loss, Mrs Martin. It was a terrible time for us all, so it was.'

'Yes...' Her throat caught at the sympathy in his voice. She hadn't trusted or liked him, but those eyes were kind now. 'I miss him very much.'

'It is hard to lose those you love,' he said solemnly and then the twinkle was back in his eyes. 'I dare say you'll be fighting the gentlemen off – a fine woman like you.'

How could he say such a thing! Andrea was speechless for a moment. Her desire to smack his face must have shown in her face because he gave a shout of laughter and that released her.

'How dare you! You abominable man! Please leave at once.'

'That's it, Mrs Martin. Get good and mad at me. I'm a cheeky devil and I don't mind if you tell me so – but it's no good letting it fester inside. Let go and look about you. The world is a good place if you give it a chance.' And with that he walked off and didn't look back.

Andrea was outraged, still fighting to get her breath. Cheek didn't cover it! She wished now that she'd told him it was highly improper to speak to her in that way... and yet she felt better for shouting at him. She'd been holding so much inside – her tension must have shown to him, so he'd taken a swipe at her. Damn him!

Returning to the main department, Andrea saw the girls had all arrived and were setting their counters to rights. Lilly had rearranged the bags in the showcase on the wall; it had not yet been moved to the shoe department, because Sally Harper was still redesigning that area. Lilly was humming a little tune and for the first time that Andrea could recall, she looked happy. It made Andrea wonder. Was it just the promotion or was there another reason she was so pleased with life?

'Stand behind your counters, girls,' Andrea instructed. 'I can see customers on their way...'

She moved behind the jewellery counter. After today, it would be her special concern and she supposed Lilly would be looking after the bags for the moment. Andrea decided that when the first customer asked for a bag she would hand over to Lilly, give her a chance and see what happened...

11

Beth was having coffee with Sally in her office when Mick arrived. He grinned at them and remarked that it was fine to see them enjoying themselves and Sally laughed.

'We're working, Mick,' she said with a challenging look. 'Aren't we, Beth?'

'Yes, we are,' Beth said firmly. 'We've been discussing the fashion department and we've decided that Sally is going to order from a French fashion designer. Maggie told us about one she met during the war and Sally has kept in touch, but she did not have enough stock to export until now. It took her a while to recover from the war – but now she has new workers and can supply the quantities that Harpers needs.'

'Chanel or Patou?' Mick asked and they looked at him in surprise. He laughed. 'Yes, I know a bit about French fashion, but not too much.'

'Well, neither at the moment,' Sally admitted. 'I am trying to stock both of them, as well as other French designers – but the only one I have managed to secure as yet is Madame Felice.'

'That's a start, but I might be able to help with Coco Chanel – I did meet her fleetingly when I was over there for a while during the war. She may not recall, but, if she does, she might agree to sell you some of her designs.'

'Mick, I love you!' Sally exclaimed just as her husband walked into the office, a sheaf of papers in his hand and a frown on his face.

'Ah, just the man I need,' he said after a quick glance at Sally. 'There's a bit of property I'd like your opinion on...' He glanced back at Sally. 'Sorry to take him away, but my need is greater than yours.'

Beth looked at Sally as the door closed behind them. 'Ben seems in an especially good mood this morning?'

'Yes, he seems happy. There is a small property adjacent to the restaurant. He isn't sure what to do with it but he wants it... He is always happy when he has a new project.'

'I know – Jack told me,' Beth said. 'They thought it would be a good place for a food hall.'

'You mean the kind of thing they have at Harrods and Fortnum and Mason?' Sally asked and Beth nodded. 'We're not big enough to do that justice yet. We have the chocolate and cake department, but that isn't like a food hall.'

'Next to the restaurant it would be exciting,' Beth went on. 'They could serve things that could also be bought to take home. If it was on sale next door, they could have it more often.'

'If you can have it at home, why go out and pay more?' Sally asked. 'It works on one level – but I always see the other side. Sometimes I think I'm too negative...'

'Of course you aren't,' Beth said. 'Far from it. I see what you mean – but it still has to be cooked or prepared if you buy it and I think everyone is more interested in going out at the moment. We all want to have some fun, don't we?'

'Yes, we do,' Sally agreed. 'I enjoyed our visit to the opera last night and Ben is taking me to see *Swan Lake* this Friday evening. I love the ballet. I could watch it for hours. He prefers the opera or a good play, but he is giving me what I want this time.'

'Good. You deserve a treat, Sally.'

'Yes, perhaps.' Sally smiled at her. 'So, tell me about the tea dances. Are they as much fun as going in the evening?'

'Yes, because I love to dance and Jack can't leave the restaurant in the evenings. He is home on a Sunday and on Mondays, and we sometimes go to a theatre on Monday – but there aren't many dances on at the beginning of the week. The tea dances are on twice a week in the afternoons and so we go there and it is fun. We have lovely cucumber and cress sandwiches and tiny cakes – little marzipan ones. You know I like them...'

'Yes, I know, but you still keep you figure, Beth?'

'Having two boys to run after keeps me slim,' she replied. 'And I've got a bicycle. Jack offered to teach me to drive, but I'm not very good. I didn't take to it the way you did, so I cycle to the shops and that helps.'

'You cycle to the shops?' Sally nodded. It must be nearly a mile to the nearest market and grocery shop from Beth's new house. When she'd lived with Jack's father, it had been just around the corner, but their new house was in a nice residential area of double-fronted houses with big gardens and the shops were not as close. 'I think that is so brave of you. I'm afraid I have quite a bit delivered.'

'I like to get out as much as I can – and when the children are out with their father or grandfather, I pop down to get whatever I need.'

'You are lucky to have a grandfather living relatively close by,' Sally sighed. 'Mum is still in Cambridge and doesn't get here as much as she'd like.'

Beth looked at her sympathetically. She knew that Sally's stepfather was often ill. It meant that her mother needed to be with him. Sally had been to visit them a few times, but she'd felt as if she was in the way, because her mother had to wait on her husband hand and foot, especially when he was laid low by a bout of illness that kept him abed.

'It's a long way to drive and getting on and off trains with Jenny and Peter isn't easy.' Sally gave her head a little shake. 'We write, send photos and telephone, so it isn't too bad – but it would be nice if I could rely on them to look after Jenny and Peter sometimes.'

'Still can't find the right children's nurse?'

'No. You know I've been casually looking for one since Pearl left last year, but now Ben is insisting I get one, because he says it is too much for Mrs Hills to do the house and look after them. I can take them to the store and I do bring Peter sometimes when Jenny is at nursery school, but they'd be better going for walks in the park... but not with some old grump who makes them afraid to move without permission.'

'Good grief, no!' Beth was horrified. 'Vera is wonderful with my boys – just the right amount of respect but plays with them too. They adore Fred... Sorry, that is tactless after what you just told me.'

'Of course it isn't. Mum loves the children and plays with them. She just doesn't have much time.'

'Where have you been advertising for a children's nurse?'

'In *The Lady* and a nursing magazine.'

'Why not put one in some shop windows locally?' Beth suggested. 'You do need a local girl if possible.'

'That is a good idea,' Sally agreed. 'I might do that...' She sighed. 'We'd better get back to work. We've decided on some French fashions, which I shall order today and hope Mick can help with Chanel. Do you think I should order these...?' She showed Beth a page in a catalogue for handbags. They were evening bags, some gold and silver leather, others beaded and some tiny ones made of silver mesh. 'What do you think? Try one or two of all of them or just the leather bags?'

'I love those silver mesh bags...'

'They are so small.'

'But right for the evening. When you go to the theatre or a dance, you don't need much. Just a handkerchief or a little money and a mirror, some lip rouge if you are daring enough to wear it – they would hold most of that.'

'These have a mirror in the lid,' Sally said, pointing to a box-shaped bag. 'You'd just need a sovereign and a hanky and perhaps the lip rouge...'

'Yes, I'd like one of those for my tea dances. You don't need to carry a load of stuff, as you do when the children are with you.'

'I think I'll try one of each of the mesh bags and two each of the leather ones and we'll see what happens.'

'Yes, although, I think I'd go for more of the mesh bags. They will look good in the glass counter and I think they will sell quickly.'

Sally beamed at her. 'Yes, I agree, Beth. One of each isn't really enough. I'm just trying not to overbuy now that more stock is available.'

'And a year ago you were desperate to fill your shelves.'

'Yes, I was. How things change,' Sally said and then laughed. 'I have got a wonderful new dress to wear for the ballet. Come back to lunch with me and I'll show you...'

'I'm supposed to be working...'

'And you will be. I have loads more catalogues at home to wade through – and the children can play together. You could even fetch Tim if you wanted...'

'Vera will keep him until I get home, and Jack is at his little school until three,' Beth said. 'Vera and Dad are making their lunch at my house so they won't mind at all.'

* * *

Beth was thoughtful as she walked home after leaving Sally's house. Sally's new dress was very modern, a gorgeous concoction of beads and very fine material that was almost transparent, but because of the pleats in the skirt, it only showed a little bit pink through the black silk when she walked; the front and back both dipped low and were made decent by bands of jet beads holding the deep V together. It was French and had come from Madame Felice's workrooms. What would Ben make of such a dress?

Beth forgot the dress as she approached her house and saw Jack playing with his children in the big front garden. He was kicking a football and their eldest boy was managing to get a foot to it most times, but Tim was still at the stumbling about stage and ran after it giggling.

Beth saw the look of love in Jack's eyes as he saw her and her heart gave a little jump of joy. There had been a time during the war when she'd wondered if the man she loved would ever come back to her. Even when he'd had leave, he'd been quiet and some-times withdrawn. His brother's cruel death in the sea had hurt him so much, but now he was her Jack again and she was so happy.

Jack was enjoying his life. He liked running the restaurant he co-owned with Ben Harper and he loved his family. They were a happy family, content with the life they had, their children and Fred and Vera.

Beth had her friends – Sally and Maggie, in particular. She was sometimes invited to tea with other women living in the area but had not made any close friends. Rachel, her one-time supervisor and older friend, was now living in the country with her husband

William. She wrote most weeks and Beth understood that William's health was up and down, but they had settled well into the life and had friends they entertained regularly.

'Had a good day at the store?' Jack teased as she went to him for a kiss and then scooped Tim up in her arms.

'Lovely. We did a lot of work over coffee and then lunch at Sally's,' she told him. 'We're going to stock French fashion – and we might even get Chanel and Patou...'

Jack's face told her that he knew nothing of the designers and she laughed.

'How did your morning go at the restaurant then?'

'Very well. We had some special guests today – a film star and a royal gentleman dining with friends.'

'One of the royal cousins?'

Jack wouldn't name his guests.

'Tell me who?'

He shook his head. The guests were entitled to their privacy and he never told her exactly who had been in.

'Spoilsport!' She laughed, not really caring. 'Let's go in and have some tea with the children...'

'We are busy this evening at the restaurant – Mr Churchill is dining with us and bringing some friends.'

'Oh, that man,' Beth said. 'I'm not sure I like him...'

'Mr Churchill has some strong opinions,' Jack said, 'but he was a good war minister and I think he will be our Prime Minister one day. We may need his skills again.'

Beth stopped in her tracks. 'You don't think there could ever be another war like the last one? Surely not?'

'I certainly hope not,' Jack said, 'but I know the Germans hated the way they were treated at the end – made to feel humiliated – and that kind of thing festers... but we won't talk about that, love. Let's enjoy life while we can. I've been given the night off this

Saturday for once, and Ben says I should book a table at the restaurant on him. Would you like to go out for a meal after the tea dance, Beth?'

'Yes. I haven't been to the restaurant yet and I should love to – but are you certain? It won't be much of a change for you...'

'It will be a lovely change to be waited on rather than the other way around,' Jack said and laughed. 'They'll give us a discreet table so we can watch but not be seen so much...'

'Shouldn't you save that for your special clients?'

Jack reached for her hand. 'There is no one more special to me than you, Beth. I hope you know that?'

'Yes, I do. I was just teasing,' she said. 'So go on, tell me – who was your royal diner? Was it the prince?'

'It might have been,' Jack said and gave her a wicked look. 'It just might have been...'

'And was he with a lady?'

'Now that, Miss Inquisitive, is not your business. The heir to the throne is safe in my restaurant and no word of gossip shall leave my lips...'

'We'll just see about that,' Beth said and giggled like a young girl. 'You wait until I get you to bed, Jack Burrows. I'll get the truth out of you...'

'I am very willing for you to try,' he said and smiled. 'But the prince's secrets are safe with me.'

'They won't be if the papers get a whiff of it,' Beth said. The young and handsome Prince Edward was at many social events and the newspapers loved to get a picture of him leaving a party late at night if they could. He would be king one day and the speculation as to who he might marry was rife – it would probably be foreign royalty in the end, but any pretty girl seen in his vicinity was photographed discreetly, because everyone wanted to know about the prince they so admired.

'Well, they won't from me,' Jack said and Beth nodded. She wouldn't tease him any more. After all, the royal family had been through the tragedy of war, too – they had many German relatives and it must have been hurtful to be at odds with them when they had been visitors and friends before it happened. In their place, Beth would have felt betrayed and let down and she thought the King must too.

'No, of course not, darling.'

He slipped an arm about her waist. 'Now, I have some special news for you. Ben told me that Colin telephoned him on a business matter. They are coming back to London for a visit in a week or two,. Maggie has been busy getting that home for wounded soldiers set up on his father's estate, but now she and Colin are returning to London... tomorrow.'

'That's lovely,' Beth said, delighted. 'It seems ages since we had a really good catch-up...'

12

'I'll be through in a minute, Mum,' Lilly called as she entered the house. She'd heard her mother call out as she opened the back door, but as she entered the kitchen, she heard her younger sister's voice, sounding alarmed. 'What is wrong?'

'I was trying to help Ma to the commode and she slipped,' Carol said, looking upset as Lilly rushed into the room to find her mother on the floor. 'I can't get her up, Lilly.'

'You should have waited for me—'

'I wanted to go bad and I didn't want to wet the bed,' Annie Ross said. 'Don't blame her, Lilly. I asked her to help me, poor love. It frightened her when I went over.'

'Have you hurt yourself?'

'No. I just went down in a heap...' Annie sighed. 'I thought my side had some feeling back and I'd manage with a bit of help, but I couldn't hold upright.'

'Oh, Mum, poor you,' Lilly said sympathetically. 'Now, just hold tight round my neck and I'll get you up."

'I've wet meself,' her mother confessed. 'It happened when I fell. I'm sorry, Lilly. I'm such a trouble to you.'

'Don't be daft, Ma,' Lilly said as she manoeuvred her mother to a sitting position. 'Go and get Ma a clean nightgown, Carol.' As her sister ran off, Lilly whipped off the soiled nightdress and used it to dry her mother's legs so when Carol brought the clean one, she just popped it over her head. 'Shall we get you back in bed now?'

'I'd like to sit up in me chair,' Annie said. 'I get fed up lying there all day. They sent the district nurse today to look at me – and they were surprised I didn't have sores. I told them it's because of the way you look after me, love. They said it would be better if I could get into the kitchen – sit in the armchair or lie on the daybed. Move me position rather than just lie here...'

Lilly looked at her dubiously. 'Me and Joe could get you through in the morning, Ma – but it's a long day sitting.'

'Effie says if there's a pot downstairs she can help me during the day – and she says her boy will help when he gets in from school...'

'Keith is fifteen,' Lilly said and nodded. 'I think he is strong, though. We can try if you think you'd rather be up, Ma.'

'I would. I've had enough of lying abed,' she said. 'It's just I know it makes more work for you and Joe.'

'We don't care,' Lilly told her. ''Sides, I might be able to pay someone to help a bit while I'm out now...'

'And how will you do that on your wage?' her mother asked.

'Remember, I told you. I've been promoted to counter assistant on thirty-five bob a week,' Lilly said triumphantly. 'And, Mr Harper told me this morning, I'm also going to learn how to be a florist in me lunch break...'

Her mother nodded. 'Are they payin' you for that too?'

'No. It's something I want to do,' Lilly said, excitement in her voice and eyes. 'It's a privilege, Ma.'

'I should've thought they'd pay you something.'

Lilly looked at her, the joy draining away. It was always how much money was coming in, never a thought for what made her happy. 'I want to do it, Ma. It will mean a better job and more pay one day...'

'Oh well, if that is the case...' Her mother smiled. 'I know you like flowers, our Lilly, and I do want you to be happy. It's just that Joe won't be here forever; he'll want to marry and we can't expect him or Ted to keep supporting us. Carol and Stevie are too young. It will be some years before they can help.' Annie let out a deep sigh. 'I used to be a good cook and I could have worked in the canteen down the factory if I wasn't such a liability...'

'It's not your fault, Ma. No one thinks it is – and both Ted and Joe will help us as much as they can.'

Annie was silent for a moment, then it came out, 'It's not right, though. Ted's wife came for a few minutes today. She says they hardly manage on what he gives her. He shouldn't have to support me – and I could go on for years. The district nurse says I'm strong. She wants me to do some exercises to help me get some movement. I can do that better in the kitchen.'

'We'll start it tomorrow. I'll tell Joe when he comes home.' Lilly heard the kitchen door. 'That will be him now. I must go and start the supper, Ma. I got a nice piece of skate cheap tonight. Will you have some?'

'No, just a cup of tea and a sandwich – cheese if we have any?'

'Yes, I bought a large piece yesterday. There should be enough left for a sandwich – though a proper dinner would give you more strength.'

Annie shook her head and Lilly turned and left. She felt close to tears. She loved her mother, of course she did, but sometimes she just wished she would think of her, show some pleasure in what Lilly tried to do for her and the family. Her mother thought it wrong Ted should give them money because he was married – but what about Lilly? Was she supposed to stay home and take care of her mother and the children forever? Would there never be a time when she could enjoy life, have fun and even marry the man she'd loved since she was a girl with pigtails? Sometimes she got so tired of trying to cope with it all that she would have liked to run away, but she was tied by the strings of love, because she could never desert her family – even if they didn't appreciate her.

Joe was standing at the kitchen table drinking beer from the jug when she got down. He wiped his mouth as he saw her looking at him.

'Sorry, I know I should've used a mug, but I was thirsty and the beer was there...'

'I don't mind. I only buy it for you and Ted – so just don't tell him.'

Joe grinned. 'You're a right one, our Lilly. What has Ma been saying to upset you then?'

'Nothing – but I'm afraid it makes more work for you. She wants you to carry her through in the mornings and the commode – and it will mean taking them back at night.'

'She ain't heavy,' Joe said and flexed his muscles. 'Don't look so sad, our Lilly. One day things will get better for you.'

'They just did – I'm going to be earning thirty-five bob from next week, so you can give us a bit less.'

Joe nodded his appreciation. 'You keep it all the first week,' he said. 'I give you a pound at the moment. If I gave you fifteen shillings, would that do?'

'Yes, of course – but can you keep giving me so much?'

'She's been on at you about it again,' Joe said with a nod of understanding. 'She was always the same with Dad – a real worrier our mum. Don't let it get to you, love. I can give you fifteen shillings all right and I will while I have a good job – so stop looking so hunted.'

'I didn't know I did,' Lilly said and stared at him.

'You look like a little deer being hunted in the woods,' her brother said affectionately. 'It ain't right you have so much to do, but we couldn't manage without you.'

Lilly's smile lit her face, banishing the anxiety. 'Thanks, Joe. Now, give over and let me get on with the supper.'

Lilly was on her way to the florist's department the next day when she met Mrs Jackson carrying an armful of silk dresses. Lilly had only seen Mrs Jackson a few times but knew she helped Mr Marco with the windows and had worked on the counters in the bag, hat and jewellery department before she had a child.

'They look lovely,' Lilly said, admiring the dresses. 'Are they real silk?'

'These are, yes. They are from our new French range and very expensive,' Mrs Jackson said. 'I'd love to wear something like this when I visit my Reggie in the rest home, but I could never afford it.'

'Me neither,' Lilly agreed and smiled at her. Mrs Jackson seemed nice. 'Was Mr Jackson wounded in the war?'

The smile vanished from Mrs Jackson's face and she hesitated, then inclined her head. 'Reggie was wounded three times in all – but it affected his nerves and that's why he's in a special home. He needs more attention than I can give him and the doctor says he is improving gradually.'

'You must miss him dreadfully,' Lilly said, feeling sad for her. 'I hope he will soon be well enough to come home.'

'So do I,' Mrs Jackson agreed but still looked sad. Then she seemed to pick herself up. 'I must get on. Mr Marco is waiting for these...'

Lilly nodded. She had no time to waste either. Her lunch break was only half an hour, but she was allowed forty-five minutes for giving up her tea breaks. It wasn't much time to learn anything, but at least she would be amongst flowers, smell their sweetness and watch how the baskets and bouquets were fashioned. One day, when she had saved enough, the knowledge would help her start her own shop. It didn't need to be as big as Harpers' florist department. Lilly would start small and build up her business. All she needed was a bit of luck...

13

Marion watched as Mr Marco completed his afternoon-themed window with the silk tea dresses; it was a perfect scene for early summer. He really was an artist and her little ideas could not compare with the sweeping scale of his, even if he did tell her quite often that he couldn't manage without her. She enjoyed her work, fetching and carrying, helping in many small ways as he created his magical scenes – and that's what Mr Marco's windows were. Scenes of everyday life but made sparkling and joyful. His evening window had brought crowds as big as they'd had pre-war. Before the conflict, people had gathered whenever a new window was revealed; that practice had tailed off during the hard times, but now there was beginning to be a new buzz in the stores. The country might still be struggling to get back on its feet, but people were shaking off the gloom of the past years.

Marion had noticed the new atmosphere in Harpers but also in other shops and the cafés too. She often heard laughter when she was out shopping. It was as if a grey curtain had been lifted and people were determined to enjoy themselves again, especially some of the young ladies who came shopping at Harpers. Not all of them could afford the expensive gowns that were going on show that morning, but there were other ranges of more affordable dresses in artificial silk. Marion thought the modern fashions were exciting, though some denounced the higher hemlines as outrageous.

She would like to buy a new dress to visit Reggie. Perhaps if he saw her looking pretty, he would love her again... The thought brought a lump to her throat. Despite the way he'd spoken to her the last few times she'd visited, and the unpleasant letter he'd sent her, Marion still loved her husband. If only the war had never happened. If she could just have Reggie back the way he always had been...

'Yes, that looks wonderful,' a voice behind Marion said and she spun round as she recognised it.

'Mrs Morgan – Maggie!' Marion's face lit up as she saw her friend. 'I heard you were coming to London again. It is lovely to see you.'

'You, too, Marion,' Maggie said and clasped her hands. 'How are you and your little boy – and Reggie?'

'We're all right, Robbie and me,' Marion replied. 'Reggie isn't much better. The doctor says it will be a slow, gradual thing – but he wants to send him to a place in the country where I can't visit and... Reggie says he's going. He may want to live in the country when he is well again and says he wants me to go with him.'

Maggie frowned. 'Why can't you see him? We allow visits at our homes.'

'This one they give them some sort of special treatment,' Marion told her. 'I didn't want him to go. I thought I might not see him again – but the doctor assured me the men do get better. It takes time and he isn't getting on where he is...'

'I'm sorry to hear that. I will have to speak to this doctor about the new treatment. If there is something that works, I want to know so we can help more of those still suffering.'

'They all went to war so willingly, eager to fight for their country,' Marion said. 'It seems wrong that they have to go on suffering long after it is all over.'

'Yes, it is very sad and some of them are still physically ill, too. We are doing what we can – but I intend to ask this doctor about the new treatment.'

'I haven't given my consent yet, but if you think it is all right, I shall.'

'If it will help Reggie, you must.'

'I was afraid he might never come home.' Marion could admit her deepest fear to Maggie. She saw understanding and sympathy in her eyes.

'That is a worry and, for some, an institution will be their home for many years, perhaps the rest of their lives. I pray that you will have Reggie home soon, Marion.'

Marion thanked her and Maggie went to congratulate Mr Marco on the window and then waved goodbye, making her way up to Sally Harper's office.

Marion sighed deeply and Mr Marco looked at her. 'Anything I can do to help?'

'I was just thinking about my husband. My visit this weekend may be the last for a while. They want to send him to a special place where they think he can be helped more.'

Mr Marco nodded. 'It can only be imagined what they suffered in the trenches under constant bombardment. I spent a short time at the Front but was swiftly injured and brought home. I was lucky.'

'You did other things though,' Marion said and looked at him with respect. 'Folk, say you were a spy – were you?'

He hesitated for a moment and then inclined his head. 'Sort of, for a while – but don't confirm it to anyone, please. I don't suppose it matters now, but I'd rather people didn't know even if they think it.'

'I shan't tell anyone,' Marion replied. 'I think you were brave to do that – but it isn't my place to speak of it.'

'I made enemies,' Mr Marco said. 'Threats were made – but although I know he is dead and the war is over... I need to keep my son safe.'

'Pierre is a lovely little boy,' Marion said. 'I saw him in the rest room the other day. He was playing happily with some toys.'

'Pierre is very good, too quiet at times. His grandmother looks after him sometimes but not often. I have to find a nurse or bring him here. This seems the best option for now.'

'You haven't thought of marrying again?'

'No, I shan't do that,' Mr Marco said. 'Sadie was special. I doubt if I could find another wife as understanding as she was...'

'I don't think I would either,' Marion spoke reflectively. 'If I lost Reggie. I would just find people to look after my child while I worked.'

'We are lucky that Mrs Harper set up a special department to care for children here – but then she is a wonderful employer.'

'Yes, she is,' Marion agreed. 'I don't think any of the other big stores would have given me the chance to do this kind of work – the window dresser is usually a man.'

'They might, because you do have talent – but they would probably expect you to work longer hours.'

'Yes, they would,' Marion replied. 'That's why I wouldn't have had the chance. I couldn't work every day.'

'As long as you come in three days a week, it is enough,' Mr Marco told her and stood back to admire his work. 'I think that is finished. Shall we have coffee in the canteen and let Mrs Harper know it is finished so that she can approve it?'

'Of course she will,' Marion said. 'It is fabulous – a tea dance. How I wish Reggie was well enough to take me sometimes...'

'I could take you to the tea dance Mrs Burrows goes to one afternoon,' Mr Marco said. 'Just as friends, naturally. I wouldn't make you feel uncomfortable.'

'I know you wouldn't. I'm not sure... May I think about it first?'

'Of course. If you think it would upset your husband...'

'I doubt if he would care at the moment,' Marion sighed. 'It is such a kind offer – and it is my birthday next week.'

'Then it is settled,' Mr Marco said. 'I see no reason why two friends should not dance and take tea together – do you?'

'No.' Marion lifted her head and smiled at him. 'I don't...'

* * *

Marion had dipped into her savings to buy some fine material to make a dress. She had satin lining in pink and a white gauze overlay. Her sister-in-law, Sarah, helped her fashion it and it was ready to wear for her next visit to Reggie.

Sarah had helped her wave her hair with setting lotion. They'd cut it a little and it looked soft and attractive as it just nestled in her nape. Her shoes were the smart black courts she wore to work and had mended regularly to keep them nice.

Marion's heart lifted as she saw herself in the mirror. Surely, Reggie would remember that he loved her now? She looked much as she had when he'd courted her. He'd been so insistent that they marry then.

Sitting in the bus that carried her to the rest home, Marion's hopes built. Perhaps he would smile and kiss her cheek and they would talk about when he might come home again.

She got off the bus and walked the last few steps, eager to see Reggie. When she passed through reception, someone said something but she didn't catch their meaning until she arrived at Reggie's room and found it empty.

Where was he? She went back into the corridor and hailed a nurse passing with another patient in a bath chair.

'Mr Jackson isn't in his room? Is he in the garden?'

'Oh, Mrs Jackson...' The nurse looked embarrassed. 'I believe the doctor has written to you – your husband has been transferred to another home. I am sure it was discussed with you?'

'I thought I had to give permission?' Marion said, startled.

'It was considered Mr Jackson was able to make the decision himself. I am sure you will get his letter. I know it was posted.'

'Where is this place? Can I visit?'

The nurse hesitated, then, 'I don't think so. I'm really not the right person to advise you. Speak to Doctor Pemberly or wait for his letter, which will explain all. Now, I must take this patient to the clinic...'

She walked off, talking to her patient, leaving Marion to stare after her in dismay. Tears came to her eyes as she walked away. She'd made this dress for Reggie, to help him remember how good it had once been, but he'd gone and no one had even told her. It was like being struck in the heart by a knife and she felt like screaming and shouting at the unfairness of it, but then she shook her head. The hurt inside her was personal; she didn't want to explain it to anyone. She just wanted to go home.

* * *

'The letters came after you left,' Sarah said, pointing to the mantelpiece. 'I'm so sorry you had that journey for nothing, love. It wasn't right that they didn't let you know in time to see him once more before he left.'

'I don't think he wanted to see me,' Marion said. She'd cried all her tears in private and there were none left. Yet as she read Reggie's few lines, telling her to get on with her life and forget him, her heart finally broke.

The doctor's letter told her that he was unable to reveal the location as the treatment was in its early stages, though proved to be beneficial – and no visitors were allowed. Reggie would be there for up to a year and then she would be informed of his progress and whether he could return to his home.

Sarah looked at the letters in disgust. 'This is awful, Marion. I can't believe Reggie would say this to you – it is so cold and emotionless. He loves you. Someone else must have written it.'

'It is his writing,' Marion said. 'He was strange the last few times I saw him – sort of distant and resigned to us being over. As if he believes he will never get better.'

'He clearly can't help himself,' Sarah said, looking at her so sympathetically that Marion almost broke into pieces. 'What will you do now, love?'

'I'll just carry on,' Marion choked, because it hurt so much, she hardly knew how to breathe. 'I'll do what I need to do to get through. I'm not the only one that lost their husband to the war...' She saw the look in Sarah's eyes. 'Yes, I know Reggie is still alive – but the man I loved, the man who loved me, has gone.'

'I am sure he is still there somewhere,' Sarah began, but Marion shook her head. 'If you feel that way, then what will you do?'

'I don't know,' Marion said. 'I shall never marry again. I know that, so there's no problem about that side of things. I might see if I can increase my hours at Harpers. I can take the little one in, so that's not a problem either. I believe I could do part time on the counters to earn extra if I asked.'

'You'll get so tired. I'll speak to Dan. He might give you some extra just so you don't need to work so hard.'

'Sarah, you are a darling and I love you – but I won't take Dan's money unless I am forced. Dickon gives me something and so does Kathy, but of course Reggie can't help me.'

Sarah shook her head at her. 'It's not right. Even his mother thinks he ought to have made more of an effort to come home...'

'She doesn't know how bad he was; he made an effort for her, because she got on to him if he didn't,' Marion said. 'I'll ask her if Milly can keep going to her after school. We'll manage—'

'Yes, but what about you – what life will you have?'

Marion's head came up. 'I'll make a life for us. It's my birthday next week and Mr Marco is taking me to a tea dance. We're just friends and it will never be more. I love Reggie, but if he doesn't love me any more – I have to find my own life.'

'A tea dance?' Sarah looked surprised and then pleased. 'Good for you, love. I hope you have a wonderful time – and your pretty new dress won't be wasted after all.'

14

Sally came downstairs dressed for the evening. They were due to pay a visit to the police ball, but she could hear the concern in Ben's voice as he spoke to someone on the telephone in the hall. She looked at him as he returned to the sitting room, seeing immediately that he was upset.

'That was Andrew,' he said. 'Jenni is very ill. I have to go up, Sally.'

'Oh no! That is terrible.' Sally was at his side in an instant. 'Of course you must, darling. What is the problem?'

'Unfortunately, the doctors aren't sure,' Ben replied. 'It came on very suddenly. She complained of pain in her head and said her vision wasn't clear, then she was violently sick and collapsed. She was rushed to hospital earlier this afternoon and is still unconscious.'

'Oh Ben, I am so sorry. That is awful,' Sally cried, shocked and distressed. It didn't seem possible that the vibrant Jenni they both loved could be so ill. 'Shall I come with you?'

He hesitated for a moment, then, 'No, I think you should stay with the children, Sally. I may be gone for a few days and we can't drag them into something like this.'

Sally inclined her head. He was being sensible, but she would have liked to go with him. 'If that's what you think best—'

'I'd rather have you with me, but I don't think you should leave the children. We still haven't got a nurse for them and it's too much for Mrs Hills.'

'I know.' Sally sighed. 'Give Jenni my love then.'

'I will if... when she wakes up.'

Sally put her arms around him, giving him a squeeze. 'She will, of course, she will. Jenni is a young woman.'

'And they can die,' Ben said, sounding harsh. 'If it is what Andrew thinks... it may be better if she doesn't wake.' He gave a little gasp. 'To lie in a bed, perhaps paralysed, perhaps knowing what is going on but not able to communicate... it is a living death, Sally. I would hate to see her that way...'

Sally nodded, understanding his agony. His first wife had been damaged in an accident and suffered a lingering death, which had caused him terrible grief. He couldn't bear the idea of something like that happening to his sister Jenni.

'Andrew believes it to be a brain haemorrhage,' Ben said. 'He says she had been suffering from headaches and dizziness for a while but refused to see her doctor.'

'Oh no, Ben. I can't believe it...'

'I can. It happened to her mother.' Jenni and Ben had the same father but different mothers and Sally hadn't known how Jenni's mother died. 'She had a severe bleed, so the doctors said, and never regained consciousness.'

'Then you think...?'

'It seems likely,' Ben replied. 'Will you pack some things for me, please, Sally? Enough for a few days. Andrew is devastated. I need to support him, if nothing more.'

'Of course I will. I'll do it now.'

Sally's throat was tight with emotion as she packed Ben's case for him, putting in the book he was reading as well as plenty of clean shirts and underwear. No wonder both he and Andrew were devastated. If there was a medical history, it made the situation even more tense.

She stopped for a moment to wipe the tear that slid down her cheek. They didn't see Jenni much these days, but she came down on the train occasionally and they went up to visit her. They'd spent a few days with her, Andrew, and the baby after the previous Christmas. It had been fun. Jenni had been full of energy and she'd been happy, telling them how well her store was doing. She couldn't be so ill. Pray God she would be all right.

Sally's chest was tight with tension and she felt actual physical pain. It was Jenni who had really helped her when she first became the buyer for Harpers. They hadn't always agreed on everything, but they'd been friends and family and she loved her.

When the case was packed, she returned to the sitting room to discover Ben playing with their daughter. Peter was still sleeping. Toys were all over the floor and Ben was pretending to bite Jenny with a stuffed lion. Sally could see how distressed he was, even though he was trying to act as if nothing was wrong. Jenni was the last tie with his American family, apart from a cousin he wasn't keen on.

'What time train will you catch?' she asked.

'There's one in an hour,' Ben said. 'I can get something to eat in the dining car, if I'm hungry.'

She looked at him anxiously. 'You will ring and let me know?'

'Yes, I will,' he promised. 'I'm sorry about this evening. You were looking forward to it...'

'It doesn't matter,' Sally assured him. 'I just wish I was coming with you, but I know you are right. I can't just abandon the children to Mrs Hills. It wouldn't be fair.'

'No, it wouldn't. You will be fine, Sally. It seems unfair to desert you again – but I know you'll cope with anything that comes up. You can ring Andrew's number if you need to get a message to me urgently, but I'll telephone every evening.'

'I shall be here waiting,' she said. 'Don't worry about anything, Ben. I'll manage.'

'I know you will.' He lifted Jenny gently to nestle beside her brother on the settee, where he was sleeping and got up carefully from beside them. 'I'd better go. I don't want to miss the last train this evening.'

'No, you mustn't,' she agreed, went to him and they kissed.

Ben hugged her, whispering against her hair. 'I love you, Sally. You know I love you. Don't ever forget that... whatever I say or do.'

Sally hugged him back. 'I love you, Ben. Please take care of yourself. I love you – and the children, and I love Jenni too. Please tell her that...'

'I will,' he promised, hugged her tight and then picked up his case and left.

Sally suddenly felt cold all over. She wanted to rush after him and tell him not to go, to stay here with her and the children, but she knew she couldn't. Ben needed to go to his sister.

* * *

'Thank you for coming over,' Sally said to Beth when she opened the door to her an hour later. She had changed out of her evening clothes into a skirt and twinset and comfortable shoes. 'I needed a friend. It is stupid of me, I know...'

'It isn't a bit stupid,' Beth said and hugged her. 'You must feel awful having to stay here while Ben goes to his sister.'

'Ben is anxious about Jenni and he has to go to her. I wanted to go as well but I had to stay for the children.'

'Yes, well, I see Ben's point there,' Beth mused. 'Jenny is very lively and you don't want another accident, but you see now why he was so worried when she banged her head... if Jenni's mother and now she...' Beth shook her head. 'But that is a different case, of course.'

'I see the connection he might make and a knock to the head is never a good thing, but my Jenny was fine; the doctors said so,' Sally replied. 'Neither Ben nor Jenni told me about the brain bleed her mother had. I thought she'd had an accident or something...'

'I don't suppose it was something either of them wanted to talk about,' Beth said thoughtfully. 'It is very worrying about Jenni. I like her, though she did get a bit bossy when you were ill the other year.'

'It's just as well she did. I could easily have died if she hadn't interfered,' Sally said, a catch in her voice. 'I just wish I could see her and tell her I love her.' It was all too sudden and shocking and Sally felt so very worried.

'Oh, Sally.' Beth squeezed her arm. 'Jenni knows that. She loves you too.'

Sally wiped the salty tears from her cheeks. 'I feel so upset over it, Beth. I want to be with Ben to comfort him – but I have to stay here. I am being silly—'

'You are not,' Beth said staunchly. 'You're upset and all mixed up. You are strong and someone needs to be here for the children and Harpers.'

'Ben said something that scared me the other day...' Sally shook her head. 'He was saying I could cope if anything happened to him...'

'Oh, Jack said that to me, too,' Beth remarked. 'I think it is because of the war. They reassure themselves that we'll manage if anything happens – but that is over now.'

Sally nodded and forced herself to smile. She couldn't tell even Beth what Ben had said about a weakness in his heart muscle. Sally had found a doctor she wanted Ben to see, but he'd refused, saying it wasn't necessary; she hadn't given up yet. It was only sensible to have another opinion. Andrew had told her about the man and agreed that it would be good to get a second consultation about something like that.

'Yes, I expect so,' Sally said now. 'I'll be fine, Beth. I shouldn't have telephoned you.'

'Of course you should,' Beth said. 'Besides, I wanted to talk to you about something different. I don't know if Maggie told you? Marion Jackson's husband has been moved to a new rest home and she hasn't been given an address for him. He is having some special treatment and they don't allow visitors. Maggie is very angry that they didn't tell Marion he was being moved – just sent her a letter. I wondered if you could find out where this place is so at least Marion could write to him and send him things?'

'Maggie didn't mention it to me... but I haven't seen her since she went to visit the rest home, though she may not have been since he was moved.' She paused then, 'Colin is worried because his father has been taken ill again. Colin may have to go back to his home and I'm not sure if she will go with him.'

'It never rains but it pours,' Beth said, shaking her head.

'Maggie says Colin and his father have been getting on better recently – he loves the children apparently, despite not wanting Colin to adopt when it was suggested.'

'Do you think they will go back to living in the country all the time?' Beth asked. 'Maggie says the children love it down there – and if Colin's father can't look after things...'

'Becky's husband, David, does that...' Sally reminded Beth.

'Becky is having another baby. She wrote to her father and he told me. She and David are thrilled.' Becky was their manager's daughter and had married the man who now managed Colin's father's estate.

'Mr Stockbridge must be excited to be a grandfather again,' Beth said. 'He had mixed feelings the first time, because she had the child before she was wed, but now he can tell everyone.'

'Minnie is very excited. She has been making lots of clothes for the new baby. She loves Becky and her granddaughter and, if she could, would live closer so she could visit more.'

'Do you think Mr Stockbridge will retire next year? He is sixty-four so he could...'

'I don't know.' Sally sighed. 'I should hate to lose him. He is our overall manager at Harpers, as you know. We have supervisors on all the floors but Mr Stockbridge is so efficient and he has that grave but pleasant manner that all the staff respect. It would be hard to find another manager as capable and honest as he is – and Minnie is a friend. We all came to love her before she married...'

'Yes, she lived with us for a while – well, I left to get married soon after she came to live with you and Maggie in the flat. I knew her at Harpers though and I loved her. I was so glad when she married the man she'd loved all those years.'

Minnie had given up her chance of marriage to be with her sister after their father had died, but she'd continued to think of the man she loved and when they met again, after her sister passed away, they had rediscovered the love between them. It was a happy ending to their story and even the upset of Mr Stockbridge's daughter, Becky, running off because she was pregnant with the child of her lover had ended well when Becky married.

'We have a lot of history together,' Beth said, thoughtfully as Sally was silent. 'Just think, if Harpers had never happened, we might never have met.'

'Oh, don't,' Sally said. 'I dread to think where I'd be if it hadn't been for Harpers. I was lonely then – I didn't even know my mother; she only found me because of a photo taken for the newspapers at Harpers...'

'How is your mother?' Beth asked. 'Have you heard from her recently?'

'She telephoned yesterday. Her husband is a little better again, so she might come and visit us soon.'

'That would be nice. I haven't seen her since last Christmas.'

'I took Jenny a few weeks back. We only stopped one night – but I'd like to see more of her.'

'It is a pity they don't live closer. Would they not consider moving here?'

'I doubt it,' Sally replied with an inward sigh. 'Her husband has his building business there – though he will probably have to sell it. Mum says she doesn't think he will be able to continue after this latest bout of chronic bronchitis.'

'I'm sorry to hear that,' Beth said and looked sad. 'They haven't been married long.'

'Not as long as Ben and me,' Sally said. 'It sometimes seems that I've been a part of Harpers forever, but it isn't really that long.'

'It's many years since the *Titanic* sank,' Beth reminisced. 'Do you remember that Jenni's friend died in that terrible accident?'

'Yes. She was so upset – and I think she married because she felt responsible for that motherless child. His father was such a cold man. I believe she was very unhappy.'

'Yes, poor Jenni,' Beth said. 'She was so much happier with Mr Alexander... and she met him because of *you*, Sally.'

'Yes...' The memory brought a smile to Sally's face. 'I persuaded him to take a look at a badly scarred patient and we became friends – and then he met Jenni in my office.' Her smile faded. 'They've had hardly any time together, Beth. It just isn't fair...'

'No, it isn't,' Beth agreed. 'Don't give up on her yet, Sally. Jenni seemed a strong person to me. She may pull through this...'

'I do hope so,' Sally said and then the tears she'd been struggling to hold back burst through. 'Oh, Beth. I can't bear to think she may die...'

Beth rushed to put her arms around her. 'You mustn't give in,' she said. 'You have to be strong. Pray for her, but be strong, Sally. If anything happens, Ben is going to need your strength.'

'Yes, I know you are right...' Sally wiped her cheeks with the lace hanky Beth gave her and laughed wetly. 'I'm daft. Jenni is going to get better, of course she is.'

15

'Mum, you look better tonight,' Lilly said as she entered the kitchen and saw her mother sitting up in her chair with a tray on her lap. She had a bowl of water on the tray and was peeling pota-toes, Carol by her side, watching and helping when one slipped to the floor.

Annie's smile made Lilly's heart lift. Bringing her mother into the kitchen in the mornings had worked so well. She moved from her chair to the daybed with Effie's help and the two spent several hours during the day just chatting. Her overall health had improved and she'd also recovered the full use of her right arm and said that she had tingling in her toes sometimes.

'The district nurse says I'm doing marvellous,' Annie told her. 'She spent an hour massaging and moving my leg this mornin' and it feels better. A bit achy but not so dead as it did. Nurse Bretton says I'll get me walkin' back if I keep on with me exercises.'

'Oh, Mum, that's wonderful,' Lilly said and went to take the bowl of peeled potatoes from her. 'I am so glad – but you needn't have done these.'

'And why not?' Annie demanded. 'I'll do whatever I can manage, our Lilly. One of these days, you'll come home and find your dinner cooked – won't she, Carol?'

'Me and Mum could do the dinner between us,' Carol said, smiling. 'I like helping her and I can put the dish in the oven if Mum tells me what to do.'

'That's lovely,' Lilly said. 'What kind of meat would you like? Shall I bring a bit of scrag end of lamb or a boiling chicken tomorrow and then we can have it the next day? They both make nice meals cooked with onions and carrots in the range. They only need a slow cooking if you put them in soon enough, don't they, Mum?'

'That's right, our Lilly. Effie made the range up when she was here so it is ready for you to cook on. What have we got for supper tonight then?'

'I bought sausages,' Lilly said, 'But there is some cheese or ham if you'd rather, Mum. We can get all sorts again now the rationing is over.'

'I think I'll have a nice sausage with some mashed potatoes and that cabbage I can see in your basket, Lilly. I feel hungry tonight...'

'That's good,' Lily said and then produced the little bunch of flowers. 'I got these for you, Mum. There weren't any violets, but these are called freesias. They smell wonderful and they were left over from a special order, so Mr Jones said I could bring them as there weren't enough to sell.'

There were just three of the delicate blooms and the perfume was sweet as Lilly placed them in a jam jar with some water and set them on the oak sideboard next to her mother's chair.

'Oh, they smell wonderful,' Annie said. 'That was nice, them letting you have them for me, Lilly. What's this Mr Jones like?'

Lilly laughed. 'He is in his sixties, Mum, and has a wife, two daughters and six grandchildren – and he treats me as if I were his grandchild. I was a bit nervous of him at first. He has white hair, tiny glasses on the end of his nose and a funny little beard – but he is kind and gentle and very clever. You should see the wonderful flower arrangements he does.'

'As long as the flowers weren't a bribe, our Lilly.'

Lilly turned away to prepare the cabbage. Why must her mother say such things? Mr Jones had just been kind, that was all.

'I didn't mean anything wrong, our Lilly,' her mother said. 'I just worry about you. Don't bring trouble home, my girl.'

'I wouldn't do anything like that!' Lilly was outraged as she turned and her mother laughed.

'Your eyes fair sparkle when you're cross,' Annie said. 'I know you're a good girl – but you can't always trust men... that Mr Harper gave you ten shillings when he broke your eggs and he promoted you. You just be careful, our Lilly.'

Lilly's laughter rang out. 'If you saw Mrs Harper, you wouldn't think he'd be after me, Mum. She is so beautiful – and she smells lovely.'

Annie nodded but said nothing. Lilly was amazed at the way her mother's mind worked. Just because someone was kind, she thought the worst.

'Why do you think things like that, Mum?' she asked, but there was no answer, just a faraway look in her eyes. Lilly made up her mind to speak to Ted about it when he came round that evening.

* * *

'It's just ten shillings this week,' Ted told her. 'We needed some new shoes for the kids, our Lilly. I'll give you more next week if I can.'

'I can manage with this,' Lilly told him. 'It's good of you to keep giving us money, Ted. I know it can't be easy for you.'

'I'd be all right if I didn't have that blighter on me patch,' Ted said. 'His last trick of tellin' folk I'd short-changed 'em didn't work after I made sure they saw what I delivered, so now he's cut the price of his coke. I can't make more than a penny a hundredweight on that, but mine's good stuff, so he's either losing money just to take over my round or it's substandard...' He shrugged. 'I've lost thirty shillings this week and if he cuts the price of coal, it will hardly be worth me continuing the business.'

'He has no right to take over your rounds,' Lilly said. 'Dad had that going for thirty years before he died...'

'I know – but there's no law against it,' Ted said. 'I might have to change me job, start doing something different...'

'What would you do?' Lilly asked him, puzzled. Ted had gone into the business straight from school. He'd never worked for a boss other than his easy-going father.

'Mebbe I'll get a barrow and sell fruit and vegetables,' Ted said on a sigh. 'To tell the truth, I don't know – but if this keeps up, I may have to...'

Lilly wasn't sure he would earn enough on the barrow. His wife expected at least two pounds a week and, with the rent for his house and what he gave Lilly, he would find it hard to make that much. The coal business had always been a good one – and Joe's wage relied on it, too.

'What about Joe?' she asked now. 'If you give up, what will he do?'

'Find work on the docks or in a factory, I suppose,' Ted said. 'To be honest, Lilly, if business doesn't pick up soon, I'll have to let him go...'

She stared at him in dismay. 'Does Joe know?'

'I expect he has some idea. He knows we're not sellin' the coke we were – if the coal goes too...'

'Can't you stop this youngster from taking your trade?'

'How?' Ted lifted his cap and scratched his head. She could see the coal dust ingrained into his scalp where his hair was receding. 'I've tried threatening him, but the cheeky little devil just says, "Make me!" What can I do? I could knock him for six, but that's not my way. Besides, with my luck, he wouldn't get up and then they would hang me for murder.'

Lilly nodded. Ted was a gentle giant, large-boned and strong. One punch from him and a young lad might never get up. If this lad wasn't scared of him and didn't respond to threats, there wasn't much he could do. As Ted said, there was no law against him working the same streets – but, surely, he must see there was no room for two?

'Have you tried talking to him, explaining that there is not enough profit for two coal merchants? Perhaps he would try somewhere else...'

'I tried that for a start – the cheeky monkey said he would take over my round if I didn't want it any longer.'

'Little devil,' Lilly said. 'I'm sorry, Ted. Look, if you need the money, I can manage without this...' She held out the ten-shilling note.

'No, not yet,' he said firmly. 'I can manage to give you that, but it's only half what I was giving you and when I start me barrow – if I do – I might not be able to give you anything for a while.'

'Ted, don't give up too soon. It was Dad's business. You should have it – and that lad wants taking down a peg or two.'

'If I only knew how...' He sighed. 'I'd best be off or my June will have words.'

'Yes – oh, just before you go, Ted. I wanted to ask if you knew why Mum doesn't trust men. She's always suspicious when someone does me a kindness and for no reason that I know.' She saw the hesitation in his face. 'Please, tell me...'

'It's not my place to tell you,' he said and then sighed. 'Somethin' bad happened to her before they were wed. Dad told me, but said I wasn't to let on that I knew. A man she thought was kind attacked her... in a way no man should. Now, don't you say a word, our Lilly, and I don't know more because that was what our dad said, and no use asking questions.'

'Thanks for telling me, Ted. I shan't feel so bad when she says things now I understand. I thought she was getting at me – but now I realise she is trying to protect me.'

'That's right. Ma is a funny one, always worrying about something. If it isn't money, it's fear that some man will take advantage of her girls – but she's all right and I'll always help if I can.'

'I know,' Lilly said and kissed his cheek. He tasted of coal. 'You're a good brother, Ted – and I'm sorry you've got all this trouble on your round...'

'I'll work it out...' Ted hesitated, then, 'If I tell the truth, our Lilly, I don't mind that much. Liftin' heavy sacks is hard work. I'd as soon do somethin' easier if I could.'

Lilly nodded, watching as he left with a sadness in her heart. Ted had had no choice about the job he did; their father had needed his young strong shoulders to help him with the round and so he'd gone straight to work for him. Perhaps he could find something better, she didn't know – but Joe would be jolted out of his safe job if Ted gave up. Lilly wondered if she should tell him when he came downstairs after his wash. It was only fair that he should know...

* * *

'Ted won't let that little runt run him out of business?' Joe stared at her in dismay. 'He just wants a clip round the ear. Ted should let me have a go at him.'

'I think he has had enough of it anyway,' Lilly said. 'He had to join Dad straight from school. He wasn't given a choice.'

'Well, I like it and I'm not giving up,' Joe said staunchly. 'If Ted wants out, I'll buy the lorry from him and take over. I'll give that little b— runt the scare of his life.'

Lilly laughed. 'You can call him a bugger. I don't mind, because that's what he is. You sort him, Joe. I'm glad you're not ready to give in – that was Dad's business all those years.'

'Aye and I don't give up what's mine.' Joe grinned at her. 'I had a real slice of luck and won the sweepstake at the pub last night. I got nearly twenty pounds and that will buy the lorry and set me up. I was going to give you half, but I'll make it up to you another time.'

'I wouldn't take it,' Lilly told him, smiling at his eagerness. 'That's a fortune and I dare say Ted won't want much for the lorry. It wouldn't still go if you weren't so clever at tinkering with the engine. You should have been an engineer on the ships, Joe.'

'Could have if I'd wanted,' he agreed. 'I don't want to go to sea, Lilly. I was lucky the war ended just as I was eighteen. I didn't have to join up and they're going to have a regular Army now of over two hundred thousand men, so I read in the paper – ready if we have another war.'

'Don't!' Lilly cried. 'The last one was bad enough. We don't want any more ever.'

'No, we don't,' her brother agreed and kissed her. He smelled of soap and she gave him a hug.

'Have a nice evening, Joe.'

'Just going to have half a pint and play a game of darts. I'll talk to Ted at work in the morning rather than go round – his June doesn't like me much.' He grinned at her. 'I reckon she wants him all to herself...'

'I am sure you're right,' Lilly said.

She smiled as he left. If Joe bought the business, he would sort it out, she thought. Ted was a lovely brother, but he just wasn't strong-minded enough to stand up for his rights; she was and so was Joe. If she could find out where this youth who was stealing their round lived, she'd go and have a word herself. Lilly would sort him out if she got the chance.

16

Sally smiled as she read an article lauding the fact that women were now permitted to sit on a jury. It had happened for the first time that July and was still remarkable enough to warrant several lines in her newspaper, though the summer had progressed and it was August now. She felt a warm satisfaction at knowing things were beginning to change, though very slowly, each concession hard-won. Reading on, she frowned as she saw a report of street battles in Ireland. What was going on there? she wondered. Why so much unrest? Shaking her head, she was about to go up and look in on the children when the telephone rang.

Sally got to her feet and answered it. 'Mum, it's lovely to hear from you – how are you?' she said when her mother spoke. 'How is Trevor now?'

'They took him into hospital this afternoon,' her mother replied with a little sob in her voice. 'The doctors say he has persistent bronchitis, which may lead to pneumonia so they took him in for observation. I've just got back from visiting him. He is being given oxygen...'

'Oh, Mum, I am so sorry. I'd like to come down to be with you, but Ben has gone to Newcastle. His sister is very ill. She is in hospital too and it may be a brain bleed. It's what her husband believes.'

'She's not much older than you?' Sally's mother sounded shocked as Sally confirmed. 'Trevor is in his sixties – but young Jenni... that's awful, Sally. I am so sorry. You mustn't think of coming here. I can manage. I just rang because I wanted to talk to you.'

'I wish we lived closer so the children could see their granny more often. They do love you so much.'

'I know and I love them. I wish we could see them more often...' She paused, then, 'How are they – and that dog of Jenny's?'

'Jenny and Peter are fine. Lulu is naughty, borrows everything that is left lying around for five minutes. If I forget to put Jenny's shoes out of reach, Lulu has them and mine – and it is a wonder Ben has any socks left.'

'She is a little imp then.' Sally's mother laughed. 'You must be run off your feet half the time with two children, the dog and Harpers to see to...'

'It can be hectic in the morning when we take Lulu to the park. I usually leave Peter with Mrs Hills. Jenny is so lively that I can't manage them both and Lulu.'

'I doubt anyone could. You need a nanny, Sally.'

'I'm trying to find one, Mum – but I want someone I can trust not to smack Jenny when she is naughty. Most of the older nannies I've interviewed are too strict. I want someone who can control her but not be unkind.'

'Yes, of course you do.' Her mother sighed. 'If we lived closer, I could look after the children sometimes...' She hesitated, then, 'Perhaps Trevor will listen to reason now he's been so ill with his chest. He had a good offer for the business but said he'd think about it. If he sold it, we could find somewhere to live near you, Sally.'

'Oh, Mum, I wish you could,' Sally cried. 'That would be wonderful. We've missed so much time together. Tell Trevor to sell – there are some nice flats going up just a short bus ride from us.'

'Oh, he'll want a garden. Trevor likes gardening when he is up to it.'

'He can come and do mine if he wants – that will keep him busy.'

Her mother laughed. 'Yes, you have a really big back garden. I couldn't believe how big it was when I saw it. You'd never think you were in a big city.'

'We were very lucky to get this house,' Sally said. 'When Ben first told me about it, I was reluctant to move, but it is perfect for the children.'

Her mother agreed, then, 'I hope his sister gets better. It must be a worry for you both.'

'I am very fond of Jenni. She has always been so bright and full of life. I can't believe she might...' Sally caught her breath. 'At least Trevor is getting the treatment he needs at last. You tell him we love him and want him to come and live near us.'

'I shall. I do already,' Sally's mother said with a laugh. 'It makes me feel better just talking to you, love. I'd better go. I have a pile of ironing to do. I let it pile up when Trevor needed me. I expect you're busy too?'

'Just making up a few orders for the store,' Sally said. 'I have a beautiful new line in evening bags and some gorgeous silk scarves. It is wonderful to be able to buy things from abroad again. I missed the fine silks and the soft leathers we get from Italy.'

'From Italy? Yes, I once had a beautiful suede bag that was made in Italy. I bought it second-hand, but it was like new. I used it until it was worn out.'

'I'll buy you a new one for your birthday,' Sally said. 'I was wondering what you'd like best.'

'Sally! You are always giving me things...'

'Because I love you and I want to,' Sally said. Lulu barked then and Sally shushed her. 'Did you hear that, Mum? Lulu wants to go out in the garden. I'll ring you tomorrow. Give Trevor my love.'

'Yes, I will. Bye then.'

* * *

After replacing the telephone receiver, Sally got up to let Lulu into the garden. The night air was chilly and the trees were blowing wildly, a few leaves whipping across the lawn. Where had the warm weather gone to? It was still summer but unseasonably cool. She shivered but stood at the door waiting for the dog to come back. It was a large walled garden and safe for Lulu to run as she pleased, but Sally waited to see her safely back inside. Feeling lonely without Ben, though she had two children and Mrs Hills in the house as well as the dog, Sally poured herself a small glass of white wine.

Why did people you loved have to get ill? If what was making Jenni ill was a problem with her brain, Sally believed it was unlikely she would recover. A kind of surgery for tumours on the brain had been performed as early as the Middle Ages but was damaging to the patient. Even now, to operate might do as much harm as good. To think of Jenni perhaps paralysed or changed mentally, slowed, no longer as bright as she had been was painful...

Sally jumped as the telephone rang. She set down her glass and rushed to answer it, sensing that this time it was the call she was waiting for.

'Sally...' Ben's voice sounded hoarse and she knew he'd been crying.

'Ben darling, how are you? Is Jenni—'

'Jenni died this afternoon,' he said brokenly and her heart caught with pain. How could that have happened so quickly? It was a thunderbolt from the blue, mind numbing. Sally couldn't quite believe it had happened but Ben's grief was evidence in itself. 'I saw her and sat with her for most of last night. I went back to Andrew's house to wash and change and he sat with her. He was with her when she died, but she never recovered consciousness. The doctors say it was a good thing because she wouldn't have been Jenni any more. She'd had a really bad stroke.'

Sally was stunned, hardly knowing what to say. 'It wasn't a tumour that caused her illness then?'

'We'll only know that if they do an autopsy and Andrew says he won't allow that, because she would hate it – and he's right.' Ben sounded terrible and Sally wished she could put her arms around him and just hold him.

'He must be devastated, as you are – and their child will never know her mother as she grows up.' Sally's words stuck in her throat. 'I'm sorry, Ben. It is too awful to take in.' She was crying and she mustn't. 'How is Andrew?'

'He just sits staring at her photograph and picks up her things. Fortunately, they have a nanny. Maria is marvellous and she is looking after little Penny.' Ben cleared his throat. 'Are you all right, Sally? Can you manage a bit longer? I need to be with Andrew, to sort things out for him. At the moment, he doesn't seem capable of making any arrangements.'

'Shall I come up, bring the children?'

Ben hesitated, then, 'I don't think so, Sally. I wish you were here, but I think you need to be at home. You have to think of the children and Harpers. You can't do anything and I wouldn't wish this on anyone...' She heard the emotion in his voice. 'I've never seen a man crumble the way Andrew is. He's usually so strong, but this just floored him. I'll keep you in touch. I do love you, Sally. Please don't feel hurt.'

'It's all right, Ben,' Sally choked, though the tears were coming fast. 'Stay for as long as Andrew needs you and give him my love.'

'Yes, I shall. Kiss our little ones for me, Sally. I never thought this would happen to Jenni. I don't understand how life can be so cruel...'

The receiver went down abruptly, as though Ben couldn't take any more. Sally wanted to ring him back immediately, but decided it would just put more pressure on him. He was battling his own emotions and trying to help Andrew, who was clearly devastated with grief.

Sally bent her head and sobbed. Jenni dead. How could it happen to a young woman so full of life? Why?

'Mrs Harper?' Mrs Hills stood in the doorway looking at her. 'I see it is bad news. I am so sorry. Is there anything I can do – make you some tea or a coffee?'

'Coffee with brandy, I think. I need something to steady me,' Sally said. 'Jenni died this afternoon. She had a massive stroke, perhaps caused by a growth on her brain; they don't know for certain whether it was a tumour and her husband is refusing the autopsy. He says she would hate it – and she would.'

'That is a terrible thing,' Mrs Hills said. 'Someone so young to die suddenly like that – it makes you wonder what it's all for. We had that wicked war and she was so good...' She gave an emotional sniff. 'I'll make that coffee and bring you a brandy, Mrs Harper.'

Sally nodded. The storm of weeping had passed but she felt heavy with grief as she wiped her face. Lulu ran up to her, pushing her wet nose into Sally's hand. She petted and stroked her, feeling slightly comforted. Dogs always sensed your mood.

'It's all right, Lulu,' she whispered. 'I'll be all right in a minute.'

It had been such a shock to hear that Jenni had been struck down by something and had died. Perhaps the doctors were right and she would never have been the same, but losing her was painful. Sally knew that neither Ben nor Andrew would ever quite get over this tragedy.

Why? Why? Why? She shook her head. Sally had come close to death when she was ill with her second child, but she'd recovered – why couldn't Jenni have got better? Anger replaced the grief momentarily. It wasn't right and it wasn't fair.

Mrs Hills returned with the brandy. 'Drink that straight down,' she commanded. 'I'll be back with your coffee in a moment.'

Taking a deep breath, Sally did as she was told. The brandy stung her throat and warmed her. She fondled the dog and Lulu crept on to her lap, nudging her as if trying to cheer her.

Mrs Hills returned with the coffee and a sandwich. 'You haven't eaten since lunch and you didn't have much then,' she said. 'No sense in you being ill as well, Mrs Harper. You have to be strong for Mr Harper and the children – and that daft dog.'

'Yes, I know,' Sally said and smiled at her. 'I am very lucky to have you, Mrs Hills.'

'I've been thinking...' Mrs Hills said. 'I don't normally put my ideas forward, Mrs Harper – but my niece is nineteen and a sensible girl. Do you remember I told you about Winnie being bored at home?' Sally nodded. 'She is looking for a job, but her mother doesn't want her to go into service or work in a shop. Winnie likes children. Would you like to meet her – perhaps take her on to help with the little ones? She's not a trained nanny, of course.'

Sally's head went up instantly. 'Yes, please. Bring her to have tea with them, Mrs Hills. If they like each other and she seems suitable I'd be glad to take her on.'

'Winnie is a good girl,' Mrs Hills said and smiled. 'I think you'll like her – and I'll be here to keep an eye out the same as usual.'

'Of course you will. I shall be going into the store in the morning. I have to tell the staff about Jenni – and to make sure everything is all right.' Sally sat up straighter and Lulu jumped down as if sensing her time was over for the moment. 'If Winnie comes to work for us, I might just get to Jenni's funeral after all.'

* * *

Sally rang her mother to tell her the sad news, then she rang Beth, Maggie and Rachel. All of them had known Jenni well and she thought they deserved to hear of her death before it became common knowledge.

'That is so sad for you all,' Beth said. 'I am really upset about it, Sally. I liked Jenni.'

'I know. That is why I am telling you, Maggie and Rachel before I tell Harpers' staff. I shall go in tomorrow morning and inform Mr Stockbridge and he can pass it on to the heads of department. It is important that everyone be told. Jenni was a part of Harpers until a couple of years ago. Besides, I don't want people asking Ben how she is and upsetting him.'

'He will take it hard. She's so young...' Beth swallowed hard. 'If there is anything I can do, Sally – have the children while you go up to Newcastle?'

'I may have found a nurse. She isn't trained as a nanny, but in some large houses it is the children's nurse who actually looks after them. Nanny just rules the nursery with a rod of iron. I didn't want that, so Winnie sounds ideal, but if I don't take her on – well, I might ask you,' Sally said. 'If you could manage them as well as your own?'

'I have Dad and Vera,' Beth said. 'It is a pity your mum doesn't live nearer, Sally.'

'Well, she might if Trevor can be persuaded,' Sally said. 'I am going to give Maggie and Rachel a call too...'

'Yes, you must,' Beth said. 'Rachel will be very sad, she thought a lot of Jenni.'

'I know...'

* * *

After speaking to Beth, Sally rang Maggie, who was sympathetic and also offered to help with the children.

'I'd be glad to have them for a couple of days,' Maggie said. 'I have my children's nurse, Mary, and she is wonderful with our two. You need someone like her, Sally. She is thirty-five and a war widow so she lives in and is glad of the job. Her only daughter is thirteen and she is at school most of the day but no trouble when she comes home. She likes playing with the children, too.'

'Thank you. I'm hoping this Winnie will be just what I need. I'll be in touch if I need help.' Sally smiled as she replaced the receiver. She had such good friends.

* * *

'Oh, Sally, that is terrible,' Rachel exclaimed when Sally told her. 'I can hardly believe it. Jenni was always so full of life. Always rushing here and there doing things. It doesn't seem possible. She sent me a lovely Shetland wool scarf and hat for my birthday...' Her voice caught. 'She was so marvellous when you were ill. Making them sponge you down when you had the fever, getting you a different doctor and taking you home to look after you. I don't think you would have your son if it hadn't been for Jenni.'

'I know...' Sally felt the tears start again. 'I can't believe it either. I am hoping to go up for her funeral.'

'You must,' Rachel declared. 'I'll come to London tomorrow and if you need help, I'll look after your children while you go – and if you have a nurse, I'll come up with you.'

'What about your William and Lizzie?'

'William is fine at the moment and so is Lizzie. Living in the country suits them both – besides, we have a housekeeper and a couple of maids, so they will be well looked after. Hazel comes for tea most days so William won't be lonely. You can't go through this alone, dearest Sally. I am coming up to London tomorrow.'

Sally laughed. 'You always did take care of me, Rachel. I would love to see you – and you can help me decide whether Winnie is suitable as a nurse for the children if you're here by tea time...'

* * *

In the end, even though Rachel had arrived and settled into her room, Sally needed no help to decide that Winnie was perfect for the job. She was a tall, well-built girl who liked all forms of sport, she informed them, and running after a lively little girl and a boy who was just beginning to run all over the place would be no trouble at all. She thought it would be fun. She loved Lulu and spent most of the interview playing with the dog and the children, crawling around the floor with them.

However, when Jenny threw something at Lulu, Winnie immediately threw it back at her, making the child look at her in shock. It was only a soft toy, but it still hit her.

'If you hit poor Lulu, she might bite you,' Winnie told her. 'It isn't nice when people throw things at you, is it?' Jenny shook her head. 'So tell Lulu you are sorry and won't do it again.'

Jenny sat down next to her dog and put her arms about her. 'I'm sorry, Lulu. I didn't means to hurt you.'

Sally was hard put to stifle the laugh that rose to her lips. Jenny was not normally that easily persuaded, but the shock combined with the calm, sensible voice – and perhaps the fact that Winnie had played with them – had combined to win Jenny's respect.

'Well, I think you have your answer,' Rachel said softly as Jenny crawled into Winnie's lap and smiled. 'So now you can ring Ben and tell him you are coming up for the funeral. Do you want me to come with you – or stay and make sure everything is all right at Harpers?'

'Come with me. You knew her, too,' Sally said. 'Mr Stockbridge told me not to worry. I don't have any appointments that can't be changed. I think if I can pay my respects at Jenni's funeral, I might start to feel better...'

17

'I'm glad you've sorted it out and are coming up,' Ben said when Sally telephoned him. 'Andrew has asked about you a couple of times – and, to be honest, I'm out of my depth here. I just can't reach him.'

'He has lost the woman he loved,' Sally said. 'He waited a long time to marry. I can't imagine how devastated he must feel. I know you are too, darling, but Jenni was really all Andrew had apart from his work.'

'He has his daughter…'

'Yes, and in time he will find Jenni again in her,' Sally agreed. 'At the moment she is too young to be much comfort to him. Thankfully, they have a good nurse so she will be looked after in that way.'

Ben murmured his agreement. 'It was a bit of luck you finding this Winnie – nice old-fashioned name, Winifred.'

'She is a nice girl but not a bit old-fashioned,' Sally told him. 'She likes to walk and play with the children and has loads of energy. Jenny respects her and does what she says.'

'That is good news,' Ben agreed. 'Did you say Rachel was coming up with you?'

'Yes. She wanted to pay her respects, Ben. I don't know if she can stay with Andrew, but if not, perhaps you could book a room for her in a nearby hotel. There's a nice small one round the corner.'

'I'm sure he has plenty of room. It is a big old house, as you know. I think he needs company, to take him out of himself. I've never seen a man break down quite like this before.'

'It must be awful for him,' Sally said. 'He expected to have so many years with her – and he should have done. It just isn't fair...'

'Life seldom is,' Ben replied harshly. 'I'm still trying to come to terms with what has happened, Sally. Jenni was younger than I am... God! It is unbelievable that she should die in such a way.'

'And have the doctors said why it happened?'

'They don't know for sure and without an autopsy they never will. She just had a massive stroke, but they don't know why – Andrew is convinced there was a growth on her brain. He says she'd been behaving out of character recently and he'd asked her to see her doctor several times but she wouldn't...'

'Could they have done anything even if she had?' Sally asked.

'Perhaps – who knows? Jenni was always stubborn. Oh hell!' Ben sounded both angry and upset. 'Get here as soon as you can, Sally. We need you.'

'We're coming up in the morning,' Sally said. 'Catching the early train. I'll get a taxi from the station. You stay with Andrew. Goodnight, darling. I wish I could hug you. We all need one...'

Sally's cheeks were wet with tears as she replaced the receiver. Andrew must be in a bad way for Ben to say he was out of his depth. She wasn't sure that she would be of much comfort to him; he'd met Jenni because of her and seeing her might only add to his pain.

Sally hoped not. He was a wonderful surgeon and a generous man and she hated to think of him in such pain. Grief was hard to bear when you lost those you loved, but he must feel cheated, because Jenni was so young. They should have had years together yet.

* * *

Andrew looked a shadow of his former self, his face haggard with grief, his eyes red and his skin grey; he seemed to have aged ten years since Sally had last seen him.

'Oh, Andrew, my dearest friend...' Sally said and moved towards him. He hesitated and then let her hug him, his arms coming around her after a few seconds and holding her tight. She felt the deep sobbing sigh he'd held inside and knew that this was what he needed, just to hold another human being in his arms. And then he was sobbing against her shoulder. Sally stroked his head as it bowed to her level. 'Yes, cry for her. She deserves that and she would understand – but she would also say she wanted you to carry on, with your work and to love your daughter.'

Andrew stiffened, drew a deep breath and then stood back, wiping his face with his handkerchief. 'I'm a damned mess,' he said. 'I needed that hug, Sally Harper. Thank you. I know you are right. I shall go back to work after the funeral tomorrow. As for little Penny... well, I'll see she is taken care of...'

'You must talk to her about Jenni,' Sally told him. 'Make sure she knows who her mother was and doesn't wonder and worry as she gets older.'

'Her mother should have been here for her!' he said, a harsh note in his voice. 'What did I do wrong, Sally?'

'You did nothing wrong,' Sally said sharply. 'You are not to blame.'

'What was it all for? Why give me a taste of happiness just to take it away?' he demanded.

'I don't know,' Sally admitted. 'I can't understand it either, Andrew. Yet I know that it happens. So many women lost their husbands in the war – why did that happen? Why do any of us have to suffer pain and grief? You see enough of it in your work...'

He drew a shaky breath, then, 'Aye, I do. At least I have that and I must thank God – if there is one – for that, I suppose.'

'Don't lose hope, my friend,' she said. 'I know it doesn't help now, but you have your lovely daughter and you have your work. Somehow you have to put your life back together again.'

'Could you do it if you lost Ben?' Andrew demanded fiercely.

Sally met his demanding look. 'I would have to. I have two children to bring up and Harpers needs a guiding hand. I would feel as you do now, Andrew, but I would do my duty – as you must now.'

'My duty?' For a moment, his eyes were rebellious and then he nodded. 'Yes, I know. I am needed, by my daughter and many patients. I shall go on – though I have wanted to end it. In my darkest hour, I wanted to die, to be with her.'

'She will always be with you, in your heart, your mind,' Sally told him. 'Jenni would expect a great deal of you, Andrew. Don't let her down.'

He gave a harsh laugh. 'You don't mince your words, Sally Harper. It's what I like – what I've always admired in you. I shan't let you down, I promise...' His eyes had a hint of his old smile in them as he glanced at Rachel. 'I think we may have met before. Forgive me for ignoring you. It's Rachel, isn't it?'

'We spoke once at Harpers when I worked there,' Rachel said. 'I hope I am not in the way? I just wanted to pay my respects to Jenni – but I could stay at the hotel...'

'Nonsense! I have plenty of room. It's a big house – far too big now, but we'll find somewhere else. Probably a small apartment nearer my work.'

Rachel nodded. 'I have a small apartment in London. We live in the country, but I visit Sally now and then and other friends so I keep the apartment. It is nicer than a hotel and William wanted me to keep it.'

'How is your husband these days? I remember Jenni... saying once that he wasn't always well?' Andrew asked.

'He has an inherited weakness in his chest,' Rachel said. 'Normally it doesn't bother him much, but we have to be careful in the winter. If he catches a chill, it can turn nasty.'

Andrew inclined his head. He still looked devastated, but the lost look had been replaced by one of acceptance. 'Sally, take Rachel up to her room please. It is the third down the landing past the bathroom. I have something I must do. I shall see you all at dinner...' He walked from the room, his step firm and determined.

Sally turned to Ben, who had been standing by the window overlooking the back garden. 'Could you arrange some tea for us, please? We had some lunch on the train, but the tea they served wasn't very nice...'

'Of course.' He came to her and kissed her lightly on the mouth. 'I'm glad you're here, Sally – and you, Rachel. Andrew needed some company. I think he may be a bit better now. I don't think he had sobbed like that before – just sat looking stunned and close to collapse. He didn't seem to know what I said to him, but you certainly got through to him, Sally.'

'If I helped at all, I am glad – but Jenni would want him to carry on. She would say he must be a good father to their daughter above all else.'

'Yes, she would,' Ben agreed, on a shuddering breath. 'I'll ask Mrs Morrison to make some tea for us all.'

As he went in search of Andrew's housekeeper, Sally took

Rachel upstairs and showed her the room that had been made ready for her. It smelled nice and there was a small vase of fragrant roses on the dressing table.

'Mrs Morrison must have picked those,' Sally remarked. 'It is the sort of thing that Jenni would have done. I expect there is a vase in my room too.'

'It is an old house, but the rooms are a lovely size,' Rachel said, looking round at the shining mahogany furniture and the rose wallpaper. 'Comfortable and fresh...' The window was open and she looked out at the garden. 'What a beautiful garden. It looks sheltered and warm.'

'That's because of the high walls round it,' Sally told her. 'Jenni said she could find a sheltered spot even in winter and if a pale sun was shining, it would be warm on her face...' She gulped. 'It seems wrong that she isn't here with us... with her little girl.' Penny was only just over a year old, too young to know what had happened, but she would sense her mother's loss, however good her nurse was.

'Don't cry,' Rachel said. 'You have to be strong for them both. You told Andrew that it was his duty – and it is yours, too.'

'Yes, I know.' Sally lifted her head. 'Let's dump our cases and go and have that tea...'

It rained the next morning. Not the heavy sheeting rain they sometimes had in Newcastle, but a fine drizzle. Everyone got a bit wet as they followed the coffin into church, which was old and smelled musty and cold despite the flowers everywhere. The service was nice enough in its way and the vicar gave a good speech about Jenni, her enterprise and the way she'd helped others. Jenni hadn't spoken to Sally about it, but apparently, she'd done some work for orphaned children since coming to Newcastle.

'Jenni will be sadly missed by many,' the vicar intoned. 'But we must not mourn her passing but celebrate her life. God giveth and God taketh away. Blessed be Thy name, O Lord God. Only Thee understands the workings of Thy love and truth. Give us faith, hope and goodness so that we may overcome our grief and believe that our dearly beloved Jenni has gone to a better place. Amen.'

Sally and Ben followed Andrew, with Rachel and other friends behind as they went out to see the interment. Thankfully, it had stopped raining and the brief blessing only took a short time. Then they were back in the cars being driven to Andrew's home, followed by the cars of other mourners. Jenni had made many friends in her short time here.

Mrs Morrison had prepared refreshments and there were the usual glasses of sherry, as well as tea, coffee, sandwiches and scones. Small talk was made, condolences given and, finally, the guests departed, leaving just Sally, Ben, Rachel and Andrew in the large parlour.

'Thank you for coming and all you've done,' Andrew said to Ben. 'I know that Jenni has left something to you, Ben. I think there is a gift for Sally too – but her main estate goes to Penny. It will be put into a trust for her until she is older.'

'What about Jenni's department store?' Ben asked now. 'Will you try to carry it on or sell it and bank the money for Penny?'

'To be honest, I haven't given it a thought,' he replied. 'I know nothing about women's fashions or children's clothes. Jenni did all that herself. I expect it will be best to sell.'

'I could do the buying for you – if you wished to keep it going...' Rachel surprised them all. 'I could stay on a few days, go round the store to see what it is all about – and then I could buy for you, Mr Alexander. I could visit about four times a year, more if necessary, and buy from the same suppliers that Sally uses.'

'I do most of my buying four times a year,' Sally agreed. 'For the seasons. If we need reorders or something new is brought to me, then I buy extras – but Rachel could do it. I would help her for a start if she wished.'

Rachel nodded as if she'd known that.

'I'll have to think about it,' Andrew replied. 'I'm grateful for the offer but not sure I want to continue it. Might be better to sell—'

'If you get a price, give me first refusal.' Ben said, making Sally stare at him. 'I'd buy it if I could get a loan.' He looked at Rachel. 'We might take you up on your offer to run the purchasing if we buy.'

'You think about it carefully, Andrew,' Sally advised. 'Try to decide what Jenni would think right.' She smiled at him. 'I'm glad the reception is all over. Socialising is hard at such times – but you must have a life, Andrew. Don't turn into a hermit. Entertain your friends sometimes, the way you always did.'

He nodded. 'I'll do what I can,' he promised. 'Just don't forget about me, Sally Harper.'

'We'll never do that, will we, Ben?' They would never forget Andrew an.d Jenni would burn forever in their memories and their hearts like a shining star, forever young and lovely.

'No – and our home is always open to you,' Ben told him. He looked at Sally. 'Are you ready? If we are leaving this evening, we'll need to go soon.'

'Yes, we should get back,' she agreed. 'Remember where we are, Andrew. You can ring whenever you like for a chat – and come and stay. Come to us at Christmas with Penny, please.'

'I might do that,' he agreed. He looked at Rachel. 'Are you leaving or staying for another day?'

'I'll move into the hotel,' Rachel replied. 'I am going to spend tomorrow looking round Newcastle and I'll visit Jenni's store. Afterwards, I'll give you a written report, Mr Alexander. It might help you decide what to do.'

'Yes, do that,' he agreed. 'No need to move to the hotel. I am going to the clinic now and I shall not be back until the morning. You will have the house to yourself – apart from Penny and my staff that is...' He turned to Ben. 'I'll drive you to the station. It is on my way.'

Sally went to kiss Rachel's cheek. 'Tell me all about it when you get back, please,' she whispered and Rachel nodded. 'You'll come to us before you return home.'

'Yes, I shall. William won't expect me until the weekend.'

* * *

'That was a surprise,' Ben said when they were safely seated on the train with some papers and magazines. 'I never thought Rachel would come out with something like that – did you?'

'I was surprised – but I think she misses Harpers,' Sally said. 'They are happy enough in the country, but Rachel is still young and energetic. I think she would manage the store for Andrew as far as the buying is concerned – but that isn't everything. He will need a good manager for day-to-day stuff.'

'If he keeps it,' Ben remarked thoughtfully. 'I think he will sell and put the proceeds in trust for their daughter.'

'What made you say you would buy it?' Sally asked. 'It would mean another loan.'

'Perhaps...' Ben rubbed the side of his nose. 'If we expand out of town, we might put shares on the stock market – make Harpers a limited company.'

'You wouldn't?' Sally was shocked. 'It wouldn't be yours any longer, Ben.'

'You forget. Mick bought Jenni's share and my cousin still has a few – I just own 75 per cent of the shares. If I floated it, I would keep a controlling interest, of course.'

'Wouldn't you have to ask Mick and your cousin?'

'Mick is in agreement,' Ben told her. 'My cousin only has 5 per cent. He could sell to me and then I'd still have a controlling interest if I sold say 35 per cent of the shares. Besides, when you float, you can increase the value of the shares by splitting them so that more people can own them.'

'I don't understand it,' Sally replied, shrugging. He must have given the idea some thought previously if he'd discussed it with Mick. 'Is it worth it just to own another store up here? If it were mine to decide, I'd keep the London store as it is and not bother to buy Jenni's.'

'It is something to think about,' Ben said, looking thoughtful. 'I'd like to keep Jenni's store in the family if I could. It is just how I do that...'

'Well, it is up to you,' Sally said. 'You should think about it, Ben. Make sure it is what you truly want.'

18

'I think I convinced Mr Alexander to continue the store, keep it for his daughter to inherit one day,' Rachel said when she arrived at Sally's home two days later. 'It is a busy store and well run, Sally. It would be a shame to let it be sold to a stranger.'

'Ben was thinking about it seriously so it would still have belonged to a Harper, but I am glad if Andrew wants to keep it now. I think we have enough with the London store and the restaurant for the moment. Besides... it would seem wrong to me. We would end up making money from something that should be Jenni's daughter's...'

'Ben wouldn't see it that way, of course,' Rachel said. 'I am looking forward to helping Mr Alexander – just until he gets used to the idea of owning the store and then I can find another buyer for him if it is too much for me.'

'What will William say to you taking more trips away?' Sally asked dubiously. 'I think it will eat up quite a bit of your time, perhaps more than you realise.'

'He is happy for me to do it. I do need to visit the store now and then to speak to the manager and see what is selling and what isn't, but I can do much of my buying at home – as you do. I know the fashions up there may need to be a little more conservative than in London, but I saw what Jenni had stocked and have a good idea of what she preferred.'

'Yes, you probably need to stock less evening wear than Harpers does, but I think fashion is much the same all over – perhaps a little slower to catch on up there,' Sally agreed. 'I use the catalogues the firms send out, but I try to speak to the representatives in person, too. I like to see the quality of what I'm buying. I can help you source the right firms if you wish?'

'That would be a help. A lot of the firms you use have their factories in the country and come to London, especially to get orders from their main customers. They may be prepared to visit me – or in some cases, I can get to their location by train.' Rachel looked determined. 'It is only for a year or two, Sally, just to help Jenni's husband. I dare say by then Mr Alexander will know what to do himself – either he'll sell or he will employ someone to do the job I've done temporarily.'

Sally nodded. 'Have you missed Harpers very much?'

Rachel let a sigh out. 'Yes, more than I imagined. Oh, we have a good life. I sit on various committees and run jumble sales and church bazaars, but I do miss the busy life we had in London.'

'William wouldn't consider returning?'

'He loves it down there and I'm happy enough, Sally. William often tells me to visit London more – well, now I shall. I'll call and see you on my way to Newcastle. It will give me an incentive to come more often and that will please my husband. I know he feels guilty for having taken me away from my friends, but he shouldn't because I went willingly. I do love him and I enjoy being with him – but country life just isn't quite enough for me sometimes.'

'Yes, I understand that,' Sally agreed. 'I love working at Harpers and I love living in town – the theatres, shops, museums. I couldn't work full-time now the children need more attention, because I don't want to leave them to their nurse all the time – even though Jenny loves Winnie.'

'That is one thing that works well for me,' Rachel told her with a smile. 'Lizzie is so happy in the country. She loves William and Hazel – you remember my first husband's mother?' Sally agreed she did. 'I never have to worry about Lizzie. She is either in school or visiting Hazel or at home with us, and mostly in William's study. He has lots of picture books – natural history with wonderful illustrations – and she loves them. So we do very well.' Rachel smiled. 'Please do not think me miserable; I am not, but this new interest will give me a little bit more...'

'Yes, and I am pleased that you offered, Rachel. I know that Andrew would be wrong to make a snap decision – and, to be honest, I don't want Ben to buy the store. Not yet, anyway. He has plans to expand, but I think we need to go more carefully for now. Yes, Harpers is doing very well at the moment, but we should still be cautious.'

'I don't believe your husband is the cautious type,' Rachel told her. 'Right from the start he has been looking to expand. Had we not experienced that terrible war, I am positive you would already have stores in other big towns.'

'Yes, I suppose we might – but we were just beginning to make a success of the store when the war came,' Sally told her. 'It has been difficult to do more than pay the bills and earn a living for the war years. Quite a few shops closed down because they just couldn't make them pay. We were lucky.'

'You had some luck, but you worked hard to hold it together...' Rachel looked at her oddly. 'Do you feel as if you have been pushed aside now that Ben is able to do so much more?'

Sally hesitated, then inclined her head. 'At times, yes. I'm sure that is foolish of me, Rachel. Ben loves me. He knows what I did – he just wants me to take things easier now that he's back.'

'Yes, I see,' Rachel said. 'Some of the women I know worked hard during the war, taking the jobs the men couldn't do while they were away fighting. Now they are expected to stay at home and be simply wives and mothers – to make do on what their husband gives them.' She frowned. 'They don't like it and some of the younger women are simply refusing to accept that kind of life. The war changed things for women and I don't see how we can ever go back.'

'Do you still belong to the Women's Movement?' Sally asked.

'Yes, I do. I know some of us have the vote, but I also know of women whose husbands tell them they must vote as they do – so what is the point? Women have the right to equality. They should have freedom to live in the way they wish, rather than agree with everything their husbands do or say. Loving someone doesn't mean you have to agree with their ideas all the time.'

'You are perfectly right,' Sally said. 'I no longer go to meetings, but I do cheer the Movement on. I'm not sure that women will ever have true equality, though. We might get the vote, but what about equal pay?'

'That is another matter altogether,' Rachel said crossly. 'I doubt employers will ever agree to that – they would simply stop employing women if they had to pay them the same. It would need to be enshrined in law before it happened.'

'A lot of women lost their jobs when the men came home,' Sally agreed. 'I've tried to keep a balance at Harpers. We need our girls on the counters. Men expect to be heads of departments, and in many of the departments they are – but not the ones I oversee. I believe it needs a woman's care to keep those as they should be. However, they do leave to get married and it isn't easy to get anyone as good at their job as you were, Rachel. I am lucky enough to have found Andrea Martin, though, but it is early days yet. I must give her time.'

'Is she not quite what you'd hoped?'

'She does her job well – but she doesn't have quite your touch with the staff.'

'Ah, I see,' Rachel nodded. 'I'll visit the department before I go home tomorrow, Sally. I want to buy a gift for Hazel's birthday – and I'll tell you what I think.'

'Yes, do that,' Sally agreed. 'As a customer, you will see things as they are. I always wonder if the best behaviour comes on when I visit...' She laughed. 'Do you recall when we had a floor walker? I was always in trouble with her.'

'Yes, I remember very well,' Rachel replied. 'You looked so rebellious at times.' She laughed. 'They were good times, though...'

'Yes, they were,' Sally agreed.

* * *

Rachel bought a leather bag, but not before she'd paid a visit to the jewellery department. Mrs Martin served her, but Rachel said nothing of having worked there before. Instead, she played the difficult customer, asking to see several pieces of jewellery before deciding to buy the bag she'd come for. She was unable to fault Andrea's manner or her politeness, but she did notice that she spoke sharply to Miss Ross when she reminded her that she was due for her break.

She'd frowned, told her not to be late back and then dismissed her all in the same tone, which seemed unnecessarily harsh to Rachel. Sally had told her of the arrangement Ben had made for Lilly Ross to learn the trade of a florist. She was working through her lunch hour, unpaid, simply because of her passion for flowers. Rachel had watched the girl serving customers earlier and thought her polite and attentive. She hardly merited that sharp note in Mrs Martin's voice.

Sally had put her finger on the flaw in the new supervisor. Rachel would confirm her opinion when she spoke to her later. Mrs Martin did her job perfectly well; she just needed a little advice about how to deal with staff, though it seemed to be Lilly Ross, in particular, who made her harsh.

Before she left the department, Rachel tried on a few hats. Sally had found a new designer a short time ago and they were beautiful, expensive but very stylish. Perhaps she would give her the designer's name so that she could buy some for Mr Alexander's store.

Rachel was thoughtful as she completed her purchases. She would return to Sally's for lunch and then go home to William and Lizzie. Her trip had been pleasant despite the reason for it. Mr Alexander was so lost without his beloved Jenni that something had propelled her to make her offer. Rachel knew that Sally was right and she would possibly find it more work than she'd expected, but if she gave him a breathing space, he would be able to make a reasoned decision. At the moment he was still too stunned by the suddenness of his wife's death to know what he wanted to do. Rachel could give him a little time to think. Jenni Harper would have approved, she was sure.

It was sad that her life had ended so abruptly. Rachel's eyes were moist with tears as she hailed a taxi and was driven to Sally's home. She knew how hard it was to lose someone you loved and Jenni had been far too young to die. It was a tragedy.

Rachel forced the sad thoughts from her mind. She had bought small gifts for William, Hazel and Lizzie, and now her thoughts were with her family. Life could throw nasty surprises at you and she would be glad to spend some time with them. Her trips to London would be regular in future but not frequent. Four or five trips to Newcastle a year should be sufficient, because it was a well-run store. She was merely doing the job that Jenni had done... just for a while.

19

It was that Irishman again! Andrea watched as he approached her counter. She caught her breath as he smiled at her, feeling pleased and yet wary. He seemed charming, but still she wasn't sure about him.

'Good morning, Mrs Martin. I've come to ask you how the new line of jewellery is selling. Have you had many comments?'

'You mean those beautiful pieces of Art Deco jewellery in silver and enamel?' Andrea found herself smiling. She loved good pieces and the new line was delightful and much admired. 'I have sold six pieces in the last two days. In fact, we have sold at least two thirds of what we had...'

His face lit up and she realised that he was quite an attractive man... if you liked the bold Irish type, of course. His eyes were very blue and lit with humour, his dark hair just sprinkled with grey at the temples.

'That's good news, Mrs Martin. It will please the man who made them and help him to settle here. He came from Russia and wondered if his work would be appreciated in England.'

'The work is meticulous,' Andrea said. 'I would very much like to own one of the brooches myself.'

'Is it the brooches that are selling the best then?' Mr O'Sullivan asked, his eyes scanning the counter.

'The pendants are very popular with younger ladies, but the older ones prefer a brooch – as I do. Of course, we are not allowed them at work, but on Sunday I wear one here.' She touched the spot on her dress where the collar met and smiled.

''Tis a beautiful smile you have, Mrs Martin. No wonder the customers are buying the jewellery if you look like that.'

'Stop teasing me, Mr O'Sullivan…' Andrea found herself blushing. 'I am sure it is the quality of these pieces that make women buy, not me.'

'Those brooches would look very well on black or dark green.' Mr O'Sullivan's eyes sparkled with mischief. 'I have a fancy to see you in dark green – it would set off your eyes and your hair—'

'Sir!' Andrea wasn't sure if she was flattered or outraged that he should speak to her so intimately. 'I am not sure—'

'That I should speak to you in such a fashion, Mrs Martin?' He laughed softly and it was a pleasant sound. 'Now, why would that be? If we were in Ireland, I would ask my nearest female relative to approach you, if I had one – but since we're not and I have no family – will you allow me to take you to tea on Sunday?'

'Well, I…' Andrea found that she was speechless. She ought to be outraged, but instead she discovered that she would rather like him to take her to tea. 'Why? You don't know me…'

'I won't if you don't agree,' he said. 'I just think we might be friends – if you have a need of a friend, as I do?'

Andrea was silent. She did need friends. It would be a shame to refuse. What could possibly be wrong in having tea with this man? He was a friend of Mr and Mrs Harper, so he must be respectable – despite that naughty twinkle and his Irish accent.

'Well, yes, why not?' she was saying before she could stop herself. 'Where shall we meet?'

'The only place for tea is the Savoy Hotel,' he said and took her breath. She had never ever been to such an exclusive hotel – and she did want to! 'Three-thirty on the dot I'll be there this Sunday. Make sure you are, too, Mrs Martin. We can enjoy a nice little walk afterwards – or I'll drive you to your home.'

'Do you have a car then?' She hadn't thought of him as someone who might drive a car.

'Yes, I have a car.' He grinned and her heart skidded. 'It is one made by Mr Bentley. It is comfortable, as cars go. We'll see if you'll trust my driving – we might go on an outing another time...'

He winked at her and walked off as another customer approached.

Andrea drew a deep breath, feeling quite shocked at herself. Had she truly agreed to have tea with a man she hardly knew? What would Philip think? Would he be hurt or angry – or would he be happy that she had begun to come out of her grief? A little smile touched her mouth as she thought that, yes, he would want her to enjoy her life.

'Mick, how lovely to see you,' Sally said when he entered her office some minutes later. 'I'm glad you've come. I need to give you an order for Kavi. His Art Decco line has almost sold out. The Aztec designs are doing well, too – but it is the silver brooches and pendants that customers can't get enough of.'

'I visited your jewellery department just now,' Mick confessed. 'It is much better now that you've separated the jewellery from the bags, Sally. I always felt it was too squashed up in that one cabinet – but you have a much bigger selection these days. I imagine you need extra staff in the department now?'

'Yes, we are taking on two new juniors,' Sally agreed. 'We've only ever had one junior on the floor before, but now we shall have two. Trade is picking up rapidly these past few weeks. It is as if people have finally shrugged off the shadow of the war. Of course, I know for some it will never fade – those injured and damaged or lost and their families – but for the luckier ones, life is improving.'

'Yes, things are looking up,' Mick replied. 'Now, I've a bit of news for you, Sally. I've invested in another restaurant. I'll be opening it next week – and I'd like to take you to lunch, see what you think of it...'

'Oh, that will be lovely,' Sally cried. 'Just like old times. I shall look forward to it, Mick. Where is it?'

'Only just around the corner from Harpers.' His eyes lit with pleasure. 'I'll call for you on Thursday then at 12.30 and drive you in myself. You'll be at home?'

'Yes, I have no appointments on Thursday,' Sally told him. 'I should also like to meet your Kavi – see his workshop. Would that be possible?'

'Why not? It isn't too far away. We could visit Kavi after lunch and then I'll take you home.'

'That is ideal,' Sally was pleased. 'I needed a little cheering up.'

Mick's expression became sombre. 'It was a sad thing losing a friend the way you did, Sally. Ben was devastated when he rang to tell me. I know he took it hard. Jenni was so young and the only family he had other than you and his children, of course.'

'He does have a cousin in America, but they aren't close,' Sally told him. 'Jenni was important to us both – she helped us in the beginning. We shall all miss her.'

'We all need our friends and loved ones,' Mick replied and she saw an echo of sadness in his eyes. 'I've just asked Mrs Martin to tea with me on Sunday. You told me her husband was killed in the war and I think she is lonely.'

'Andrea Martin?' Sally was surprised. 'Yes, I think she may be...' She hesitated, then, 'I'm not sure she is your sort of person, Mick...'

'Now, why would you be saying that?' Mick looked at her strangely.

'Oh... she may be a bit... old-fashioned and tight-lipped,' Sally said. 'No, I'm not decrying her, Mick. I do like her but... I may have to speak to her about the way she treats the girls under her supervision. I'd rather not have to, as, like you, I believe her to be lonely, but she can be a little harsh to them.'

'And might that not be because of her situation? Mebbe she's grieving hard still and wanting to do well in her job and that makes her sharp with the young ones?'

'You might be right,' Sally agreed. 'I shall be very careful what I say, because I don't want to hurt or upset her – but the girls need fair treatment too.'

'Aye, they do,' Mick agreed. 'Mebbe she'd loosen up a bit if she has a friend – you might ask her to one of your tea parties, too, Sally.'

'Yes, I could,' she agreed. 'I used to ask Rachel and Beth when they worked for us, so there is no reason why I can't ask Andrea too. I'll invite Beth and Mr Marco and some of the other heads of department, Marion Jackson, too. She is having a bad time, Mick. They moved her husband to a new hospital or convalescent home, without telling her – and she isn't allowed to see him while he is having some special treatment.'

Mick's gaze narrowed and he inclined his head. 'I've heard of that place and a doctor called Charles Myers. I don't know where it is – but I met someone who was there and he says the treatment helps. John is back home now and he says he was a total wreck before he went there.'

'Perhaps it will help Marion's husband then,' Sally said. She looked up as her door opened and her secretary looked in. 'Yes, Phyllis?'

'There is a new representative here, Mrs Harper. He doesn't have an appointment, but he says he has some French-designed dresses to offer you if you are interested?'

'Yes, tell him I'll be five minutes,' Sally said. 'I'll be interested if you can discover the whereabouts of that treatment centre, Mick.'

'You'd tell Mrs Jackson where to find her husband?'

'No. I would try to find out if he was getting better and get a message to him from her,' Sally told him. 'I think she deserves that much...'

Mick nodded his understanding. 'I'll see if I can discover the address for you – and the name of the man running it.'

'Thank you.' Sally went to kiss his cheek. 'Take care of yourself, my friend, and I'll see you for lunch next week.'

'Yes. Sally—' Mick broke off as the office door opened and Ben walked in.

'Phyllis says there's a representative waiting... Oh, hello, Mick. How are you?'

'It's good I am,' Mick told him and they shook hands. 'I'm taking your wife to my new restaurant for lunch next Thursday – and we'll be visiting Kavi if you'd like to come along?'

Ben seemed to hesitate and then shook his head. 'I have appointments myself most of next week. You must come for dinner one evening – say next Friday? Would that be all right, Sally?'

'Yes, of course.'

'I'll be there,' Mick promised. 'If you were wanting that extra investment, I still have funds available, Ben.'

'Thank you. I'll think about it – but Jenni's husband is keeping her shop for the moment. I believe he will sell to us eventually, but it's natural that he should need time to make up his mind.'

'Of course. It is a terrible thing for you all.' Mick looked sad. 'You all need time to grieve.' Mick nodded to them and went out.

Sally looked at Ben curiously. 'Did you approach Mick about investing in Jenni's store?'

'Yes, I did,' Ben told her. 'He'd mentioned that he still has a large sum to invest – and I thought you'd rather have him as our main partner than put Harpers on the stock market.'

'Yes, I think it more sensible,' Sally said and hesitated. 'Did Mick tell you how he came by the money he has now? He only told me he had a bit of luck...'

'Apparently, he was left it by an Irish-American relative. Mick went to stay with him when he was recovering from his war injuries – and this uncle took a fancy to him. It turned out he had no sons, only some distant cousins and Mick. When he died, he left almost everything to Mick.'

Sally laughed. 'I thought he'd found gold or won it in a casino or something...'

'Don't think so – Mick isn't the gambling type, at least not that sort of gambling. He takes risks investing at times, but we all have to do that...'

Sally was thoughtful. 'What changed your mind about the stock exchange, Ben?'

'Your doubts and instincts,' Ben said and moved to put his arms around her. 'I trust them, Sally. They haven't let us down yet. Please, always tell me if you don't agree with what I'm thinking of doing. I have ideas and sometimes they are good, but others... well, it is best to keep Harpers a family firm.'

'Yes, it is,' she agreed. 'Mick is like a brother to me. We are good friends and I like him. We can trust him, Ben.'

'I know that,' he agreed and gazed down into her eyes. 'I used to be jealous of him, but I'm not now. I know you love me and the last thing you would do is ruin what we have.'

Sally reached up and kissed him. 'Thank you for trusting me, darling,' she said. 'I'm sure you've done the right thing – and if Andrew does want to sell, I'll be in agreement this way.'

'I know – but perhaps I rushed in too quickly. I just didn't want to see Jenni's shop, that I believe meant so much to her, go to a stranger...' His eyes were bleak in that moment. 'She was so young, Sally...' A shudder went through him. 'Andrew must be in agony. I know I should be if anything happened to you.'

'We need each other,' she said and kissed him. 'And now I'd better see that poor man waiting outside. He has some French fashion to offer me...'

20

Lilly was returning from the florist department when Mr Harper stopped her. He was on his way out of the lift and nearly bumped into her again.

'This is becoming a habit,' he said, his eyes dancing with laughter. 'How are you, Lilly? Are you enjoying your time in the florist department? Is it still what you want to do?'

'Oh yes, sir,' Lilly exclaimed, her cheeks a little warm as she saw several pairs of eyes turn their way. 'I can't thank you enough for what you've done for me.'

He nodded. 'Once you've learned the tricks of the trade, we might transfer you there – would you enjoy that?'

Lilly hesitated. 'Would I earn the same there, sir?'

'When you are trained, yes – perhaps a little more,' he replied.

'Then I should love it – it would be my dream,' Lilly told him and now she was blushing hard. 'I can't believe I'm so lucky, sir.'

'Not at all,' he replied. 'We like to look after our staff.'

And then he was on his way without a backward glance.

Lilly was conscious that one or two of the female staff were looking at her oddly as she got into the lift and went up to the bag

department. She hoped they wouldn't start talking about her –
getting the wrong idea. Mr Harper was very kind, but Lilly knew
people could soon see something that wasn't there.

She shrugged it off as she reached the department and saw Mrs
Martin at her counter. She very pointedly looked at the watch she
wore pinned to her dress. Lilly was a few minutes overdue and she
knew she was in for a telling-off later.

* * *

'You look tired, our Lilly,' her sister Carol said when Lilly put her
shopping basket down on the kitchen table that evening. 'And it's
6.30 – did you miss your bus?'

'My supervisor made me stay ten minutes past time to help her
tidy up and put things away,' Lilly said. 'I was five minutes late back
from lunch so she punished me – and when I'd done my shopping,
I missed my bus and walked rather than wait for the next.'

'Mean old thing,' Carol cried crossly. 'I won't work for someone
like her when I leave school.'

'What are you going to do then, miss?' Lilly asked, shrugging
off her tiredness. 'Marry the King of England?'

'I might,' Carol said and giggled. 'No, I want to be a school
teacher. My teacher is lovely and she says I'm clever enough to go
to high school and then college.'

'We'll see…' Lilly smothered a sigh. It would be a much better
job for Carol – but to pay for the uniform they needed in high
school and then support her through college –Lilly wasn't sure she
would be able to afford it, even if she worked harder than she did
now. Perhaps if she earned a few shillings more. 'You'll probably
change your mind when you're older – think you want to earn
some money rather than spend more years at school.'

Carol looked at her and nodded. 'It's not fair on you, is it, our Lilly?'

'What isn't fair?' Joe asked, entering the kitchen in all his dirt and shedding coal dust on the slate floor. 'What 'ave you been up to, miss?'

'I want to go to college and be a school teacher,' Carol said, 'but it isn't fair on Lilly. She would have to support me for years and years.'

'I don't think we need to worry about that yet,' Lilly told her.

'I'll be earnin' a fortune by the time you need to go to college,' Joe said and grinned. 'I'm the proud owner of Dad's coal business now – and I've sorted that little runt out what was ruinin' our round.'

'How have you done that then, Joe?' Lilly asked.

'I told him he 'ad a choice. I'd put him in the canal and drown him or he could come and work for me – with an option to be a partner when we'd doubled the round.'

'He's going to work for you?' Lilly was astounded.

'He is – and I know why he was up to tricks, too.'

'Tell us then...'

'His mother is an invalid. Sam is the only breadwinner in the family – there's two younger girls at home. He couldn't get a job that paid him enough so he tried to take over our round, but he wasn't doin' that well – by the time he sold his stuff cheap to undercut us, he hardly earned a decent wage.'

'But you've promised him a partnership?' Lilly still couldn't get over it.

'I like him,' Joe said. 'He's a bright nipper – and when I've knocked him into shape, he'll do. He can use his cleverness to help build up the round rather than struggling alone and ruining it for both of us.'

'But if Ted had done that, he could've kept the business—' Carol blurted.

'Aye, he could – but, as it is, he preferred to sell to me,' Joe said. 'He'd got it in his head he could do better with a barrow – and now he's got one. I wished him luck, but I wanted to keep Dad's business goin'...'

'Well, as long as this Sam doesn't cheat you,' Lilly said. 'Are you sure you can trust him, Joe?'

'He'll do as I bid him,' Joe replied. 'I'm not soft like Ted.'

'Can I go next door to play until supper?' Carol asked as Lilly was silent.

'Yes.' Lilly glanced round. 'The food will be ready in half an hour – so tell Stevie if you see him.'

'He's playin' football down the lane,' Joe told her. 'That lad will play for a big club afore he's finished.'

'Let's hope so,' Lilly said. 'Get upstairs and wash, Joe – but pop through first and ask Mum if she wants anything. I'll be there in a moment with a cup of tea for her.' Annie had decided to stay in bed that day as she had a bit of a cold.

'Yes, our Lilly.' He looked her in the eyes. 'If Carol wants to be a teacher, it would be good for her – and you know I'll help, but she is right. It isn't fair on you, not if you want to get wed.'

'No one has asked me to marry them yet,' Lilly quipped. 'I'll let you know when I decide between my suitors...'

'No, maybe not asked, but that Jeb is sweet on you,' Joe said, surprising her. 'I met him this afternoon. He sold his barrow to Ted – he's got his own shop now. On the corner of Little Lane, next to Dressmaker's Alley, where the sweatshop is...'

Lilly stopped and stared. Little Lane connected to the busy Commercial Road and Dressmaker's Alley was round the corner, near Mulberry Lane. 'Jeb has his own shop?'

'Aye. He was full of it – told me to be sure to tell you. He says when you marry him you can run it for him...'

'That's never, the cheeky monkey!'

'Ah, well, never is a long time. You could do worse, our Lilly,' Joe said and dodged the cushion she threw at him, just as he disappeared through the door leading to the stairway, completely forgetting to visit his mother before he went up to wash.

Lilly smiled and shook her head as she picked up the boiling kettle and made the tea. Fancy Jeb having a florist shop of his own. She knew he'd talked about it for ages, but she hadn't believed he could do it... and that started the dreams in Lilly's head. Perhaps one day she could have a florist shop herself. She was learning so much at Harpers and she liked it there – but she would rather have her own little shop.

She shook her head. That could never happen. She had her mother to look after and the little ones to take care of – and Annie hadn't felt well this morning. She'd refused Joe's offer to carry her through.

Lilly carried the tray of tea and a nice little cheese sandwich into her mother's room. She would try to coax her to eat something...

* * *

Mrs Martin was waiting for Lilly the next morning when she walked into the department and from the look on her face, Lilly knew she was in trouble. She'd gone in early, hoping to make up for her late return from lunch the previous day, but her supervisor looked at her as if she loathed her.

'I wish to speak to you alone please, Miss Ross,' she said in an icy tone. 'Please come through to the jewellery department...'

Lilly followed, quaking inside as she tried to think what she'd done wrong. She wasn't habitually late and it hadn't been her fault that Mr Harper had delayed her the previous day, even though she hadn't used that as an excuse.

'Something disturbing has come to my attention,' Mrs Martin was saying as Lilly hastily brought her mind back to the present. 'I have been informed that you have behaved inappropriately towards your employer...'

Lilly stared at her blankly. 'What did I do?' she asked, frantically searching her mind.

'You were late back yesterday because you were flirting with Mr Harper – and that is inexcusable—'

'No! That isn't true,' Lilly blurted indignantly. 'He nearly bumped into me and stopped to ask me how I was getting on at the florist...'

Mrs Martin looked angry. 'And why should he be interested in a girl like you, Lilly Ross? Surely you cannot be so ignorant that you don't know a man in his position would only want one thing...'

'No, Mrs Martin,' Lilly denied. 'Mr Harper has never said a word wrong to me. He wouldn't – I wouldn't even if...' She broke off, feeling hot and bothered. 'I don't know who said such nasty things, but it isn't true.'

Mrs Martin looked at her a few moments longer and then nodded. 'I am inclined to believe you – mainly because I do not think Mr Harper would be interested in a girl like you, however much you flaunt yourself at him. If this is a lie, then I can only say – be careful, young lady. If you encourage men to think you are easy, you will regret it. I am aware that young girls today think they should have more freedom – but a reputation lost cannot be regained. I say this for your own good, believe me.'

Lilly swallowed hard and thanked her. What else could she say? Someone had reported the incident to her and Mrs Martin had acted on it. Even though she considered the matter resolved, it was clear she'd believed the wicked lie at the start. Lilly's eyes stung with tears she was too proud to shed. How could her supervisor think Lilly was a bad girl? Just because she'd stopped two minutes to speak to her employer?

It wasn't fair. Lilly sensed that Mrs Martin didn't like her – but now she realised that it was since she'd started at the florist in her lunch break that she'd been really down on her. Why? It didn't interfere with her – so why didn't she like Lilly? She never cheeked her or giggled behind her back like some of the others did – what had she done wrong?

21

Andrea looked at herself in the mirror as she prepared to meet Mr O'Sullivan for tea. Three times she'd changed her dress and then her hat, but it was a fine day and she'd finally settled on a grey linen dress, a light wool jacket and her best red felt hat with a curling feather that she always felt was a bit too jaunty for church but sometimes wore if she treated herself to a cream tea. It wasn't often that she did anything nice, so the hat was still almost new. She'd bought it from Harpers in a sale once and it was the prettiest one she'd owned for years.

Her mood lifted as she set out for the bus that would take her up to the posh end of town. She'd never been in the Savoy Hotel and she was so excited – and she needed that lift, because she'd been feeling out of sorts this past couple of days. If she was honest with herself, she was feeling guilty for having been so sharp with Lilly Ross. Andrea had known the story about Mr Harper flirting with Lilly couldn't possibly be true. He had a charming smile, which was easy to respond to, as she knew only too well, but she still didn't think he was the type to take advantage of a girl like Lilly.

There were bound to be rumours when the boss took an interest in one of the girls, of course there were. Andrea knew that spiteful tongues could ruin a girl's reputation and it had annoyed her that one of her girls should have attracted that kind of attention. It was probably jealousy on the part of whoever had started the tale she'd happened to overhear. There was always jealousy when one girl seemed to be luckier than others – though she wasn't sure that really applied to Lilly Ross. Mrs Harper had explained to her that Lilly had to care for her invalid mother as well as her younger siblings so it might mean that she was occasionally late in to work in the morning. It hadn't happened much.

Andrea really shouldn't have blamed Lilly for the few minutes she'd spent talking to Mr Harper. He had delayed her. Yet she'd felt a spark of jealousy herself when she heard the spiteful tale. Mr Harper hadn't so much as looked her way since the day he'd asked her to see that salesman.

It was ridiculous and Andrea was ashamed of herself for picking on Lilly – but it was hard sometimes. The young girls in her department had everything to live for; love in the future, and the promise of happiness with the man of their choice, a family and home. All the things Andrea had lost. Sometimes, she envied them their freedom. She was still young, but everything she earned went into supporting her son at his exclusive boarding school and paying rent for the home he came back to in the holidays. Clothes, small luxuries and even sometimes a nice meal had to be considered and planned to make sure she could afford them. Every month there seemed to be something extra Paul needed for his school regulations.

A sigh escaped Andrea. Mrs Harper had been into the department and praised how neat and tidy it all was, but then, just before she left, she'd said something that made the back of Andrea's neck prickle with unease.

'At Harpers we try to keep our staff happy. Girls who are nervous or afraid of making mistakes often do, I find. While I wouldn't condone blatant rudeness or careless behaviour, I try to be a little forgiving over small things – it makes life more pleasant all round, wouldn't you say?'

'Oh, yes, I am sure you are right,' Andrea had no option but to agree, though it made her feel a little uneasy. She had the feeling she was being warned in the nicest possible way – so who had complained?

Of the three girls who worked in her department, Lilly had the most right and cause, but she was so anxious to keep her job for the sake of her family that it hardly seemed likely. Someone must have said something to Mrs Harper for her to go out of her way to bring the subject up.

It had caused Andrea to do some soul-searching and she'd realised her mistake in speaking to Lilly Ross as harshly as she had. If Mrs Harper had heard the spiteful gossip about her husband and the young girl he'd promoted some months sooner than she could have expected, she would instantly dismiss it – or would she?

Remembering the morning when Mrs Harper had been late for an appointment because of her daughter needing to be taken to the hospital, Andrea wondered: was their marriage as solid as she'd assumed at the beginning?

As she got down from her bus near to the Savoy, Andrea's thoughts dismissed Harpers and the shop girls. This was one of the most exciting days of her life and she intended to enjoy it!

* * *

Andrea had wondered if Mr O'Sullivan would be there. Had he just been flirting with her or teasing her? Would he forget all about his arrangement to meet her for tea?

Her doubts fled as she saw him sitting in the foyer waiting for her to arrive and her heart fluttered like a young girl's. Mr O'Sullivan wasn't as handsome as Mr Harper; he was a little older and he had a sprinkling of grey in his hair, perhaps because of what he'd suffered in the war. She knew that he'd done a very dangerous job and been wounded more than once; she had made it her business to find out a little more about him and Mrs Harper had willingly given the information after a casual enquiry.

'Oh yes,' she'd said. 'Mick O'Sullivan was in the thick of it – his team were always the advance; tunnelling is a dangerous job for many reasons.'

'Mrs Martin,' he said, smiling as he came to meet her on her rather hesitant arrival. 'I am glad you've come. I wasn't sure you would risk meeting a wicked-tongued rogue such as meself.'

Andrea saw the spark of humour in his eyes and laughed. She felt light and happy – happier than she had since Philip had gone. His death had taken all the joy from her, but now, at this moment, she felt the grey of her life suddenly brighten.

'I've never been here, so of course I had to come,' she said, a teasing note in her voice.

'Ah, it's the Savoy you've come to see.' Mr O'Sullivan's eyes sparked with mischief. 'And why wouldn't you? I like it myself. I have a new restaurant, Mrs Martin – but it isn't as posh as this…'

Andrea looked at the stylish Art Deco decor of the tea room as Mr O'Sullivan took her arm and escorted her through. Someone was playing a piano softly, dreamy music fitted to a pleasant afternoon and such elegant surroundings. She sat on one of the soft plush chairs, sinking into its comfort as he sat opposite her.

'Are you hungry, me darling?' he asked, picking up the menu. 'Shall we have the full tea?'

Andrea's heart raced as he used the word of endearment, but, after a few seconds, she realised that he'd done so without thinking – it was just his way, she imagined. A little blush touched her cheeks. Was she so starved of affection and company that she could be affected by a careless word?

'Yes, please,' she said. She hadn't eaten lunch because she wanted to enjoy whatever was on offer. 'That would be lovely... but whatever you wish...'

'Then we'll settle on the full works,' he replied. 'That is a very fetching hat you're wearing, Mrs Martin – or may I call you Andrea when we are out?'

That sounded as if he wanted to meet her again.

She hesitated and then graciously inclined her head. 'Yes, if you would like to. At Harpers, of course, we must be more formal.'

'Oh, of course,' he said, but his eyes had that wicked sparkle. 'And how do you like working there, Andrea? Are you settling in well?'

'Yes, I think so,' she replied. 'I had worked on the counters before I married Philip, but this is my first job as a supervisor.'

'It takes a while to get used to giving orders and being in charge,' he said, nodding at her. 'It's getting the balance right between securing their respect and keeping order. Not always easy, especially when you have your own counter.'

'No, that is true,' Andrea agreed. 'I try to talk to the girls when they arrive, before their lunch break and when they leave in the evening. Otherwise, it depends how busy I am. I do have a clear view of the whole department, because my counters are at the rear, so I could see if anything was untoward – but mostly it is all as it should be without my interference.'

'Yes, best to let them get on with things unless you see someone making a mistake,' Mick said. His attention turned then as the waiter came to ask for his order. 'I did tell you my name is Michael, didn't I? Mick to most of my friends... If you'd like to use my name, Andrea, I'd appreciate it.'

'Oh, well, if you wish... Michael,' she said. Andrea really didn't feel she could say Mick. 'I like that name...'

'Aye, it's what my mother called me back in Ireland when I was a lad – God rest her soul. It was when I came to England to make my fortune that people started to call me Mick.'

'Because you're Irish, I suppose,' Andrea acknowledged.

'The very reason,' he said with a chuckle. 'What sort of a life have you been having since you lost your man? Can you bear to talk about him – or shouldn't I ask?'

'I'd like to talk about Philip,' Andrea said. 'No one mentions him except our son Paul when he is home from boarding school.'

'Ah, the poor lad. Is there no way you can keep him at home?'

'I'd be happier if he was at home,' Andrea found herself confiding. 'I sent him there because it was what Philip wanted; he came from a good family and had that kind of education himself – but it is so expensive. I know it must be done, so I do it – but I do miss him.'

'I'm no believer in those kinds of schools,' Mick told her. 'I think children should be at home with their mother and father. This war has left a lot of women without their husbands and children without their fathers – 'tis a terrible shame, so it is.'

'Yes. I miss Philip so much, but he would have sent Paul to this school. It was planned when he was born...'

Mick nodded. 'Well, that was his choice. It wouldn't be mine – but I suppose if the lad is happy...'

'I am not certain he is,' Andrea said hesitantly. 'I think some of the other boys come from far better homes and he is made to feel like the poor boy; he won his scholarship to go there. I couldn't have afforded the fees; the uniforms and sports equipment are as much as I can manage.'

'Did your husband not make provision for the fees?' Mick raised his brows at her.

'Philip said there was no need – he earned a good wage, but then the war came. There was a small amount of savings, but I had to use that for various expenses. We had to move out of our big house into a smaller one and...' She sighed. 'I have a little put by in case, but it isn't as easy as it was when my husband was alive.'

'I dare say he thought he had plenty of time,' Mick said sympathetically. 'No one expected the war to be quite so brutal or claim so many lives.'

'Philip's family disowned him when he married me...' Andrea blurted out the truth without intending it. 'I wasn't the right sort for them – a shop girl from the East End of London. He was meant to marry a girl of his own class, but he came into Selfridges and bought some gloves from me and then hung around until I left for the evening. It sort of just developed from there. We were in love and we married. Philip should have inherited part of his family's fortune, but he was cut off without a penny and had to find a job. He was intelligent and clever and he would have made a good life for us, but he didn't have time...' She shook her head. 'It is stupid to look back.'

'It's sorry I am for your loss,' Mick said and then a waitress arrived with their tea. There were stands of dainty sandwiches, scones with butter, jam and cream and a selection of tiny cakes. 'Well, this looks all right. Shall we eat?'

Andrea agreed and they shared the sandwiches, which were hardly more than a mouthful, and then the scones, following them with marzipan fancies, delicate strawberry tarts and rich fruit cake slices. Andrea poured tea into porcelain cups and used the silver tongs to put three lumps in his tea and one in her own.

'Very nice,' Mick approved as he popped an almond fancy into his mouth. 'I do enjoy good food. I serve lunches at my restaurant, well, I shall when it is open – but Ben Harper is thinking of opening his for tea as well – and I'm considering it.'

'Have you owned it for long?' Andrea enquired.

'Not this one – I had some but sold them after the war. I invested the money elsewhere. Wasn't sure I would ever want to live here again, but after some time in America, I decided to give it another try.'

'I thought you had a jewellery workshop?'

'A small one – I got it for Kavi who makes that wonderful silver jewellery you sell at Harpers. It's just him for the moment and I'll sell the place to him when he's ready. He needs support for the time being.' Mick looked thoughtful. 'Kavi is a nervous chap – don't know why...' He shook his head. 'I'll take care of him.'

Andrea looked at him. He must be quite well off. She hadn't thought so when he first came asking to speak to Mrs Harper, but he spoke of owning property, so obviously he had money. 'You seem to do all kinds of things...'

'Aye, that I do...' he laughed. 'A Jack of all trades, that's me, Andrea. The secret is to employ those who know their business and let them work for you.'

'That doesn't sound quite fair,' she objected.

'It's what makes the world go round,' Mick told her. 'There are those who do and those who don't in this world. If you gave a hundred men a thousand pounds each, some of them would soon have doubled and trebled it and others would be left with nothing. You get what you work for – and I work at my businesses, even if I don't wait at tables or make jewellery or the cars I plan to sell.'

'Cars too? I don't like them much – noisy smelly things...'

Mick threw back his head and laughed. 'You haven't lived

much, have you, Andrea? Wait until I take you for a ride in my Bentley. You'll change your mind.'

She found herself joining in his laughter, because it was infectious. 'I shall look forward to it,' she said. 'I'm not sure I shall change my mind, but we'll see…'

* * *

Andrea was forced to admit the journey back to her home was more comfortable than the bus she'd ridden on to get to their meeting. She was still unsure she liked cars; they were undoubtedly smelly and still a little noisy, but the one Mick drove her in was very comfortable.

He got out to open the door for her and assisted her from her seat, taking her gloved hand and bowing over it as they stood at her door for a moment. 'It has been a pleasure, Andrea,' he told her. 'I hope you enjoyed the Savoy?'

'I did,' she assured him, hesitated, then, 'I enjoyed your company too, Michael.'

'Then I'm pleased,' he murmured. 'We will do it again – in two weeks' time, perhaps. I've business that takes me to Ireland next weekend, but I'll be back by the next week – so the following Sunday. If you're free?'

'I think so,' Andrea told him. 'Thank you for taking me somewhere I'd never been. It was lovely.'

'There's a lot of places we might go,' he said, hesitated and then turned back to his motorcar and got in, giving her a little wave before he drove off.

Andrea wondered why he'd hesitated. Was he waiting for her to ask him in? She didn't feel able to do that – it was her strict upbringing. Her parents might have come from the East End of London, but they had tight moral rules they had taught their daughter. Philip had shown her how to relax a little, but then he'd gone to war...

Shaking her head at the memory, Andrea went into her modest terraced house. It did not look much from outside, but the street was respectable and clean and inside it was as neat as a new pin. Taking her hat off, she deposited it on the table in the hall and went through to her kitchen at the back. Her small garden was mostly paving with a square of lawn and flower beds at the side and along the back. In the house she'd shared with Philip before the war, she'd had wide lawns, trees and shrubs and beautiful French windows to look out of.

Sighing, she felt the tears trickle down her cheeks and dashed them away with the back of her hand. She was so lucky to have been taken out for tea at the Savoy. The prices had shocked her, but Mr O'Sullivan – Michael – hadn't batted an eyelid. He was obviously well off. A self-made man by his own admittance. She wondered what he needed to go over to Ireland for, but then forgot it as she started to prepare her clothes for the next day, when she would be back at work at her counter.

Andrea had two similar black dresses she wore for work. One was a stiff but subtle brocade with a fitted collar and the second was a fine wool and that had a lace collar, because it didn't wash well, she usually sponged it clean and left it to air. It would be so much easier if somebody could find a material that washed as easily as cotton but was stiffer. In the summer, linen or cotton was more comfortable, but that kind of dress wasn't correct for her work. A fine suiting was necessary then and she had seen some material that would make up into a new dress that she could wear to work and would wash if she was careful.

Perhaps by next year she would be able to afford to buy enough material to make two such dresses. She sighed deeply again. It had opened her eyes being taken to the Savoy and she knew it would live long in her memory, but it did make the reality of her life even harder to bear.

'Don't be a misery,' Andrea told herself aloud. She was lucky to have her job at Harpers and it was stupid to dwell on what might have been.

22

Lilly had missed her bus again that Monday evening and, as the nights shortened, it was dark so much earlier now. It was because she worked in the florist that she had to do her shopping after work instead of in her lunch break and just lately she'd missed her bus three times. It was a pleasant evening, so she decided she would walk home rather than wait for the next one. She was lucky enough that it would only take her about twenty minutes or so and she often walked it on summer nights, but her basket was heavy with the vegetables she'd bought that evening and after she'd been walking for a while, her arm ached and she wished she'd waited for the bus.

She decided to take a short cut through Barrel Alley, which was a narrow, smelly little walkway between a sweatshop on one side and a boot factory on the other and there were two public houses, one at either end. Lilly normally took the longer route to avoid having to walk down this particular alley as it was ill lit and there were sometimes drunks standing around. It had got worse the past few months and Lilly knew that was due to the men who had returned from the war and were unable to find work, perhaps because they were ill, maimed or in some other difficulty. She walked quickly, wanting to get home and again wishing she'd caught her bus.

'Who is this then?' A huge shape loomed up at her out of the gathering gloom, making Lilly start. 'What yer doin' 'ere then, flower?'

'Nothing. Just going home,' Lilly retorted. 'Please don't stand in my way. I'm late and my family needs me—'

'Do they now?' The man leered at her, thrust his face close to hers. She saw the broken bent nose and the ugly blistered scar on his cheek. Lilly could smell the whisky on his breath and his eyes were bloodshot. 'Well, happen I need yer more… give us a kiss and mebbe I'll let yer go.'

Lilly gave a squeal of fear, cursing herself for coming this way. She'd noticed men hanging around on the rare occasion she'd walked through the alley, but she'd never been spoken to before. Her heart was racing as she tried to force her way past him, but he grabbed hold of her arm, slamming her against the wall and pushing his face into hers. His mouth was wet and smelled foul as he placed it on hers, his tongue inside her mouth as she tried to scream. He was clawing at her skirt, forcing it up above her knees, his hand pushing between her legs, touching her where Lilly had never been touched before. She beat at him with her basket, but he snatched it away, sending it and the contents flying.

Lilly screamed, but then his hand was over her mouth, preventing her from making a sound. She struggled, kicking and scratching his face, biting his hand as he tried to quieten her, and then he banged her head against the wall so hard that all the fight went out of her and she felt herself fainting. As she collapsed to the floor, losing all conscious thought, she felt his weight on top of her and before she fell into the void, she knew that he had violated her.

* * *

It was so dark... Where was she? As Lilly came to herself once more, she was aware that she felt bruised and sore all over – but worse than ever between her legs. She struggled to sit up, her head whirling, still dizzy, still unsure of where she was and what had happened to her. Then, all of a sudden, it came rushing back and she knew – she knew that she had been attacked in a way that was too awful to think about.

Lilly pulled herself unsteadily to her feet. She kicked against something and reached out, discovering it was her shopping basket. Some things were still inside, though not all she'd bought, but she couldn't think of looking for lost items. She pulled her skirt down, feeling the soreness between her thighs again.

It was her worst nightmare come true! What was she going to do? Her mother would kill her – and if she told her older brothers what had happened, they would go looking for the man and likely kill him. Lilly knew she could describe him – his bloodshot eyes, bent nose and the scar on his right cheek. She mustn't tell them! They would kill for her. Lilly knew it and she also knew they would hang if they were caught.

It was very late. She must be in a state. Her hair was falling down round her shoulders and she felt there was dirt or blood on her cheek. Then the solution came to her. She'd had an accident! That was it. As she began to walk, gingerly at first and then gritting her teeth at the pain, Lilly made up the story she would tell her family. She'd taken a short cut through the alley and someone had come riding through on a bicycle and knocked her down. She'd hit her head and passed out for a while. Well, part of it was true. She had fallen into an unconscious state as he had raped her... that word! It was so terrible.

She paused and vomited, feeling the world rush round her and nearly falling again. Determinedly, she pushed the memory and the word from her mind. She'd just had an accident that was all... her brother Joe had to believe that. Joe would go mad if he knew what had truly happened to her.

* * *

'We have been looking for you,' Joe yelled as she entered the kitchen some minutes later. He was alone there, no sign of her mother and younger siblings. 'My God! What happened, Lilly? If some man did this, I'll kill the bugger.'

'I was knocked down by an old man on a bicycle, Joe,' Lilly lied. She had to sit down because her legs had started shaking. 'I may have lost your supper. I hit my head and was out for a while...'

'We had a bit of bread and dripping. It's past nine,' Joe said. 'You're never this late. Didn't this old man stop to help you?'

'It was in that dark alley. I took a short cut because I missed the bus and I didn't see him. Perhaps he didn't see me...' Lilly couldn't meet his eyes she was so shamed.

'He must have known...' Joe suddenly looked at her through narrowed eyes. He lowered his voice, soft but urgent, 'You've been attacked, our Lilly. Oh, don't worry, I shan't tell Ted or the others – but I can see it in your face. Do you know who did it? If you did, I'll make him sorry he was born.'

She hesitated, then nodded slightly, because she knew that he had already guessed some of the truth. 'I didn't see him properly,' Lilly lied desperately. 'I don't want Mum or the kids to know. Please, promise not to tell Ted or the others.' He mustn't tell her mother; she would be so angry and Lilly was shamed as it was without a scolding.

'They don't need to know,' Joe said. 'I know and I'll find him.

Just give me one clue, Lilly. He doesn't deserve to get away with this; it will be someone else next time if he does...'

Lilly sighed. 'He had bloodshot eyes and he was drunk. That's all I saw before I went down. I fought him, Joe...' Her voice broke on a sob. 'I promise I fought with all my strength, but he was too big, too strong...' Now she'd given him another clue. 'I don't want you in trouble over it, Joe.'

'Don't you worry about me, Lilly. The kids are next door. Ma had a hot drink just now, but she'll have heard you come in. I'll tell her you had an accident – you get yourself cleaned up in the scullery before you go to her. No sense in lettin' her worry herself sick over it – and she will just in case...'

Lilly stared at him, the vomit rising inside her as she realised what could be the consequences. 'It won't happen,' she said. 'It can't – it's not fair, Joe. I didn't ask for it—'

'Do you think I don't know you?' her brother said. 'You're a victim, Lilly, but we're going to keep it between us. If there are consequences – well, I might know someone. We'll just have to hope nothing more 'appens.'

Their mother's voice calling from the other room had Joe going through to her with his story of Lilly's accident. She went quickly into the scullery and filled a bowl with cold water. She washed the dirt and blood from her cheek and the blood from between her thighs and then sponged the skirt of her dress. She smoothed her hair back and twisted it up into its usual style. Now only her eyes gave her away – the wide scared eyes of a girl who knew her life had been ruined. She had been violated and no one would want her now. A tear slid down her cheek as she pushed aside her dreams. She would never marry Jeb, because if she did, she must tell him of her shame...

Lifting her head, Lilly went into the parlour where Annie was in bed waiting.

23

Marion Jackson stood back to admire the window they had just finished and revealed to the public. It depicted a circus and featured toys that had just arrived to restock the department. Teddy bears swung from a trapeze and toy elephants performed tricks with balls and hoops, while pretty dolls sat and watched and a clockwork train circled the arena. Several clockwork pieces were set in motion and a small crowd of children had gathered outside.

It had been revealed that Saturday morning and the smiles, laughter and cries of joy from the parents and children had been a pleasure to behold. Marion went back into the store, where Mr Marco was waiting. He looked at her, anticipating her reaction.

'It is wonderful,' Marion told him. 'I think we may cause a hazard on the pavement if the children spread the word. They and their parents are loving it – it's so different.'

'It will cheer folk up,' Mr Marco said. 'It's time to be happy again. Speaking of which, I was thinking we might go to another tea dance – providing you enjoyed the last one?'

'You know I did,' Marion said and smiled at him. Mr Marco was fun to work with and a charming companion to be with at any time. 'It was so lovely to dance and have tea.'

'I think a nice tea while music plays is a pleasant way to spend an afternoon. I am free next Tuesday – if you are?'

'I am sure Sarah or Kathy will look after my son,' Marion said. 'I will be ready, Mr Marco.'

'I shall look forward to it – and now you'd best get off home to your family. We've done our work for this week and I have to plan the next one...'

'Yes, everyone will be eager to see what you do next,' Marion agreed and went off to fetch her coat.

As she entered the staff cloakroom, she heard the sound of crying. The young girl was washing her hands at the basin and as soon as she saw Marion, she turned away.

'Is there something wrong?' Marion asked, sensing her deep distress. 'It is Miss Ross – Lilly Ross, isn't it? Can I help you?'

The girl turned towards her and Marion saw that her eyes looked red, as if she had cried a lot. 'No, it's all right, thank you, Mrs Jackson. I'm just being silly.'

'I'm sure you're not,' Marion said. 'I know what it feels like to feel miserable and I can see that you are unhappy. I would like to help if I can.'

'No one can,' Lilly said and bit her lip. She shook her head and turned away. 'I'm sorry. I'm just—'

'Did someone hurt you? Have you been to the police station?' Marion asked and saw Lilly shudder as she shook her head. She thought she understood and went to her side, placing a gentle hand on her arm. 'I am sorry if something bad happened to you, Lilly, and if ever you need help, come to me. I really would like to help.'

'Thank you...' Lilly's response was muffled, but she took the large white handkerchief Marion offered and wiped her face. 'You are very kind.'

'I know how it feels to be unhappy, to believe that no one cares and you are alone, but at Harpers that isn't true. Most of us are good people and we would help you. If you need to talk, Lilly, I am here at least three days a week and sometimes more.'

'My supervisor isn't kind like you,' Lilly said as she offered the handkerchief back. 'Shall I wash this and give it back then?'

'You keep it in case you need it,' Marion told her. 'Why isn't Mrs Martin kind? Is she unpleasant to you often?'

'Most days,' Lilly admitted. 'I don't seem to be able to please her – but I don't mind so much only... perhaps she is right. Perhaps I am a bad girl and that's why...'

'I am sure you are not,' Marion replied instantly. 'I don't think Mrs Harper would like it if she knew Mrs Martin wasn't being kind to you, Lilly.'

'Oh, please don't tell her!' Lilly said. 'I don't want to cause trouble.'

'I shan't tell her,' Marion said, 'but I am right in thinking someone has caused trouble for you – was it a man?'

Lilly hesitated and then nodded, the words tumbling out of her. 'He just attacked me. I think he was drunk and—' She swallowed a sob, looking frightened. 'I shouldn't have said that. Please, don't tell anyone. I should lose my job—'

'Of course you wouldn't, but I'd never tell. You can trust me, Lilly – and I will help, if you should need me.'

'Thank you.' Lilly smiled and put the handkerchief in her dress pocket. 'I'd better go or Mrs Martin will keep me late again.'

'Yes, you mustn't be late back from your lunch break,' Marion said and smiled. 'Keep your chin up, Lilly. Nothing is ever quite as bad as it seems. There is always a way to manage your troubles.'

Lilly nodded and went off.

Marion put on her coat. She was thoughtful as she left Harpers. If she was right, Lilly had been attacked and harmed in a way that should never happen to a young woman – or any woman. She must be feeling devastated and yet she'd come into work as usual. Of course she had no choice; she had a family to support.

For the moment, there was nothing she could do but sympathise. Lilly would be too ashamed to report the attack to the police or anyone who might do something about it. From something she'd said, Marion knew that she was half-blaming herself, perhaps because of a careless word from Mrs Martin.

She shook her head. Marion had no authority, but she knew someone who did. Mrs Martin had to keep her staff in order, but she had no need to be unkind to a girl like Lilly who was too frightened of losing her job to say a word out of place. If Mrs Harper knew, she would probably ask her to leave – or at least move Lilly to another department.

Ought she to say something to Sally Harper, who had been so kind to her? Marion had said she wouldn't, but she would keep an open mind. If she thought Lilly was being victimised, then it was surely the right thing to tell the one person who could stop it.

* * *

'Yes, I'll have Robbie for you,' Sarah said when Marion mentioned the tea dance. 'He is never any trouble. I would have him when you go to work if you weren't able to take him in with you. You are lucky to be able to do that, Marion. Most women have to either give up work or find someone to care for their children. Harpers is a lovely place to work.'

'Yes, it is, and I am lucky to have my job there,' Marion agreed.

'I have good friends too and... Oh, Sarah, you should see the window we finished this morning.' She described it in detail and saw her sister-in-law's face light up. 'There was a crowd of children and parents outside when I left.'

'How lovely,' Sarah said. 'I'll take my Pamela to see it on Monday. I am coming up to Oxford Street to do some shopping. I need some material for an order for my sewing, so I will visit Harpers while I am there.'

'We don't have a haberdashery department yet,' Marion said. 'I'm not sure we'd have room. You need a lot of shelves for rolls of material.'

'I shall go to Selfridges or one of the other stores,' Sarah said. 'I love Harpers, though. It is different and it has that special atmosphere that you don't get in the bigger shops. I hope it never changes.'

'I think Mr Harper will buy or rent more property if he can. There is one building on the other side of us that he believes will be available soon. If he takes that over, he will have quite a lot more space. We might start to sell materials then. He was talking to Mr Marco about it the other day, saying he thought we could have a furniture department as well as one for other household items.'

'You like Mr Marco, don't you?'

'Yes, as a friend,' Marion said and shook her head at Sarah's raised brows. 'It isn't anything more, Sarah, believe me. I love Reggie – even though he has cast me off.'

'He is ill, Marion,' Sarah told her. 'I know you are hurt and I wouldn't blame you if you were angry, too.'

'I'm not angry. I was when they moved him without telling me – but I know that Reggie wasn't getting better. I can only pray that this new treatment, whatever it is, will help him.'

'Would you take him back if he came home?'

'Yes.' Marion's head came up. 'If I have to make a life without him, I will, but I still love him. I say a prayer for him each night and I write letters to him, telling him how much I love him, but I know that he may never come back to me.'

'You are so brave, my love.' Sarah moved to hug her. 'Dan and I love you – and we are proud of you. Never forget that you are loved.'

'I love you, too,' Kathy said, coming into the kitchen from the scullery. 'You're the best sister ever.'

'Thank you – both of you,' Marion said and smiled mistily. 'I love you both. I have a good family, I know that.'

'I've been promoted at work,' Kathy told her. 'I am working with the chef now, Marion. He says I can make pastry as well as he can and he's teaching me lots of things. I made a flaky-pastry apple tart today, which I brought home for you. It didn't get used and we don't keep food at the restaurant – so I was told I could bring it home.'

'That's wonderful news, love,' Marion said. 'I don't think I've had flaky pastry. I shall look forward to it, Kathy. Do we need custard to go with it?'

'It has fresh whipped cream on it to decorate,' Kathy told them proudly. 'It is really delicious. That is why I brought it home. I made three of them and two sold, but the cream doesn't keep so we have this one for ourselves.'

'Fresh cream! I love that,' Sarah cried. 'Can I have a piece before I go, Kathy?'

'Of course,' Kathy said. 'We'll all have a piece with a cup of tea.'

* * *

Later, when she had done all her chores, bathed and fed her son, Robbie, and seen him sleeping peacefully, Marion had time to sit over a magazine Sarah had left for her. Rather than concentrate on the knitting patterns and cookery tips, Marion read a story about a young girl finding love.

Her mind wandered, because it was so obviously heading for a happy ending and life often wasn't like that in her experience. Marion sighed. She missed Reggie so much and had looked forward to spending quiet evenings at home with him now the war was over – but for him it wasn't finished. His mind still held the torturous pictures that had him quivering every time he heard a loud noise.

Shaking her head, Marion forced away her unhappy thoughts, only to have the picture of a young woman's tearful face enter her mind. Poor little Lilly. She was only a slight girl. She would have had no chance of fighting off a drunken man if he attacked her.

What would she do if that attack resulted in more bad news? To have a child out of wedlock was a shameful thing, even if, as in Lilly's case, she was violated. A lot of people would point the finger and wouldn't believe that she was innocent. It was always, 'There's no smoke without fire,' when it happened to a young woman. She was blamed for flaunting herself, even if she'd done no such thing.

Was that what Mrs Martin had said to her? Lilly would never tell her what had happened. She'd confided in Marion because of her sympathy and because of her despair. Lilly believed herself ruined. Not many men would be interested in putting a ring on her finger now – she was spoiled goods. It was the attitude that prevailed and, although unfair, it was likely that Lilly would never marry because of what had happened to her.

Sarah had had a great-aunt who had been attacked as a young woman. Her family had sent her to an institution for bad girls, where she had stayed for most of her life. She had not been released until she was in her fifties and then lived alone in a small room with few friends and little money until she died of pneumonia one winter.

'It may have been one of the reasons my father was so strict with me,' Sarah had told her. 'Though, mostly, he just wanted to keep me at home for himself. He thought I would be his nurse when he was old. I believe he has a young woman as a nurse now, though he will still not see me or answer my letters.'

Marion thought that if she were Sarah, she would not bother to write or visit the man who had been so unkind to her. Life could be cruel and Marion had suffered with a drunken father herself. He'd killed her mother through one of his brutal beatings and done other bad things that led to his arrest.

Feeling the tears on her cheeks, Marion turned the page of her magazine and saw the article about young women being more independent these days. It had been written by a member of the Women's Movement and said that they were continuing their campaign for women's rights and equality.

'Still up?' Dickon's voice asked as he entered the kitchen. 'I'm glad, Marion. I've been wanting a quiet moment to talk to you...'

'I've got the kettle on and I am about to make some cocoa,' Marion said. She did so and put his mug in front of him. 'What did you want to talk about?

'I'm leaving my job at the docks,' Dickon told her. 'I've been given a chance to sign on a ship as crew. The captain and his crew are going on a diving exploration and they need someone with my skills. I'll be gone for a year at least, perhaps more...'

'Dickon! Is that wise?' Marion asked and saw the pleading for understanding in his eyes. He had been forced to work on the docks throughout the war, because he was needed both at his job and at home. Now he wanted an adventure and this was his chance. 'What are they looking for?'

'Buried treasure...' Dickon laughed as he saw her face. 'A ship that was sunk hundreds of years ago carrying all kinds of things.'

'Sounds like something out of a boy's adventure story,' Marion said. 'It might be dangerous...' She saw the answer in his eyes. He'd been denied his chance to fight in the war and had both resented and regretted that, perhaps even felt guilt at being alive when many of his school friends had fought and died. 'If you're sure it's what you want, then you must do it.'

Dickon's face lit up as if a candle burned inside him. 'They are going to pay me well and I'll get some money before I go – I'll give half of it to you, Marion. I'll have to keep the rest for things I'll need.'

'Don't give me more than you can afford,' Marion told him. 'You did your share all through the war, Dickon. Go and have your fun. I can manage. Kathy is working now and I'm earning more. Keep what they give you. It's your time to enjoy life.'

'You're the best, Marion,' Dickon said and let out a little whoop of joy. He was just a boy still, though he'd been forced to work like a man and he'd helped her all through the war. She smiled as he grabbed her and lifted her into the air. 'I thought you might not let me go...'

'I couldn't stop you and I wouldn't try,' Marion said. 'I'm glad you have a chance to do something you want for once, Dickon. Just let me know you're all right when you can, please.'

He promised he would and went off upstairs.

Marion washed the cups, glanced around the kitchen and headed upstairs. She peeped in at her younger sister Milly, who was almost eleven now, and then at her son, sleeping peacefully in his cot next to her bed.

Marion would need to give him his own room soon – perhaps the one Sarah had used until she and Dan had moved into their new home when he'd returned from the war. Dan had left the sea now and was working in a factory. It was better for them than spending months apart.

Once again Marion's thoughts went to her husband and she sighed. Would Reggie ever be well enough to come home? Her eyes stung with tears, but she refused to let them fall. She would manage. Even if Reggie never came back to her, she had her son. She would manage somehow...

24

Sally examined the little silver trinket that Kavi had given her when she had visited the workshop. It was a model of a Russian peasant and the workmanship was intricate and perfect, the legs, head and arms movable. At the top, it had a little ring so that she could attach it to a chain if she wished, but she thought it too delicate and wonderful to use and kept it in a box in her dressing-table drawer.

'Mikel told me you come,' Kavi had said as he presented his gift. 'I make for you, Mrs Sally Harper.'

'Oh, it is beautiful – charming. I shall treasure it,' Sally had exclaimed. 'It must have taken so much time?'

Kavi had shaken his head. 'It is nothing. I make more beautiful toys for the Czarina and the grand duchesses...'

'Yes, I understand you worked for the firm that made beautiful Easter eggs for the Romanov family. I was so sorry when I learned what happened to them during the war.'

Kavi's eyes had glittered for a moment, making him look unusually fierce. 'It was a wicked evil thing they did to them... Once, I see the Grand Duchess Anastasia. I go to the summer palace with my master to deliver a gift and I see the girl in the garden. She is playing hide-and-seek and she put her finger so...' Kavi had placed a finger to his mouth. 'She young and beautiful and they kill her.'

'Yes, that is terrible,' Sally had agreed. 'It must have been a desperate time for you then, Kavi?'

'I leave my country. I never go back,' he'd said and then turned abruptly to Mick. 'I need more materials for my work. You buy, yes?'

Sally had left them to talk business, looking at some of the other trinkets and jewellery Kavi had been working on. He really was a remarkable craftsman and they were lucky to have him. For a moment, she'd wondered at the look in his eyes when he'd spoken of the Grand Duchess Anastasia, but it had gone in an instant.

Sighing, Sally closed her jewellery box and glanced in the mirror. Winnie was staring in at her from the doorway and the look on her face was a little strange – angry or resentful perhaps.

'Yes, Winnie?' she said, forgetting Kavi and the tragedy of the Romanovs. 'Did you want something? Are the children all right?'

'I just came to tell you that Peter has been sick. Do you want me to take him to the doctor?'

'I'll have a look at him. If he needs to go, I'll pop him down myself.'

'Yes, Mrs Harper, as you wish...'

* * *

Peter was a little red in the face but not crying or running a temperature. Just to be safe, Sally took him to her doctor's surgery and was given an appointment by the receptionist. However, the kindly doctor told her there was nothing to worry about after examining the small child.

'We often get little tummy upsets at our age, don't we, young man?' he said and then to Sally, 'Perhaps he had too many sweeties?'

'I don't allow them to have sweets all the time, just now and then,' Sally said. 'But it might have been some kind of food that upset his tummy. I have noticed that if he eats too much too quickly, he can bring it back up.'

'There you are then,' the doctor told her. 'Nothing to worry about, but I am glad you brought young Peter. Better safe than sorry, Mrs Harper.'

'Yes, I agree,' Sally said.

She was thoughtful as she walked home. Had Winnie been letting the children eat too many sweets or cakes and biscuits? Perhaps she should warn her that it wasn't good for them to overindulge? After all, she was only nineteen and had no experience of caring for children, even though she was good at playing with them – but that wasn't everything...

'Of course I wouldn't let them eat lots of sweets and cakes,' Winnie said indignantly when Sally told her what the doctor had suggested. 'I only give them what Aunt Jean sends to the nursery for their meals.'

'Well, that is all right then,' Sally said. 'Mrs Hills knows just what they should have. It was just a little tummy upset, Winnie. I suppose most children get them.'

'Yes, Mrs Harper...'

Sally had dismissed the girl then, but again she'd seen a flash of something in her eyes that resembled resentment. Did Winnie dislike her? It made her feel a little uncomfortable as she considered the possibility.

* * *

Later, Sally was reading the headlines in the evening newspaper that autumn night, frowning over an article about Sylvia Pankhurst, who had called upon the dock workers to loot the docks and was now to be charged with sedition. She shook her head over it, never having been in favour of some of the more extreme actions taken by the Women's Movement, while supporting their aims to achieve equality for women.

Putting the paper to one side when her children's nurse entered the sitting room, Sally looked up and smiled. She saw Winnie's gaze directed at the article and nodded.

'Do you support the Women's Movement, Winnie?'

'I'm not sure, Mrs Harper. I suppose they mean well but... I don't think I should like to go to prison for speaking out the way Sylvia Pankhurst did.'

'I am not sure it is the right way to get what we want, though very brave of her...' Sally sighed. 'If only these ladies would be more sensible. We should make reasoned arguments, not cause damage to property if we want to attract the right people to our cause.'

'Not all women are rich and privileged,' Winnie spoke sharply, making Sally look at her. What was that supposed to mean? Winnie flushed as if she'd spoken without thinking. 'I mean – most of the suffragettes are, aren't they? My mother says it is wealthy women who have nothing better to do with their time—'

'Then your mother is wrong,' Sally said in a calm, flat tone. 'I know quite a few women who belong to the Women's Movement and most of them are not wealthy or privileged at all.'

'I didn't mean anything wrong, Mrs Harper...' A half-guilty look flashed across Winnie's face and disappeared. 'The children are in bed – if you don't mind, I'll go home now.'

'Yes, of course,' Sally agreed. 'You should go to one of the meetings, Winnie. Mrs Burrows often attends. You could go with her if you felt nervous about going on your own.'

'Oh no,' Winnie said instantly. 'My mother wouldn't approve. Goodnight, Mrs Harper.'

'Goodnight, Winnie...' Sally reached for her newspaper again as the girl left the room. That was a strange thing for Winnie to come out with – *rich and privileged...* Was that how she thought of Sally?

Sally dismissed the uncomfortable thought. She'd been anything but privileged as a child, her life in the orphanage unhappy and austere. It had been a struggle to find a good job when she left the institution at sixteen, but she'd worked hard and her luck had turned when she was given a position at Harpers.

Winnie had looked at her almost with dislike for a moment, but then the expression had gone in an instant. No, Sally wouldn't let herself think that way – yet, if Winnie disliked her employer, because she thought her rich and privileged, was she the right sort to look after her children?

That was stupid! Winnie was wonderful with the children and Sally would find it difficult to employ another girl that Jenny liked as much as she did Winnie.

* * *

Mrs Harper just didn't know how lucky she was! Winnie felt disgruntled as she caught her bus home, shivering in the cool breeze. The Harpers kept their house warm, with big fires in all the main rooms, but her mother's house would be cold everywhere apart from the kitchen, where the old range was all they had for warmth and cooking. Winnie's mother never lit a fire in the parlour, because it was a waste when they could sit in the kitchen, and a fire in the bedroom was unheard of. Mrs Harper had a fire in her bedroom and so did Aunt Jean...

'You could have your own room here if you wished,' Winnie's aunt had told her. 'Mrs Harper would be pleased for you to stay with us, I am sure.'

'I couldn't leave my mother alone at night,' Winnie had replied. 'She wouldn't like that...'

Mrs Harper was so lucky! Winnie thought as she stared out of the bus window at shops blazing with light. It was still autumn so they hadn't yet started to display Christmas themes, but they would soon, because she knew from listening to Sally Harper that they had to be planned months ahead. Winnie wondered what the Harpers were planning for Christmas. Her mother would expect her to spend as much time as she could with her, but there would be only a plain dinner and Winnie's present would probably be a new pair of woollen stockings.

Sally Harper had silk stockings. Winnie had seen them lying on the bed in her room when she was out. Jenny had run in there looking for her mother. In truth, Winnie had let her so that she could follow her in and have a good look round. It was such a beautiful room! All pale pinks, cream and rich reds. Luxurious. Like the clothes and jewellery, she wore – so many smart dresses, shoes and pretty underwear too. Winnie envied her those clothes...

Why did some people have so much and others so little? Winnie's mother said it was an unfair society, but she didn't think the suffragettes would do much good. She didn't approve of them. Winnie wasn't sure what she thought. Sometimes when she read about a dramatic act of defiance on the part of one of the suffragettes, she admired them – but she would never have the courage to chain herself to the railings outside Buckingham Palace. If she dared to do such a thing, her mother would never forgive her.

Winnie sighed as her bus stopped and it was time for her to get off. The kitchen would smell of wet washing, because that was how her mother made any money – washing for other people. It was her way of supporting herself. Winnie's wage should have made that unnecessary, but her mother had told her to save it.

'You don't know how long they will keep you on,' she'd told her daughter. 'These posh folk are all right, Winnie, but you can't trust them – they will turn you off the minute it suits them.'

'Is that what happened to you?' Winnie had asked and her mother had scowled.

'I was daft enough to marry a soldier,' she'd said. 'As soon as the mistress knew, she sent me packing. It wasn't allowed to have followers or marry when I was in service. Your father was away half the time and then he went and got himself killed. No thought for me left with a teenage girl to bring up alone.'

Winnie's feet dragged the last few steps. If only she had a lovely big warm house to come home to – and a husband like Ben Harper. A deep sigh escaped her. He was so lovely and when he smiled at her, Winnie went all funny inside.

Sally Harper just didn't know how lucky she was...

25

'Lilly... Wait on a bit!' Lilly heard Jeb call to her as she neared her house. She was tempted to hurry on and pretend she hadn't heard him, but he came running up to her and she couldn't just walk off without speaking. 'I've been wanting to see you... I'd like you to see my shop now it's set up proper.'

Lilly's throat tightened with tears. She would love to see Jeb's flower shop, but she knew she mustn't encourage him. That eager light in his eyes would die if he knew what had happened to her. She was spoiled goods and she couldn't bear him to know it.

'I've no time for visiting,' she said, wanting to put him off. 'I've got Mum and the kids to see to – and I never get a minute to myself.'

'You must get a break now and then,' Jeb reasoned, his eagerness dying away to be replaced by disappointment as she shook her head. He stared at her for a long moment. 'What is it, Lilly – what has changed? Have you found another fella?'

'Don't talk daft,' she said. 'Anyway, what is it to you if I have?'

'You know the answer to that,' Jeb shot back at her and took hold of her arm. 'You are my girl, Lilly, and you always have been.'

'I'm not anyone's girl. I can't be,' she said, her tears spilling as she wrenched away from him and hurried to her house, rushing round to the back kitchen. Once safely inside, the tears ran down her face. Then she became aware of her mother and Carol sitting at the kitchen table watching her. Lilly sniffed, took off her coat and wiped her eyes with the sleeve of her dress.

'What's wrong, our Lilly?' Carol asked, looking at her anxiously.

'It's just the wind out got in my eyes,' Lilly said. 'I might have a bit of a cold.'

'Let's hope you're not sickening for anything,' her mother said. 'We can't afford to have you laid up, Lilly.'

'I'll be all right, Mum,' Lilly replied. 'Carol, unpack the basket for me while I make a cup of tea.'

'Kettle's nearly boiling,' her young sister said with a look of triumph. 'I filled it and put it on the range ready and I got a shovel of coke for the range, didn't I, Mum?'

'You were a good girl,' Annie confirmed. 'We made a pie with that rabbit you bought yesterday, Lilly. The cabbage and carrots are ready. You've only got to put them on the stove.'

'Thanks, Carol, thanks, Mum,' Lilly said and turned away to make the tea with water that was now boiling. Her mother hadn't asked questions, but that would probably come later when she was putting her to bed...

* * *

'So what were you really crying over?' Annie asked when Lilly helped her undress. 'It wasn't the wind, was it?'

'It was Jeb,' Lilly replied. 'He wanted me to see his flower shop and I said no. He said I'd always been his girl and that's daft...'

'Why is it daft?'

'Because I can't be his girl. I don't have time,' Lilly replied as she helped her mother into bed.

'Has he asked you to wed him?'

'No – and I'd say no if he did, Mum. Don't worry, I shan't run off and leave you.'

'No, you wouldn't do that,' her mother agreed after a moment's silence. 'You're a good girl to me – to us, Lilly. I don't say it, but it's true. Not many would take as much care of me as you do, love.'

'I love you, Mum,' Lilly said and bent to kiss her as she settled back against the pillows. 'Are you all right now? Comfortable?'

'Yes. You get off and do whatever you need to, Lilly.'

'Have a good night and call me if you want me,' Lilly said.

'I always do. I couldn't manage without you, Lilly.'

'I know that, Mum...'

Lilly left her mother to rest. She still had some ironing to do and the washing to put in the copper to soak. The kitchen floor needed a wash, where Joe had shed his clothes earlier, spreading coal dust everywhere. Sighing, she blinked away her tears. It would have been impossible for Lilly to think of marrying the man she'd loved since he was a young boy, even if she hadn't been shamed and ruined. Her family needed her, which meant she was tied to them. Sometimes she felt it wasn't fair, because her brothers could all come and go as they pleased, but then she shut such wicked thoughts away. She loved her mother and her younger siblings and she would never desert them.

* * *

Mr Marco and Mrs Jackson were working on Harpers' windows when Lilly arrived at the ground floor the next lunchtime. She washed her hands in the cloakroom before nodding to Mrs Jackson and making her way to the florist department. Mr Jones was looking at his paper but looked up and smiled at her as she went in.

'I was just reading the football results. They set up a new league in August and I was thinking I'd like to watch a match one day...'

'Do you like football, sir?' Lilly asked, interested.

'I played as a youngster but haven't had time to watch or play in years. Maybe I will when I retire.'

'I've only ever seen the lads play in the street.' Lilly rubbed her hands to warm them.

'It is a cold one today, Miss Ross. How about we have some of my cocoa to warm ourselves up?'

'Yes, please, sir,' Lilly said, responding to his kindness. 'I love your cocoa.'

'That's because I make it with mostly milk,' he told her. 'Nothing like a warm milky drink on a cold day.' He glanced down at his work list. 'We've got all the displays for the restaurant to do today, half a dozen bouquets to go out – and then I want to teach you how to make a Christmas wreath; there will be no time to teach you when the season starts.'

'I've never seen one of those close up,' Lilly said. 'Some folk put them on their front doors, don't they?'

'They do indeed,' he told her jovially. 'It's to show visitors they are welcome. A nice custom, though only if you can afford the expense; they are not quite as easy to make up as the baskets, but you'll soon get the hang of it.'

'I shall enjoy learning,' Lilly said.

He handed her a mug of hot cocoa and she warmed her hands on it. Would Jeb have Christmas wreaths in his shop? She couldn't help wondering about it and half-regretted refusing to visit. He would think she didn't like him and she did – she really did...

26

Sally finished reading about the success of the first women students to be admitted to Oxford and nodded in satisfaction. It seemed that at last the Women's Movement was making a difference. Women were gradually gaining more privileges and in America they had the precious vote they had so long campaigned for. Perhaps she would visit with Ben one day. He had spoken of it, but they were always too busy to take a long holiday.

Her mind turned to other things as she folded the newspaper. There were only two months to go until Christmas, Sally thought as she looked through the latest batch of catalogues to arrive at Harpers. She was already making plans for the spring stock, the goods for Christmas in the basement waiting to be brought up when the moment was right. They decorated the store towards the end of November and that was the signal for all the extra merchandise to be put out on the shelves. It would ensure the atmosphere that the store needed for the festive season.

This year, Ben had decided he would restore the customs they'd had before the war, with Father Christmas and presents for the children who came to visit him.

'I don't feel like playing him myself this year,' he'd told Sally when he mentioned his intention. 'Do you think Fred Burrows would come in for a couple of weeks for us?'

'I will telephone and put the idea to Beth,' Sally had replied with a smile. She'd suspected that Fred would love the idea and he had. Fred was enjoying his retirement but couldn't resist the chance to return to Harpers for such an occasion.

Sighing, Sally put down her catalogue without making any decisions. It would be the first year for a long time that they wouldn't see Jenni at Christmas and that was a sad thought. She would, of course, ask Andrew to come with Penny, but she wasn't sure he would feel able to this year, though she hoped he would. The ache of Jenni's sudden illness and death would stay with them all forever but life had to go on despite the grief and loss.

The telephone shrilled beside her and she answered it, 'Sally Harper...'

'Sally love, it's Mum,' the familiar voice came over the line. 'I don't know how to say this...' Sally heard the catch in her voice and trembled. Not more bad news! 'Trevor has agreed to sell and move nearer to you – so could you look for a place for us?'

Relief swept over Sally and she gave a hysterical giggle. For a moment, she'd thought her mother was about to tell her that Trevor had become suddenly worse.

'That's wonderful, Mum. Yes, of course, we'll look round for somewhere nice for you. I'm so glad. I thought for a moment it was bad news and it's the best news ever.'

'I'm so excited,' her mother said. 'He suddenly told me this morning that he's had enough and wants a quieter life. Apparently, the chap who made him the offer upped it by another three thousand pounds, so he decided to grab it while he can.'

'Better and better,' Sally trilled. 'It will be wonderful to have you living near us, Mum. You will see so much more of the children.'

'And you, Sally,' her mother agreed. 'I missed so many years – and that's why Trevor made up his mind. He wants me to be near you if anything should happen to him.'

'He isn't worse?' Sally's heart caught because she liked her mother's husband – the man she called dad.

'No, he's home and feeling more himself, but his bronchitis can be pretty bad and it has made him think.'

'I know...' Sally's breath caught in her throat. 'Ben has been thinking on the same lines since we lost Jenni.'

'He's so young... but then his sister was even younger.' Sally's mother paused, then, 'You are all right – the children, Ben, and you?'

'Yes, we are, Mum,' Sally said. 'Truly, so don't worry. Jenni's death has just been hard for us – especially Ben. He will be pleased with your decision to live closer. I'll make some enquiries, look at a few houses, and then let you know what I think – that way you needn't go to view lots of unsuitable properties. I am so excited. I was just thinking of Christmas...'

'I'm not sure we can move by then, but we'll certainly visit – fingers crossed,' her mother said and Sally laughed. 'We're having a Father Christmas at Harpers this year again with presents for the children – and Fred Burrows is going to wear the Santa suit.'

'I should like to see that,' her mother said, laughing. 'Perhaps I could take the children. That would be fun, wouldn't it?'

'It certainly would,' Sally agreed. She heard the door and voices in the hall. 'I think Ben has just got in...'

'I'll ring off now, but we'll talk again soon,' her mother said, but Sally stopped her.

'Just have a word with Ben – tell him the good news.' She

handed the receiver to her husband as he walked in and mouthed the word 'Mum,' to him.

Ben chatted to her for a moment then, 'I've seen a nice house just around the corner from us, Mum. I'll have a look at it and let you know what we think...' He was smiling as he replaced the receiver a moment or two later. 'That will be nice for you, Sally, having them here.'

'Yes, I'm so pleased,' she replied, getting up and kissing his cheek. 'It will be good for the children too. Mum wants to take them to see Father Christmas...'

Ben nodded and went to pour himself a drink. 'I think I deserve this – I've just bought us that property we wanted adjacent to Harpers...'

'Ben!' Sally looked at him in surprise. 'I thought they turned your offer down – said they were going to let rather than sell?'

'They did. I considered taking a lease on it – but then they came back to me and said they'd changed their minds and would accept my offer. No explanations.'

'Well, that is good – although...' Sally hesitated. 'Have you considered there may be some fault in the structure... to change their minds so quickly?'

'It won't matter that much as I'm going to gut the place anyway,' Ben said. 'It is old-fashioned, Sally, dark and dreary. Mick knows builders who will do what we need at a reasonable rate and not hold us to ransom, as some are doing at the moment. They start a job and then put it on hold until you agree to pay them more. I had a similar experience before the war, but Mick says it won't happen with these lads.'

'He has a lot of useful contacts,' Sally replied. 'What would you like for supper?'

'I was thinking I would take you out,' Ben told her with the slow smile she loved. 'We haven't been anywhere much for ages... neither of us has felt like it.'

'No, but I suppose we have to get on with things,' Sally said. 'I would love to go. I'll ask Mrs Hills if she needs to go anywhere...'

'Winnie has agreed to stay,' Ben told her. 'I met her in the hall and asked if she would and she said yes.'

'Poor Winnie has been looking out for them all day,' Sally laughed. 'Still, they should sleep for most of the time...'

'She didn't seem to mind. I don't think she gets out very much,' Ben informed her. 'Told me she didn't have a boyfriend – or girl-friends either.'

'Really? I can't imagine why. She is pretty enough and wonderful with the children. I wonder why she has no friends.'

Ben shrugged. 'It's what she said.' He frowned. 'I saw Lilly Ross looking a bit miserable this afternoon as I left Harpers. She didn't see me and seemed in a hurry, so I didn't speak to her. You don't know why she's upset, I suppose?'

'I haven't seen her recently,' Sally replied thoughtfully. 'Do you think she is finding it a bit too much, learning the art of floristry?'

'I wouldn't have thought so,' he said, 'but there is something. I'd ask her myself, Sally – but I don't want to pry or start rumours. You know how spiteful tongues can wag... you'll do it so much better.'

Sally looked at him. 'You like young Lilly, don't you?'

'Yes. In one way, she reminds me of you, Sally...' He walked to her and put his arms around her. 'It was my lucky day when you came to work at Harpers, my love.'

'You didn't even look at me for ages...'

'Oh, I looked,' he said. 'You know why I kept a distance, Sally.'

'Yes, I do,' she agreed. 'You've had a lot of grief, Ben.'

'Yes...' he sighed, 'but I've also had a lot of luck, finding and marrying you, the children and the store. I want to think of the future, not the past – and tonight is a celebration.'

'Yes, it is,' Sally said and went into his embrace, broken only when the door shot open and Jenny came bundling in with Winnie rushing after her.

'I am so sorry, Mrs Harper, but she wanted to see her daddy...'

'That's all right, Winnie. Her daddy wanted to see her too.' Ben bent down and swept Jenny up in his arms. He threw her into the air and caught her, then tickled her, making her trill with laughter.

At that moment, Sally glanced at Winnie. She wasn't sure what drew her attention, but a little shock ran through her as she saw the girl's rapturous look of adoration as she stared at Ben. Her children's nurse was in love with her husband!

Winnie seemed to become aware of her and turned to look at her. The expression in her eyes instantly changed to one that puzzled Sally, but she'd seen that look and for some reason it sent a chill down her spine.

27

'You're looking a bit peaky,' Mr Jones said to Lilly when she handed him the bucket of carnations and roses. They stored the spare flowers in buckets of water in the back room, because it was cool and the blooms kept well, only displaying a few vases and arrangements in the shop. Today, he was making up a large basket of roses and carnations for a birthday gift. 'Are you sure you feel up to it?'

'I'm all right, sir,' Lilly said. 'I just felt a little bit queasy this morning. It must have been something I ate.'

'Well, if you still feel unwell, you should go to the rest room. Mrs Simpson might give you something to help settle your stomach. I always take liver salts myself if I get a funny tummy.'

'Yes, my father used to do that,' Lilly said and her smile peeped out. She liked Mr Jones. He was clever at his work and kind to her and she thought how lovely it would be to work with him all the time. 'I can manage. I like coming here and watching you work.'

He nodded and picked up a tall and perfect pink rose. 'Now, where would you put this, Lilly?'

'I think I would have that one in the centre because it is so tall,'
she said after looking at the basket. He had crushed wire in the
mouth of the round vase that stood in the well of the basket and
flowers splayed out at angles as he built up the arrangement piece
by piece.

'Yes, so would I,' he agreed and removed the rose that was
already in the centre, replacing it with the perfect pink one. 'So,
where shall we put this one?'

'If we cut it, it could go here on this side,' Lilly suggested. 'It
gives it a sort of lop-sided look but follows the shape of the basket,
which is like a fan at the back.'

'That is exactly right,' Mr Jones gave his approval. 'I think you
could finish the basket on your own now, Lilly.'

He stood and watched as she placed each flower after careful
deliberation and then clapped his hands.

'I think we can say that you've reached stage one of your train-
ing, Lilly.' He looked at her thoughtfully, then, 'Supposing I asked
Mr Harper if you could be my full-time assistant? Would you like
that?'

'Do you really mean it?' Lilly looked at him with delight. 'I
should love that, sir – if Mr Harper would permit it...'

'Oh, I think he might,' Mr Jones said and then laughed. 'Why
do you think he sent you to me, Lilly? I'm sixty-four and I won't be
here forever. You could take my place if you work hard and learn
all I have to teach you. It isn't just the arrangements – you need to
be able to care for your flowers and know all about them, what
goes with what, and how to keep them fresh for longer, but you are
the right sort and you learn quickly.'

'I'll work hard and learn everything,' she said eagerly. Her
excitement shone out of her.

She helped him clear up the bits and pieces, not realising the time until he said, 'You'd better go, Lilly. You don't work here yet and it's five minutes over your time...'

Lilly gave a little start, thanked him and left. She walked as quickly as she could through the main store and took the lift up to the bag department, but it was more than ten minutes over her time when she reached it.

Lilly threw a scared glance at the clock on the wall and then at Mrs Martin, who was serving a customer. The expression on her supervisor's face told her that she was in trouble.

* * *

They were busy the whole of the afternoon so it wasn't until closing time that Mrs Martin approached her. 'Miss Ross, I need to speak to you now.'

'Yes, Mrs Martin. I am very sorry that I was late back, but I was helping Mr Jones and I didn't realise the time.'

'That is not good enough. I have warned you before, and this is your last chance. If it happens again, I shall speak to Mr Stockbridge about whether or not we can continue to employ a bad girl like you.'

The tone of her voice made Lilly wince inwardly. Mrs Martin so obviously thought she was a careless, lazy girl who didn't deserve her job at Harpers, but that wasn't true. She tried not to take advantage of the privileges given her and prayed that Mr Harper would agree that she could work for Mr Jones, because she wasn't sure how much longer she could bear Mrs Martin's disapproval.

* * *

Lilly met Jeb on her way home that evening. He was loitering at the end of her lane and came towards her, giving her no chance to avoid him. Her heart caught as she saw the uncertainty in his eyes. After their last meeting, he wasn't sure that she liked him, but she did – oh, she did, even though she could never let him know how much.

'Evening, Lilly,' he said and produced a small bunch of violets from behind his back. 'I got these for you. I know you like them.'

'Oh, Jeb, thank you,' Lilly cried and accepted them. 'It is so kind – Mum will love them.'

'I gave them to you.'

Lilly saw the disappointment in his eyes and sniffed their perfume. 'We both love them,' she said. 'I like to give them to her because she isn't well. She doesn't get much pleasure in her life...'

Jeb's irrepressible smile returned to his face. He wasn't a handsome man – not like Mr Harper – but he had a lovely smile and a nice nature. Lilly liked him and she'd always hoped that one day... but it couldn't ever be now. Remembering what had happened to her, Lilly's face clouded. She tried not to think about that night and some of the time she was able to forget – but now it all came back to her.

She mustn't encourage Jeb, because she could never marry him. She was shamed and he deserved a decent girl, not trash like Lilly. Mrs Martin thought her trash and only bad girls got attacked the way Lilly had.

'Thank you for the violets, Jeb,' she said in a small voice, 'but please, don't do it again...'

Lilly walked away as fast as she could, leaving Jeb to stare after her in dismay. 'Lilly – What's wrong? What did I do?' he called after her.

Lilly didn't turn her head. It wasn't what he'd done, it was her. She was a bad girl and she didn't deserve his love...

* * *

Joe came in about ten minutes after Lilly and found her crying in the scullery. She jumped as she saw him and dabbed at her eyes with her apron.

'Lilly...' Joe said and frowned. 'I thought we said you wouldn't let it upset you? It wasn't your fault, love. Don't think I've forgotten. I'll kill the bugger if I ever find out who did it.'

'You never will,' Lilly said in a choked voice. 'I don't think he was local. He may have come in off one of the ships and is probably long gone.'

'Better for him if he has cleared off,' Joe said grimly. 'I told you I'd look after you, Lilly, and I will. Are you in trouble?'

'No, thank goodness!' She shook her head emphatically, because she dared not even think what would have happened if she had been pregnant. 'It was my supervisor at work, Joe. I was late back at lunch and she said I wasn't the sort of girl they need at Harpers – called me a bad girl...'

'She is an old battleaxe,' Joe said. 'Ignore her, Lilly. I don't think she made you cry – so tell me the truth.'

'Jeb bought me some violets...' Lilly said. 'I know he likes me – but he wouldn't if he knew what I am... what happened to me.'

Joe swore beneath his breath. 'Jeb is all right, our Lilly. He would understand.'

'Please don't tell him...'

'Tell me what...?' They both turned as they heard their mother's voice. She was standing at the door that led upstairs. 'Why are you upset, Lilly? I thought I heard you crying...'

'Mum! Have you been upstairs – how did you get down?' Joe said.

'I thought you were in bed when I got home...' Lilly added.

'I came down on my bottom,' Annie replied, a pleased look in her eyes. 'I can't walk downstairs alone yet, but Effie has been helping me and I got upstairs with her help.' Her gaze narrowed. 'You have been crying, Lilly. Why?'

'It was her supervisor at work,' Joe said. 'She's a right horror, Ma. Lily was late back from her work in the florist at lunch and she called her a bad girl.'

'That's wicked,' Annie exclaimed. 'My Lilly isn't a bad girl. If I had the use of my legs proper, I'd go in there and tell her so.'

Lilly gave a watery chuckle. 'Oh, Mum. Please don't. She would have me sacked – but I might not have to put up with her much longer. Mr Jones has asked if I would like to work with him all the time and I said yes. He is sixty-four and he says when he retires, I could have his job...'

'That's lovely,' Annie said. 'Don't you let that woman upset you, our Lilly. I know you're not a bad girl, whatever she thinks.'

* * *

Lilly looked at herself in the mirror as she undressed that evening. What would her mother say if she knew the truth? She'd believed Lilly's story about being knocked down by a bicycle. If she ever discovered what had really happened, she would be shocked and hurt.

Lilly's monthlies had come as usual a few weeks after the attack in answer to her fervent prayers. It was what had made her feel a little unwell when she was working with Mr Jones. She'd told him she felt a little sick because she'd been too shy to say it was just women's trouble.

At least Lilly would not have a child because of what had happened to her. Joe was relieved when she told him. She knew he'd worried about what they'd do if she did. He'd said he knew a woman who got rid of unwanted babies, but that seemed so cruel to Lilly. She wasn't sure she could have gone through with it, even though the alternative was to be publicly shamed...

28

Lilly was serving in the bag department the next day when she saw Mrs Harper enter. She stood watching for a few moments, and then, when Lilly's customer had gone, she approached her counter.

'Well done, Miss Ross. You sold an expensive bag and I wasn't sure that lady would buy. I tried to sell her something once, years ago when I worked here, but she went away without purchasing it.'

Lilly blushed with pleasure. 'Thank you, Mrs Harper. I just told her that the same bag cost more elsewhere and was excellent value.'

'And does it?'

'Yes. Shirley told me she saw the same one in Selfridges, but it was two pounds and ten shillings more.'

'They had the same bag?' Mrs Harper frowned. 'I shall have to ask my supplier about that; they are supposed to be exclusive to us... but that isn't why I came, Miss Ross. Mr Harper tells me you would like to work in the florist's department and Mr Jones says you are bright and clever and he would like you to be his assistant

– so I have to tell you that you may start next Monday full-time. I shall move a young woman from the clothes department here.'

'Oh, thank you, Mrs Harper,' Lilly exclaimed and saw Mrs Martin look at her sharply. 'That is wonderful. I am really happy.'

'Good. Now, I must pass the news on to Mrs Martin – but I thought I would make sure it was what you wanted first.'

Lilly had a customer almost immediately and she was busy so did not see Mrs Martin's reaction to the news. However, when it was time for her lunch break, she saw disapproval in her supervisor's eyes, but she gave no sign of noticing.

It was when she was leaving that evening that her supervisor approached her. 'So, you've got you what you wanted,' she said. 'I just hope you appreciate how lucky you are and do not take advantage.'

Lilly took a deep breath and then looked at her. 'Why do you dislike me so much, Mrs Martin? I don't know what I've done to deserve your scorn.'

For a moment, Mrs Martin stared at her and then shook her head. 'If you don't know, then I can't tell you,' she said and walked off.

Lilly raised her head, refusing to let her upset her. She only had two days more to endure Mrs Martin's unkindness and then she would be working somewhere else. It was a dream come true. Yet she still didn't understand why her supervisor disliked her so much.

* * *

Andrea didn't like herself very much. The look in Lilly Ross's eyes when she'd asked why Andrea disliked her had made her ashamed. She wasn't sure why she'd picked on the girl right from the beginning – unless it was because Lilly reminded her of how she'd been when she met Philip.

A girl from the East End, looked down at and ignored by his family. That had stung her to the quick and she had never quite got over the fact that they had cut Philip off without a penny. He had tried to make light of it, but she'd always felt that he resented it. Sometimes, when he'd looked at her, Andrea had fancied he was asking himself if she was worth all he'd given up for her sake.

Yet they had been happy. Philip had been over the moon when Paul was born, buying her flowers and perfume and promising her the earth when he made his fortune. If it hadn't been for the war, perhaps he might have kept his promise.

Was she jealous of Lilly, because she was young and pretty and popular? Lilly had everything in life to look forward to. Yes, she had to care for her invalid mother, but that was only temporary. One day she would get married – and working in the florist's, she would very likely meet a better class of young man.

Andrea acknowledged she was indeed jealous. She had very little to look forward to. Mr O'Sullivan had taken her to tea once but she hadn't heard from him since. It was several weeks now since he'd taken her out and she knew he was back from his business trip, because she'd seen him leaving the store with Mrs Harper. They were old friends and she'd been told that they often went out for lunch together. It was his seeming neglect that had eaten at her and made her sharper than she should be. She realised that she would have to apologise to Lilly.

Did Mr Harper approve of his wife going to lunch with Mr O'Sullivan? Philip would certainly not have approved of his wife being taken out to lunch by another man. Mr Harper must be very tolerant, Andrea thought – and yet he'd been angry with his wife when their daughter fell and hurt herself. Perhaps he didn't know that his wife went out to lunch with Mr O'Sullivan? It was none of her business either way.

Andrea told herself that it didn't matter if Mr O'Sullivan never asked her out again, but it did! She'd enjoyed their tea at the Savoy and looked forward to being taken somewhere again – even if it meant riding in a motorcar.

Telling herself not to be a fool, Andrea walked home alone. She went into her small house and turned on the tiny gas ring she used to both heat the room and boil her kettle. She'd had something to eat in her lunch break; at home, she normally heated a little soup with a sandwich or a piece of toast. In the morning, she just had a cup of coffee and toast. There was no point in lighting the oven to cook for just her. When Paul came home for the holidays, she might cook something nice – or they might just go out and have a meal. He wouldn't stay long; he never did, because he preferred to stay at his friend's house in the country.

'Why did we move here?' he'd asked several times. 'I preferred where we were before, Mother.'

He spoke so well now. That posh school taught their boys to be polite and correct, but Andrea missed the fun they'd had together in the countryside, going for long walks and listening to the birds. Paul liked animals. In the country, he'd had several pets, but they couldn't keep them in town. It had upset him when she'd given them away – but what else could she do?

Tears of self-pity stung Andrea's eyes as she glanced around her neat little room. Was this how she must spend the rest of her life – alone and unloved?

* * *

Andrea was serving a customer the next morning when Mr O'Sullivan entered the department. He stopped by the bag counter and spoke to Lilly, asking to see a bag, which she showed him. He bought it and stood chatting to her for a bit longer, and then, as Andrea's customer left, promising to think about the piece of jewellery she'd spent twenty minutes or so looking at, he approached her.

'That's a bright young woman you've got,' he said cheerfully. 'I wanted a good bag for a friend of mine. Marlene lost her favourite bag somehow – thinks she left it on a bus – so I bought her a new one...'

Andrea nodded politely. Who was this Marlene? He hadn't mentioned her before. Was she the reason he hadn't bothered to visit Andrea until now?

'I am sure she will like it. That is one of our best ones.'

'Yes, that is what Miss Ross said,' he agreed. 'I was wondering whether you would like to come out to lunch with me this Sunday?'

Andrea hesitated. She wanted to go so much, but she wasn't going to be used as a second string. 'I have other arrangements this weekend,' she said frostily.

'Ah, well, it will have to be postponed for a while then,' he said and nodded to her. 'I'll be away for a few weeks after this Sunday. Take care of yourself, Mrs Martin.'

She watched as he walked away, cursing herself for her foolish pride. She had nothing planned, of course she didn't, and now he would think she wasn't interested and wouldn't ask her again.

Andrea's throat was tight with misery. She was lonely and unhappy at weekends and lunch with Mick O'Sullivan would have been a delight. What a fool she had been to turn him down!

Her glance fell on Lilly, who had just sold another expensive bag. What right did she have to look so happy when Andrea was miserable? If Mrs Harper knew that her husband flirted with that girl, she might not be so happy to promote her to a better job...

And what about Mr O'Sullivan? He was obviously a flirt, taking a married woman to lunch, buying an expensive bag for another woman friend while asking *her* to lunch. Well really, what kind of a man was he?

Andrea sighed with frustration as she saw the customer returning to look at the jewellery she'd said she would think about and painted on a smile. 'Have you decided, madam?' she asked.

'Yes, I am going to buy the silver bangle with the Art Nouveau decoration,' the woman said. 'I am sure my daughter will love it.'

Andrea said she was certain anyone would love it and packed the delicately engraved bangle for her, giving her one of the distinctive Harpers' bags. A sigh left her as the woman walked away. She could never afford to buy a bangle like that even if she'd had a daughter. Feeling her throat tighten, she saw Lilly looking at her in a puzzled way and glanced at her watch.

'You may as well go for your lunch break,' she told her.

Lilly inclined her head and left.

The new junior went to stand behind the counter. She looked nervous. Andrea realised that she was going to miss Lilly's efficiency when she left, the new girl did not have half Lilly's personality when it came to selling bags.

Lilly was back on time. She came over to Andrea's counter, one hand behind her back. 'Yes, is there something you wanted, Miss Ross?' she asked.

Lilly brought her hand forward and she saw she held a rose arranged on a piece of trailing lace with a pin. 'The head was broken off one of our roses when it arrived,' Lilly told her. 'Mr Jones told me to bring it for you.'

'Oh...' Andrea swallowed hard. She'd never spoken to Mr Jones and he didn't know her. Lilly must have made the decision. 'Thank you. That was very thoughtful of... Mr Jones.'

Lilly nodded, handed it to her and walked away.

Andrea hesitated and then pinned the flower to her dress. It smelled lovely and looked so bright that she couldn't resist wearing it.

Her next customer was a man. He smiled at her and nodded at the rose. 'I love roses and so does my wife. It's her birthday. I shall buy her some roses, but what else can I get her?'

'She might like this,' Andrea suggested, taking out an enamelled pink brooch in the style of a rose set with a rose quartz at the centre, 'there is a matching bracelet and necklace, too.'

He looked at the exquisite workmanship and nodded. 'Yes, they are just right. I will take all three please – and that rose you are wearing is lovely. It's a pity more people don't wear them. It brightens the day to see them...'

Andrea smiled, packing his purchases carefully into leather boxes and then the smart bags. He went away looking pleased with himself.

Andrea was busy the whole afternoon. She sold far more than normal and put it down to the rose she was wearing. Most of the customers had commented on it and she'd told them it had come from Harpers' florist. She thought one or two might have decided to buy flowers because of it.

Just as she was putting away the more valuable pieces for the evening, someone entered the department. He walked over to her and stood looking at her.

'If you won't have lunch with me on Sunday, will you come out to tea with me now?'

'I'd love to come to lunch with you, Mr O'Sullivan,' Andrea said, feeling relieved. 'I will cancel my other arrangement.'

Mick's smile lit up his face and her heart. 'That's what I wanted to hear,' he said, 'Now I'll take you home in my car...'

Andrea didn't argue. She'd almost lost any chance of being with him and she wasn't going to make the same mistake again.

As she saw Lilly leaving for the evening, she nodded and smiled. She would probably miss the young woman more than she'd thought possible and she would thank her properly for the rose the next morning – Lilly's last in her department...

29

'Are you still free for the tea dance this week?' Mr Marco asked Marion as they were finishing their latest window, which was an autumn scene with a backdrop of trees with their leaves turning red, gold and brown, some scattered on the ground. The models were all wearing winter coats, hats, scarves and gloves, and there were two stuffed toy dogs playing in fallen leaves. On the backdrop, there was also the outline of a window reflecting a cosy fire burning. It was one of the simpler window displays they'd done and Marion's idea, but it wouldn't have worked if Mr Marco hadn't painted the backdrop so beautifully.

'Yes, if you are?' she said and smiled at him. He was such an easy person to be with and she never felt uncomfortable with him when they were dancing. 'The window has turned out well, hasn't it? I think you should be an artist and paint pictures, Mr Marco. That autumn scene is so comforting and warm.'

'You gave me the idea,' he said, looking pleased. 'I enjoy my work. It gives me a feeling of satisfaction to see a finished window – but I do paint now and then. I've painted a few pictures of Pierre. I've done one of his mother from a photograph, but I'm not sure it looks like her – perhaps it is more the way I saw her...'

'I'm sure it is beautiful. I should love to see the pictures,' Marion said and he nodded.

'I will bring some in one day,' he replied. 'I've had an idea... but I must run it by Mr Harper first. I thought we might do a memorial window for those fallen in the war – or who fought in the war and have since died. We could invite customers to bring in their photographs and do a collage of them surrounded by flowers. It would be a window dedicated to those loved ones lost either to the war or, like Sadie, to the pandemic they called Spanish flu.'

'So it wouldn't have any merchandise in it at all?' Marion asked.

'No, it wouldn't feature Harpers' stock, which is why I must ask for permission to do it... Only perhaps an antique chair or sofa or something like that... I haven't finished planning it yet, but I would bring in some paintings that I did of the war from memory.'

'I think it is a wonderful idea. Would you do it for Armistice Day?'

'Yes, perhaps. I'll have to talk to Ben Harper and see what he thinks. I believe Mrs Harper would approve – but it does mean a loss of display of stock for a week or so...'

'Yes, but think how much people would like the idea of having their loved ones honoured in Harpers' window,' Marion said. 'I would love my brother, Robbie, to be featured. I have a lovely picture of him in his uniform. I have one of Reggie too...' Her throat caught. 'It's almost as if I've lost him, too.'

'Don't give up,' Mr Marco told her. 'He is receiving treatment and there is always a chance that he will return to you.'

'Yes, I know.' Marion's head went up. 'I try to believe that he will come home and be as he used to be – but sometimes I think it will never happen.'

'You can only hope and pray,' Mr Marco told her. 'Now we are finished, I think we can raise the blind and let the public see – and we deserve a nice cup of coffee and a bun, I think...'

* * *

There was a little chill in the air that evening when Marion got down from her bus and walked quickly along the street to her home. She could smell smoke and saw that some people had lit their fires, perhaps for the first time since the previous winter. She was glad that she kept her range going on a low heat while she was at work; it only took a few minutes to get it roaring away when she got in ready to cook their tea. Sarah might even have made it up before she left. She'd been looking after Marion's son that day and would have brought her home when Kathy got back at four in the afternoon. Kathy worked mornings three days and three in the afternoons and early evenings. She was on mornings that day and Sarah would have left little Pamela with her.

As she opened the back door, Marion caught the smell of baking. Kathy often cooked something nice for them when she got home early, especially cakes and puddings, which was what she most enjoyed making.

'Kathy...' Marion's words died on her lips as she saw the man sitting at the kitchen table. 'Reggie! You're home... you're home at last!' She rushed towards him, dumping her shopping basket on the table, and then halted as he stood up, something in his eyes preventing her from throwing herself into his arms. 'Reggie – are you home for good? Are you better?'

'I'm home if you'll have me?' Reggie said in a hesitant voice. His eyes were begging her for understanding and her heart felt so full, she thought it would burst. 'I know I treated you badly, Marion. I wouldn't blame you if—'

'Don't be daft, love,' she said, a smile bubbling up from inside her. 'Of course, I'll have you. I love you. I love you so much...'

'Still? Even after what I did and the way I hurt you?' He looked at her sadly. 'I'm sorry for what I said, Marion. I couldn't help myself...'

She moved forward, gently putting her arms around him. 'Are you really better?' she asked, looking up at him. 'I never stopped loving you, Reggie, but I almost gave up hope. Mr Marco told me to keep believing and praying and he was right.'

Reggie gazed down at her. 'He is the chap you work with at Harpers?'

'Yes. Mr Marco is a good friend, Reggie. He took me to a tea dance a few times to cheer me up when I was down, but that was all it was – just a friend being kind. I love you and if you hadn't come back to me, I still wouldn't have taken another man. You're the only one I'll ever want...'

A tiny shiver went through him. 'I thought I might have lost you, my love.'

'Have you seen Robbie?'

Reggie nodded and smiled.

'And your mum? How are you? Are you hungry?' The questions poured out and he laughed.

'Yes, yes, I'm much better and I am hungry.'

'I'll have supper ready soon, but I can make a sandwich now...'

'Kathy made a treacle tart and gave me a slice with a cup of tea, so I'll wait for supper. She is upstairs changing the boy...' He hesitated, then, 'My father and brothers want me in the building business, Marion. I'm not sure...'

She took a deep breath. 'If you want to go and live in the country, I will come with you, Reggie.'

'Thank you,' he said and reached for her hand. 'I need a little time to get used to everyone again, before I decide – but I thought I might do better running a country pub or a little corner shop rather than land work – be my own boss...'

'Would you let me help you run whatever you choose?' Marion asked him just as Kathy brought their little boy down. Still less than four years old, he was pink and chubby and smelled of soap and baby powder.

Reggie sat down and Kathy placed the child in his arms. He nodded as he looked down at his son and then turned to Marion. 'He has my eyes and your nose...' he said.

'Yes, he does.'

'He is beautiful – just like his mum.'

Marion just nodded, but her eyes told him all he needed to know. 'I'm so glad you're home,' she managed at last.

Kathy spoke then. 'I've made a cottage pie for supper. Whatever you've brought can wait for tomorrow, Marion. I'll be on tea and early evening service then – home at nine in the evening.'

'You make sure you catch the bus,' Marion told her. 'It is getting dark earlier now and you shouldn't walk home late at night alone.'

'Well, I don't,' Kathy said with a little note of triumph in her voice. 'I've got a new friend.'

'Oh... what is his name?' Marion asked and Kathy frowned.

'It isn't a he, it is a she. Jill is one of the pastry chefs at the hotel and she is looking for lodgings. She has a room near us but doesn't like it – I said I would ask if she could have Robbie's room. Now that Dickon has left us, there are two empty rooms, Marion. Jill can pay ten shillings a week for her room and extra for food – well, she'll probably cook us nice things... if you say yes...'

'I'm not sure...' Marion looked at Reggie for approval, but he shrugged. She hesitated, then, 'All right, Kathy. This is your home as much as mine – and it is possible that Reggie and I will be moving away, perhaps to the country, perhaps just to a nice quiet area in the suburbs...'

Kathy looked pleased. 'That's what I thought. If you go – what about Milly? Will you take her with you?'

'She can choose,' Marion said decisively. 'If she wants to stay here, Reggie's mum will look after her when you're not around.'

'I'd rather she went with you,' Kathy said and looked stubborn. 'I'm not you, Marion. You've looked after us all since Mum was ill, but I don't want that responsibility. Dan doesn't live here any more; Robbie is dead and Dickon has gone off on a mad adventure – and I want my turn to have fun with Jill. We don't want to look after Milly.'

Marion took a deep breath and counted to ten. Kathy was being selfish, but she couldn't force her to take on the responsibility.

'Milly will come with us wherever we go,' Reggie said into the silence. 'She is your sister, Marion. If we have a business to run, she can learn to help. It's only fair Kathy should have her freedom if she wants it… and Milly is just one more for us. She'll help with Robbie too…'

'That's settled then,' Kathy said. 'I'll tell Jill she can move in with us – and you'll look for somewhere else to live…'

'If we decide to,' Marion reminded her.

'Well, you said…' Kathy said. 'I'm never going to marry a man. I told you that, Marion. I won't forget what Dad did to all of us, even if you can. So if I want a woman friend – who I care about a lot – what is wrong in that? We are just friends if you're wondering, but we enjoy each other's company.'

'So I would imagine. There is nothing wrong at all in having a friend to stay,' Marion said. 'It's your life, Kathy. I'd like to see you happy and if you really don't want to marry, it might work for you to share a home with a friend.'

'Thank you, Marion!' Kathy's face lit up. 'I hoped you would understand. I just can never marry. I need a companion and Jill is the one – perhaps not forever, because she might get married, but for now.'

'Well, she can teach you quite a bit about fancy cakes and stuff, I suppose,' Marion said, nodding as she saw some iced buns on the dresser. 'Is that cottage pie ready yet? I am hungry...'

* * *

Later, when they were alone in their bedroom, Reggie drew Marion into his arms and kissed her softly, just the way he had when they were courting.

'I love you, Marion,' he told her. 'I never stopped. I just couldn't make myself believe in a future and it made me angry and bitter – but I've been taught to live and to trust again by a wonderful man. I don't know what he did that was different to the other doctors, but he gave me time – and he made me whole again. He even made me fire a gun to get over my fear of loud noises and somehow that worked. I am sorry for the things I did and said to you. Can you truly forgive me?'

'Yes, of course I can,' Marion said. 'Where do you think you would like to live, Reggie?'

'Ideally, it would be a country village, far away from the noise and bustle of a town,' he told her. 'I know that isn't fair to you, Marion. You love your job at Harpers and I should try to help my father and brothers in the business they began after the war.'

'Shall we give it until Christmas?' Marion asked. 'I can give in my provisional notice and help out over the busy period and you can try working with your family. If you hate it, we'll go wherever you wish, Reggie.' She smiled up at him. 'I quite like the idea of running a little village shop.'

'Yes, I'll try for a while,' Reggie agreed. 'It wouldn't be fair to rush you away, Marion. I do love you and I want you to be happy, too.'

'I am happy now,' she said, gazing up at him. 'I've got my Reggie back and I thought I never would. Will you make love to me? Can it be as it always was?'

For answer, Reggie bent his head and kissed her passionately. Marion gave a little gurgle of delight as he swept her up in his arms and carried her off to their bed. She clung to him, feeling the sweet happiness of having her husband back. Reggie had truly returned to her and if he needed to live in the country then Marion would go wherever he wished. She had loved her job at Harpers but she loved Reggie more...

30

'We haven't been to the theatre in ages,' Ben said as he presented the tickets for the opera to Sally that evening. 'These are for tomorrow. Will Winnie or Mrs Hills look after the children?'

'Yes, I am sure Mrs Hills will be glad to,' Sally said and kissed him. 'Thank you, darling. I've been wanting to see *La Boheme* for ages.'

'I was going to take you months ago,' Ben said. 'I bought tickets and then Jenni...' A sigh escaped him. 'I gave the tickets to Jack. I believe he passed them on to a customer at the restaurant; he said the opera wasn't Beth's thing...'

'No, I think Beth prefers the Music Hall to opera – but she does love the ballet. I thought we might take her one night, Ben. Jack won't, because he hates it – but we could. Fred would look after her children.'

'Yes, remind me of dates and I'll get them,' Ben said and smiled. 'Fred is looking forward to playing Father Christmas this year. He came to see me – and to have a look at his old department. He said it was all in order.'

'Yes, the basement storage is well run,' Sally replied. 'I still miss my chats with Fred, though. I think we all used to pop down for a cuppa and a bit of his homespun advice now and then.'

'So, what did you think of my plans for the extension to Harpers?' Ben asked as he sipped the glass of red wine she'd poured for him. 'Will they do? I thought we'd have a food hall on the ground floor, furniture on the second and the haberdashery on the top?' Ben looked at her for approval, but she shook her head.

'I feel the furniture should be on the ground floor,' Sally told him, 'But—' What she intended to say next was lost as the door burst opened and Jenny came running in, followed by Winnie with Peter in her arms.

'I'm sorry, Mr Harper,' Winnie said. 'But she heard your voice and she would come. Jenny loves her daddy...'

Ben laughed and scooped up his daughter, holding her high and tossing her so that she giggled with delight. Lulu scampered in, not wanting to be left out, and jumped up at them, barking.

'I'll take Peter,' Sally said and held out her arms to take her son, who was now wriggling madly, wanting to get down. 'Thank you, Winnie. You can go if you wish. We'll put them to bed this evening.'

'Oh, but...' Winnie looked at her, the dislike in her eyes barely concealed. 'As you wish, Mrs Harper – though it is really no trouble...'

'I know. We are lucky to have such a kind nurse for our children,' Sally said, 'but we're going to the opera tomorrow – and perhaps you might stay later then. Mrs Hills will be here, of course, but you could see they are asleep before you leave.'

Winnie hesitated for a moment and then inclined her head. 'Yes, of course, Mrs Harper.'

Ben was busy tickling his daughter, but after the girl left and the door was shut, he looked at Sally. 'Something wrong? She hasn't done anything you don't like?'

'No, of course not,' Sally replied. 'Winnie is excellent with the children.'

'Yes, she is – but you're not sure about her?'

Sally hesitated, then, 'It's probably nothing, Ben—'

'But?'

'I doubt you've noticed the way she looks at you – but I've seen a certain look in her eyes a few times now and I think... I know it seems daft, but I think she has a crush on you, Ben.'

'No? Really?' He laughed. 'Poor girl. I really don't think you should be jealous, Sally. I hadn't even noticed...'

'That is the problem,' Sally replied. 'I don't want the poor girl to feel hurt – and I'd rather she didn't leave because her heart is broken. She is very good with Jenny...'

'Yes, she is. Pity. Let's give it a little while. If it is just a schoolgirl crush, and I am sure it is, she will get over it. She will have to or leave.'

* * *

Outside the door, which she'd left open just a crack, Winnie listened. She was mortified that her secret feelings for Ben Harper had been discussed as a source of amusement! Her skin crawled as she heard them laughing at her, calling her a poor girl. That Sally Harper was so smug! Everyone did what she wanted and she got all her own way. Why should she have everything? Winnie never got anything she wanted. In that moment, she wanted to run away and hide, but she loved her job and knew she would hate the alternative, which was to work in the biscuit factory. She would have to swallow her embarrassment if she wanted to go on as the children's nurse.

Walking away, fighting tears of humiliation, anger began to

replace the humiliation. Winnie thought she'd like to wipe the smile off Sally Harper's face!

'Ah, there you are, Winnie love,' her aunt's voice called to her. 'Will you give your mum a message for me? Tell her I'll be pleased to come on Sunday for lunch. Mrs Harper says she doesn't mind cooking lunch for herself and Mr Harper is going to some kind of an automobile fayre with Mr O'Sullivan, so he'll be gone most of the day.' She looked at Winnie hard. 'Is anything wrong?'

'No, I just had an eyelash in my eye. I'll tell Mum,' Winnie agreed, swallowing back her distress. 'She will be pleased. She looks forward to your visits, Aunt Jean.'

'I know. I do too,' Mrs Hills replied. 'Off home early tonight then?'

'Yes. Mrs Harper said they will put the children to bed this evening. They are going to the opera tomorrow. I'll stay a bit later then.'

'Yes, you do that,' her aunt replied with an approving smile. 'Get off home then – unless you're going out?'

'I never do,' Winnie told her. 'I don't like young men, they are all so callow. I prefer older men – but the war killed so many...' She sighed. 'I don't think I'll ever find the right sort...'

'Someone will come along one day,' her aunt said, smiling. 'You're young yet, Winnie.'

Winnie walked away, shaking her head silently. Her aunt didn't understand. There was only one man that would do for Winnie – and he belonged to that awful woman. She'd laughed at Winnie! She hated Sally Harper! She couldn't help herself. She really did hate her. Sally Harper had everything that Winnie wanted and knew she would never have.

* * *

Saturday morning was Winnie's free morning. She would go in after lunch and take the children out, either to the park or just into the garden for some fresh air. The Harper family had a large garden and Winnie enjoyed playing games with the children. She loved her job – but the trouble was, she wanted more. She wanted all that Sally Harper had. During the night, she'd let her anger take over. She wouldn't give up her job – let them sack her if they didn't want her.

Winnie was curious about Ben Harper's store. She had never been there, but that Saturday she'd decided to buy a new dress for herself now that she'd saved some of her generous wages and thought she would go to Harpers and see what they had in stock.

It was nearly November now and chilly, but Winnie was warm enough in her thick coat, tweed skirt and warm stockings, a scarf wrapped around her neck and a red beret set jauntily on her dark curls. She caught a bus into Oxford Street and wandered along window-gazing until she came to the store, a flutter of excitement in her stomach. She'd seldom come shopping as a young girl, because her mother was a widow and had made all her clothes, claiming she couldn't afford to buy them. Winnie had never seen clothes like Sally Harper wore until she went to work for the Harper family. Their softness and elegance filled her young heart with envy. Why should some people have so much and others, like Winnie and her mother, have so little?

Immediately on reaching Harpers, she was entranced by one of the windows. It was a circus scene but all the artistes tumbling and on the trapeze were toys. The audience was made up of teddy bears dressed in clothes and the elephant trainer was a toy soldier. Dolls sat on a seesaw and there were lots of coloured balls, rattles and all kinds of mechanical trains and model cars.

Winnie lingered at the window for ages, drinking in the colour and richness of the display. How lucky some children were to have things like these to play with. Her own life had been sad and bleak and had become much worse after her father died in the war. Before that, her life had been better when he was home from his regiment, but there had never been much money to spare and the hard times were freshest in her mind.

She sighed, once again feeling envy, and then her eyes were drawn to the florist department just a short distance away. The nape of her neck prickled as she saw a man enter and realised it was Mr Harper himself. Quickening her steps, she walked towards the florist shop and gazed in through the glass window. Mr Harper was talking to a girl at the counter. She was laughing as she showed him some roses and he was chatting to her, smiling and talking animatedly. Winnie felt a sharp prick of jealousy. Why was he so interested in that girl?

He purchased a large number of red roses and paid for them, and then he plucked one from the bunch and handed it to the girl behind the counter. Her face lit up and she smiled and thanked him, lifting the rose to smell it.

Winnie lingered as he came out of the shop looking pleased with himself. 'Hello, Mr Harper,' she said and he glanced at her in surprise. He started to smile, but then seemed to check himself and nodded to her.

'Your morning off, Winnie,' he said. 'Have a nice time.'

She watched him walk away, roses in his hand, feeling slighted and resentful. He'd given that girl in the shop one of his roses. Why her and not Winnie? She hesitated and then went into the shop. She had come to buy a new dress but seeing Ben Harper buy the roses, she wanted some for herself. She could pretend someone had given them to her. The young woman looked at her politely as she entered.

'May I help you?' she asked.

'I'd like some of those roses,' Winnie said, pointing to the red ones. 'How much are they?'

'They are very special roses,' the girl told her. 'I'm afraid they are two shillings each...'

'I'll take just one then,' Winnie said, then, abruptly, 'Do you like working here?'

The girl looked surprised and then nodded. 'Yes, it is lovely. Mr Harper helped me get the job. He is so kind...'

'Lilly,' an older man said, coming through from the back, and then saw Winnie. 'Oh, I beg your pardon, miss. I just need you when you have time, Miss Ross.' He nodded to Winnie and disappeared the way he'd come.

Winnie paid for her one rose and left. She was seething inside as she walked away. What did Mr Harper see in that girl to get her a job like that? Why had he just walked away from Winnie, instead of chatting and asking how she was, as he normally did? She felt a surge of anger and disappointment. She'd thought his special smiles were just for her – but he'd smiled at Lilly Ross the same way.

She suddenly threw the rose into the gutter in a fit of temper. He was obviously a flirt and... She stopped and smiled to herself. Ben Harper might not be what he seemed; he might be having a dirty little affair with Lilly Ross. Perhaps Sally Harper wasn't as fortunate as she thought she was...

31

Andrea almost bumped into Lilly as they were both leaving Harpers that evening. Mist was curling though the air and it was bitterly cold. Andrea saw that her former salesgirl was carrying a beautiful red rose wrapped in delicate silver paper.

'Oh, that is lovely,' she said. 'Does it smell nice?'

'Yes, gorgeous,' Lilly replied happily. 'It is for my mother. Mr Harper bought his wife a huge bouquet of them and he gave me this one for Mum – wasn't that kind of him?'

'Yes, very kind,' Andrea replied. It was on the tip of her tongue to add that Lilly shouldn't abuse her privileges, but she stopped herself just in time. It was wrong of her to feel jealous of the girl and she wouldn't be nasty to her again. 'You enjoy your new job then, Lilly? Is it all you hoped for?'

'Yes, even better,' Lilly replied. 'I enjoy helping people choose flowers for their wives, mothers or aunts.'

Andrea nodded. 'Yes, I suppose that is what most people who buy flowers do, buy them for wives or relatives. I was so pleased with the rose pin you gave me, Lilly. It brought me luck...'

'Really?' Lilly smiled. 'I am so glad. We all need a little luck in our lives, Mrs Martin.'

'Yes, we do, and I'm glad you've had some, too, Lilly. Goodnight, I must go to catch my bus. I am being taken out to the theatre this evening...'

Andrea walked away, reflecting that it was easier to be kind when something good was going on in your own life. She regretted now that she'd been so harsh to Lilly. Her only excuse was that she had been feeling uncertain and lonely, but she hoped she'd made up for it a little now. She was truly pleased that Lilly had the job she wanted. The red rose from Mr Harper had made her wonder about that relationship for a brief moment, but then she'd reflected that perhaps Mr Harper was just being kind. He'd given Lilly the rose for her mother, not for herself. If he was behaving badly with her, he would more likely have given the girl a more extravagant gift. Yes, she decided. She had been wrong to doubt him or Lilly. He was just a pleasant friendly man. People could be friendly without anything bad going on between them... of course they could.

Andrea climbed aboard the bus that came to a halt at her stop, her thoughts still with Lilly for a few moments, before moving on to the evening ahead. She was so looking forward to being taken out to the theatre by Mick. It was years since she'd had the pleasure of an evening out, but she still had a nice dress to wear, because she'd kept her figure.

She was smiling as she got down from the bus and walked the short distance to her front door, shivering and glad to be in the warm. It was foggy that evening but not too bad. It shouldn't interfere with their trip to the theatre...

* * *

Andrea sat waiting until an hour after Mick O'Sullivan had promised to pick her up, dressed in her smart black dress with the lace inserts and wearing her single strand of pearls that had been Philip's wedding gift. As the marble mantel clock ticked round to 8.30 p.m., she knew that Mick wasn't coming. They would have missed the first half of the show, so there was no point in going now.

Why hadn't he arrived when he'd made such a point of wanting to take her to the theatre? At first, she'd been unsure, because he'd suggested a play by Shakespeare and she wasn't truly enthusiastic, but then he'd told her it was a comedy and she'd agreed to go.

'We can see the play and dine out afterwards,' Mick had suggested. 'It is a Saturday night, so you don't have to work in the morning... Come on, Andrea, live a little...' He'd teased her into it with that twinkle in his eye and so she'd said yes, and now he hadn't arrived.

To her surprise, Andrea discovered that she was anxious rather than angry. Remembering the last time, they'd seen each other, something told her that Mick wasn't the sort to just stand her up unless he couldn't help it – so what had happened to him?

She decided to make herself a cup of cocoa, and then, if she heard nothing in the next hour, she would go to bed as she normally did. Her disappointment was sharp, but she was sure that Mick had been delayed for some reason and would contact her as soon as he could...

* * *

It was nearly 10 p.m. when Andrea decided to retire for the night. She had no way of contacting Mick, because she didn't know where he lived. To sit here waiting and worrying was foolish. No doubt he would come to see her in the morning or at Harpers on Monday.

She went slowly upstairs. The house seemed very lonely and Andrea sniffed back her tears. Why was life so unfair? She'd been looking forward to this evening and now...

Hearing a knock at her door, she paused at the top of the stairs and then hurried back down.

'Who is there?' she called, opening the door just a little with the chain on.

'I'm sorry I am so late...'

Recognising his voice, Andrea opened her door and allowed Mick to enter. She gave a little cry of distress as she saw the bandage around his hand and blood on his white shirt.

'Don't worry; I'm all right. I stopped off on my way here for a little bit of business and was attacked and robbed.'

'Oh, Mick,' she said, beckoning him in. 'Are you badly hurt? Where have you been all this time?'

'I was taken to hospital because I had a knock on the head,' he said ruefully. 'I fought back, didn't want to give in – but there were three of them. I was sitting in the hospital fretting, thinking you'd be sure I'd stood you up and finish with me entirely...'

'Oh no, I wouldn't do that,' she exclaimed. 'I had a feeling something bad must have happened. Why didn't you go home to bed or stay in hospital? Are you sure you are well enough to be here?'

'I wanted to see you,' he said simply. 'I do have a headache and I'd like to sit down if I could?'

'You'll come upstairs and get into bed,' Andrea told him. 'I'm not having you wandering about in this state, Michael O'Sullivan, so don't argue. The sheets are clean in my son's room.'

A little to her surprise, he didn't argue but followed her meekly up to the spare room. Andrea always kept her son's bed aired in case he came home unexpectedly, and she pulled the sheets back for Mick, promising a cup of cocoa when he was settled.

'Get undressed while I make it,' she told him. 'Did the doctors give you anything for pain? I have a headache powder if not...'

'They gave me something to take,' Mick said. 'I'll have it with my cocoa.'

'I'll be back soon,' she promised, but as she reached the door, she heard his voice.

'Thank you for not being angry. I do want us to be good friends...'

Turning, she smiled at him. 'I dare say I'll be angry many times in the future, Mick, but this isn't one of them...'

Mick's look made Andrea's heart quicken. She turned away and went quickly downstairs to make his cocoa, but when she returned, he was in the bed and fast asleep. Sitting on the chair next to the bed, Andrea looked at his face as he rested. Her lonely heart had reached out to him, his kindness and charm bringing warmth back to her cold existence. She realised then that she had come to feel affection for him, which might, given a little time, be love, and tears filled her eyes, but she blinked them away. It wasn't the careless, sweeping, passion she'd known with Philip when they were so much in love, but a sweet and tender emotion – it was because of Mick that her bitterness had drained away, Andrea thought. She'd been suppressing all her natural warmth, consumed by her anger and self-pity, but somehow he had teased it out of her.

Fancy him coming here at this hour when he'd been attacked and must have been badly hurt to be taken to hospital. As soon as they'd patched him up, he'd come straight to her because he didn't want her thinking he'd stood her up. She smiled at the thought. Mick must care a little for her too or he would have waited to give her the news.

She sat for a little longer, but he was fast asleep, so she rose quietly and went to her own room, undressing and sliding into her bed. For a moment, she wished she'd let Mick sleep here with her, because then she could have had him beside her all night. Her heart missed a beat as she thought it might happen in the future and she drifted into sleep with a smile on her face.

* * *

Andrea awoke on Sunday morning to the smell of coffee brewing and bacon frying. She jerked awake as she heard voices down in the kitchen. Who had broken into her home? Her heart raced and then she remembered that Mick had come to her late the previous night – and surely that high-pitched laughter was her son Paul's? What was her son doing home?

Throwing on her dressing robe and slipping into soft shoes, she went downstairs to see Mick in his evening suit trousers and blood-stained shirt making bacon sandwiches for Paul and himself. He looked up and smiled as he saw her.

'Paul was going to bring a tray up and surprise you in bed,' he told her. 'He's home because there was a misunderstanding at school and they were going to expel him. He found your spare key and walked into the kitchen just as I came down. I explained why I was sleeping in his bed.'

'Mick sells motorcars,' Paul told her. 'He's going to take us for a ride in his new Bentley after breakfast. They've only been available for a couple of months. He's one of the first to own one! He'll fetch it and show me after he goes home and gets changed – and then he'll take us all out to lunch. He says we can go for a ride into the country somewhere...' His excitement was bubbling out of him.

Andrea looked from one to the other. They both had the guilty look of conspirators and she ought to be angry with Paul for just coming home without leave from his school, and with Mick for aiding and abetting him. But she felt laughter bubbling up inside her as she saw the way they looked at her. 'Well, that sounds a good plan,' she said. 'So why was the headmaster of your school going to expel you?'

'Because there was a midnight feast two nights ago and one of the boys got drunk and put the headmaster's wife's drawers on the flagpole. He thought it was me, but it wasn't, Mum. I just pinched the drawers from her washing line as a lark – I didn't know Steve was going to run them up the flagpole.'

Andrea's laughter rang out. 'Well, I don't think that was too terrible and certainly not a reason to expel you...' Paul's head went down. 'He didn't actually expel you, did he?'

Paul raised his head to look at her. 'He said, if I did anything else as disgusting, he would expel me – but I don't want to go to that school, Mum. I would rather come home and live with you, go to a local school... please?'

'It was what your father wanted,' she said, but the pleading expression in his eyes, stopped her. 'Let's think about that later. We'll eat breakfast and then we can go for a ride in Mick's car – and I'll have time to think...'

'I'll be away and pick up my car and make myself decent,' Mick said with a nod of his head. 'I'll be back by the time you've had breakfast – and you need a wash, too, lad.'

He looked across the room at Andrea for approval.

'We'll be waiting for you.'

After he'd gone, Paul paused in consuming his bacon sandwich and looked at her curiously. 'He's all right,' he said. 'Are you going to marry him, Mum?'

'Paul! What a thing to ask. We are just friends...'

'You wouldn't let anyone you didn't trust stay the night,' Paul said. 'I reckon you like him a lot.'

'Yes, I do like him,' Andrea confessed with a little blush. 'If he ever asked me – and I'm not at all sure that he will – what would you think?'

Paul shrugged. 'I'd be fine if you were happy. You will let me leave that toffee-nosed school and come home, won't you?'

'Have you been unhappy there all the time?'

'I hate it,' her son said truthfully. 'They ask me who my mother is and when I tell them they go all superior because you work in a shop.'

'It isn't any old shop. It's Harpers and I had to work to pay the bills,' Andrea said defensively. 'I'm sorry if you were miserable. You said you wanted to stay with friends in the holidays...' She saw the way his eyes avoided hers. 'You meant the friends we used to have, didn't you?'

Paul nodded. 'I worked on a farm last holiday and it was fun,' he said, 'but I thought you would be angry if I told you, so I let you think I'd gone with a school friend.'

'Would you prefer to live in the country?' she asked and he hesitated.

'I liked it where we were when Dad was alive, but I'm not sure. I just want to go to an ordinary school and live at home with you.'

'Let me ring your headmaster and sort things out then,' she said, making up her mind. 'It would be better for both of us if you were at school near me. I'll make enquires and then we'll decide what to do for the best...'

'Thanks, Mum,' he said and sent her a grateful look. 'Is there any more toast?'

'Yes, I expect so,' she said. 'Go up and get washed and changed, ready to go for a ride with Mick, and I'll make some – do you want more bacon or marmalade?'

'Marmalade please,' he said and grinned before running off to do as she'd asked.

Andrea became aware that she was still in her dressing gown. She would need to be washed and dressed when Mick returned. The prospect of a lunch out with her son and her friend was pleasing.

It was too soon to be thinking of anything more than friendship, but at least she had something to look forward to now.

32

'Lilly...' Jeb stopped her as she was on her way to work the following Monday. He stood in her way and when she tried to pass him, he moved to the left and then the right to block her. 'What have I done that has made you turn against me?' he asked and there was a look of determination on his face. His dark hair was cut short and his eyes were grey and clear, his suit an old one that had come from a second-hand stall but looked clean and freshly pressed. 'I'm not letting you go until you tell me.'

'It's not you, Jeb,' Lilly said and a little sob escaped her. 'It's me – I'm not worthy of you...'

His gaze intensified. 'I thought somethin' was up. Some bugger hurt you, didn't he?' His eyes flashed with anger as she inclined her head slightly. 'I asked Joe and he wouldn't tell me, but I knew he was lyin' when he said you were all right. Tell me who done it and I'll thrash the devil until he's crawlin' in the gutter where he belongs.'

'I can't... I don't know,' Lilly muttered, her cheeks flaming. 'Don't shame me, Jeb. I'm shamed enough...' She tried to push past him, but he caught her wrist and held her. 'Please let me go...'

'No,' he said, his face set stubbornly. 'Not until you understand that you're my girl, Lilly. You've always been my girl and whatever that bugger done to you...' He swore as he saw her look of desperation and shame. 'It doesn't matter, except that I'll stick him wiv a knife; a beating is too good for the likes of him.'

Lilly shook her head. The last thing she wanted was for Jeb to commit murder for her sake. 'Please don't,' she whispered. 'Let me go now, please. I'll be late for work—'

Jeb looked into her eyes. 'I love you, Lilly Ross, and I want you to be my wife. There, I've said what I should've said a long time ago.'

'No, I can't, not after...' Lilly jerked away from him and went running down the street, arriving at the bus stop just in time to jump on the bus before it pulled away. She looked back and saw Jeb watching her and swiped the tears from her cheeks. Why had he told her he loved her now when she couldn't be his wife? How could she, after she'd been defiled the way she had? She felt dirty and used and wasn't sure she could let any man touch her – even the one she'd loved ever since she was a little girl at school and he stopped one of the bigger girls pulling her hair.

It wasn't fair! Lilly loved Jeb and now she could never marry him, even if her mother was beginning to get a little better. There was just no hope for her. None at all.

* * *

Lilly had got over her tears by the time she reached Harpers. She washed her face in the cloakroom. Her eyes were a little red still, but she'd mastered her emotions by the time she entered the flower department. Her kind but elderly boss looked at her and nodded to himself.

'Now what has been making you cry like that, young Lilly?' he asked, genuinely concerned. 'You're not in trouble, are you?'

'No, sir,' Lilly said and felt the hot flush in her cheeks. 'Someone told me they loved me and wanted to marry me and I can't... that's all...'

'Don't you love him?' he asked, looking closely at her. 'Of course you do, that's why you cried – you want to but can't. Now, why would that be? A lovely young lady like you would make any man a good wife.'

'I'm not worthy of him,' Lilly said in a muffled voice. Mr Jones' kindness was bringing her close to tears again. 'You don't understand...'

'Oh, I think I probably do, Lilly,' he said gently. 'I haven't got this old without knowing how cruel life can be. Did some brute force himself on you?'

Lilly swallowed hard and nodded. She could never have told him, but he'd guessed, just the way Jeb had earlier. 'I'm so ashamed. You won't tell Mrs Harper. I don't want to lose my job...'

'It wasn't Mr Harper that forced you?' he said with sudden suspicion.

'No!' Lilly was indignant. 'Mr Harper is a gentleman and has been kind to me – it was a drunken stranger when I was walking home. He just came out of nowhere and...' She gave a little cry of distress. 'I tried to stop him. Honestly, I did – he was just too strong.'

'Ah, I see – and now you think you can't ever marry?'

She nodded and he shook his head at her.

'Why break your young man's heart? I am sure he will understand if you tell him the truth.'

'He already knows, but I thought...' Lilly looked at him hopefully through her tears. He was so kind and gentle, giving her renewed hope. 'Do you really think I still could? Jeb deserves someone who hasn't been spoiled...'

'You haven't been spoiled, Lilly. It wasn't your fault and you deserve to be happy. Now, dry your eyes. We have a lot of work to do, but when you next see your young man, you tell him you love him. That is all he wants to hear, believe me.'

Lilly swallowed hard. She almost did believe him, but a part of her still felt shamed and sad that such a bad thing had happened to her. It must have been her fault, why else would that brute have picked on her?

* * *

When Lilly left work that evening, she saw Jeb standing on the pavement. He was obviously waiting for her and his eyes were questing as they met hers. Lilly gave him a half-smile and he came to her immediately.

'What are you doing here?' she asked softly.

'I've come to walk you home, make sure you're safe.' He presented her with a perfect pink lily, his gaze firmly fixed on her face.

'Oh, that is beautiful,' she exclaimed. 'We have them in the shop... but they are so expensive, because they're grown in a hothouse.' She looked at him shyly, hoping he could see the love inside her.

'You are the beautiful one,' Jeb said. 'That lily is perfect and so are you...' He put a finger to her lips as she would have protested. 'To me, you will always be perfect, Lilly. I meant it when I said I loved you – and I know you can't wed me just yet, because of your mum, but we might be able to work somethin' out.' He looked into her eyes. 'If you love me, Lilly, nothing else matters to me.'

'You know I do. I always have...' Her words brought back the cheeky grin and he grabbed her hand. 'I always hoped we might marry one day.'

'That's settled then,' he said. 'I spoke to Joe and he says your mum is gradually getting better and we might manage if we all lived together for a while.'

'I think we'd need a bigger house for that,' Lilly told him, but she clung to his hand. 'Perhaps we could find somewhere close by...'

'Well, I've got my shop,' Jeb said. 'There's a flat over the top where I'd thought we might live one day – but if I sold it, we could get a bigger house.'

'No, Jeb. You worked hard to get that shop,' Lilly objected. 'What would you do if you sold it?'

'I'd go back on the barrow until I could get another,' he said promptly. 'I'd do anythin' for you, Lilly.'

'Oh, Jeb, I don't deserve you...' she said, her eyes misty with tears. 'You should forget me and find a decent girl...'

'I'll have none of that,' Jeb's voice was harsh with anger. 'You're as decent a girl as any, Lilly Ross, my best girl, and don't you forget it.' He fixed her with a stern look that almost made her giggle. 'We might have to wait a while to sort out where we'll live and what's best to do for your mother – but you're going to marry me and I shan't take no for an answer.'

'Do you really want to marry me?' Lilly asked. They had been walking slowly as they talked and were now at the bus stop. 'I do love you so much...'

She got no further. Jeb reached out right there in the street, put his arms around her and kissed her softly on the mouth. For a moment, she froze but then as she smelled his familiar fresh scent and the faint tang of his hair cream, she relaxed. This was Jeb – the boy who had protected her at school, the youth she'd watched shyly as he played football with his mates in the street, the young man she had fallen in love with over the years.

Someone wolf-whistled and then the bus drew up and Jeb helped her on board and paid their fares. She sat beside him on the double seat and held his hand as they travelled the three stops to their destination.

Jeb walked her up to her front door. 'I'll be callin' for you on Sunday afternoon to go walkin',' he told her. 'Tell your mother we're courtin' – let her get used to the idea gradually.' He looked into her eyes and then bent his head and kissed her firmly on the lips once more. 'You're mine now, Lilly Ross, and, no matter what happens or how long we have to wait, you'll marry me – won't you?'

Lilly drew a long sigh and then nodded. 'Yes, I'll marry you, Jeb. Thanks for asking me.'

'Thanks for sayin' yes,' he replied and touched her cheek lightly. 'Keep that lovely head up, Lilly Ross. You're as good as anyone and better, and don't you forget it.'

'You're the best, Jeb,' she whispered as he sauntered off down the street. 'You always were...'

* * *

Lilly was smiling as she entered the kitchen. Her mother was sitting at the kitchen table peeling carrots. She looked up as Lilly entered and nodded.

'Jeb give you that, did he?' she asked.

'Yes... he's coming to call for me on Sunday afternoon—' Lilly faltered, her nerves jumping.

'About time he spoke up,' her mother said with a little sniff. 'He has been moochin' after you since you were in short petticoats. I was beginning to wonder if he would ever ask.'

'Mum! You've never said anything...' Lilly stared at her, astonished.

'It was your business,' her mother said. 'So, has he asked you to wed him?'

'Yes – but not until...' Lilly faltered. 'I shan't go off and leave you in the lurch, Mum.'

'No need to,' her mother said. 'Joe says there is a house to let just down the road. If you're quick, you can get that and then you'll be near enough to pop in and do a few jobs for me, when you have time. Jeb won't expect you to go to work every day once you're wed. He'll likely want you to work with him some days – but you can have more time off if you need it... until you have a family and then you'll give up, same as I did.'

'Mum!' Lilly stared at her. She hadn't expected this reaction at all. 'What happens if you're poorly again or need to get up in the night?'

'Joe can help me – and Effie was sayin' that when you get wed, she could have your room. Her lad can sleep in Stevie's room – and that will make it easier all round. She's finding it a struggle to manage now she's a widow. Her money will go further if she lives with me...'

'You've got it all worked out, haven't you?' Lilly said. 'How long have you known?'

'About Jeb – or what happened to you a while back?' her mother asked. 'Don't look so shocked. I'm not daft, Lilly. I might be weak in the body, but my head's as clear as a bell. Do you think I don't know what that shamed look in your eyes was all about?'

'Oh, Mum. I didn't want you to know...' Lilly's eyes filled with tears. 'Joe didn't tell you?'

'He never breathed a word, but I saw him looking at you, sad and unsure of how to comfort you. You were lucky, Lilly. When it happened to me... Ted isn't your dad's son. I was raped and thought I'd die of the shame when I knew I was carryin' a child – but your dad married me and never said one word wrong about it all his life.'

'Ted isn't...' Lilly stared at her. 'Is that why he—?'

'It's why I never wanted to take more from him than I was forced,' her mother said, 'and why he didn't much care about your father's coal round. He's doing all right with his barrow and Joe loves the coal business – and now you'll be all right with Jeb. He will look after you.'

Lilly nodded but made no reply as Carol came running in. 'Is tea ready yet? Stevie is playing football with some of the lads. I'm hungry...'

'You can have a piece of bread and jam,' Lilly told her. 'We're having egg and chips later with fried tomatoes and mushrooms.'

'Ooh, lovely,' Carol said and seized the slice of bread and strawberry jam Lilly quickly prepared with delight. 'Is it true you're goin' to marry Jeb, our Lilly? I just saw him and he gave me sixpence to spend on sweets. I haven't spent it yet. I'm saving it for Christmas...'

'You should have a Christmas wedding,' Lilly's mother suggested. 'That would be something to celebrate, wouldn't it, Carol.'

Carol gave a squeal of excitement. 'Can I be your bridesmaid, our Lilly? Can I have a new dress for it?'

'I'm not sure about that,' Lilly said. 'It's a bit quick. I think we might wait until next spring, give me a chance to save for our new dresses – and perhaps Mum will be able to walk better by then, so she can come.'

'Aye, there is that,' her mother agreed. 'As long as there's no hurry?'

'No, Mum, no hurry,' Lilly told her. 'I think we'll let Jeb decide when we'll marry, but I doubt it will be before the spring. And I'll need to give plenty of notice at Harpers. They've been good to me and I don't want to let them down...' She would be a little sorry to leave Harpers, because they had given her a wonderful opportunity to learn about the flowers she loved, but her aim had always been to have her own flower shop. If she let them know now, they could have another girl trained in her place by the spring.

* * *

Lilly was smiling as she entered the florist's department the next morning. She could hardly believe her luck. After what had happened to her that never-to-be-forgotten night, she'd thought all chance of being a wife and having a family had passed her by. Jeb's insistence that she would be his wife had made her respect and love him more than ever, but her mother's reaction had shocked her. After Annie Ross' revelations, a lot of things had become clearer.

'Good morning, sir,' she said as Mr Jones entered the back room where she was removing her coat. 'It is cold out, isn't it?'

'Yes, Lilly, it is,' he said and looked at her in a strange way. 'Mrs Harper just sent a message down. She would like to see you in her office before you start work.'

'Mrs Harper wants to see me?' Lilly felt a chill at the nape of her neck. 'Am I in trouble, sir?'

He shook his head, looking anxious. 'I don't know, Lilly. I can only tell you what Mrs Harper said... but I can't think you've done anything terrible. I certainly have no complaints.'

'I'd best go immediately,' Lilly said and smoothed her dress. 'I'll just put my coat in the cloakroom and go straight up...'

'I've got a flask of hot cocoa. We'll have some when you get back.'

Lilly gave him a nervous look. What had she done that she was being summoned to Mrs Harper's office?

33

Your husband is having a dirty little affair with that slut Lily
Ross...

Sally looked at the horrid letter again and frowned. Someone had
cut the letters from a magazine or newspaper; it had taken time
and been done with malice and spite. Who could have done such
an unpleasant thing?

Her first thought on seeing it was to feel a little sick. Who could
hate her and Ben so much that they would try to make her believe
that he was having an affair with Lilly Ross? Sally had dismissed
the idea instantly. It was true that for a time she'd felt that Ben was
pushing her aside when it came to decisions about Harpers – but
she'd never imagined he was having an affair and she didn't
believe it. Yes, he'd been kind and considerate towards the girl,
especially after she'd told him of Lilly's situation at home – and it
was Sally who had suggested that Lilly be given an opportunity to
learn the art of floristry.

Was it possible that one of their staff had done this out of jealousy? Sally felt chilled. She had believed that all Harpers' staff

were loyal to her as well as Ben – but someone had wanted to hurt them, to rip their marriage apart.

Sally had known that she must speak to Lilly personally. She too was being targeted, because if Sally had been deceived by this nasty insinuation, she would have felt compelled to dismiss her.

Sally had coffee and biscuits sent up ready. She sat sipping hers and going through how she would tell Lilly that she had an enemy in the store. It was a difficult situation. When a knock came at the door, she invited Lilly to enter and saw from her scared expression that she was nervous.

'Will you have a cup of coffee?' she asked and saw the surprise in the girl's eyes. 'Please do – and please do not be upset by what I must tell you.'

'Have I done something wrong?' Lilly asked. She sat in the chair Sally set for her, still apprehensive.

'No, Lilly, I don't believe you have – but someone has tried to make trouble for you, my husband and me. I am perfectly certain it is just a cruel trick to upset me – but I wanted to see you and to ask if you know of anyone who would do this...'

She handed Lilly the sheet of paper with its crude message made of cut-out letters stuck to a piece of paper. Lilly stared at it for a moment, her face pale, and then she looked up. Her bottom lip trembled, but she spoke bravely, head raised.

'It is all lies, Mrs Harper. Mr Harper is always polite and kind when I see him, but he has never said one word... not even a touch on my hand or anything. Some men pat you as you pass them, but he doesn't. Not ever. It is a horrible cruel lie.'

'Yes, it is,' Sally said. 'Had I not been confident of my husband's love and loyalty, it might have hurt me badly – and then I might have had no choice but to ask you to leave. However, we shall just ignore this. If I get more, I shall go to the police, but for now I would like to know if you have any idea of who might have done this out of spite?'

Lilly hesitated, almost spoke and then shook her head. 'No, I can't think of anyone who would be this unkind, Mrs Harper.'

'You don't think Mrs Martin might have done it?' Sally asked and saw her start of distress. 'I know she was not always kind to you, Lilly. It was one of the reasons you were moved – but I would not have thought her capable of this...'

'She was a little... harsh sometimes if I was late,' Lilly bit her lip. 'Please, I don't wish to get her into trouble but... she did once imply something... like that letter, only she said I was flirting with him, because he stopped and spoke to me once in the store and I was late back and... and she called me a bad girl.'

Sally nodded. 'Then I think I must ask her if she was behind this,' she said. 'I shall not mention anything you've said, Lilly. Very well, go back to your work. You may be needed.'

'Thank you, Mrs Harper. Thank you for knowing I wouldn't do anything like that...'

'Of course you wouldn't, Lilly, and neither would Ben.' Sally smiled at her. 'No blame attaches to you – but someone has been unnecessarily cruel.'

'Yes. It was a bad thing to do,' Lilly said, put down her coffee cup, its contents hardly touched, and went out.

Sally frowned as the door closed behind her. She'd wondered briefly if it might be Andrea Martin but hoped she was wrong. The woman was good at her job – apart from her sometimes severe treatment of her staff – but she could not keep her if she was a trouble-maker. This was deliberate and nasty. It was downright spiteful!

Sally sighed and then asked her secretary to do two things. One was to take a message down to the jewellery department and the other to bring fresh coffee after Mrs Martin arrived.

* * *

Andrea was surprised and then concerned when she was asked to go straight up to Mrs Harper's office. 'But my department!' she exclaimed. 'I can't just leave the counter unattended.'

'Mr Stockbridge is sending a senior assistant to take over for a while,' she was assured. 'Mrs Harper requests you come now.'

Andrea bit her lip. What had she done to be summoned this way? She could think of nothing untoward in her work; the stock was immaculate, her records neat and correct and nothing had been stolen or mislaid in months.

She summoned one of the juniors and told her to expect senior help within a few minutes. Her heart was beating a little too rapidly and she felt a bit sick. Had Mrs Harper heard that Mr O'Sullivan was courting her? Because he was; he'd made that very clear on their Sunday out as a family. Would that make Mrs Harper angry? Would Andrea be told that it was not permitted for staff to have followers? Was she going to lose her job?

She knocked at the office door and was invited to enter. Sally Harper was looking at something on her desk and frowning.

'Mrs Martin – Andrea,' she said and looked up. 'Come in and sit down please. I wanted to ask you a few questions. First of all, how are things in the department? Are you happy at Harpers?'

'I think everything is as it should be – and I enjoy my job...' She took a deep breath. 'I can see you are upset, Mrs Harper. Have I done something wrong? If it is because I have been out with Mr O'Sullivan...'

'Oh, no. I know he likes you. He told me so... No, this is something else. Something unpleasant.' Sally Harper hesitated, then, 'Someone has tried to harm both me and Lilly Ross...' She handed Andrea the sheet of paper she had been frowning over. 'I must tell you that I do not believe this for one moment, but it is rather spiteful, do you not think so?'

Andrea scanned the brief and disgusting message, the colour draining from her cheeks. 'That is wicked!' she exclaimed. 'How could anyone send you such a horrible letter?' Her eyes widened as she looked at Sally Harper. 'You don't think that I... surely you can't?'

'I don't know what to believe,' Sally replied. 'I know that you were harsh to Lilly once or twice but...' She looked at Andrea intently for a moment, then sighed. 'No, I don't think you could have done this. Perhaps you might know of someone who is jealous of Lilly? This could have harmed her had I believed it...'

'Yes, I see that...' Andrea breathed deeply. Her throat was tight with anger and indignation, but she knew she had to swallow it and to accept that she'd brought it on herself. She had been unkind to Lilly. 'Mrs Harper, I know that I was hard on Lilly – but I felt she needed it at times. I believe now that I was wrong but...' She took another breath. 'There was some talk amongst staff when Miss Ross began working in the florist's department. She was seen talking to Mr Harper and jealous tongues will wag, I'm afraid. I did speak sharply to Lilly over it because I didn't want her to get into trouble – but I would never have done this wicked thing.'

'I see...' Sally said. 'Why did you not tell me about the gossip at the time?'

'I saw no point in it. Lilly denied any wrongdoing and I believed her. I did not wish to distress you for no reason.'

'Yes, I see your reasoning,' Sally agreed. 'Can you tell me who began this gossip?'

'No, Mrs Harper, I can't,' Andrea said and rose to her feet in a dignified manner. 'Nor would I do so if I could. Enough trouble and suspicion have been cast without starting more. Do you wish me to leave Harpers?'

'There is absolutely no need for that,' Sally Harper said. 'I believe your word, Andrea. I felt I had to ask, given that I knew you had spoken sharply to Lilly – and I have to find the person who did this, even though it is most unpleasant to question any of my staff.'

'I imagine it must have given you a nasty feeling when you opened that disgusting letter,' Andrea agreed. 'Whoever sent that must be full of hate, Mrs Harper. I am sorry you have been distressed – but I do wonder if I can continue to work here. I trust I shall receive a reference from Mr Stockbridge if I leave?'

'Yes, of course,' Sally replied. 'I am truly sorry I have hurt you...'

Andrea inclined her head and walked from the room with dignity. She left the office and went to the lift, holding the desire to burst into noisy tears inside. She would let no one see that she was frightened and miserable inside, because she really did not know if she could continue to work for someone who obviously did not trust her. Sally Harper had apologised, but for Andrea, the trust was broken.

* * *

Sally sat alone in her office, her thoughts muddled and distressing. She had offended Andrea Martin and wished that she'd handled the situation better. Sally should have known that her supervisor wouldn't do such a thing, despite her sometimes unnecessary severity towards the girls in her department – but who would? It was impossible to pick out a member of her staff at Harpers that she thought capable of such meanness. What good could it possibly do any of them to see a split between their employers? A little gossip was one thing; it happened all the time and was a source of amusement for a while and then forgotten. But this was something different altogether.

Sally tried to think of anyone who wanted to harm her – and Lilly Ross – and couldn't. There just wasn't any connection. Why should anyone link Lilly's name with Ben's? If it had been just a vague message that he was having an affair, it might have come from anywhere – but this was centred on Harpers. So, it must be one of the staff – and yet Sally could think of no one who had cause to hate her or Ben.

Sally's thoughts went round and round. She hadn't told Ben about the letter. He would have demanded that she take it straight to the police and perhaps she would have done better if she had consulted them. Sally had believed she could handle this herself, but now she'd made a mess of things. Andrea was indignant and had spoken of leaving. If she did, Sally would have to employ someone else and it wasn't always easy to find a good supervisor.

Oh, blow it! The whole thing was an unpleasantness that she could do without. She would make sure that Mr Stockbridge wrote Andrea Martin a glowing reference; it was the least she could do.

Sally decided to go home. She had a headache and was feeling at odds with herself. Placing the letter in her desk, she reached for her coat. She would take a walk in the park to clear her thoughts first...

* * *

The grey fog of previous days had cleared. Sally sat for a moment on a bench, enjoying the wintry sunshine and watching a grey squirrel gathering acorns. Most of them had disappeared long before, but this squirrel had manged to find some and was busy burying them underneath some bushes. Leaves – golden, red and brown – littered the pathways and rustled across the wide expanse of grass as people walked their dogs. Hearing laughter, her gaze moved to a couple strolling arm in arm and looking at each other ardently. They were so obviously in love. Watching the girl's face as she looked up into the eyes of her lover, Sally was reminded of the look in another girl's eyes when she'd looked at Ben without realising that she was observed. Something clicked in her mind and she remembered the look of dislike Winnie had given her recently.

It occurred to Sally that Lilly's name had been wrongly spelled in the poisonous letter. Something she'd noticed earlier but dismissed. Winnie would only have heard the name; she wouldn't have seen it written down. Andrea had, of course. How stupid Sally had been not to realise that at once. It had to be someone who did not know that Lilly's name was not spelled like the flower.

'No! It can't be...' she said out loud and the couple turned their heads to look at her.

Sally shook her head, got up and started to walk away. She must be wrong, but she had to confront Winnie and ask her straight out. Yet how could her children's nurse know anything of Lilly Ross?

She couldn't. Sally stopped walking. It was stupid of her. If she accused Winnie of sending the letter, she would lose her, as she might already have Andrea Martin – and perhaps Mrs Hills, too.

No, she couldn't ask her outright. It seemed impossible that it could be her children's nurse and yet something told her it must be. There simply was no one else who might mistakenly think they could gain from destroying her faith in Ben. Sally knew she couldn't accuse the girl without evidence, but she would watch her and she would ask questions in a roundabout way. Perhaps Winnie had heard them discussing Lilly... she must have put two and two together, and come to the wrong conclusion.

Remembering the way Winnie had looked at her with such malice and dislike, the conviction grew in Sally's mind. She was reluctant to admit it, but it was just possible that the girl did hate her that much...

34

When Sally walked into her house, she could hear the children crying. Jenny was screaming her head off and Peter was wailing. The noise came from the children's nursery and Sally ran upstairs, her heart pounding. Had something happened to her children? If they had been harmed to spite her...

She burst into the room to discover Mrs Hills looking harassed as she tried to quieten Peter while begging Jenny not to scream.

'What on earth is going on? Where is Winnie?' Sally asked, her heart racing.

'I am so sorry, Mrs Harper. She has gone...' Mrs Hills looked stricken. 'If I'd known what a little viper she was, I would never have recommended her...'

Sally picked Jenny up and the screams stopped immediately. Peter continued to wail. 'What did she do?' she asked, a sick feeling building inside her.

'I discovered her in your room, Mrs Harper. She was trying on your jewellery and clothes and when I admonished her, she said they would soon be hers. I told her not to be stupid, but she looked at me in such a way... I lost my temper with her and told her to leave – and, out of spite, she told Jenny she would never come back and made her scream.'

'She won't be back,' Sally said. 'What you just told me has confirmed something in my mind...' She shook her head as Mrs Hills looked at her. 'We'll talk later. Why don't you make us a pot of tea and I'll put the children to bed?'

'Yes, of course,' Mrs Hills murmured and looked relieved.

It took Sally half an hour or so to bath Jenny and settle her. Peter had fallen asleep in his cot by this time, so she left him to rest and then went down to the kitchen. Mrs Hills moved the kettle onto the big range to bring it to the boil and Sally sat down and waited while the tea was made. She explained that she thought Winnie might have a young girl's crush on Ben and told her about the letter she'd received, though not the awful words that had been used.

'I can't understand how she knew Lilly's name,' Sally told her. 'I'm not sure I ever mentioned it in front of her.'

'I think she listened at doors – oh, and she went shopping in Oxford Street on her morning off,' Mrs Hills said. 'I thought she was going to buy clothes in Harpers, but she came home with nothing but a pile of magazines and she was in a sullen mood...'

Sally nodded. 'The letters were cut from magazines, not written. I might have recognised her handwriting. I could hardly think it was her, but after what you've told me—'

'I told her to replace all your jewellery, but she may have taken something,' Mrs Hills said sadly. 'I thought she was such a lovely girl – and so good with the children.'

'She was,' Sally agreed. 'I am only sorry it happened. I can't believe she really thought Ben would turn to her if she caused trouble between us...'

As she spoke, her husband walked into the kitchen. He looked angry.

'What's wrong, Ben?' she asked.

'This came to Harpers for me this morning,' he said and placed a piece of paper in front of her. Sally saw instantly that it was similar to the one she'd received, only it accused her of having an affair with Mick O'Sullivan and the language was foul. 'It is disgusting! What kind of depraved mind would write something like that?' he demanded. 'I can't think anyone would imagine I'd believe these lies. Who could have sent it?'

'The same person that wrote this...' Sally placed hers beside his. 'I very much fear it was Winnie. I told you I thought she had a schoolgirl crush on you...'

'At nineteen, she is hardly a schoolgirl – but this language, Sally. I mean – does Winnie know that kind of language?' He looked furious. 'You know it is all lies?'

'Yes, of course, Ben. I don't know if it was her, but it seems likely.'

Mrs Hills spoke thoughtfully. 'Her father was in the Army. As a child, she might have heard him use words that were not fit for her, but he died a few years ago.' She looked distressed. 'I feel responsible, Mr Harper – Mrs Harper. I recommended her to you, because I wanted to help her. My sister-in-law had a hard time after her husband died and I felt sorry for Winnie. I am so sorry.'

'Where is the girl – not with the children, I hope?' Ben spoke sharply.

'No. I sent her home,' Mrs Hills confirmed. 'She was in Mrs Harper's room trying on her clothes and jewellery. I just hope she hasn't stolen anything.'

'She mustn't be allowed near the children again,' Ben said firmly. 'If she could deliberately set out to try to wreck our marriage, goodness knows what more she might do. We'll have to get another nurse quickly, Sally – or you will need to be at home more often...'

'Oh, that reminds me,' Mrs Hills said. 'The argument with Winnie put it out of my head – your mother telephoned, Mrs Harper. She and her husband have bought the house Mr Harper recommended and they will be moving to London as soon as possible. She wanted to know if they could come and stay until the purchase was completed, as her husband wants to oversee some renovations before they move in.'

'Oh, thank goodness,' Sally exclaimed. 'I shall feel safer with them living here for a while. Jenny loves Winnie and it would be only too easy for her to entice her away, but if she has her granny here, it can't happen.'

Ben looked relieved. 'I can't understand why she did it... unless, might she have overheard us talking about her the other evening. She left and you told me to be careful not to hurt her... she may have thought we were laughing at her.'

'Winnie's mother was always very proud,' Mrs Hills said. 'She will be wanting to know why Winnie has lost her job. Oh, dear. I wish I had never recommended her to you.'

'Not your fault,' Ben assured her. 'She seemed ideal. I thought she would be with us for years.'

'I did too until I realised that she had fallen for you,' Sally agreed. 'It is sad and I feel sorry for her.'

'Well, I don't,' Ben said sharply. 'Not after what she tried to do. Remember, Sally. This girl tried to set us against each other. She might be capable of anything.'

A wail from the nursery made them all look at each other in alarm. Ben went running up the stairs, Sally and Mrs Hills just behind him. When they got there, he had his son in his arms. Jenny was awake and staring at them.

'Where is Winnie?' she asked, a rebellious look on her face. 'I want Winnie.'

'Winnie has gone away,' her father told her. 'Granny and Grandad are coming to stay. They will play with you...'

'I want Winnie...'

Ben handed his son to Sally, who took him into the next room to change him and comfort him. Ben sat down beside Jenny on her little bed.

'Winnie did something very naughty,' he told her. 'She might hurt you if she came back. If she does tell you to go with her, say no – will you do that for me, Jenny?'

Jenny stared at him; eyes wide with distress as she struggled to understand. 'What did Winnie do – did she hurt Lulu?'

'No, she hurt Mummy,' he said. 'You wouldn't like her to do that, would you?' Jenny shook her head. 'Good girl. You just remember what I said – promise me?'

'I promise,' Jenny said solemnly. 'I don't like her any more. Will you read me a story, Daddy?'

'Yes – which one do you want?'

'One from my book of fairy tales...'

'The one by Hans Christian Andersen,' Ben said, smiled and picked it up, beginning to read her favourite book as Sally returned with the now sleeping Peter. She placed him in his cot and then went to kiss Jenny, who clung to her for a moment and then curled up, her eyes closing. Sally went quietly from the room. She could hear Ben's voice getting softer. He wouldn't leave until he was certain that Jenny was asleep.

Mrs Hills was sniffing into her handkerchief when Sally reached the kitchen. She looked at her tearfully. 'Do you want me to resign, Mrs Harper?'

'Certainly not,' Sally said instantly. 'I couldn't manage without you. You mustn't blame yourself. You couldn't possibly have known what Winnie would do.'

'I never dreamed she had so much malice in her,' Mrs Hills confessed. 'Even when I saw her meddling with your things, I never thought... but she was so rude to me, and those terrible letters...'

'Yes, they are nasty,' Sally said. 'Just imagine what might have happened if I hadn't been confident of Ben's love – and he of me.'

'That Lilly Ross... she could have lost her job. How could Winnie have done such a cruel thing to a girl she doesn't even know? I can hardly believe it.' She blew her nose hard. 'It just shows you never know someone as well as you think you do.'

'Winnie must have been unhappy,' Sally said. 'It is the only explanation.'

'But to hurt you and Mr Harper – when you'd both been so kind to her. I simply don't understand. She'd had a difficult life at home for a while, but you would think she would be grateful.'

'Perhaps she envied us our life...'

'But even so – to send letters like that... I feel let down and that's the truth. If she did you any real harm...'

'We must be vigilant for a while,' Sally replied. 'If she was willing to see a girl she didn't even know sacked for no reason – there is no telling what she might do...'

* * *

'Oh, Sally,' Beth cried when she told her what had happened later that evening. 'I can hardly believe it. She seemed such a nice girl, exactly what you needed.'

'Yes, I thought so too,' Sally sighed over the phone. 'Now I have to look for a new girl all over again. It is such a nuisance – and I'm anxious in case Winnie tries to snatch one of the children...'

'She wouldn't!' Beth exclaimed. 'Oh, Sally, you must be careful. It's a horrid thought. If you need me to come and look after them when you're at work sometimes, I can.'

'Thank you, Beth. I may ask you now and then – but the good news is that Mum and Trevor are going to move in for a while, just until their new house is ready. I am even more grateful they are coming to live near us now.'

'Yes, that will be a big help,' Beth agreed. 'I am so sorry that girl let you down. She seemed so perfect. I can't imagine why she wanted to hurt you like that...'

'I think she had a crush on Ben – but she may have overheard us talking about it, and perhaps when she realised that he wasn't interested she decided to punish us both.'

'I suppose you are right,' Beth said, 'but it still seems such a nasty thing to do. It just shows that you can't be too careful. I mean, we all thought Winnie was trustworthy.'

'Yes, I know. It makes me wonder if I should give up my work and look after them myself...'

'No! If you do that she has won,' Beth said. 'I am sure you will find someone else – perhaps look for someone a bit older next time. Winnie was only nineteen, wasn't she?'

'Twenty this coming January – and I was going to make her birthday a special day. Oh, well, she has gone now and I just hope she won't come near us again.'

'Be on your guard,' Beth warned. 'When are your parents coming?'

'Not until the weekend...'

'Then I'll come over on Friday and stop with the children. I know you have an appointment with a sales representative that day. I'll bring Timmy and Vera will fetch Jack from his infants' school. If that girl dares to try anything, I'll make her sorry!'

'Oh, Beth,' Sally laughed. 'You sound so fierce. Yes, please come over. I'll be back for lunch and we can have the afternoon together...'

35

'Have you said anything to your boss about us getting wed in the spring yet?' Jeb asked when he walked Lilly home that evening.

'I've told my supervisor, but I haven't spoken to anyone else yet. Mr Jones said he would have a word with Mr Stockbridge about it. He says he'll have time to train up a new girl before he leaves in the summer if I go once we are wed.' She smiled up at him. 'I'm looking forward to seeing where we'll live when we're married. It's so exciting, Jeb. I never thought I'd be so happy!'

'I'm glad you're happy,' he told her and put his arm about her waist. 'You know I love you, Lilly.'

'Yes, I do, and I love you,' she murmured. 'I was thinking though – Mum says I should leave Harpers when we marry, but what do you think?'

'I think I want you to be happy,' Jeb replied. 'You can come and work in our shop, love, if you want – but if you'd rather stay at Harpers, I'll not make a fuss.'

'You'd like me to manage the shop for you?' Lilly asked and he nodded.

'I want to make a good life for us,' he said. 'I've got the shop, but it only makes a small profit. I've got ideas, but I can't be in two places at once.'

Lilly tipped her head to one side. 'What else are you planning on doing?' she asked, a teasing look in her eyes.

'I'm going to clear houses,' Jeb told her. 'I can charge for clearing rubbish to the tip or burning it – but I can also make money from stuff other folk throw away.'

'But surely people want their furniture and personal bits?' Lilly was puzzled.

'They don't always need the stuff their relatives leave behind. All they want is the house cleared quick so they don't have to pay the rent.'

Lilly's eyes widened. 'That's dead folks' stuff...' She gave a little shiver. 'Aren't you frightened to go in where people have died?'

'Some of it is dead folks' stuff,' Jeb agreed. 'Some of it is stuff that has been out in a shed forever. People just want it out of the way...'

'But if they don't want it, will anyone else?'

'They will by the time I've done with it,' Jeb told her. 'I polish things up and repair them and then they look beautiful – and I find lovely things in old boxes what 'ave been forgotten. Just wait until you see some of the things I've got stored in my flat, Lilly.'

'I didn't know you could repair stuff,' Lilly said. 'There is an old table in our shed. It belonged to my granny but the leg broke – it would be pretty if it was mended.'

'I'll have a look at it,' Jeb promised. 'I reckon we should get married in early April, Lilly. That house, near your mum, Joe told me about is all right – but it wants a bit of sprucing up before I'd take you there. Joe and me will make it decent between us. He's all right, your brother.'

'Yes, Joe is a good brother. Ted is, too – but not like Joe.'

'Ted is a good bloke, but he doesn't have enough go in him,' Jeb said. 'He's not getting on with his barrow as he should. I've offered to give him some help, but he says he can manage. I could tell him where to get better stuff and cheaper – if he'd listen.'

'I'll have a word,' Lilly told him. 'Thanks for offering, Jeb. I appreciate it, even if Ted doesn't.'

'A bit touchy, your Ted,' Jeb replied. 'He had a good coal round if he'd known how to handle it – look at the way your Joe is getting on. He's already doubled the size of his round. Joe will go places, if you ask me.'

'Yes, I believe he will do well,' Lilly said. 'I feel a little sad for Ted, though.'

'I'll see if I can throw some business his way,' Jeb promised. 'I could do with another pair of hands on the days I clear houses.'

Lilly nodded. She wasn't sure she liked the sound of Jeb's sideline, but he knew what he was doing. Her mother would say he was a good provider and that's what you wanted in a husband.

'I think I'll tell my boss that I'll be wed in the spring and will leave Harpers then.'

'Like I said, you don't have to leave if you don't want to,' Jeb said, looking at her anxiously. 'I want you to be happy, love.'

'And I shall be,' Lilly said, hugging his arm. 'I'll be working in our shop doing what I love – and if I need time off, I'll have an understanding boss.'

'Aye, I can do my other stuff as and when I please,' Jeb agreed. 'I just want to make a good life for us – and any kids we may have.'

'I know and I love you for it,' Lilly said, smiling at him. 'Come on, Mum will be waiting. She and Carol have made a casserole for our supper.'

* * *

Lilly told Mr Jones the next morning. He nodded as if he had expected it. 'I'm pleased for you, Lilly, and I wish you all the happiness and luck in the world. I shall miss you, but I'll be leaving next summer myself. Mr Harper will have to look for new florists to take our place. He knows of my retirement plans, but I think he will be sorry to lose you, Lilly.'

'I feel bad about letting him down,' Lilly confessed. 'I wouldn't leave, but Jeb has so many plans and he really needs me to help out in the shop. It won't be like it is here, though. We'll sell more little bunches of violets than big bouquets of roses.'

'In time you'll build it up,' Mr Jones told her encouragingly. 'Customers come back for a lovely smile like yours, Lilly.' As if to confirm his statement, the door opened and one of their regular customers entered. Lilly went to serve him and was soon making up a beautiful bunch of chrysanthemums.

After the customer left, she and Mr Jones worked on several orders for a hotel who wanted ten perfect arrangements by that afternoon, so they were kept busy, working right through the lunch hour and making do with a snatched sandwich and a cup of cocoa from Mr Jones' flask.

'Well, that was quite a rush,' he said to her when the last arrangement had been taken out to the delivery van. 'That should teach you something about the trade, Lilly. If you want more business, get a contract with a hotel. Most of the bigger ones need flowers in all their reception rooms – and if you can secure it, you have a good steady trade.'

'Yes, I see that,' Lily replied thoughtfully. 'I'm surprised Jeb hasn't thought of that himself. He is keen on making money for us for our future.'

'Sounds like you've found yourself a good one,' Mr Jones said with a little chuckle. 'How did you meet Jeb then?'

'At school – on my first day. I was being bullied by one of the older girls and he stopped her. He walked me home that day and most days after that...' Her eyes lit up at the memory. 'I always knew he was the one for me... but I wasn't sure Jeb saw me that way. He stopped coming round once I left school and I never knew why, but it was because he was working so hard on the barrow. He was determined to get his first shop...'

'His first shop? Does he have more than one then?' Mr Jones' eyebrows went up.

'Not yet, but he will have soon – a second-hand shop, he calls it. Joe calls it a junk shop, but Jeb says there is money in junk. Sometimes he finds good stuff. He buys anything and knows where to sell it...'

'An enterprising young man then – as I said, you've found yourself a good one.'

'Yes, I think so.' Lilly smiled as she got on with her work. She was happy serving customers right up to closing time and wished Mr Jones a pleasant evening as she prepared to leave. For a while, her world had fallen to pieces but now it was mended.

* * *

Jeb wasn't set to meet Lilly that evening as he had a clearance job to do, but he'd told her to be sure to take the bus and not walk home. Lilly saw the headlines on the newspaper hoarding as she walked to her bus stop.

MURDER IN THE EAST END

A little shiver went down her spine as she bought a paper and read that a young woman of about Lilly's age had been murdered – and not far from where she lived. She continued scanning the article as she took her seat. Reading between the lines, she guessed that the girl had been raped as well as murdered, though the report just said 'abused'. The man had been seen running away and police were asking for anyone who had seen him to tell them. Lilly's heart raced as she read the description of him and she knew – she knew that it was the man who had attacked her.

Her throat felt tight with fear and distress. A feeling of guilt entered her mind, because if she'd told the police about what had happened to her, the girl might still be alive.

Tears were streaming down her cheeks as she got off the bus and ran the short distance to her house. Joe was in the kitchen talking to her mother and they both turned to look at her as she entered. Joe's eyes went to the paper and he nodded.

'He's the one, isn't he?' he demanded and she nodded. 'We reckon we know him. One of my mates saw him runnin' away and several people heard her screams. We're going to search for him – we know the pubs he goes to and we'll find him—'

'Joe! Just tell the police,' Lilly begged, but she could see from his face that he was determined. 'Please don't do anything foolish...'

'We're just goin' to find him and then we'll hand him over,' Joe said, nodded to his mother and went out.

'There's no stoppin' him,' Annie muttered as he shut the door behind him. 'I just hope you haven't brought more trouble to us, Lilly.'

'Mum! That isn't fair,' Lilly replied. 'I did nothing wrong.'

'I know – but if our Joe does something foolish it will be for your sake.'

'He won't, Mum. He said they will just hand him over to the police...'

'If you believe that one, you'll believe anythin',' her mother said sourly. 'Oh, I know it isn't your fault – but it is because of you that Joe wants revenge on that bugger.'

Lilly nodded. Her mother didn't have to tell her. She knew it would be her fault if Joe got into trouble – or, worse still, was killed. That man had killed once already.

* * *

Lilly lay in bed, unable to sleep. She was awake when, in the early hours of the morning, the kitchen door opened. Flinging off the bedclothes, she pulled on a dressing robe and ran down the stairs. Joe he looked as if he'd been in a fight. His lip was split and bloody and his cheek and knuckles were bruised.

'Joe! What happened?' Lilly asked, her breath catching in her throat.

'We had the bugger and we thrashed him, but then the coppers came charging in and he got away...' Joe said bitterly. 'The daft sods arrested us and took us down the station. It was hours before they finally listened.'

'Oh, Joe...' Lilly fetched a bowl of clean water. 'Let me bathe those cuts for you. You're lucky they let you go.'

'We got a stern warning,' Joe said. 'They insisted we should have told them where to find the suspect, but they let him slip through their fingers and they would again, the daft so-and-sos.'

'Not as daft as you and your vigilante group,' Lilly said. 'You could all have gone to prison. We don't want to lose you, Joe. Please leave it now – you thrashed him. Let the police do the rest.'

'Maybe I will,' Joe agreed. 'I just wanted to punish him for what he did to you, Lilly, but I couldn't kill him. I had him by the throat and I could have slit him with my knife but I didn't – I couldn't...'

'Good. I don't want you to kill anyone for me,' Lilly said. 'I'm going to marry Jeb and be happy – so don't ruin it all and get yourself locked up, please.'

Joe laughed and inclined his head as she finished bathing his face. 'That's my Lilly. I didn't like to see you lookin' so shamed and miserable. I wanted to get even and when I heard about that other girl... but it's best left to the police. I just hope they get him...'

'They will,' Lilly told him. 'Sometimes they are slow, but with the information you've given them now – you have, haven't you?' He nodded. 'They will get him, you'll see.'

'I hope you are right,' Joe replied but looked anxious.

'What?' she asked, but Joe shook his head. She sensed he knew something more. 'What aren't you telling me?' she persisted, but whatever it was, he wasn't telling.

'Nothing. You get back to bed, our Lilly. You need to get to work in the morning.'

'So do you,' she retorted, 'but I will, because I haven't slept a wink all night...'

36

'You get off to your appointment,' Beth said when she arrived at Sally's home that Friday morning. 'I shall be here with the children and that leaves Mrs Hills free to do whatever she needs to do.'

'Thanks, Beth,' Sally said. 'I'll return the favour if you and Jack want to go out.'

'Just stop worrying,' Beth told her and gave her a hug. 'I know you, Sally. Don't let that awful girl make you feel guilty for leaving your children. Harpers is a successful business because you helped make it that way. Go and do what you do so well.'

'I will,' Sally replied and put on her jacket. 'I'll be back for lunch.'

Beth waved her off and settled down on the carpet to play with the children. Peter was happy knocking down the brightly coloured building blocks that Jenny had set up for him. Beth's youngest son, Timmy, went to join her and they started to build a grand castle. Lulu sauntered up to Peter, now playing with a toy train, and turned over on her back, wriggling and begging for a tummy rub. Beth was on her knees, obliging him when the glass door leading to the garden was flung open and someone burst in.

Shocked, Beth got up quickly, causing Lulu to bark. Winnie stood there looking slightly wild, her hair windblown and disordered, her eyes darting about the room. She didn't seem to see Beth but called to Jenny to come to her.

'Come on, I'm going to take you to the park,' Winnie said, her voice high-pitched and sounding strange.

'No, Jenny,' Beth warned as the girl moved two steps forward. 'You can't take her, Winnie. You no longer work here.'

Jenny stopped and then retreated to Timmy's side. He took a sturdy step forward, as if to protect his friend.

'What is it to you?' Winnie demanded rudely and suddenly snatched at Peter. He screamed as she took hold of his arm, yanking him up from the floor where he was playing.

Beth moved towards her, but before she could do anything, Lulu flew at Winnie's ankles and bit her. She screamed and let go of the little boy. Peter fell back to the carpet on his bottom with a bump and started screaming. Winnie was kicking at Lulu, but she hung on, growling and continuing to bite.

Beth ushered the children behind her. 'Lulu, stop!' she commanded and was surprised when the dog obeyed. She hadn't thought it would but it backed off, though continued to growl.

'You let that beast attack me,' Winnie accused. 'My ankle is bleeding!'

'If you sit down, I will bathe it for you,' Beth said and rang the bell for Mrs Hills. However, the noise had brought her and she was there almost immediately.

'I thought I heard her,' she said and looked at the girl crossly. 'What are you doing here, Winnie?'

Beth had bent to pick up Peter, who was wailing, but although she examined him anxiously, it was fright more than anything else. His little bump hadn't harmed him, but he clung to her tearfully.

'That savage beast bit my ankle,' Winnie muttered. 'I was just going to take the children to the park...'

'After those dreadful letters you sent?' Mrs Hills said accusingly. 'How could you think we would let you? You are a naughty girl and you should apologise for what you've done...'

'Why are you taking her side?' Winnie demanded. 'You don't care about me – you only care about her and her brats.'

'Winnie that is a disgusting thing to say,' Mrs Hills reprimanded. 'You were shown nothing but kindness in this house – taken on by Mrs Harper with only my reference and no experience.'

'Oh, go on, defend her,' Winnie cried and then burst into tears. 'It isn't fair. Why should she have it all and I have nothing?'

'That is a foolish way to talk,' Mrs Hills said. 'Come to the kitchen with me, Winnie. I'll bathe your ankle and then take you home.'

'I hate you!' Winnie cried. 'I hate you all...' With that, she got up and ran back the way she'd come through the double glass doors, which were still wide open.

'She is naughty,' Jenny said into the stunned silence. 'Daddy told me so...'

'I'd better go after her,' Mrs Hills said. 'If she goes home in that state, her poor mother will have a fit. I don't know what has got into her. I'll get my coat and come back as soon as I've seen her safe, Mrs Burrows.'

'Yes, please do,' Beth said. 'The poor girl. Her ankle must hurt – but I can't understand why she has taken against Sally that way!'

Mrs Hills shook her head and went back into the hall. Beth heard the kitchen door close a few seconds later. After locking the door to the garden, she sat down on the chair with Peter on her lap. Jenny and Timmy resumed the building of his grand design and Lulu came and sat at Beth's feet, looking pleased with herself.

'Yes, you're a good dog,' Beth said and stroked her brown curls.

'I'm sure Sally has no idea what a good guard dog you are...'

Lulu huffed and licked her hand and then settled down to sleep.

* * *

It was nearly two hours later when Mrs Hills returned. She was apologetic and worried as she brought in a tray of tea and biscuits.

'I am so sorry, Mrs Burrows. I'll get on with the lunch now, but my sister-in-law was so distressed when I told her what Winnie had been up to...'

'Did she get home safe?'

'She went up to her room and locked the door,' Mrs Hills said. 'She wouldn't come down no matter what her mother or I said... I really don't know what has happened to her. I always thought her a good quiet girl, but her mother says she is resentful... They've had it hard I know, but...' Mrs Hills shook her head. 'There are a good many folk, who have to struggle for a living, but they don't go around sending nasty letters.'

'Winnie is young and...' Beth shook her head. 'No, I shan't make excuses for her. I know Sally was kind and generous to her – she shouldn't resent her for that.'

'It's what I told her mother.' Mrs Hills sighed. 'I think she's let Winnie do much as she likes most of her life. It was too much for her when she was widowed. I can only say I wish I'd never recommended her.'

Beth agreed but didn't say so.

Mrs Hills went off to cook lunch and when Sally arrived home, everything was peaceful.

'No trouble then?' she asked as she took off her jacket with its fur collar and laid it down. She saw Beth's expression and her eyes widened. 'What happened?'

'Winnie came and tried to grab Peter. Lulu bit her ankle and she went home. Mrs Hills says she is locked in her bedroom and will not come out.' Beth shrugged. 'I think she is a very resentful young lady, Sally. She wants what you have.'

'Oh, damn,' Sally said. 'I hoped it was just a stupid prank...' Beth looked at her and she made a face. 'What am I going to do, Beth? Must I go to the police?'

'Perhaps the brush with Lulu will have cautioned her,' Beth suggested. 'At least you have a good guard dog there...'

'I never thought she would bite anyone,' Sally said, looking at the bundle of fur rolling on the ground and hanging its tongue out. 'Good girl, Lulu.' Lulu sprang up and ran around her, barking and jumping up to be stroked. 'I shall speak to Ben when he comes home. Perhaps we should tell the police what has happened...'

* * *

Before Ben arrived that evening, Mrs Hills came to the sitting room to tell Beth and Sally that she had news.

'That silly girl has run away from home,' she announced. 'Her mother just came and told me. She went up to her room to tell her lunch was ready and discovered that she'd taken most of her things and gone. She left a note to say she was never coming back.'

'How can she possibly manage on her own with no job and no money?' Beth asked and Sally frowned.

'She took two pieces of jewellery when she left the other day. A gold and lapis lazuli pendant on a chain and a diamond ring that Ben bought me...' Sally bit her lip as Beth and Mrs Hills looked at her. 'I wasn't going to tell anyone. I didn't want to get her into more trouble – but she could sell them for a few pounds. Enough to get away and start a new life...'

'Her mother is going to the police,' Mrs Hills said. 'She thinks

Winnie is not herself – too emotional and mixed up to be on her own, and I agreed she should.'

'Yes, perhaps that will be for the best,' Sally concurred. 'Oh, how upsetting and distressing for everyone. I do wish it hadn't happened. I am so sorry, Mrs Hills. I feel it must be my fault...'

'Nonsense! You were nothing but kind to her,' Mrs Hills stoutly denied. 'It is the way she's been allowed to do as she pleased. If she'd had a father to see to her, she might have been different.'

* * *

Ben agreed when he got home. 'You did nothing wrong – except trust a girl we all liked and thought kind and caring. You should tell the police about the missing jewellery, Sally. It might help them to trace her if she tries to sell them. We won't press charges if you prefer not.'

'I feel the girl has enough to cope with as it is,' Sally said. 'I don't know why she turned against us, Ben. Perhaps it was the hard life she'd had that made her so resentful of what we have. I am just sorry for her.'

'Well, don't be,' he said sternly. 'If Lulu hadn't bitten her and Beth couldn't stop her, she might have stolen our son. What do you think might have happened then?'

A shiver went down Sally's spine. 'Thank God that Beth was here and Lulu,' she breathed. 'I couldn't bear to lose either of them, Ben.'

'Just be careful for a bit longer. I was willing to overlook those foolish letters – but an attempt to snatch Peter and Jenny is different. I'll be contacting the police myself.'

'I suppose you must,' Sally replied. 'Yes, Ben. I know you are right – but I also know how it feels to be alone and believe no one cares for you...'

'Exactly. You had a tougher childhood than Winnie – and you just got on with it. Had she been content to work for us, we would have given her a good life and she might have made a good marriage one day if she wanted.'

Sally sighed. 'What was going on in her mind to make her think the way she did? I just don't understand...'

* * *

Beth told Jack what had happened when she got home. He looked anxious and drew her into his arms. 'That was an unpleasant experience for you. A good thing you had the dog there to help you guard the children.'

'She looked a bit wild,' Beth said. 'I think she knew what she was doing was wrong, but she was so miserable that she just went ahead and did it.'

'Well, let's hope she learned her lesson,' Jack said and hugged her. 'She might have harmed you and the children...'

'I don't think she is really evil,' Beth replied thoughtfully. 'I think she is lost, Jack – lost and lonely and unhappy. She needs someone to love her...'

'You've been through a lot yourself, but you don't take it out on other people,' Jack said. 'I don't think you should feel sorry for her, Beth. She knew what she was doing all right.' He bent his head and kissed her. 'Cheer up, love. Nothing terrible happened. Remember we are going dancing tomorrow. Be happy for us and forget that girl. She isn't worth it.'

Beth inclined her head and kissed him back. Perhaps he was right, but she couldn't help feeling sympathy for Winnie. She'd looked so wild and desperate and her ankle must be hurting. Where had she gone? And what would become of her now?

37

Winnie was tired of carrying her suitcase; it was so heavy that it made her shoulder ache. After wandering around for a couple of hours, she decided to leave it in a left-luggage area at the station in Oxford Street. She didn't know why she had taken the underground to Oxford Street in the first place, but once she'd deposited her case, she wandered down, past the brightly lit shops, many of them now showing Christmas displays.

As she approached Harpers, she stopped to look at the latest window and scowled. It was all his fault – Ben Harper. He'd smiled at her and talked to her in a way that made her feel he cared for her and then she'd heard them laughing about her! It was that that made her resentment flare after years of simmering inside her.

As she gazed into the glowing window, Winnie's anger built and built in her head. Suddenly, without truly thinking, she took off her shoe and attacked the store window with the heavy heel. To her astonishment, it shattered and cracked. Laughing, she hit it harder, again and again, her fury at her situation coming out.

The sound of a police whistle made her stop and look over her shoulder. In the light of the street lamps, she could see a policeman running towards her; he was shouting and waving his truncheon. Suddenly realising what she was doing, Winnie hastily put on her shoe and ran. The policeman was determined and followed her; he was getting closer and closer and obviously not going to give up.

In fright, Winnie ran and ran for several streets, turning this way and that until she dodged down a dark lane and into a shop doorway. She was trembling and shaking, terrified by what she'd done and the chase. Had the policeman seen her face? Would he arrest her?

It was very dark in the narrow alley that she'd stumbled into and she could no longer hear the sound of running steps behind her. Closing her eyes, Winnie allowed the hot tears to fall. What had she done? If she was arrested, she might go to prison and then she would have no reputation and no chance of ever finding a decent job again.

Why had she been so foolish? Winnie didn't know why she'd broken the store window. She hadn't expected it to shatter like that – and she didn't know why she'd done the other things either. Jealousy wasn't a good enough reason for sending those awful letters and stealing – and her plan to take the children and worry Sally Harper had been a stupid one. She wouldn't have hurt them, of course she wouldn't...

Winnie bent down to touch her sore ankle, feeling sorry for herself. She'd bandaged it herself after using warm water and salt to bathe it, but it hurt, especially after running.

She had been so stupid. Aunt Jean was angry with her and her mother had reproached her through the bedroom door. Winnie felt wretched. She was ashamed now. Ashamed of her behaviour. As her mother had told her, she'd had a really good job and the prospect of a better future – why had she let her silly longings to be loved rule her head? She should never have let herself build up dreams of Ben Harper in her heart. Now she was ruined... no one would ever forgive her...

Leaving the shelter of the doorway, Winnie walked desolately down the dark lane. Where could she go? What could she do?

Suddenly, the man was in front of her. A big solid man who smelled of strong drink. She looked up, startled, seeing the close-set eyes and the scar on his face, which was bruised and battered as if he'd been in a fight. He leered at her, grinning as he reached out for her.

'What pretty little morsel is this then?' he said, his voice thick and slurred. 'Come here, my little whore, and I'll teach you a thing or two...'

'No! Help!' Winnie screamed at the top of her voice.

He was grabbing her round the throat, lifting her half off her feet. He banged her up against the wall and pressed his body into hers, half-suffocating her as his face came closer to hers and she smelled the stink of his breath.

Winnie screamed again and brought her knee up sharply, catching him in the groin. He gave a growl of rage but recoiled slightly, giving her access to her shoe. She reached down and pulled it off and attacked him with the heel she'd used to break Harpers' window. He jerked back, his hand to his eye, and Winnie wondered if perhaps a piece of glass had embodied itself in her heel when she broke the window. She hit him again as near to his eye as she could manage and he shouted in rage and pain.

At that moment, Winnie heard the sound of a police whistle and pounding feet. She screamed for help, although her attacker was holding his hand to his eye and yelling blue murder.

'He attacked me,' she cried as not one but three policemen arrived all at once and started hitting the man with their truncheons. He went down on his knees under the flurry of blows, his arms about his head. One of the policemen yanked his hands together and cuffed him as he knelt before them, his head bent. When he at last raised it to look at Winnie, she saw that his face was cut and bleeding and one eye was half closed.

'Bitch,' he muttered before he was dragged to his feet and pulled off by two of the policemen.

'Are you all right, miss?' the third police officer asked and then his eyes narrowed in recognition. 'I reckon you're the young woman who smashed that glass window. One of those suffragettes, I dare say?'

Winnie raised her head. 'What of it if I am?' she said. 'When men like that are allowed to walk freely, women have to protect themselves.'

'Happen I agree with you on that one,' the police officer said. 'However, I'll have to arrest you, miss...'

'It's Winnie,' she replied and held out her hands. 'Go on, arrest me. You might as well...'

'I'm not going to cuff you, Miss Winnie,' he said and grinned at her. 'I reckon I'll just take you down the station and give you a cup of tea. My wife belongs to the Women's Movement and she'd skin me alive if I cuffed one of her friends.'

'I haven't got any friends,' Winnie said and a tear trickled down her cheek. 'I deserve to be arrested for what I've done.'

'Well, we need you down the station to give us your account of what happened,' the kindly officer said. 'Afterwards, if my sergeant says it is all right, I might take you home. You can talk to my wife. I reckon a girl like you is just what they need in the Movement. My wife will tell you all about it...'

* * *

Three hours later, Winnie was sitting in front of a warm fire talking to Mrs Winston about the wicked things she'd done and sipping hot cocoa with a ham sandwich on a plate on the table beside her.

'Well, Winnie, I think you've been a very foolish girl, don't you?' Mrs Winston said. 'You can call me Mary by the way. I believe you are going to have to apologise to Mr and Mrs Harper – but after that... well, you have spirit and courage. You fought off that wicked man, who, my husband says, has already attacked several young women and murdered one. The police think your brave action makes it possible to overlook the damage you did to Harpers' window – but that will be for Mr Harper to decide. If they decide to press charges, you could get a custodial sentence – but if you do, the Women's Movement will stand by you.'

'I didn't do it for women's rights,' Winnie confessed, wanting now to be honest. 'I was just angry and resentful – jealous, I suppose. Why should some folk have so much and others have nothing?' Her job at the Harpers' house had only made her more aware of all the things she'd never had and she'd let herself dream for a while that it could be hers. When the dream was shattered, she'd just struck out like a spiteful child.

'A question many have asked,' Mary said with a wry look. 'All I can say is that you should harness that resentment of yours to a cause, Winnie. Women are gradually winning their small freedoms, but we want more concessions – every woman over the age of twenty-one should be able to vote and there are many other things that need putting right. Are you willing to join us – to go to prison for your beliefs if you have to?'

'Yes, I am,' Winnie replied. She caught back a sob. 'You and your husband have been very kind and I don't deserve it.' Winnie was ashamed of what she'd done and knew she could be in big trouble but now it looked as if she might get a second chance.

'Everyone deserves a second chance,' Mary Winston told her. 'Now, where are you staying?'

'I haven't found anywhere yet.' She couldn't go home to her mother, to return to that old life of ceaseless complaints and dreariness. She wanted to be free, to find a new home where she could grow and find something to fill her empty life.

'Then you will stay here with us until everything is settled – and we'll find you a place in one of our organisations. What kind of work would you like to do?'

'I've only ever done sewing and looking after the Harpers' children,' Winnie said with a little gulp.

'Can you spell and add up?'

Winnie nodded.

'You can work in one of our charities then. We help all kinds of needy folk, Winnie, and we'll soon have you settled and happy. You'll be one of us and helping us to make life more equal for women,' Mary said. 'Now, I'm going to send you to bed. You need a good night's sleep. Tomorrow you and I will go to Mr and Mrs Harper and you will apologise and then we'll see...'

'It will serve me right if they say they think I should go to prison...'

'If they are the kind of people I believe them to be, I doubt it. That's why my husband chased you so hard, Winnie. Mrs Harper has done a lot for our charities. I don't think she is the vindictive sort.'

* * *

Winnie swallowed hard as her aunt opened the door to them the next day. She couldn't find the words, but Mary Winston stepped forward.

'Winnie is here to apologise for all the trouble she has caused. May we please come in?'

'I'm not sure I should let you...'

'I will stand surety for her good behaviour.'

'And you are?'

'Mary Winston. Mr Harper knows my husband – Constable Winston. He witnessed the attack on Harpers' window and gave chase. I think you should allow Winnie to apologise.'

'Please wait there...' Mrs Hills shut the door firmly in their faces and Winnie looked at Mary.

'She won't see me...'

'She might,' Mary reassured as the door was quickly reopened and Mrs Hills gave an audible sniff.

'I wouldn't have you in, my girl – but Mrs Harper says she will see you.'

She stood back and allowed them to follow her into a small sitting room where Sally Harper had been working alone, an array of papers in front of her on the desk. She stood up as they entered.

'Winnie... how is your ankle?' Sally asked. 'I hope it isn't too sore?'

'It hurts, but it is all right,' Winnie said. She looked down at her hands. 'Thank you for seeing me, Mrs Harper. I have been very foolish and I am sorry. I was upset and jealous... but what I did was very wrong.'

'Yes, it was, not least because you named Lilly Ross – that wasn't nice, Winnie. She could have lost her job because of it.'

'I wish I hadn't done it,' Winnie admitted. 'I'm giving you back the things I took.' She removed the pieces of jewellery from her coat pocket and placed them on the desk. 'Will you press charges against me?'

Winnie held her breath as Sally Harper looked at her for a few seconds. 'No, I shan't, Winnie. Mr Harper is very angry, more about the way you tried to snatch Peter than the broken window. He may still do so, but I will ask him to give you another chance.' She looked at Mary Winston. 'Is Winnie staying with you?'

'Yes, for the moment. We intend to find her a place with the Women's Movement, where I think she will settle. I believe she is genuinely sorry, Mrs Harper.'

'I believe I owe you some wages,' Sally said. She turned to the desk and took five one-pound notes from the top drawer. 'I hope you have a good future, Winnie. I am sorry if we made you unhappy.'

'You didn't,' Winnie replied, flooded with remorse. What a fool she had been to envy Sally Harper and throw away all that she'd been given! 'That happened when my father died and my mother just gave up – but thank you for not pressing charges. I shan't bother you again. I give you, my word.'

'Then we shall forget it,' Sally said and nodded. 'You must forgive me. I have some work to finish and I'm expecting my parents this afternoon.'

'Thank you for seeing us.' Mary took Winnie's arm and they left the room. Mrs Hills saw them firmly to the door and closed it after them.

Winnie looked at Mary. 'She didn't forgive me, did she?'

'She did her best, Winnie. I think you have to forgive yourself now and get on with life.'

'Yes, I know,' Winnie said and smiled. 'Perhaps with your help, I shall.

38

'She apologised to you – to us?' Ben looked at Sally doubtfully. 'Do you believe in her change of heart?'

'Not completely,' Sally admitted. 'However, Mrs Winston was with her and she seemed chastened. I think if she joins the Women's Movement it may give some purpose to her life and be the making of her.'

'You mean Mary Winston – Constable Jim Winston's wife?' Ben nodded. 'I know Jim well. I bought tickets for the Police charity ball from him, but we couldn't go if you remember.'

'It was held just after Jenni became suddenly ill. Yes, I do remember,' Sally said. 'I wouldn't have wanted to go then and you had to go up there immediately.'

'I still can't believe she has gone,' Ben said and sighed. 'It knocked me for six, Sally, made me realise how precarious life can be. I enjoy owning Harpers and I know you do, too – but I think we must make more time for ourselves next year. Now Mick is a partner, I feel we can trust him to look after things if we're away.'

'Yes, I am sure that is true... only...' Sally bit her lip. 'He rang me just before Winnie and Mary Winston arrived. I haven't told you, but I asked Andrea Martin if she knew anything about that letter accusing you of having an affair with Lilly Ross and she was upset and threatened to resign... and, well, Mick is courting her, it seems, and he was angry that I'd upset her.'

'Good grief! What made you do that?' Ben asked, genuinely astonished.

'Well, she was a bit harsh with Lilly a few times for being late and...' Sally sighed. 'Of course, I shouldn't have asked Andrea and I never meant to upset her – unfortunately, Mick is angry with me because of it. It seems he is planning to ask her to marry him...'

'Really? Well, good for him.'

'Ben?' Sally was taken aback. 'Mick sounded so angry because I'd hurt her feelings – doesn't that worry you?'

'Well, if anyone accused you of something like that, I'd be pretty angry too. I'm glad Mick was prepared to stand up for her. It sounds as if he has found someone he can care for. I just hope she says yes when he asks her.'

Sally was silent for a moment, then, 'Yes, I agree. I should like to see Mick married to a woman he loves – but I don't like him being angry with me, Ben.'

'He will get over it,' Ben replied. 'I don't think he'll suddenly sell all his shares and refuse to have anything to do with us, Sally. Have you apologised to Andrea?'

'I did try and I explained to Mick what had happened and what I mistakenly thought... but he is right, I should have known better.'

'Yes, you should, but there is no use in crying over spilled milk. I'll have a word and see if we can sort it out,' Ben said. 'I could do with a sandwich and a drink. I skipped lunch today.'

'Mrs Hills is cooking supper. There is a chicken casserole this evening...'

'I'll eat that too,' Ben said. 'I'm feeling much better. That niggling little pain in my chest has cleared up.' He hesitated, then,

'I went to the doctor Andrew recommended. He said the Army doctor was wrong and there isn't much wrong with my heart or lungs and suggested the pain might be indigestion. He gave me some pills to take and I'm feeling more like myself and hungry again.'

'Oh, thank God!' Sally said as relief poured through her. She'd been keeping her worry inside. 'As long as it isn't serious.'

'Darling Sally,' Ben said and took her in his arms to kiss her. 'I am sorry you were worried, but I was convinced it was the hereditary trouble my father and uncle had... but it seems the military doctor was wrong. Probably overworked, as they all were then.'

'As long as I'm not going to lose you,' she said and hugged him. 'I love you so much, Ben.'

'I'm more than relieved,' he told her with a wry smile. 'Especially after Jenni died so suddenly. I'd begun to think my family were cursed.'

'Oh no, don't say things like that,' she reprimanded. 'Andrew must be feeling so lonely and miserable. Shall we take a few days off to visit him?'

'I was going to suggest that,' Ben agreed. 'I'll ring him and see what he thinks. If he'd like us to go up – but you know how busy he is...'

'I really want him to come to us for Christmas,' Sally said, 'but he may not feel up to it.'

'I'll ring him while you make my sandwich.'

* * *

Ben was still talking to Andrew when Sally brought his sandwiches and put them on the occasional table beside him.

'So you will come for Christmas?' Ben nodded at her. 'That's wonderful, Andrew. We're looking forward to seeing you all... Yes,

I'll give Sally your love and she sends hers. Glad that things are a little better... See you soon.'

'Andrew is definitely coming at Christmas, then?' Sally asked as he replaced the receiver and sipped the sherry Ben had poured for her.

'Yes, and bringing Penny's nurse with him,' Ben said. 'She is a young Scottish girl and very good with the child. He sounded much more cheerful – says that Rachel has been helping him with Jenni's shop, which is doing well, and he is busy at the hospital as always.' Sally could see the call had lifted Ben's spirits, too, because he'd worried a lot about Andrew's mental state after they'd left him. Jenni would not have wanted him to be so desperately unhappy.

'Good. The last time I rang him, he was still very down, so that is an improvement. Did he say what the nurse was called?'

'Morag,' Ben informed her. 'He says she is a nice quiet girl and he doesn't have to worry about Penny now. I'm relieved, I really thought at first that he wouldn't cope.'

'I knew you were concerned about the possibility,' Sally said. 'I'm so glad it didn't happen. One tragedy was enough.'

'More than enough for me,' Ben said and ate one of the tiny finger sandwiches. 'This is delicious, Sally. Smoked salmon and cream cheese – you are spoiling me.'

'I was lucky to get it. I hadn't seen any for a long time.' She looked pleased. 'When the rationing finally ends this month, we'll be able to get a lot more luxuries again.'

'Just in time for Christmas,' he sighed with pleasure. 'I think I'll go up and change before dinner – just look in on the children.'

'They are both fast asleep,' Sally told him. 'Mum put them to bed after we had tea and they were as good as gold, so excited that Granny was here.'

'They got here nice and early then.' Ben glanced around the room. 'Where are they?'

'They went over to look at the house, check on a few things, but they will be back for dinner.'

'Good. I shall see them later.'

Sally smiled as he went out. She knew he couldn't resist kissing the children, but hopefully they would not wake.

A little sigh escaped her. What was she going to do about Mick and Andrea? She didn't want to be at odds with her old friend and she was sorry she had upset Andrea. Perhaps if she went to see her to apologise...?

Hearing her mother's voice in the hall, Sally got up to welcome her as she entered. 'Mum, Trevor, everything all right?'

'Perfect,' her mother replied. 'The house hardly needs anything done to it, apart from a slate off the roof and a leaking tap in the kitchen. Such a lucky find on Ben's part, Sally. I just have to choose some wallpaper, paint, carpets and colours for the curtains and then we can move in.'

'Well, you know you are welcome here for as long as you wish,' Sally said and kissed her. 'Trevor – would you like a drink before dinner. Mum, I know you like sweet sherry.'

'Trevor will have orange juice or lemonade,' her mother said. 'He doesn't drink anything stronger than a half of beer and only now and then – his doctor told him it wasn't good for him.'

'I am sure we have some beer in,' Sally said.

'I'll have a half with my dinner,' Trevor said and nodded at her. 'Never was much of a one for spirits or wine.'

'Ben enjoys beer sometimes, too,' Sally agreed. 'You must say what you fancy, Trevor. This is your home until you move into your new house.'

'Aye, I know that, lass,' Trevor said. 'You're a good girl and I'm glad we've moved to be near you.'

Sally went to give him a hug and he grunted with pleasure and hugged her back. 'It will be so good having you both around,' she told him. 'I think our little crisis with Winnie is over – but that means we can all relax and enjoy ourselves.'

'Where is Ben?' her mother asked, glancing round. 'Not still at work I hope?'

'He went up to see the children. He will be down shortly.'

Even as she spoke, Ben's voice could be heard in the hallway, speaking to Mrs Hills. He entered a moment or two later and greeted Sally's parents with a smile of welcome.

'I thought I heard you arrive. Mrs Hills says dinner is almost ready.'

* * *

Later that evening, when the men had gone for a little stroll with Lulu, Sally sat with her mother talking by the fire.

'So how is Trevor really now, Mum?' she asked.

'Better than I expected when he was rushed off to hospital with his chest. He couldn't get his breath and I thought it might turn to pneumonia, but thankfully they pulled him through – but I think it is why he agreed to give up work. He thought it would be better for me to be close to you and the children, should the worst happen.'

'Surely it won't, Mum? He seems quite well now?'

'It came on suddenly last time,' her mother said. 'Look what happened to Jenni – and she was half Trevor's age.'

'Yes, that upset Ben a lot. She was younger than him and he couldn't accept it for a while, but I think he is beginning to.'

'Not much else you can do,' her mother said. 'Do you really think you've heard the last of that young woman?'

'It is difficult to be sure. I think she has been given a second chance and I hope she makes the most of it for her sake.'

'Ben won't press charges for the damage she did at Harpers?'

'No. He was very angry at first, but a broken window is a small thing compared to a girl's life, Mum. We have to let her have her chance...'

Her mother sniffed in disapproval. 'I think she had her chance when you took her on, Sally, but I suppose you are right – just as long as she doesn't cause more trouble.'

'I think Mary Winston will keep an eye on her – and if she gets involved in the Women's Movement, she will be too busy to bother about us.'

'Let's hope so.' Her mother smiled and changed the subject again. 'What shall I buy Jenny and Peter for Christmas?'

'Puzzles and games,' Sally replied. 'Jenny is a bright little girl and she needs to be doing something to keep her out of mischief, but Peter is content with some bricks to build up. Jenny asked Father Christmas for a bike, so Ben is getting her a tricycle and I shall give her something pretty to wear; Peter will have some toy soldiers and a train set – but I am also making a donation to a children's home this year, Mum. Jenny and Peter have all they need and there are so many who don't, so I thought I'd take some toys to Dr Barnardo's for the children there. We give sweets to children who come to see Father Christmas at the store, but there are so many who have no homes or very poor ones.'

'The war didn't help,' her mother agreed. 'With so many men killed fighting for their country, it leaves a lot of widows struggling to bring up a family alone.'

'Yes, it does,' Sally said. 'When the war ended, we thought primarily about the men suffering from mental stress as well as physical injury, but I've noticed an increase in children going barefoot on our streets, Mum.'

Her mother tutted in distress. 'What can we do to help, Sally? We can't feed or clothe them all...'

'No, but I've been talking to Maggie and Beth about this and we thought we might organise a flag day and give the money to Barnardo's. They will know how to use it.'

'I always think the Sally Army do a good job,' her mother said. 'We could collect for a jumble sale – or run a bazaar before Christmas and give it to the Sally Army. They are out on the streets and it is there that the children really need help.'

'Would you like to help organise that?' Sally asked. 'We could hire the mission hall and hold the bazaar there. I know Maggie will help if she is in town and Beth is always up for anything that is worthwhile. I might ask Marion Jackson too if she has time...' She broke off as she heard the door and then Mrs Hills speaking to someone. The next moment, the door of the sitting room opened and she entered, followed by a visitor.

'Mrs Martin said it was important...' she said. 'I'm sorry, Mrs Harper. I knew you didn't want to be disturbed...'

Sally rose to her feet in surprise. 'Andrea – what can I do for you? You look upset?'

'It's Mick – Mr O'Sullivan,' Andrea burst out. It was clear she had been crying. 'I came to you, because I knew you were friends – he has been attacked and badly beaten. He is in hospital and...' She caught a sobbing breath. 'I am not sure how bad he is...'

'Oh no! That is terrible,' Sally said, jumping to her feet. 'Andrea, I am so sorry. Where is he?'

'In the London Hospital,' Andrea answered. 'It was the nearest one when he was set upon.' A little cry escaped her. 'This is the second time he's been attacked recently!'

'Have you been able to see him?' Sally asked.

'No. I'm not family and they will only allow family...' Andrea looked at her. 'Apparently, he has your name down as closest family...'

'I'll telephone the hospital now and see if I'm allowed to visit.'

She went quickly to her desk, flicked through her index and then picked up the receiver and asked for the number she needed. It took a few minutes of explanations before she was finally put through to the ward and was able to speak to the sister on duty.

Her mother had gone to Andrea and brought her to the fire, pouring her a small glass of sherry and doing her best to look after her while Sally phoned.

'You say he is still unconscious?' Sally spoke into the receiver. 'What other injuries does he have? I see... yes... yes, I understand. I will ring again in the morning. Thank you so much...' She looked at Andrea as she replaced the receiver. 'Mick is still unconscious, so no one can visit. He has a broken nose and ribs, but his lungs are all right, and he is breathing normally. It is mainly the head injury that concerns them...' She hesitated, then, 'How did you know he'd been attacked?'

'A note was pushed through my door an hour ago. I panicked and rang the hospital but was told I couldn't visit and they wouldn't give me any real information after I told them I wasn't Mrs Sally Harper...' She bit her lip. 'I couldn't think what to do, so I came to you.'

'I am glad you did,' Sally told her. 'I'm sure we can arrange for you to visit when Mick is well enough. I know Ben will want to get to the bottom of this – why has he been attacked twice? If it was just robbery... it surely wouldn't happen twice?'

'I don't know – he said he was robbed the first time, but...' Andrea shook her head. 'I'm not thinking straight – but could he be involved in some criminal activity?'

'I doubt it,' Sally replied with a shake of her head. 'I know Mick and he's pretty straightforward.' She looked at Andrea hesitantly, then, 'I wanted to apologise to you for what I did, Andrea. I should not have even considered that you had sent that letter... Would you feel able to forgive me and be friends? I'd really love you to stay on at Harpers.'

Andrea hesitated and then looked relieved. 'I was a little hasty, Mrs Harper. I don't truly wish to leave but... with Mick ill and my son at home—'

'Why don't you take a couple of weeks paid sick leave?' Sally suggested. 'Come back to us when you've sorted yourself out.' She offered her hand. 'Are we friends again?'

'Yes, we are,' Andrea said and clasped hands. 'I may have deserved your suspicion. I was too harsh with Lilly Ross, I know that and I am sorry for it.'

'We shall all start afresh,' Sally said. 'You haven't touched your sherry – can I get you a cup of tea before I ring for a taxi to take you home?'

At that moment, Ben and Trevor walked in with the dog. Ben looked at Sally and she explained swiftly about Mick's beating. He swore softly.

'It will be that protection gang,' he said, looking angry. 'They have been trying to make Mick pay them to protect his businesses and he refused – told me he wasn't going to give into their blackmail.'

'Oh, Ben!' Sally cried. 'Gangsters like that are dangerous. Mick could easily have been—' She broke off because Andrea was looking scared. 'Did he tell you who they were?'

Ben nodded. 'One of them used to be in the building trade. He tried to blackmail me before the war over some work they were supposed to do – remember Mick sorted it for me? Looks as if he moved up a level.' He glanced at Andrea. 'Not Mick – this other chap...'

'I think I'll go home,' Andrea said, looking shocked. 'I don't need a taxi, Mrs Harper.'

'I'll run you home myself,' Ben offered but she shook her head.

'Thank you, but I can catch a bus just up the road.'

'You are upset and I prefer that Ben takes you in the car,' Sally said. 'Mick would never forgive me if anything happened to you.'

'Oh well...' Andrea sighed and then nodded. 'I suppose you are right, thank you. I didn't want to be any trouble.'

'No trouble at all,' Ben replied. 'I'll have the car out in a couple of minutes. In the meantime, try not to worry and sit by the fire.'

'You must be extremely worried,' Sally's mother said as Andrea did as she was told. 'It is an unpleasant thing to happen, but he is a strong man and I am sure he will recover.'

'Thank you. I do hope so,' Andrea replied. 'We haven't known each other long, but I have become very fond of him.'

'Good, that is exactly what Mick needs,' Sally said. 'I should like to see him settled and happy – and you, too, Andrea. What does your son think of him?'

'Paul is fascinated by him...' Andrea began and then Ben was back and she stood up. 'Thank you for helping me, Mrs Harper. I was so desperate when the hospital wouldn't let me visit.'

'Do you know who put the note through your door?' Andrea shook her head.

'It is a little strange. As far as the hospital is concerned I'll make sure they understand you are Mick's close friend,' Sally reassured her. 'You have more right to visit than I do – but I suppose Mick had us down as his next of kin since he has no one else.' She corrected herself, 'He *had* no one else. I have a feeling he does now.'

Andrea smiled. 'Yes, he has someone now,' she said and followed Ben from the room.

'Well, that was unexpected,' Sally's mother said after she had gone. 'It never rains but it pours. Just one thing after another recently.'

'Yes, it has been,' Sally replied. 'I do hope Mick recovers consciousness soon, Mum. Head injuries can be so nasty.'

'Let's hope he is all right for his sake and that young woman's. Am I right in thinking her a war widow?' She looked sad as Sally nodded. 'I thought that might be the case. That awful war has a lot to answer for, Sally.'

'It certainly does,' Sally agreed. 'Which brings me back to what we were saying concerning the children's charity, Mum. May I put your name down for the committee – and you too, Trevor, if you would feel able to help?'

'I'm more the practical sort,' he told her with a nod. 'If you want any work done anywhere, I'll help – setting up tables for a bazaar or building work.'

'That's splendid,' Sally said. 'Now, how about I make us some coffee?'

* * *

The news from the hospital was better the next morning. Mick had recovered consciousness during the night and there was no lasting damage, other than the pain of broken ribs, which was bad enough in itself.

'I've rung the hospital and Mick wants to see you,' Sally told Ben. 'He says there is something important he needs to speak to you about – so I said you would go in at about eleven this morning, is that all right?'

'Yes, of course. I have a couple of meetings later, but my secretary can rearrange them. I'll certainly visit him. I want to get to the bottom of this.'

Sally nodded. She was relieved that Mick was conscious but

still worried over what had happened to him. For him to be attacked twice in a short space of time was concerning.

Sally spent the morning with her mother and the children. They took them to the park and then for a visit to an ice cream parlour, where they had cakes and dishes of ice cream and jelly. Ben was at home reading the paper when they returned. He greeted them with a kiss but said nothing of Mick until Sally's mother had gone upstairs.

'He's fine, a bit sorry for himself over the broken bones, but angry more than anything,' Ben said. 'I was wrong to assume it was the builder who had beaten him. He says he has some Irish friends who handle them – no, it was because of Kavi. The first time he was attacked he thought it was just a robbery, but this time, he realised what it was all about...'

'Kavi – but he wouldn't hurt a fly, surely? He seemed a gentle, rather timid young man.'

Ben nodded. 'You knew that he worked as a goldsmith in Russia and was supposed to have left because of a purge against his people?'

'Yes. Mick told me.'

'Well, apparently, he worked for a very famous goldsmith and before he left Russia, he stole something extremely valuable – it was a Fabergé egg and had been intended for the royal family before they were murdered.'

Sally's hand flew to her mouth in shock. 'No! Something like that would be almost priceless...'

'Exactly. Someone – Russians, Mick thinks – knew about the egg and they've been looking for Kavi. They must have discovered he was working for Mick and thought he was involved in it some-how... and yesterday they went into the workshop when Mick was there and attacked both him and Kavi. They ransacked the place and only left when Kavi revealed its hiding place.'

'It is a wonder they aren't both dead...' A shiver went down Sally's spine.

Ben's expression showed his agreement. 'Mick was hurt the worst because he fought to protect Kavi – he only had some bruises.'

'It must have been him who put the note through Andrea's door,' Sally said. 'I wondered who might have done it. Mick must be furious...'

'He will be when he learns that Kavi has now disappeared and taken much of the stock with him. Mick's good deed has earned him a beating and lost him several thousand pounds.'

'You went to the workshop?'

'Mick asked me to; he was worried about Kavi. Well, he has gone and so has all of the gold and silver from the safe.'

Sally gasped in dismay. 'How could he do that to Mick? After he brought him here and set him up in business? I can hardly believe it – Mick will be so disappointed. I am too. Kavi is a skilled craftsman – though it seems also a thief.'

'It doesn't seem fair,' Ben agreed and poured himself a drink of sherry. Sally shook her head when he asked if she wanted one. 'It won't affect Mick too much. He has plenty of irons in the fire, but it knocks your faith in others – first Winnie and now this Kavi...'

'Winnie returned what she took and apologised,' Sally reminded. 'I think she is just a mixed-up young woman who needs to find her way – Kavi seems to be a habitual thief, so not quite the same.'

'I suppose that is true,' Ben acknowledged. 'Mick will get over it. He's asked for Andrea to be allowed to visit, so that's sorted.'

'Good. I don't think Mick will worry too much over the workshop, Ben. He intended to give it to Kavi when he was able to stand on his own two feet, but he will feel let down. I am just glad he has Andrea now...'

'Yes, there is that,' Ben agreed. 'He will have someone to look after him when he leaves hospital if Andrea will have him.'

'Oh, I think she will,' Sally replied and smiled. 'Mick may have lost some gold and silver, but he has gained much more.' They looked at each other in agreement and then Ben sighed.

'I must go, love. I have some business meetings – why don't you visit Andrea this afternoon and see how she is?'

'Yes, I will,' Sally replied. 'Mum will look after the children and I am sure Andrea is anxious for news.'

39

'That is a terrible thing to happen,' Andrea said when Sally explained what had occurred. 'Mick thought a lot of Kavi. I am so sorry he has been let down.'

'The main thing is that he is recovering and would like to see you.'

'I'll visit this evening.' Andrea perked up immediately. 'Paul has been asking about him. He really likes Mick...'

'So there will be no problem there if you marry,' Sally said. 'I wish you all the happiness in the world, Andrea.'

'Thank you.' Andrea smiled. 'I think we shall be happy together. I didn't like him at first, but he has a certain charm that wins you over.'

'Yes, you are quite right,' Sally agreed. 'I didn't like Mick when we first met, but he became my friend and I think he always will be – once he forgives me for suspecting you of sending those letters.'

'I am sure he will. I have,' Andrea said. 'Will you stay for a cup of tea?'

'I can stay for a bit longer,' Sally told her. 'My mother is looking after the children for me. She enjoys that so much because she missed most of my childhood. Through no fault of her own, she was forced to give me up as a small child, but she never forgot me and, when she was able, came looking for me – though it took her years to find me.'

Andrea was silent for a moment. 'Who brought you up then?'

'I was in a children's home until I was sixteen, when I left and started work, first of all in a factory and then in Selfridges. My luck changed when I started to work at Harpers and I found friends – and then love...'

'I see – then I misjudged you, too,' she said. 'I imagined you as a spoiled only child...'

Sally's laughter rang out. 'Oh no,' she said. 'I was never that, Andrea.'

* * *

Sally was thoughtful as she drove herself home after chatting to Andrea some more. They were well on the way to becoming friends, which was good because if Mick married her, they could not remain distant with each other. She knew she had reached a good place in her life. There were still difficulties, but there always would be. Her marriage had settled down after a slightly bumpy passage and Sally knew that she would be content to hand over the reins she had carried during the war. She would continue to oversee her own departments, but Ben would be the driving force for Harpers now and that was how it should always have been. Sally would have more time to spend with her friends, her family and her good causes. There were still too many children living in homes that were not what they should be. Some orphanages were good, others were not. Sally would turn some of her energy towards them.

She was smiling as she got out of her car and locked it. Mrs

Hills had put the front porch light on so that she could see her way to the front door without tripping over, but she was startled when a figure came rushing at her out of the darkness. About to scream, her instincts held back the cry as something heavy was thrust into her arms.

In the light of the lamps outside the porch, Sally could see a pale scared face staring at her. 'Kavi...?' she whispered. 'What are you doing here?'

'Give to Mick. I thank him,' Kavi said, his accent heavy, but his broken English was easy enough to understand. 'I take because lock broken. People might steal. Tell him I go where I not be found...'

'I'll tell him,' Sally said but as he turned away, 'Why did you steal the egg, Kavi?'

'It not belong those who rule my country now. For the Czarina and her children.'

'But she is dead with all her family. They were all shot by the Bolsheviks...'

Kavi shook his head. 'No. I believe one lives.' He looked furtively over his shoulder. 'I go to find her and I take what I keep from workshop. Mick understand...'

'Who – where?' Sally asked, but Kavi had turned, disappearing into the shadows as swiftly as he had appeared. The bundle he had thrust into her hands was heavy and must contain a considerable amount of gold and silver.

Feeling a little breathless and bewildered, Sally went into the house. She was greeted by Mrs Hills, who took the bundle from her, remarking on its weight with a smile.

'Yes, it is a surprise,' Sally replied. She couldn't wait to tell Ben when he arrived home.

* * *

They opened the parcel together later that evening. Sally gasped in delight as she saw all the beautiful pieces of silver and gold jewellery, pendants, bracelets set with precious stones and plain but elegant brooches.

'Did you know all this existed?' Ben asked as she examined the wonderful workmanship.

'No. I think this is some of Kavi's best work,' she told him excitedly. 'He brought them to me because he knew how much I admired his work and obviously the hospital was too public a place for him to give them to Mick. This is wonderful, Ben. If I can buy these from Mick, it will keep us stocked for a year or more.'

'I am sure he will be only too pleased to let you buy them. You said Kavi told you he had kept some stock from the workshop for this mysterious Russian princess?'

'He believes one of the family is still alive,' Sally said. 'It hardly seems possible...'

'There have been rumours, but no one believes them,' Ben replied thoughtfully. 'Perhaps if Kavi truly knows where she is that may be the reason for the attack on the workshop rather than the Fabergé egg...'

'Who knows?' Sally said a little wistfully. 'It is a romantic idea and you can't help hoping that it is true one of the Romanov family escaped death, but we shall never know the truth.'

'No, we shan't,' Ben agreed. 'I dare say she is the heiress to a fortune if she lives, but will anyone ever accept her?' He shrugged. 'At least Mick hasn't lost as much as we thought – and Kavi wasn't a habitual thief after all.' He smiled at her. 'Life is good sometimes, isn't it, Sally?'

'I think it can be rather wonderful,' Sally agreed. 'I believe we have so much to look forward to, Ben. Our family is strong and Harpers is doing well. Beth and Jack are happy, as are Maggie and

Colin. I think Rachel is happier now she has something to bring her to town more often and Andrew is getting better.'

'I saw Lilly at the store today,' Ben said. 'She is getting married after Christmas and then she will be leaving us to work in her husband's little flower shop.'

Sally nodded. 'Marion Jackson is leaving after Christmas too. She and her husband, Reggie, have decided to try living in the country for a while. They feel it may suit him better and, apparently, he has found a nice little corner shop they are going to run themselves.'

'Well, that is nice to know,' Ben said and reached out to take her in his arms. 'I wonder how soon we shall be dancing at Mick's wedding? I am sure it won't be long.'

'Which reminds me, you haven't taken me dancing for a long time,' Sally said and lifted her head for his kiss. 'Why don't we go somewhere for a holiday after Christmas, Ben? We could take the children – perhaps up to Scotland? I've never been there...'

'Then we should go,' he agreed. 'Although January is a busy time at Harpers for the sales... but we have good people to take care of that. We will take a little holiday in the early spring when the weather will be better...'

Sally nodded, feeling happy. Kavi's surprise visit had restored her faith. After Winnie's behaviour and Kavi's theft from Mick, she'd felt disappointed and unsure of her judgement in people, but Winnie had apologised and she sincerely wished her well for the future, and now it seemed that Kavi had only stolen the egg for his Czarina and her children. Perhaps whatever he'd kept from the workshop was something special he'd made and perhaps he would find the princess he believed still lived. Sally smiled. Sometimes good things could happen, so you never knew what was around the corner...

MORE FROM ROSIE CLARKE

We hope you enjoyed reading *Changing Times at Harpers*. If you did,
please leave a review.

If you'd like to gift a copy, this book is also available as an ebook, large
print, hardback, digital audio download and audiobook CD.

Sign up to Rosie Clarke's mailing list for news, competitions and updates
on future books.

https://bit.ly/RosieClarkeNews

Explore the rest of the Harpers Emporium series...

ABOUT THE AUTHOR

Rosie Clarke is a #1 bestselling saga writer whose most recent books include *The Mulberry Lane* and *Blackberry Farm* series. She has written over 100 novels under different pseudonyms and is a RNA Award winner. She lives in Cambridgeshire.

Visit Rosie Clarke's website: http://www.lindasole.co.uk

Follow Rosie on social media:

twitter.com/AnneHerries
bookbub.com/authors/rosie-clarke
facebook.com/Rosie-clarke-119457351778432

Sixpence Stories

Introducing Sixpence Stories!

Discover page-turning historical novels from your favourite authors, meet new friends and be transported back in time.

Join our book club
Facebook group

https://bit.ly/SixpenceGroup

Sign up to our
newsletter

https://bit.ly/SixpenceNews

Boldw∞d

Boldwood Books is an award-winning fiction publishing company seeking out the best stories from around the world.

Find out more at www.boldwoodbooks.com

Join our reader community for brilliant books, competitions and offers!

Follow us
@BoldwoodBooks
@BookandTonic

Sign up to our weekly deals newsletter

https://bit.ly/BoldwoodBNewsletter

Made in United States
Orlando, FL
02 May 2023

32690145R00176